W9-CEC-243

KILLING MOON

Also by Jo Nesbø

Headhunters

The Son

Blood on Snow

Midnight Sun

Macbeth

The Kingdom

The Jealousy Man and Other Stories

Books in the Harry Hole series

The Bat

Cockroaches

The Redbreast

Nemesis

The Devil's Star

The Redeemer

The Snowman

The Leopard

Phantom

Police

The Thirst

Knife

Jo Nesbø

KILLING MOON

Translated from the Norwegian
by Seán Kinsella

Alfred A. Knopf   New York   2023

THIS IS A BORZOI BOOK PUBLISHED BY ALFRED A. KNOPF

English translation copyright © by 2023 Seán Kinsella

www.aaknopf.com

Knopf, Borzoi Books, and the colophon are registered trademarks of
Penguin Random House LLC.

Library of Congress Control Number: 2023934044
ISBN: 978-0-593-53696-4 (hardcover)
ISBN: 978-0-593-53697-1 (ebook)

Jacket image by Yellow_stocking/Shutterstock
Jacket design by John Gall

Manufactured in the United States of America
First United States Edition

The sun shall be turned into darkness, and the moon into blood, before the great and terrible day of the Lord come.

Book of Joel 2:31

PROLOGUE

"OSLO," THE MAN SAID, RAISING the glass of whiskey to his lips.

"That's the place you love the most?" Lucille asked.

He stared ahead, seeming to think about his answer before he nodded. She studied him while he drank. He was tall; even sitting down on the bar stool next to her he towered above her. He had to be at least ten, maybe twenty years younger than her seventy-two; it was hard to tell with alcoholics. His face and body seemed carved from wood, lean, pure and rigid. His skin was pale, a fine mesh of blue veins visible on his nose, which together with bloodshot eyes, the irises the color of faded denim, suggested he had lived hard. Drunk hard. Fallen hard. And loved hard too, perhaps, for during the month he had become a regular at Creatures she had glimpsed a hurt in his eyes. Like that of a beaten dog, kicked out of the pack, always on his own at the end of the bar. Next to Bronco, the mechanical bull that Ben, the bar owner, had taken from the set of the giant turkey *Urban Cowboy*, where he had worked as a propman. It served as a reminder that Los Angeles wasn't a city built on movie successes but on a garbage heap of human and financial failure. Over eighty per cent of

1

all the films made bombed completely and lost money; the city had the highest homeless population in the USA, living at a density comparable to Mumbai's. Traffic congestion was in the process of choking the life out of the city, though street crime, drugs and violence might get there first. But the sun was shining. Yes, that damn Californian dentist's lamp never switched off, but shone relentlessly, making all the baubles in this phoney town glitter like real diamonds, like true stories of success. If only they knew. Like she, Lucille, knew, because she had been there, on the stage. And backstage.

The man sitting next to her had definitely not been on the stage; she recognized people in the industry immediately. But neither did he look like someone who had stared in admiration, hope or envy up at the stage. He looked more like someone who couldn't care less. Someone with their own thing going on. A musician, perhaps? One of those Frank Zappa types, producing his own impenetrable stuff in a basement up here in Laurel Canyon, who had never been—and would never be—discovered?

After he had been in a few times, Lucille and the new guy had begun to exchange nods and brief words of greeting, the way morning guests at a bar for serious drinkers do, but this was the first time she had sat down next to him and bought him a drink. Or rather, she had paid for the drink he had already ordered when she saw Ben hand him back his credit card with an expression that told her it was maxed out.

"But does Oslo love you back?" she asked. "That's the question."

"Hardly," he said. She noticed his middle finger was a metal prosthetic as he ran a hand through a brush of short, dirty-blond hair, tinged with gray. He was not a handsome man, and the liver-colored scar in the shape of a J running from the corner of his mouth to his ear—as though he were a fish caught on a hook—didn't help matters. But he had something, something almost appealing and slightly dangerous about him, like some of her colleagues here in town. Christopher Walken. Nick Nolte. And he was broad-shouldered. Although that might have been down to the rest of him being so lean.

"Uh-huh, well, they're the ones we want the most," Lucille said. "The ones who don't love us back. The ones we think will love us if we just try that *little* bit more."

"So, what do you do?" the man asked.

"Drink," she said, raising her own whiskey. "And feed cats."

"Hm."

"What you really want to know, I guess, is who I am. Well, I'm . . ." She drank from her glass while considering which version to give him. The one for parties or the truth. She put down her drink and decided on the latter. Screw it.

"An actor who played one big role. Juliet, in what remains the best film adaptation of *Romeo and Juliet*, but which nobody remembers any more. One big part doesn't sound like much, but it's more than most actors in this town get. I've been married three times, twice to well-off filmmakers who I left with favorable divorce settlements, also more than most actors get. The third was the only one I loved. An actor, and an Adonis, lacking in money, discipline and conscience. He used up every penny I had then left me. I still love him, may he rot in hell."

She finished the contents of her glass, put it on the bar and signaled to Ben for one more. "And, because I always fall for what I can't get, I've invested money I don't have in a movie project with an enticingly big part for an older lady. A project with an intelligent script, actors who can actually act, and a director who'll give people food for thought, in short, a project that any rational individual would realize is doomed to failure. So that's me, a daydreamer, a loser, a typical Angelino."

The man with the J-shaped scar smiled.

"OK, I'm all out of self-deprecation here," she said. "What's your name?"

"Harry."

"You don't talk much, Harry."

"Hm."

"Swedish?"

"Norwegian."

"You running from something?"

"That what it looks like?"

3

"Yeah. I see you're wearing a wedding ring. You running from your wife?"

"She's dead."

"Ah. You're running from grief." Lucille raised her glass in a toast. "You wanna know the place I love the most? Right here, Laurel Canyon. Not now, but at the end of the sixties. You should've been here, Harry. If you were even born then."

"Yeah, so I've heard."

She pointed towards the framed photos on the wall behind Ben.

"All the musicians hung out here. Crosby, Stills, Nash and . . . what was the name of that last guy?"

Harry smiled again.

"The Mamas and the Papas," she continued. "Carole King. James Taylor. Joni Mitchell." She wrinkled her nose. "Looked and sounded like a Sunday-school girl, but she laid some of the aforementioned. Even got her claws into Leonard—he shacked up with her for a month or so. I was allowed to borrow him for one night."

"Leonard Cohen?"

"The one and only. Lovely, sweet man. He taught me a little something about writing rhyming verse. Most people make the mistake of opening with their one good line, and then write some half-decent forced rhyme on the next one. The trick is to put the forced rhyme in the first sentence, then no one will notice it. Just take a look at the banal first line of 'Hey, That's No Way to Say Goodbye' and compare it with the beauty of the second line. There's a natural elegance to both sentences. We hear it that way, because we think the writer is thinking in the same sequence as he writes. Little wonder really; after all, people are inclined to believe that what is happening is a result of what's gone before, and not the other way around."

"Hm. So what happens is a result of what will happen?"

"Exactly, Harry! You get that, right?"

"I don't know. Can you give me an example?"

"Sure." She downed her drink. He must have heard something in her tone because she saw him raise an eyebrow and quickly scan the bar.

"What's happening, at present, is that I'm telling you about how I owe money on a movie in development," she said, looking through the dirty window with the half-closed blinds at the dusty parking lot outside. "That's no coincidence, rather a consequence of what *will* happen. There's a white Camaro parked next to my car outside here."

"With two men inside," he said. "It's been there for twenty minutes."

She nodded. Harry had just confirmed that she was not mistaken in what she guessed to be his line of work.

"I noticed that car outside my place up in the Canyon this morning," she said. "No big surprise, they've already given me a warning and told me they'd send collectors. And not the certified type. This loan wasn't taken out at a bank, if you follow me. Now, when I walk out to my car these gentlemen are probably going to want to have words with me. I'm guessing they'll still make do with that, warnings and threats, that is."

"Hm. And why tell me this?"

"Because you're a cop."

Once more he raised an eyebrow. "Am I?"

"My father was a cop and, clearly, you guys are recognisable the world over. The point is I want you to keep an eye out from here. If they get vocal and turn threatening, I'd like you to come out onto the porch and . . . you know, look like a cop, so they beat it. Listen, I'm pretty sure it's not going to come to that, but I'd feel safer if you kept an eye out."

Harry studied her for a moment. "OK," he simply said.

Lucille was surprised. Hadn't he allowed himself to be persuaded a little too easily? At the same time there was something unwavering in his eyes that made her trust him. On the other hand, she had trusted the Adonis. And the director. And the producer.

"I'm leaving now," she said.

Harry Hole held the glass in his hand. Listened to the almost inaudible hiss of ice cubes melting. Didn't drink. He was broke, at the end of the line, and was going to drag this drink out and enjoy it. His gaze settled on one of the pictures behind the bar. It was a photograph of one of the favorite authors of his youth, Charles Bukowski, outside Creatures. Ben had told him it was from the seventies. Bukowski was standing with his arm around a buddy, at what looked like dawn; both were wearing Hawaiian shirts, their eyes swimming, pinpricks for pupils, and grinning triumphantly, as though they had just reached the North Pole after a gruelling journey.

Harry lowered his eyes to look at the credit card which Ben had tossed on the bar in front of him.

Maxed out. Emptied. Nothing left. Mission accomplished. Which had been this, to drink until there was indeed nothing left. No money, no days, no future. All that remained was to see if he had the courage—or the cowardice—to round it all off. There was an old Beretta handgun underneath the mattress in his room back at the boarding house. He had bought it for twenty-five dollars from a homeless guy living in one of the blue tents down on Skid Row. There were three bullets in it. He laid the credit card in the flat of his hand and curled his fingers around it. Turned to look out the window. Watched the old lady as she strutted out to the parking lot. She was so small. Slight, delicate and strong as a sparrow. Beige slacks and a short matching jacket. There was something 1980s about her archaic, but tasteful, clothing style. Walking the same way as how she swept into the bar every morning. Making an entrance. For an audience of between two and eight people.

"Lucille is here!" Ben would proclaim before, unbidden, he began mixing her usual poison, whiskey sour.

But it wasn't the way she took a room that reminded Harry of his mother, who had died at the Radium Hospital when he was fifteen, putting the first bullet hole through his heart. It was the gentle, smiling, yet sad look, in Lucille's eyes, like that of a kind, but resigned soul. The concern she displayed for others when she asked for the latest news about their health problems, love lives, and their nearest and dearest. And the consideration she showed by letting Harry sit in peace at the far end of the bar. His mother, that taciturn woman who was the family's control tower, its nerve center, who pulled the strings so discreetly one could easily believe it was his father who called the shots. His mother, who had always offered a safe embrace, had always understood, whom he had loved above all else and whom therefore had become his Achilles heel. Like that time in second grade when there had been a gentle knock on the classroom door and his mother was standing there with the lunch box he had left at home. Harry had brightened up automatically at the sight of her, before hearing some of his classmates laugh, whereupon he had marched out to her in the hall and, in a fury, had told her she was embarrassing him, she had to leave, he didn't need food. She had merely smiled sadly, given him the lunch box, stroked his cheek and left. He didn't mention it later. Of course, she had understood, the way she always did. And when he went to bed that night, he also understood. *She* was not the reason he had felt uncomfortable. It was the fact they had all seen it. His love. His vulnerability. He had thought about apologizing several times over the following years, but that would probably just have felt stupid.

A cloud of dust rose up on the graveled area outside, enveloping for a moment Lucille, who was holding her sunglasses in place. He saw the passenger door of the white Camaro open, and a man in sunglasses and a red polo shirt emerge. He walked to the front of the car, blocking Lucille's path to her own.

He expected to observe a conversation between the two. But instead the man took a step forward and grabbed hold of Lucille's arm. Began pulling her towards the Camaro. Harry saw the heels of her shoes dig into the gravel. And now he also saw that the Camaro didn't have an American license plate. In that instant he was off the bar stool. Running towards the door, he burst it open with his elbow, was blinded by sunlight and almost stumbled on the two steps down from the porch. Realized he was far from sober. Then zeroed in on the two cars. His eyes gradually adjusting to the light. Beyond the parking lot, on the other side of the road winding its way up the green hillside, lay a sleepy general store, but he couldn't see any other people apart from the man and Lucille, who was being dragged towards the Camaro.

"Police!" he shouted. "Let her go!"

"Please stay out of this, sir," the man called back.

Harry surmised the man must have a similar background to his own, only policemen employed polite language in this type of situation. Harry also knew that a physical intervention was unavoidable, and that the first rule in close combat was simple: don't wait, he who attacks first and with maximum aggression wins. So he didn't slow down, and the other man must have realized Harry's intention, because he let go of Lucille and reached for something he had behind him. His hand swung back around. In it he held a shiny handgun Harry recognized instantly. A Glock 17. Now pointed directly at him.

Harry slowed down but continued moving forwards. Saw the other man's eye aiming from behind the gun. His voice was half drowned out by a passing pickup on the road.

"Run back to where you came from, sir. Now!"

But Harry kept walking towards him. Became aware he was still holding the credit card in his right hand. Was this how it ended? In a dusty parking lot in a foreign country, bathed in sunlight, broke and half drunk, while trying to do what he hadn't been able to do for his mother, hadn't been able to do for any of those he had ever cared about?

He almost closed his eyes and squeezed his fingers around the credit card, so his hand formed a chisel.

The title of the Leonard Cohen song swirled through his mind: "Hey, that's no way to say goodbye."

Fuck that, the hell it wasn't.

1

FRIDAY

EIGHT O'CLOCK. HALF AN HOUR since the September sun had gone down over Oslo, and past bedtime for three-year-olds.

Katrine Bratt sighed and whispered into the phone: "Can't you sleep, darling?"

"Gwanny is singing wong," the child's voice answered, sniffling. "Whe ah you?"

"I had to go to work, darling, but I'll be home soon. Would you like Mama to sing a little?"

"Yeah."

"Well, then you have to close your eyes."

"Yeah."

"'Blueman'?"

"Yeah."

Katrine began singing the melancholy song in a low, deep voice. *Blueman, Blueman, my buck, think of your small boy.*

She had no idea why children had, for over a century, felt happy to be lulled to sleep by the story of an angst-ridden boy who wonders why

Blueman, his favorite goat, hasn't returned home from grazing, and who fears it's been taken by a bear and now lies mutilated and dead somewhere in the mountains.

Still, after just one verse she could hear Gert's breathing become more regular and deep, and after the next verse she heard her mother-in-law's whispered voice on the phone.

"He's asleep now."

"Thanks," said Katrine, who had been squatting on her haunches so long she had to put her hand on the ground. "I'll be back as soon as I can."

"Take all the time you need, dear. And I'm the one who should be thanking you for wanting us here. You know, he looks so much like Bjørn when he's asleep."

Katrine swallowed. Unable, as usual, to respond when she said that. Not because she didn't miss Bjørn, not because she wasn't happy that Bjørn's parents saw him in Gert. But because it simply wasn't true.

She concentrated on what lay in front of her.

"Intense lullaby," said Sung-min Larsen, who had come and crouched down next to her. "'*Maybe now you lay dead*'?"

"I know, but it's the only one he wants to hear," Katrine said.

"Well, then that's what he gets." Her colleague smiled.

Katrine nodded. "Have you ever thought about how as children we expect unconditional love from our parents, without giving anything in return? That we are actually parasites? But then we grow up and things change completely. When exactly do you think we stop believing that we can be loved unconditionally just for being who we are?"

"When did *she* stop, you mean?"

"Yeah."

They looked down at the body of the young woman lying on the forest floor. Her pants and underwear were pulled down to her ankles, but the zipper on the thin down jacket was pulled up. Her face—which was turned to the starry skies above—appeared chalk-white in the glare of the Crime Scene Unit's floodlights, which were positioned among the trees. Her makeup was streaked, and looked like it had run and dried out several times. Her hair—bombed blonde by chemicals—was sticking to one side of her face. Her lips were stuffed with silicon, and false eyelashes protruded like the eaves of a roof over one eye, which was sunken down in its socket, staring glassily up and past them, and also over the other eye, which was not there, only an empty socket. Perhaps all the barely degradable synthetic materials were the reason the body had remained in as good condition as it had.

"I'm guessing this is Susanne Andersen?" Sung-min said.

"I'm guessing the same," Katrine replied.

The detectives were from two different departments, she was with Crime Squad at the Oslo Police and he was with Kripos. Susanne Andersen, twenty-six years old, had been missing for seventeen days and was last spotted on a security camera at Skullerud metro station around a twenty-minute walk from where they were now. The only lead on the other missing woman, Bertine Bertilsen, twenty-seven years old, was her car, which was found abandoned in a parking lot in Grefsenkollen, a hiking area in another part of the city. The hair color of the woman in front of them tallied with the security camera footage of Susanne, while Bertine was, according to family and friends, currently a brunette. Besides, the body had no tattoos on the naked lower body, while Bertine was supposed to have one—a Louis Vuitton logo—on her ankle.

So far, it had been a relatively cool and dry September, and the discoloration on the corpse's skin—blue, purple, yellow, brown—might be consistent with it lying outdoors for close to three weeks. The same went for the smell, owing to the body's production of gas, which gradually seeped out from all orifices. Katrine had also noted the white area of thin hair-like filaments below the nostrils: fungus. In the large wound on the throat, yellowish-white, blind maggots crawled. Katrine had seen it so often she no longer had any particular reaction. After all, blowflies were—in Harry's words—as loyal as Liverpool fans. Turning up at a moment's notice no matter the time or place, rain or shine, attracted by the smell of dimethyl trisulfide which the body begins to excrete from the moment of expiration. The females lay their eggs, and a few days later the larvae hatch and begin gorging on the rotting flesh. They pupate, turning into flies, which look for bodies to lay their own eggs in, and after a month they have lived their life to the end and die. That's their life cycle. Not so different to ours, Katrine thought. Or rather, not so different to mine.

Katrine looked around. White-clad members of Krimteknisk, the Forensics Unit, moved like soundless ghosts among the trees, casting eerie shadows every time the flashes on their cameras lit up. The forest was large. Østmarka continued on, for mile after mile, virtually all the way to Sweden. A jogger had found the body. Or rather, the jogger's dog, which had been allowed off the lead and had disappeared from the narrow gravel road and into the woods. It was already getting dark. The jogger—running with a head lamp—had followed after while calling out to the dog and had eventually found it, next to the body, wagging its tail. Well, no wagging had been mentioned, it was something Katrine had pictured.

"Susanne Andersen," she whispered, not knowing quite to whom. Perhaps to the deceased, as comfort and assurance that she had finally been found and identified.

The cause of death appeared obvious. The cut that had been made across her throat, running like a smile over Susanne Andersen's narrow neck. The fly larvae, various forms of insects and perhaps other animals had probably helped themselves to most of the blood; however, Katrine still saw traces of blood spatter in the heather and on the trunk of one tree.

"Killed here *in situ*," she said.

"Looks that way," Sung-min replied. "Do you think she was raped? Or just sexually assaulted after he killed her?"

"After," Katrine said, shining the flashlight on Susanne's hands. "No broken nails, no signs of a struggle. But I'll try and have them undertake a forensic post-mortem over the weekend and we'll see what they think."

"And a clinical autopsy?"

"We won't get that until Monday at the earliest."

Sung-min sighed. "Well, I guess it's only a question of time before we find Bertine Bertilsen raped and with her throat slit somewhere in Grefsenkollen."

Katrine nodded. She and Sung-min had become better acquainted over the past year, and he had confirmed his reputation as one of Kripos's best detectives. There were many who believed he would take over as Senior Inspector the day Ole Winter stepped down, and that from then on the department would have a far better boss. Possibly. But there were also those who voiced reservations about the country's foremost investigative body being led by an adopted South Korean and homosexual who dressed like a member of the British aristocracy. His classic tweed hunting jacket and suede-and-leather country boots stood in stark contrast with Katrine's thin Patagonia down jacket and Gore-tex sneakers. When Bjørn was alive, he had called her style "gorpcore," which, she had been given to understand, was an international term for people who went to the pub dressed as though they were headed up the mountains. She had called it adapting to life as the mother of a small child. But she had to admit that this more subdued, practical style of dress was also owing to the fact that she was no longer a young, rebellious investigative talent but the head of Crime Squad.

"What do you think this is?" Sung-min said.

She knew he was thinking the same as her. And that neither of them intended to say those words out loud. Not yet. Katrine cleared her throat.

"The first thing we do is stick to what we've got here and find out what happened."

"Agreed."

Katrine hoped "agreed" was a word she would hear often from Kripos in future. But she did, of course, welcome all the help they could get. Kripos had let it be known they were ready to step up from the point Bertine Bertilsen was reported missing exactly a week after Susanne, and under strikingly similar circumstances. Both women had gone out on a Tuesday evening without telling any of those the police had spoken to where they were going or what they were doing, and had not been seen since. Besides, there were other circumstances linking the two women. When these came to light, the police shelved their theory of Susanne being in an accident or having taken her own life.

"All right, then," Katrine said and stood up. "I'd better notify the boss."

Katrine had to remain standing for a moment before regaining the feeling in her legs. She used the light on her cell phone to ensure she trod on more or less the same footprints they had made on their way into the crime scene. Once beyond the cordon tape, which was strung between trees, she tapped in the first letters of the name of the Chief Superintendent. Bodil Melling picked up after the third ring.

"Bratt here. Sorry for calling so late, but it looks like we might have found one of the missing women. Murdered, her throat is cut, probable arterial spatter, likely raped or sexually assaulted. Fairly certain it's Susanne Andersen."

"That's too bad," Melling said, in a voice lacking any tone. And at the same time Katrine pictured the lack of expression in Bodil Melling's face, the lack of color in her attire, lack of emotion in her body language, guaranteed lack of conflict in her home life and lack of excitement in her sex life. The only thing that triggered a reaction in the newly appointed Chief Superintendent, she had discovered, was the soon-to-be vacated office of Chief of Police. It wasn't that Melling wasn't qualified, Katrine just found her unbearably boring. Defensive. Gutless.

"Will you call a press conference?" Melling asked.

"OK. Do you want to . . . ?"

"No, as long as we don't have a positive ID on the body, you take it."

"Together with Kripos, then? They have people at the scene."

"All right, fine. If there's nothing else, we have guests."

In the pause that followed Katrine heard low chatter in the background. It sounded like a genial exchange of views, the kind, that is, where one person confirms and elaborates on what the other has said. Social bonding. That was how Bodil Melling preferred it. She would almost certainly be annoyed if Katrine brought up the subject again. Katrine had suggested it as soon as Bertine Bertilsen was reported missing and suspicion arose that the two women might have been killed by the same man. She wouldn't get anywhere either, Melling had made that very clear, had, in effect, put an end to the discussion. Katrine ought to just let it go.

"Just one thing," she said, letting the words hang in the air as she drew a breath.

Her boss beat her to it.

"The answer is no, Bratt."

"But he's the only specialist on this we have. And he's the best."

"And the worst. Besides, we don't *have* him any longer. Thank God."

"The media are bound to look for him, ask why we're not—"

"Then you just tell them the truth, which is we don't know his whereabouts. Moreover, considering what happened to his wife, coupled with his unstable nature and substance abuse, I can't imagine him functioning in a murder investigation."

"I think I know where to find him."

"Drop it, Bratt. Resorting to old heroes as soon as you're under pressure comes across as an implicit disparagement of the people actually at your disposal in Crime Squad. What will it do to their self-esteem and motivation if you say you want to bring in a wreck without a badge? That's what we call poor leadership, Bratt."

"OK," Katrine said and swallowed hard.

"All right, I appreciate that you think it's OK. Was there anything else?"

Katrine thought for a moment. So Melling could actually be antagonized and bare her teeth after all. Good. She looked at the crescent moon hanging above the treetops. Last night, Arne, the young man she had been dating for almost month, told her that in two weeks there would be a total lunar eclipse, a so-called blood moon, and they should mark the occasion. Katrine had no clue what a blood moon was, but apparently it occurred every second or third year, and Arne was so eager that she hadn't had the heart to say maybe they shouldn't plan something as far in the future as two weeks, seeing as they barely knew each other. Katrine had never been afraid of conflict or of being direct, something she had probably inherited from her father, a policeman from Bergen who'd had more enemies than that city had rainy days, but she had learned to choose her battles and the timing of them. But now, having thought about it, she understood that unlike a confrontation with a man she didn't know whether she had any future with, this was one she had to face. Now rather than later.

"Yes, actually," Katrine said. "Would it also be OK to say that at the press conference if anyone asks? Or to the parents of the next girl who is killed?"

"Say what?"

"That the Oslo Police District is declining the assistance of a man who has cleared up three serial killer cases in the city and apprehended the three culprits? On the grounds we think it may impact on the self-esteem of some colleagues?"

A long silence arose, and Katrine could not hear any chatter in the background now either. Finally, Bodil Melling cleared her throat.

"You know what, Katrine? You've been working hard on this case. Go ahead and hold that press conference, get some sleep over the weekend, and we'll talk on Monday."

After they hung up, Katrine called the Forensic Medical Institute. Rather than go through the proper channels, she called the direct line of Alexandra Sturdza, the young forensic medical officer, who had neither partner nor child, and wasn't too averse to long working hours. And sure enough, Sturdza replied that she and a colleague would take a look at the body the following day.

Afterwards, Katrine stood looking down at the dead woman. Maybe it was the fact that in a man's world she had gotten where she was on her own that would not allow her to set aside her contempt for women who willingly depended on men. That Susanne and Bertine lived off men was not the only circumstance that bound them, but also that they had shared the same man, one more than thirty years their senior, the real estate mogul Markus Røed. Their lives and existences relied on other people, men with the money and the jobs they themselves did not have, providing for them. In exchange, they offered their bodies, youth and beauty. And—insofar as their relationship was exposed—their selected host could enjoy the envy of other men. But, unlike children, women like

Susanne and Bertine lived with the knowledge that love was not unconditional. Sooner or later their host would ditch them, and they would have to seek out a new man to feed upon. Or allow themselves to be fed upon, depending on how you viewed it.

Was that love? Why not, simply because it was too depressing to think about?

Between the trees, in the direction of the gravel road, Katrine saw the blue light of the ambulance, which had arrived noiselessly. She thought about Harry Hole. Yes, she had received a sign of life in April, a postcard—of all things—with a picture of Venice Beach, postmarked Los Angeles. Like a sonar pip from a submarine in the depths. The message had been short. "*Send money.*" A joke, she wasn't sure. Since then there had been silence.

Complete silence.

The final verse of the lullaby, which she had not reached, played in her head.

Blueman, Blueman, answer me, bleat with your familiar sound. Not yet, my Blueman, can you die on your boy.

2

FRIDAY

Value

THE PRESS CONFERENCE TOOK PLACE as usual in the Parole Hall at Police HQ. The clock on the wall read three minutes to ten, and while Mona Daa, *VG*'s crime reporter, and the others waited for the police representatives to take to the podium, Mona could conclude that the attendance was good. Over twenty journalists, and on a Friday evening. She'd had a brief discussion with her photographer on why double murders sold twice as well as single ones, or if it was a case of diminishing returns. The photographer believed that quality was more important than quantity, that as the victim was a young, ethnic Norwegian, of above-average attractiveness, she would generate more clicks than—for example—a drug-addicted couple in their forties with previous convictions. Or two—yes, even three—immigrant boys from a gang.

Mona Daa didn't disagree. So far only one of the missing girls was confirmed killed, but realistically it was only a matter of time before it turned out the other had suffered the same fate, and both were young, ethnic Norwegians and pretty. It didn't get any better. She wasn't sure what to make of that. If it was an expression of extra concern for the young, innocent and defenseless individual. Or if other factors played a part, factors pertaining to the usual things that got clicks: sex, money and a life the readers wished they themselves had.

Speaking of wanting what others had. She looked at the guy in his thirties in the row in front. He was wearing the flannel shirt all the hipsters were supposed to be wearing this year and a porkpie hat à la Gene Hackman in *The French Connection*. It was Terry Våge from *Dagbladet*, and she wished she had his sources. Ever since the story broke, he'd had his nose in front of the others. It was Våge, for instance, who had first written about Susanne Andersen and Bertine Bertilsen having been at the same party. And Våge who had quoted a source as saying both girls had had Røed as a sugar daddy. It was annoying, and for more reasons than simply that he was competition. His very presence here was annoying. As though he had heard her thoughts, he turned and looked right at her. Smiling broadly, he touched a finger to the brim of his idiotic hat.

"He likes you," the photographer said.

"I know," she said.

Våge's interest in Mona had begun when he made his improbable comeback to newspaper journalism as a crime reporter, and she had made the mistake of being relatively friendly towards him at a seminar on—of all things—press ethics. Since the other journalists avoided him like the plague, her attitude must have come across as inviting. He subsequently got in touch with Mona for "tips and advice," as he termed it. As if she had any interest in acting as a mentor for a competitor—indeed, had any desire to have anything to do with someone like Terry Våge; after all, everybody knew there had to be *something* in the rumors circulating about him. But the more stand-offish she was, the more intense he became. On the phone, social media channels, even popping up in bars and cafes, as though from nowhere. It had, as usual, taken a little time before she understood it was *her* he was interested in. Mona had never been the boys' first pick, stocky and broad-faced as she was, with what her mother had called "sad hair" and a defective hip, which gave her a crab-like gait. God knows if it was an attempt to compensate, but she had begun training with weights, grown even more stocky, but had pulled off two hundred and sixty pounds in the deadlift and a third place in the national bodybuilding championships. And because she'd had to learn that a person—or at least she—didn't get anything for free, she had developed a pushy charm, a sense of humor, and a toughness which the Barbie dolls of this world could just forget about, and which had won her the unofficial throne of crime queen—and Anders. Out of the two, she valued Anders higher. Well, just about. No matter, even though the type of attention from other men which Våge displayed was unfamiliar and flattering, it was out of the question for Mona to explore it any further. And she was of the opinion that she—if not in so many words, then in tone and body language—must have made this clear to Våge. But it was as though he saw and heard what he wanted. Sometimes when she looked into those wide-open, staring eyes of his, she wondered whether he was on something or if he was all there. One night he had shown up at a bar, and when Anders went to use the men's room, he had said something to her, in a voice so low it couldn't be heard above the music, but still not quite low enough. "You're mine." She had pretended not to hear, but he just stood there, calm and confident, wearing a sly smile, as if it were now a secret they shared. Fuck him. She couldn't stand drama, so she hadn't mentioned it to Anders. Not that Anders wouldn't have handled it just fine, she knew he would, but still she hadn't said anything. What was it Våge imagined? That her interest in him, the new alpha male in their little pond, would grow in proportion with his position as a crime reporter who was always one step ahead of the others? Because he was, that wasn't open to discussion any longer. So yes, if she wanted something someone else had, it was to be leading the race again, not downgraded to one of the pack chasing behind Terry Våge.

"Where does he get it from, do you think?" she whispered to the photographer.

He shrugged. "Maybe he's making it up again."

Mona shook her head. "No, there're good grounds to believe what he's writing now."

Markus Røed and Johan Krohn, his lawyer, had not even attempted to refute any of what Våge had written, and that was confirmation enough.

But Våge had not always been the king of crime. The story lingered about him, always would. The girl's stage name was Genie, a retro glam act à la Suzi Quatro, for those who remembered her. The incident had occurred about five or six years prior, and the worst part of it was not that Våge had manufactured pure lies about Genie and had them put in print, but the rumor he had dropped Rohypnol into her drink at an after-party in order to have sex with the teenager. At the time, he had been a music journalist for a free newspaper and had obviously become infatuated with her, but had—in spite of his eulogizing her in review after review—been turned down repeatedly. Nevertheless he had continued showing up at gigs and after-parties. Right up to the night when—if the rumors were to be believed—he had spiked her drink and carried her off to his room, which he had booked at the same hotel as the band were staying at. When the boys in the band realized what was happening, they barged into the hotel room where Genie lay unconscious and in a state of half-undress on Terry Våge's bed. They had given Terry such a beating that he suffered a skull fracture and was hospitalized for a couple of months. Genie and the band must have figured Våge had had punishment enough, or may not have wanted to risk prosecution themselves; in any case, the matter was not reported to the police by any of the parties involved. But it was the end of the glowing reviews. In addition to panning her every new release, Terry Våge wrote about Genie's infidelity, drug abuse, plagiarism, under-payment of band member, and false information on applications for grants for tour support. When a dozen or so stories were referred to the Press Complaints Commission, and it turned out that Våge had simply made half of them up, he was fired and became *persona non grata* in the Norwegian media for the next five years. How he had managed to make it back in was a mystery. Or maybe not. He had realized he was finished as a music journalist, but had been behind a crime blog that gathered more and more readers, and eventually *Dagbladet* said that one could not exclude a young journalist from their field just because he had made some mistakes early in his career, and had taken him on as a freelancer—a freelancer who currently got more column inches than any of the newspaper's permanent reporters.

Våge finally turned away from Mona when the police made their entrance and took their places on the podium. Two from Oslo Police, Katrine Bratt—the inspector from Crime Squad—and Head of Information Kedzierski, a man with a Dylanesque mane of curly hair; and two from Kripos, the terrier-like Ole Winter and the always well-dressed Sung-min Larsen, sporting a fresh haircut. So Mona assumed they had already decided that the investigation would be a joint effort on behalf of the Crime Squad, in this case the Volvo, and Kripos, the Ferrari.

Most of the journalists held their phones up in the air to record sound and pictures, but Mona Daa took notes by hand and left the photographs to her colleague.

As expected, they didn't learn much other than a body had been found in Østmarka, in the hiking area around Skullerud, and that the deceased had been identified as the missing woman Susanne Andersen. The case would be treated as a possible murder, but they had, as yet, no details to make public about the cause of death, sequence of events, suspects and so on.

The usual dance ensued, with the journalists peppering those on the podium with questions while they, Katrine Bratt for the most part, repeated "no comment" and "we can't answer that."

Mona Daa yawned. She and Anders were supposed to have a late dinner as a pleasant start to the weekend, but that wasn't going to happen. She noted down what was said, but had the distinct feeling of writing a summary she had written before. Maybe Terry Våge felt the same. He was neither taking notes nor recording anything. Just sitting back in his chair, observing it all with a slight, almost triumphant, smile. Not asking any questions, as though he already had the answers he was interested in. It seemed the others had also run dry, and when Head of Information

Kedzierski looked like he was drawing breath to bring things to a close, Mona raised her pen in the air.

"Yes, *VG*?" The head of Information wore an expression that said this better be short, it's the weekend.

"Do you feel that you have the requisite competence should this turn out to be the type of person who kills again, that is to say if he's—"

Katrine Bratt leaned forward in her chair and interrupted her: "As we said, we don't have any sound basis to allow us to state that there's any connection between this death and any other possible criminal acts. With regard to the combined expertise of the Crime Squad and Kripos, I dare say it's adequate given what we know about the case so far."

Mona noted the inspector's caveat of *what we know*. And that Sung-min Larsen, seated in the chair next to her, had neither nodded at what Bratt said nor given any indication of his view on this expertise.

The press conference drew to a close, and Mona and the others made their way out into a mild autumn night.

"What do you think?" the photographer asked.

"I think they're happy they have a body," Mona said.

"Did you say *happy*?"

"Yeah. Susanne Andersen and Bertine Bertilsen have both been dead for weeks, the police know that, but they haven't had a single lead to go on apart from that party at Røed's. So, yeah, I think they're happy they're starting the weekend with at least one corpse that might give them something."

"Bloody hell, you're a cold fish, Daa."

Mona looked up at him in surprise. Considered it for a moment.

"Thanks," she said.

It was a quarter past eleven by the time Johan Krohn had finally found a parking spot for his Lexus UX 300e in Thomas Heftyes gate, then located the number of the building where his client Markus Røed had asked him to come. The fifty-year-old lawyer was regarded among colleagues as one of the top three or four best defense attorneys in Oslo. Due to his high media profile, the man in the street regarded Krohn as unquestionably the best. Since he was, with a few exceptions, a bigger star than his clients, he did not make house visits, the client came to him, preferably to the offices of the law firm of Krohn and Simonsen in Rosenkrantz gate during normal working hours. Still, there were house calls and there were house calls. This address was not Røed's primary residence; he officially resided at a 2,800-square-foot penthouse on the top of one of the new buildings in Oslobukta.

As he had been instructed on the phone half an hour ago, Krohn pressed the call button bearing the name of Røed's company, Barbell Properties.

"Johan?" Markus Røed's out-of-breath voice sounded. "Fifth floor."

There was a buzz from the top of the door, and Krohn pushed it open.

The elevator looked sufficiently suspect for Krohn to take the stairs. Wide, oak steps and cast-iron banisters with a form more reminiscent of Gaudí than a venerable, exclusive Norwegian town house. The door on the fifth floor was ajar. It sounded like a war was taking place within, which he understood to be the case when he stepped inside, saw bluish light coming from the living room and peered in. In front of a large TV screen—it had to be at least a hundred inches—three men were standing with their backs to him. The biggest of them, the man in the middle, was wearing VR goggles and had a game controller in each hand. The other two, young men in perhaps their twenties, were apparently spectators, using the TV as a monitor to look at what the man in the VR goggles was seeing. The war scene on the TV was from a trench, in the First World War, if Krohn was to judge by the helmets on the German soldiers rushing towards them, and who the large man with the game controllers was blasting away at.

"Yeah!" one of the younger men shouted, as the head of the last German exploded inside his helmet and he fell to the ground.

The larger man removed the VR goggles and turned to Krohn.

"That's *that* taken care of, at least," he said with a grin of satisfaction. Markus Røed was a handsome man, his age taken into consideration. He had a broad face, a playful look, his permanently tanned complexion was smooth, and his swept-back, shiny black hair as thick as a twenty-year-old's. Granted, some weight had spread to his waist, but he was tall, so tall that the stomach could pass as dignified. But it was the intense liveliness in his eyes that first caught your attention, a liveliness indicating the energy which meant most people were initially charmed, then flattened, and eventually exhausted by Markus Røed. Within that time he had probably got what he wanted, and you were left to your own devices. But Røed's energy levels could fluctuate, as could his mood. Krohn assumed both had something to do with the white powder he now saw traces of under one of Røed's nostrils. Johan Krohn was aware of all this, but he put up with it. Not just because Røed had insisted on paying half of Krohn's hourly rate up front to—as he had put it—guarantee Krohn's undivided attention, loyalty and desire to achieve a result. But mostly because Røed was Krohn's dream client: a man with a high profile, a millionaire with such an odious image that Krohn, paradoxically, appeared as more courageous and principled than opportunistic by taking him on as a client. So he would—as long as the case went on—just have to accept being summoned on a Friday night.

The two younger men left the room at a signal from Røed.

"Have you seen *War Remains*, Johan? No? Fucking great VR game, but you can't shoot anyone in it. This here is a sort of copy the developer wants me to invest in . . ." Røed nodded in the direction of the TV screen while he lifted a carafe and poured whiskey into two crystal rocks glasses. "They're trying to retain the magic of *War Remains*, but make it so you can—what would you say?—influence the course of history. After all, that's what we want, right?"

"I'm driving," Krohn said, raising a palm to the glass Røed was holding out to him.

Røed looked at Krohn for a moment as if he didn't understand the objection. Then he sneezed powerfully, sank down onto a leather Barcelona chair, and placed both glasses on the table in front of him.

"Whose apartment is this?" Krohn asked, as he settled into one of the other chairs. And immediately regretted the question. As a lawyer it was often safest not knowing more than you needed to.

"Mine," Røed replied. "I use it as . . . you know, a retreat."

Markus Røed's shrug and scampish smile told Krohn the rest. He'd had other clients with similar apartments. And during an extramarital liaison, which had fortunately come to an end when he realized what he was in danger of losing, he had himself considered buying what a colleague called a bachelor pad for non-bachelors.

"So what happens now?" Røed asked.

"Now Susanne has been identified, and murder has been established as the cause, the investigation will enter a new phase. You need to be prepared to be called in for fresh interviews."

"In other words, there'll be even more focus on me."

"Unless the police find something at the crime scene that rules you out. We can always hope for that."

"I thought you might say something like that. But I can't just sit here hoping any longer, Johan. You do know Barbell Properties has lost three big contracts in the last two weeks? They offered some flimsy excuses, about waiting for higher bids and so on, no one dares say right out that it's because of these articles in *Dagbladet* about me and the girls, that they don't want to be associated with a possible murder, or are afraid I'll be put away and Barbell Properties will go under. If I sit idly by hoping that a gang of public-sector, under-paid knucklehead cops will get the job done, then Barbell Properties might go bust long before they've turned up something that gets me off the hook. We need to be proactive, Johan. We need to show the public that I'm innocent. Or at least that I believe it serves my interest for the truth to come out."

"So?"

"We need to hire our own investigators. First-rate ones. In the best-case scenario they find the killer. But failing that, it still shows the public that I'm actually trying to uncover the truth."

Johan Krohn nodded. "Let me play devil's advocate here, no pun intended."

"Go on," Røed said, and sneezed.

"Firstly, the best detectives are already working for Kripos, as they pay better than the Crime Squad. And even if they were to say yes to quitting a secure career to take on a short-term assignment like this, they'd still have to give three months' notice, plus they'd have an obligation of confidentiality covering what they know about these missing persons cases. Which in effect renders them useless to us. Secondly, the optics would be pretty bad. An investigation being bankrolled by a millionaire? You'd be doing yourself a disservice. Should your investigators uncover so-called facts that clear you, this information would automatically be questioned, something which would not have happened if the police had uncovered the same facts."

"Ah." Røed smiled, wiping his nose with a tissue. "I love value for money. You're good, you've pointed out the problems. And now you're going to show me that you're the best and tell me how we solve those problems."

Johan Krohn straightened up in his chair. "Thank you for the vote of confidence, but there's the rub."

"Meaning?"

"You mentioned finding the best, and there is one person who is perhaps the best. His previous results certainly point to it."

"But?"

"But he's no longer on the force."

"From what you've told me that ought to be an advantage."

"What I mean is that he's no longer in the police for the wrong reasons."

"Which are?"

"Where do I begin? Disloyalty. Gross negligence in the line of duty. Intoxicated on the job, clearly an alcoholic. Several cases of violence. Substance abuse. He's responsible, although not convicted, for the death of at least one colleague. In short, he's probably got more crimes on his conscience than most of the criminals he's hauled in. Plus, he's supposed to be a nightmare to work with."

"That's a lot. So why are you bringing him up if he's so impossible?"

"Because he's the best. And because he could be useful with regard to the second part of what you were saying, about showing the public you're trying to unearth the truth."

"OK . . . ?"

"The cases he's solved have made him one of the few detectives with a public profile of sorts. And an image as uncompromising, someone with don't-give-a-damn integrity. Overblown, of course, but people like those kind of myths. And for our purposes that image could allay suspicions of his investigation being bought and paid for."

"You're worth every penny, Johan Krohn." Røed grinned. "He's the man we want!"

"The problem—"

"No! Just up the offer until he says yes."

"—is that no one seems to know exactly where he is."

Røed raised his whiskey glass without drinking, just frowned down at it. "What do you mean by 'exactly'?"

"Sometimes in an official capacity I run into Katrine Bratt, the head of Crime Squad where he worked, and when I asked, she said the last time he gave a sign of life was from a big city, but she didn't know where he was in that city or what he was doing there. She didn't sound too optimistic on his behalf, let's put it that way."

"Hey! Don't back out now that you've sold me on the guy, Johan! It's him we want, I can feel it. So find him."

Krohn sighed. Again regretted opening his mouth. Being the show-off he was he had of course walked right into the classic prove-you're-the-best trap that Markus Røed probably used every single day. But with his leg stuck in the trap it was too late to turn. Some calls would need to be made. He worked out the time difference. OK, he might as well get right on it.

3

SATURDAY

ALEXANDRA STURDZA STUDIED HER FACE in the mirror above the sink while routinely and thoroughly washing her hands, as though it were a living person and not a corpse she would soon touch. Her face was hard, pockmarked. Her hair—pulled back and tied in a tight bun—was jet black, but she knew the first gray hairs were in store—her Romanian mother had gotten them in her early thirties. Norwegian men said her brown eyes "flashed," especially when any of them tried to imitate her almost imperceptible accent. Or when they joked about her homeland, a place some of them clearly thought was a big joke, and she told them she came from Timişoara, the first city in Europe to install electric street lighting in 1884, two generations before Oslo. When she came to Norway as a twenty-year-old, she had learned Norwegian in six months while working three jobs, which she had reduced to two while studying chemistry at NTNU, and now just one, at the Forensic Medical Institute while also concentrating on what would be her doctoral thesis on DNA analysis. She had at times—although not that often—wondered what it was that made her so obviously attractive to men. It couldn't be her face and direct—at times harsh—manner. Nor her intellect and CV, which men seemed to perceive as more threatening than stimulating. She sighed. A man had once told her that her body was a cross between a tiger and a Lamborghini. Odd how so cheesy a comment could sound totally wrong or completely acceptable, yes, wonderful even, depending on who said it. She turned off the faucet and went into the autopsy room.

Helge was already there. The technician, two years her junior, was quick-minded and laughed easily, both qualities Alexandra viewed as assets when one worked with the dead and was tasked with extracting secrets from a corpse about how death occurred. Helge was a bioengineer and Alexandra a chemical engineer, and both were qualified to carry out forensic post-mortems, if not full clinical autopsies. Nevertheless, certain pathologists attempted to pull rank by calling post-mortem technicians *Diener*—servants—a hangover from German pathologists of the old school. Helge didn't care but Alexandra had to admit it got to her now and again. And especially on days like today, when she came in and did everything a pathologist would do in a preliminary post-mortem—and equally well. Helge was her favorite at the institute, he always showed up when she asked, not something every Norwegian would on a Saturday. Or after four o'clock on a weekday. Sometimes she wondered where on the index of living standards this work-shy country would have been placed if the Americans hadn't discovered oil on their continental shelf.

She turned up the light on the lamp hanging above the naked body of the young woman on the table. The smell of a corpse was dependent on many factors: age, cause of death, if medication was being taken, what food had been eaten and—of course—how far along the process of decay was. Alexandra had no problems with the stench of rotting flesh, of excrement, or urine. She could even tackle the gases created by the process of decomposition that the body expelled in long hisses. It was the stomach fluids that got her. The smell of vomit, bile and the various acids. In that sense, Susanne Andersen was not too bad, even after three weeks outdoors.

"No larvae?" Alexandra asked.

"I removed them," Helge said, holding up the vinegar bottle they used.

"But kept them?"

"Yeah," he said, pointing to a glass box containing a dozen white maggots. They were saved because their length could be indicative of how long they had fed on the corpse, in other words, how long it had been since they hatched, and therefore, something about the time of death. Not in hours, but in days and weeks.

"This won't take long," Alexandra said. "Crime Squad just want the probable cause of death and an external examination. Blood test, urine, bodily fluid. The pathologist will perform a complete post-mortem on Monday. Any plans for tonight? Here . . ."

Helge took a photograph of where she was pointing.

"Thought I might watch a movie," he said.

"What about joining me at a gay club for a dance?" She made notes on the form and pointed again. "Here."

"I can't dance."

"Bullshit. All gays can dance. See this cut on the throat? Starts on the left side, gets deeper farther along, then shallower towards the right. It indicates a right-handed killer who was standing behind and holding her head back. One of the pathologists was telling me about a similar wound that they thought was murder, and it turned out the man had cut his own throat. Pretty determined, in other words. What do you say, want to go dance with some gays tonight?"

"What if I'm not gay?"

"In that case . . ." Alexandra said, taking notes, ". . . I wouldn't actually want to go out anywhere with you again, Helge."

He laughed out loud and snapped a picture. "Because?"

"Because then you'll block other men. A good wingman needs to be gay."

"I can pretend to be gay."

"Doesn't work. Men notice the smell of testosterone and back off. What do you think this is?"

She held a magnifying glass just below one of Susanne Andersen's nipples.

Helge leaned closer. "Dried saliva, maybe. Or snot. Not semen, in any case."

"Take a photo, then I'll take a scrape sample and check it at the lab on Monday. If we're lucky, it's DNA material."

Helge took a picture while Alexandra examined the mouth, ears, nostrils and eyes.

"What do you think has happened here?" She raised a penlight and shone it in the empty eye socket.

"Animals?"

"No, I don't think so." Alexandra shone the light around the edges of the eye socket. "There's nothing remaining of the eyeball inside and no wounds around the eye from the claws of birds or rodents. And if it was an animal, why not take the other eye as well? Take a photo here . . ." She illuminated the eye socket. "See how the nerve fibers look like they've been cut at one place, as though with a knife?"

"Jesus," Helge said. "Who does something like that?"

"Angry men," Alexandra said, shaking her head. "Very angry and very damaged men. And they're on the loose out there. Maybe I should stay in and watch a movie tonight as well."

"Yeah, right."

"OK. Let's see if he's assaulted her sexually too."

They took a cigarette break on the roof after determining there were no obvious signs of injury to the exterior or interior of the genitalia nor any traces of semen on the outside of the vagina. If semen had been present within the vagina, it would have been drawn into the rest of the body long ago. The pathologist would go over the same ground as them on Monday but she was pretty certain they would not arrive at a different conclusion.

Alexandra was not a regular smoker, but had a vague belief in cigarettes smoking out any potential demons from the dead that had taken up residence within. She inhaled and looked out over Oslo. Over the fjord, glittering like silver beneath a pale, cloudless sky. Over the low hills, where the colors of autumn burned in red and yellow.

"Fuck, it's nice here," she said with a sigh.

"You make it sound like you wish it wasn't," Helge said, taking over the cigarette from her.

"I hate getting attached to things."

"Things?"

"Places. People."

"Men?"

"Especially men. They take away your freedom. Or rather, they don't take it, you bloody well give it away like a wuss, as if you're programmed to. And freedom is worth more than men."

"You sure?"

She snatched the cigarette back and took a long, angry drag. Blew the smoke out just as hard and gave a harsh, rasping laugh.

"Worth more than the men I fall for anyway."

"What about that cop you mentioned?"

"Oh, him." She chuckled. "Yeah, I liked him. But he was a mess. His wife had kicked him out and he drank all the time."

"Where is he now?"

"His wife died and he skipped the country. Tragic business." Alexandra stood up abruptly. "Right, we better finish up and get the body back in the refrigerator. I want to party!"

They returned to the autopsy room, collected the last samples, filled out the rest of the fields on the form and tidied up.

"Speaking of parties," Alexandra said. "You know the party this girl and the other one were at? That was the same party I was invited to, the one I then invited you to."

"You're kidding?"

"Don't you remember? A friend of one of Røed's neighbors asked me. She said the party was taking place on *the* best rooftop terrace in Oslobukta. Told me it would be crawling with the well-heeled, with celebrities and party people. Said they'd prefer women came in skirts. *Short skirts.*"

"Ugh," Helge said. "Don't blame you for not going."

"Fuck that, course I would've gone! If I hadn't had so much work on here that day. And you would have come with."

"Would I?" Helge smiled.

"Of course." Alexandra laughed. "I'm your fag hag. Can't you picture it, you, me and the beautiful people?"

"Yes."

"You see, you are gay."

"What? Because?"

"Tell me truthfully, Helge. Have you ever slept with a man?"

"Let me see . . ." Helge wheeled the table with the corpse towards one of the cold lockers. "Yes."

"More than once?"

"Doesn't mean I'm gay," he said, opening the large metal drawer.

"No, that's only circumstantial evidence. The proof, Watson, is that you tie your sweater over one shoulder and under the other arm."

Helge chuckled, grabbed one of the white cloths on the instrument table and flicked it at her. Alexandra smiled as she ducked down behind the top end of the table. She remained like that, stooped over, her eyes fixed on the body.

"Helge," she said in a low voice.

"Yeah."

"I think we've missed something."

"What?"

Alexandra reached out towards Susanne Andersen's head, lifted the hair and pulled it to the side.

"What is it?" Helge asked.

"Stitches," Alexandra replied. "Fresh stitches."

He came around the other side of the gurney. "Hm. Guess she must have hurt herself then?"

Alexandra lifted away more hair, followed the stitches. "These weren't carried out by a trained doctor, Helge, no one uses thread this thick or stitches this loosely. This was done in a hurry. And look, the stitches continue all the way around the head."

"As though she's . . ."

"As though she's been scalped," Alexandra said, feeling a cold shudder go through her. "And then the scalp has been sewn back on."

She looked up at Helge, saw his Adam's apple rise and fall. "Will we . . ." he began. "Will we check what's . . . underneath?"

"No," Alexandra said firmly, straightening up. She had taken home enough nightmares from this job, and the pathologists earned two hundred thousand kroner a year more than her, they could earn it.

"This is outside our field of competence," she said. "So it's the kind of thing *Diener*s like you and me leave to the grown-ups."

"OK. And OK to partying tonight too, by the way."

"Good," Alexandra said. "But we need to finish the report and send it along with the photos to Bratt at Crime Squad. Oh fuck!"

"What is it?"

"I just realized that Bratt is bound to ask me to run an express DNA analysis when she reads about that saliva or whatever it is. In which case I won't make it out on the town tonight."

"Come on, you can say no, everyone needs time off, even you."

Alexandra put her hands on her hips, tilted her head to one side and looked sternly at Helge.

"Right." He sighed. "Where would we be if everyone just took time off?"

4

SATURDAY

Rabbit hole

HARRY HOLE WOKE UP. THE bungalow lay in semi-darkness, but a white strip of sunlight, coming from under the bamboo blind, stretched across the coarse wooden floor, via the stone slab serving as a coffee table, and over to the kitchen worktop.

A cat was sitting there. One of Lucille's cats; she had so many of them up in the main house that Harry couldn't tell one from the other. The cat looked like it was smiling. Its tail was waving slowly as it calmly observed a mouse scuttling along the wall, stopping now and then to stick its snout in the air to sniff, before continuing. Towards the cat. Was the mouse blind? Did it lack a sense of smell? Had it eaten some of Harry's marijuana? Or did it believe, like so many others seeking happiness in this city, that it was different, special? Or that this *cat* was different, that it meant well and wouldn't just eat him?

Harry reached for the joint on the nightstand while keeping his eyes on the mouse, who was headed straight towards the cat. The cat struck, sinking its teeth into the mouse and lifting it up. It writhed a few moments in the predator's jaws before going limp. The cat laid its prey on the floor, then viewed it with its head cocked slightly to one side, as though undecided on whether to eat the mouse or not.

Harry lit the joint. He had come to the conclusion that joints didn't count with regard to the new drinking regimen he had embarked upon. Inhaled. Watched the smoke curl upward to the ceiling. He had dreamed about the man behind the wheel of the Camaro again. And the license plate that read Baja California Mexico. The dream was the same, he was chasing them. So not exactly hard to interpret. Three weeks had passed since Harry had stood in the parking lot outside Creatures with a Glock 17 aimed at him, fairly certain his imminent demise was a second or two away. Which had been just fine by him. So it was strange that the only thing that had been in his head after those two seconds had elapsed, and every day since, was *not* to die. It had begun with the hesitation on the part of the man in the polo shirt, perhaps he was considering the possibility that Harry was a mental case, a manageable obstacle to be overcome, who didn't need shooting. He would hardly have had more time to think before Harry's chisel punch struck him in the throat and put him down for the count. Harry had physically felt the man's larynx give way. He had lain squirming on the gravel like a worm, his hands to his throat and eyes bulging while he gasped desperately for air. Harry had picked the Glock up off the ground and stared at the man in the car. Due to the tinted windows he hadn't seen much, only the outline of a face, and that the man looked to be wearing a white shirt buttoned right up to the neck. And that he was smoking a cigarette or a cigarillo. The man made no move, just looked calmly out at Harry, as though evaluating him, committing him to memory. Harry heard someone shout "Get in!" and noticed Lucille had started her own car and pushed open the door on the passenger side.

Then he had jumped in. Down the rabbit hole.

The first thing he asked as she turned down towards Sunset Boulevard, was who she owed money to and how much.

The first answer—"The Esposito family"—didn't mean much to him, but the next—"Nine hundred and sixty thousand dollars"—confirmed what the Glock had already told him. That she wasn't in a little trouble but a lot. And that from now on that trouble included him.

He explained that under no circumstances could she go back home, and asked if there was anyone whose place she could lay low at. She said, yes, she had a lot of friends in Los Angeles. But after thinking about for a minute, she said none of them would be willing to run the risk for her. They stopped at a gas station, and Lucille called her first husband, whom she knew had a house he hadn't used in several years.

And that was how they had ended up on this property, with its dilapidated house, overgrown garden and guest bungalow. Harry had installed himself in the bungalow with his newly acquired Glock 17 because from there he had a view of both gates, and because it was fitted with an alarm that went off should anyone break into the main house. Any prospective intruders wouldn't hear that alarm, meaning hopefully he could take them from the rear, given that he would be coming from the outside. Up until now, he and Lucille had hardly left the property, just short trips for the absolute essentials: alcohol, food, clothes and cosmetics—in that order. Lucille had taken up residence on the first floor of the main house, which after just a week was full of cats.

"Aw, in this town they're all homeless," Lucille told him. "You put some food out on the stoop a few days in a row, leave the front door open, some more food in the kitchen, and before you know it you've got enough pet friends for an entire lifetime."

Yet not quite enough it seemed, because three days previously Lucille decided she couldn't endure the isolation any longer. She had taken Harry to a former Savile Row tailor she knew, to an elderly hairdresser in Rosewood Avenue and then—most important of all—to John Lobb's shoe store in Beverly Hills. Yesterday, Harry had picked up the suit while Lucille got ready, and a few hours later they had gone to eat at Dan Tana's, the legendary Italian restaurant where the chairs were as worn-out as the clientele, but where Lucille seemed to know everybody and had beamed all evening.

It was seven o'clock. Harry inhaled and stared at the ceiling. Listened for sounds that shouldn't be there. But all he heard was the first cars on Doheny Drive, which was not the widest street, but popular because it had fewer traffic lights than the roads running parallel. It reminded him of lying in bed in his apartment in Oslo, listening to the sounds of the city wake outside the open window. He missed it, even the ill-tempered ringing and the shrill screech of a braking tram. *Particularly* the shrill screech.

But Oslo was behind him now. Following Rakel's death he had sat at the airport, looked at the departure board, and rolled a dice that determined his destination would be Los Angeles. He had figured it was as good as anywhere. He had lived in Chicago for a year while attending the FBI's course for serial homicides, and thought he was familiar with American culture and their way of life. But not long after arrival, he realized that Chicago and LA were two different planets. One of Lucille's movie friends, a German director, had described Los Angeles with bluster in a broad accent at Dan Tana's the night before.

"You land at LAX, the sun is shining and you're picked up by a limousine which drives you to a place where you lie down by a swimming pool, get a cocktail, fall asleep and wake up to discover that twenty years of your life have gone by."

That was the director's LA.

Harry's introduction to LA had been four nights at a dirty, cockroach-infested motel room without AC in La Cienega, prior to his renting an even cheaper room in Laurel Canyon, also without AC, but with larger cockroaches. But he had settled in somewhat after discovering Creatures, the neighborhood bar, where the liquor was cheap enough for him to deem it possible to drink himself to death.

But after staring down the barrel of a Glock 17 this desire to die had ceased. As had the drinking. That type of drinking at any rate. If he was to be capable of keeping watch and looking out for Lucille, he would have to be somewhat sober. He had, therefore, decided to test out the drinking regimen his childhood friend and drinking partner Øystein Eikeland had recommended, although frankly it sounded like bullshit. The method was called Moderation Management, and was supposed to turn you into a substance user, meaning a substance abuser who exercises moderation. The first time he had told Harry about it, the two of them had been sitting in Øystein's taxi at a stand in Oslo. His enthusiasm had been such that he had hammered on the steering wheel while proclaiming its virtues.

"People have always derided the alcoholic who swears that from now on he's only going to have a drink in social settings, right? Because they don't think that's possible, they're sure it isn't, almost as if you'd be defying the law of gravity for, like, alcoholism, yeah? But you know what? It is possible to drink to just the right level of drunkenness even for a full-blown alkie like you. And me. It's possible to program yourself to drink to a certain point and stop. All you have to do is decide beforehand where to draw the line, how many units. But, it goes without saying, you have to work at it."

"You have to drink a lot before you get the hang of it, you mean?"

"Yeah. You're smirking, Harry, but I'm serious. It's about that sense of achievement, of knowing that you can. And then it's possible. I'm not kidding, I can offer the world's best substance abuser as living proof."

"Hm. I presume we're talking about that overrated guitarist you like so much."

"Hey, have some respect for Keith Richards! Read his biography. He gives you the formula right there. Survival is about two things. Only the purest, best dope, it's the stuff mixed in with it that kills you. And moderation, in both drugs and alcohol. You know exactly how much you need to get sufficiently drunk, which in your case means pain-free. More liquor after doesn't help soothe the pain more, now does it?"

"Suppose not."

"Exactly. Being drunk isn't the same as being an idiot or weak-willed. After all, you manage not to drink when you're sober, so why shouldn't you manage to stop when you're at just the right level. It's all in your head, brother!"

The rules—in addition to setting a limit—were to count the number of units and decide on set days where you abstained completely. As well as take a naltrexone an hour before your first drink. Putting off drinking for an hour when the thirst suddenly hit actually helped. He had kept to the regimen for three weeks now and had yet to crack. That was something in itself.

Harry swung his legs out of bed and stood up. He didn't need to open the fridge, he knew it was empty of beer. The Moderation Management rules specified a maximum of three units per day. That meant a six-pack from the 7-Eleven down the street. He looked in the mirror. He had actually put a little more meat on his bones in the three weeks since the escape from Creatures. As well as a gray, almost white, beard. It hid his most conspicuous feature, the liver-colored scar. Whether that would be enough for the man in the Camaro not to recognize him again was doubtful, however. Harry peered out of the window towards the garden and the main house while he pulled on a ragged pair of jeans and a T-shirt starting to tear at the neckline reading "Let Me Do One More illuminati hotties" on it. Put the old, non-wireless earphones in his ears, his feet in a pair of flip-flops and noted that nail fungus had created a grotesque artwork of sorts on the big toe of his right foot. He walked out into a tangle of grass, bushes and jacaranda trees. Stopped by the gate and looked up and down Doheny Drive. Everything seemed fine. He turned on the music, "Pool Hopping" by illuminati hotties, a song that had lifted his spirits ever since he had heard it for the first time live at Zebulon Café. But after walking a few yards down the sidewalk, he caught sight of a car pulling away from the curb in the side mirror of one of the parked cars. Harry continued on, turning his head ever so slightly to check. The car was moving slowly behind at the same speed about ten yards back. While living in Laurel Canyon, he had been stopped twice by police cars simply because he was on foot and therefore deemed a suspicious individual. But this wasn't a police cruiser. It was an old Lincoln, and as far as Harry could make out only one person was in the car. A broad bulldog face, double chin, small moustache. Fuck, he should have taken the Glock! But Harry couldn't envision the attack happening in the middle of the street in broad daylight, so he continued walking. Turned off the music discreetly. Crossed the street just before Santa Monica Boulevard and entered the 7-Eleven. Stood and waited while scanning the street. But he didn't see the Lincoln anywhere. Maybe it had been a prospective house buyer cruising slowly along while checking out the properties on Doheny.

He made his way between the aisles towards the refrigerators with beer at the back of the premises. Heard the door open. Remained standing with one hand on the handle of the glass door, but without opening, so he could see the reflection. And there he was. In a cheap, check suit and a body to match his bulldog face: small, compact and fat. But fat in the way that might mask speed, strength and—Harry felt his heart beat faster—danger. Harry could see the man behind him hadn't drawn any weapon, not yet. He kept the earphones in, figuring he might have a chance if the man believed he had the element of surprise on his side.

"Mister . . ."

Harry pretended not to hear and watched the man approach and stop directly behind him. He was almost two heads shorter than Harry, and was now reaching out, maybe to tap Harry on the shoulder, maybe for something else entirely. Harry wasn't planning on waiting to find out what it was. He turned halfway towards the man, quickly threw an arm around his neck at the same time as he opened the glass door with his other hand. He twisted back while simultaneously kicking the man's feet from under him, causing him to fall into the shelves of beer. Harry released his hold on the man's neck and drove his own bodyweight against the glass door, squeezing the man's head against the shelves. The bottles toppled over, and the man's arms were pinned between the door and the jamb. The eyes in his bulldog face widened and he called out something from behind the door, his breath misting the cold glass on the inside. Harry eased up slightly so the man's head slipped down to the shelves below, then he pushed again. The edge of the refrigerator door pressed against the man's throat and his eyes bulged. The man had stopped shouting. His eyes had stopped bulging. And the glass was no longer misting in front of his mouth.

Harry gradually eased off the pressure on the door. The man slid life-lessly onto the floor. He clearly wasn't breathing. Harry had to quickly assess priorities. The man's health weighed against his own. He chose his own and put his hand into the inside pocket of the fat man's check suit. Fished out a wallet. Opened it and saw a photo of the man on an ID card: a Polish-sounding name and—of more interest and in large letters at the top of the card—*Private Investigator Licensed by the California Bureau of Security and Investigative Services*.

Harry looked down at the lifeless man. This wasn't right, this wasn't how debt collectors operated. They might use a private detective to find him, but not to make contact or rough him up.

Harry flinched and ducked his head when he noticed a man standing between the shelves in the aisle. He was wearing a 7-Eleven T-shirt, and his arms were raised and pointing towards Harry. His hands gripped a revolver. He could see the man's knees were trembling and the muscles in his face twitching uncontrollably. And he also saw what the 7-Eleven man saw. A bearded guy, dressed like a homeless person, holding the wallet of a guy in a suit who he'd obviously just assaulted.

"Don't . . ." Harry said, putting the wallet down, lifting both hands in the air and getting to his knees. "I'm a regular here. This man—"

"I saw what you did!" the man said in a shrill voice. "I shoot! The police is coming!"

"OK," Harry said, and nodded down at the fat man. "But let me help this guy, OK?"

"Move and I shoot!"

"But . . ." Harry began, but held back when he saw the revolver being cocked.

In the silence that followed only the humming of the fridge and the sirens in the distance could be heard. Police. Police and the unavoidable consequences that brought, of interrogations and charges, were not good. Not good at all. Harry had outstayed his welcome long ago and had no papers to prevent them throwing him out of the country. After they had thrown him into prison, of course.

Harry took a deep breath. Looked at the man. In the vast majority of countries he would have made a defensive retreat, in other words, got to his feet with his hands above his head and calmly walked out of there, secure in the knowledge that the individual wouldn't put a bullet in him, even though he appeared to be a violent thief. But this was not one of those countries.

"I shoot!" the man repeated, as though in response to Harry's deliberations, and moved his legs farther apart. His knees had stopped trembling. The sirens were getting closer.

"Please, I must help . . ." Harry began, but his voice was drowned out by a sudden fit of coughing.

They stared down at the man on the floor.

The detective's eyes were bulging again, and his whole body shook from a continued bout of coughing.

The 7-Eleven man's pistol swung this way and that, unsure if the hitherto presumed dead man now also represented a danger.

"Sorry . . ." the detective whispered as he gasped for breath, ". . . for sneaking up on you like that. But you are Harry Hole, right?"

"Well." Harry hesitated while considering which of the evils was lesser. "Yes, I am.

"I have a client who needs to get in touch with you." The man, groaning, rolled onto his side, took a phone from his trouser pocket, tapped a key and held the phone out to Harry. "They are eagerly awaiting our call."

Harry took the already ringing phone. Placed it against his ear.

"Hello?" a voice said. Strangely, it sounded familiar.

"Hello," Harry answered, glancing at the 7-Eleven man, who had lowered the revolver. Was Harry mistaken or did he look slightly more disappointed than relieved? Maybe he was born and raised here after all.

"Harry!" the voice on the phone exclaimed. "How are you? This is Johan Krohn."

Harry blinked. How long had it been since he had heard Norwegian?

5

SATURDAY

Scorpion tail

LUCILLE SHOOED ONE OF THE cats off the four-poster bed, stood up, drew the curtains and sat down at the makeup mirror. Studied her face. She had recently seen a picture of Uma Thurman, she was over fifty now, but looked like a thirty-year-old. Lucille sighed. The task seemed more insurmountable with each passing year, but she opened the Chanel tub, dipped her fingertips in and began spreading foundation from the center of her face outwards. Saw how the increasingly loose skin was being pushed together in folds. And asked herself the same question she asked every morning. Why? Why begin every day in front of the mirror for at least half an hour in order to look like you're not close to eighty but perhaps . . . seventy? And the answer was the same every morning too. Because she—like every other actor she knew—needed to do whatever it took to feel loved. If not for who they were, then for who they—with makeup, costume, and the right script—pretended to be. It was an illness which aging and lower expectations never quite managed to cure.

Lucille put on her musk perfume. There were those who thought musk was such a masculine aroma that it didn't belong in a perfume for women, but she had used it with great success ever since she was a young actress. It made her stand out, it was a fragrance you didn't forget easily. She tied her bathrobe and walked downstairs, taking care to avoid two cats who had settled on the staircase.

She went into the kitchen and opened the fridge. Almost immediately, one of the cats rubbed against her legs in an attempt to curry favor. No doubt it smelled the tuna fish, but it was easy to imagine there was a sliver of affection there as well. At the end of the day, it was more important to feel loved than to be loved. Lucille took out a tin, turned to the kitchen counter and gave a start as she caught sight of Harry. He was sitting at the kitchen table with his back leaned against the wall and those long legs of his stretched out in front of him. He was squeezing the gray titanium finger on his left hand. His blue eyes were squinting. He had the bluest eyes she had seen since Steve McQueen.

Harry shifted in the chair.

"Breakfast?" she asked, opening the tin.

Harry shook his head. He tugged at his titanium finger. But it was the hand he was tugging with that caught her eye. She swallowed. Cleared her throat.

"You've never said it but you're really a dog person, aren't you?"

He shrugged.

"Speaking of dogs, did I ever tell you I was supposed to co-star with Robert De Niro in *Mad Dog and Glory*? Do you remember that movie?"

Harry nodded.

"Really? Then you're one of the few. But Uma Thurman got the part. And she and Bobby, Robert that is, started dating. Which was pretty unusual, given that he mostly went for black women. There must have been something about the roles that brought them together, we actors do go so very into what we do, we *become* those we play. So if I'd gotten the role like I'd been promised, then Bobby and I would have become an item, you get me?"

"Mm. So you've said."

"And I would have been able to hang on to him. Not like Uma Thurman, she . . ." Lucille upended the tin can onto a plate. "Did you read how everyone 'praised' her after she came forward and spoke about how Weinstein, that pig, had tried it on with her? Wanna know what I think? I think when you're Uma Thurman, millionaire actor, and you've known what Weinstein's been up to without blowing the whistle, that when you finally step forward to kick a man when he's down, who other less powerful and braver women have brought down, that you shouldn't be praised. When, for years, you've tacitly allowed all those young, hopeful actors to walk into Weinstein's office alone because you with all your millions, by speaking out might—*might*—miss out on yet another million-dollar role, then I think you should be publicly whipped and spat upon."

She paused.

"Something wrong, Harry?"

"We need to find a new place," he said. "They'll find us."

"What makes you think that?"

"A private detective found us within twenty-four hours."

"Private detective?"

"I just spoke to him. He's gone."

"What did he want?"

"To offer me a job as a private investigator for a wealthy guy who's suspected of a murder in Norway."

Lucille swallowed hard. "And what did you say?"

"I said no."

"Because?"

Harry shrugged. "Because I'm tired of running, maybe."

She placed the plate on the ground and watched the cats crowd around. "I'm well aware that you're doing it for my sake, Harry. You're heeding that old Chinese proverb about how once you've saved someone's life you're responsible for it forever."

Harry gave a crooked smile. "I didn't save your life, Lucille. They were

47

after the money you owe, and they're not going to kill the only person who can get it for them."

She smiled back. Knew he was saying that so she wouldn't be scared. Knew that he knew that they knew she could never get her hands on one million dollars.

She picked up the kettle to fill it with water, but realized she couldn't be bothered, and let go of it. "So you're tired of running."

"Tired of running."

She remembered the conversation they'd had one night while drinking wine and watching a VHS copy of *Romeo and Juliet* she had found in a drawer. For once, she had wanted to talk about him and not herself, but he hadn't said much. Only that he had fled to LA from a life in ruins, a wife who'd been murdered, a colleague who'd taken his own life. No details. And she had understood there was no point in digging any further. It had actually been a pleasant, almost wordless evening. Lucille propped herself up on the kitchen counter.

"Your wife, you never told me her name."

"Rakel."

"And the murder. Was it solved?"

"In a sense."

"Oh?"

"For a long time I was the prime suspect, but finally the investigation identified a known offender. One I'd put behind bars before."

"So . . . the man who killed your wife did it to take revenge . . . on you?"

"Let's just say that the man who killed her . . . I'd taken his life from him. So he took mine from me." He got to his feet. "Like I said, we need a new hiding place, so pack a bag."

"We're leaving today?"

"When private detectives are looking for someone they leave behind tracks of their own. And that visit to the restaurant last night was probably a bad idea."

Lucille nodded. "I'll make some calls."

"Use this," Harry said. He placed a cell phone on the kitchen counter, obviously newly purchased and still wrapped in plastic.

"So he took away your life but let you live," she said. "Did he get his revenge?"

"The best kind." Harry said, striding towards the door.

Harry closed the door of the main house behind him and stopped dead. Stared. He was tired of running. But he was even more tired of staring down the barrels of guns. And this one had two. It was a sawn-off shotgun. The man at the other end was Latino. As was the man with the pistol beside him. Both of them had prison muscles and both a scorpion tattooed on the side of his neck. Harry towered enough over them to see the cut strip of alarm cable dangling on the side of the gate behind them and the white Camaro parked on the other side of Doheny Drive. The tinted window on the driver's side was halfway down, and Harry could just discern cigarillo smoke seeping and a white shirt collar.

"Shall we go inside?" the man with the shotgun said. He spoke with a distinct Mexican accent while he flexed his neck on each side, like a boxer before a match. The motion stretched out the scorpion. Harry knew the tattoo symbolized an enforcer, and the number of squares on the tail the number of people killed. The tails of both men's tattoos were long.

6

SATURDAY

Life on Mars

"'LIFE ON MARS'?" PRIM SAID.

'The girl on the other side of the table looked at him with incomprehension.

Prim burst into laughter. "No, the *song*, I mean. It's called 'Life on Mars'."

He nodded in the direction of the TV where David Bowie's voice emanated from the sound bar below it into the large loft. From the windows he had a view over Oslo's central west side and towards Holmenkollen Ridge, glittering like a chandelier out there in the night. But right now he only had eyes for his dinner guest. "A lot of people don't like the song, they think it's a little odd. The BBC called it a cross between a Broadway musical and a Salvador Dalí painting. Perhaps. But I agree with the *Daily Telegraph*, who named it the best song of all time. Imagine! The *best*. Everybody loved Bowie, not because he was a lovable person, but because he was the best. That's why people who haven't been loved are willing to kill to be the best. They know that will change everything."

Prim took hold of the wine bottle standing on the table between them, but instead of pouring from where he sat, he got up and walked around to her side.

"Did you know that David Bowie was a stage name, that his real name was Jones? I'm not actually called Prim, it's just a nickname, but only my family call me that. But I'd like to think that when I get married my wife will also call me Prim."

He was standing directly behind her and, while filling her glass, he stroked her long, fine hair with his free hand. Had it been a couple of years ago, even a couple of months ago, he would not have dared touch a woman like this for fear of rejection. Now he had no such doubts, he was in total control. Having his teeth fixed had helped, of course, as well as starting to go to a proper hairdresser and taking advice on which clothes to buy. But it wasn't that. It was something he exuded, something they were unable to resist, and knowing that endowed him with a confidence which was in itself such a strong aphrodisiac it alone could have carried him, that placebo effect that was self-perpetuating with every turn as long as he kept the cycle going.

"I'm probably old-fashioned and naive," he said, walking back to his side of the table. "But I believe in marriage, that there's a person out there who's the right one for each of us, I really do. I was at the National Theater recently seeing *Romeo and Juliet*, and it was so beautiful I cried. Two souls nature intended to be inextricably linked. Just look at Boss over there."

He pointed to an aquarium atop a low bookshelf. A single shimmering gold-and-green fish was swimming within. "He has his Lisa. You can't see her, but she's there, the two of them are one and will be until they both die. Yes, one will die *because* the other dies. Like in *Romeo and Juliet*. Isn't that beautiful?"

Prim sat down and slid his hand across the table towards her. She seemed weary tonight, empty, off. But he knew how to brighten her up, all he had to do was flick a switch.

"I could fall in love with someone like you," he said.

Her eyes lit up immediately, and he could feel the warmth from them. But he also felt a little pang of guilt. Not in manipulating her in this way but because he was lying. He might fall in love, but not with her. She was not the one, the Woman who was meant for him. She was a stand-in, someone he could use to practice on, test approaches out on, say the right things to, in the right tone of voice. Trial and error. Erring now didn't really matter, it was on the day he would declare his love to the Woman that everything had to be properly in tune, perfect.

He had also used her to rehearse the act itself. Well, used might not be the right word, she had been the more active of the two. He had met her at a party where there were so many others above him in the pecking order that, upon seeing her peering over his shoulder, he realized he would only get the chance to say a few words before she was gone. He had, however, been effective, had complimented her on her body, and asked which gym she went to. When she answered tersely SATS in Bislett, he said it was strange he hadn't seen her as he went there himself three days a week, but perhaps they went on different days? She made a curt reply about going there in the mornings, and looked annoyed when he said he did too, so on which days did she train?

"Tuesdays and Thursdays," she replied, as though to conclude the conversation, and turned her attention to a man in a tight-fitting black shirt who had wandered over in their direction.

The following Tuesday, he had been standing outside the gym when she came out. Pretended he happened to be passing and had recognized her from the party. She didn't remember him, had smiled and was about to be on her way. But then she stopped, turned around to face him, giving him her full attention as they stood there on the street. Looked at him as though only now really becoming aware of him, no doubt wondering how it could have escaped her notice at the party. He did the talking, she wasn't exactly the most communicative. Not verbally, at least, her body language told him what he needed to know. It was only when he said they should meet up that she spoke.

"When?" she said. "Where?"

And when he told her, she just nodded in response. It was that simple.

She came as arranged. He had been nervous. So much could go wrong. But she was the one who took the initiative, who unbuttoned his clothes, fortunately without saying too much.

He knew this could happen, and even though he and the Woman he loved had not exchanged any promises, this was a form of infidelity, was it not? A betrayal of love, at least. But he had convinced himself that it was a sacrifice on the altar of love, something he did for Her, that he performed the deed because he needed all the practice he could get, so that on the day it counted he would meet the requirements She demanded of a lover.

But now the woman on the other side of the table had served her purpose.

Not that he hadn't enjoyed making love to her. But any repeat of it was out of the question. And—if he was being honest—he didn't like her smell or her taste. Should he say it out loud? Tell her this was where they would part ways? He stared down at his plate in silence. When he looked up again she had tilted her head a little to the side, still with that inscrutable smile in place, as though she were viewing his monologue as an amusing performance. And suddenly he felt like a prisoner. A prisoner in his own home. Because he couldn't just get up and leave, he had nowhere else to go. And he couldn't very well ask her to leave, could he? She didn't look like she was planning on going anywhere just yet, not at all, and the almost unnatural intensity of the gleam in her eyes dazzled him, made him lose perspective. It occurred to him there was something warped and confused about the entire situation. She had taken control, and without uttering a single word. What was it she actually wanted?

"What . . ." he began. Cleared his throat. "What is it you actually want?"

She made no reply, just tilted her head slightly more to the side. Looked like she was emitting silent laughter, with teeth shining blue-white in that beautiful mouth of hers. And then Prim noticed something he hadn't seen until now. That she had the mouth of a predator. And it struck him:

this was a game of cat and mouse. And it was he, not she, who was the mouse.

Where had that absurd thought come from?

Nowhere. Or, the place where all his crazy thoughts came from.

He was frightened, but knew he mustn't show it. He tried to breathe calmly. He had to go. *She* had to go.

"This was nice," he said, folding his napkin and putting it on the plate. "Let's do it again sometime."

Johan Krohn had just sat down at the dining table with his wife, Alise, when the phone rang. He had yet to call Markus Røed with the bad news that Harry Hole had declined their generous offer. That's to say, Harry had already declined before Krohn had time to mention the fee. And he hadn't changed his mind after Krohn had presented the conditions to him and told him they had booked him a business-class seat on the 09.55 flight to Oslo via Copenhagen.

He saw by the number that the incoming call was from Harry's old phone, the one he had only gotten messages from saying "unavailable" when he had tried to call. So perhaps his saying no had merely been a negotiating tactic. That was fine, Røed had given him carte blanche to raise the amount.

Krohn stood up from the table, gave his wife an apologetic look, and went into the living room. "Hello again, Harry," he said cheerfully.

Hole's voice sounded hoarse. "Nine hundred and sixty thousand dollars."

"I beg your pardon?"

"If I solve the case, I want nine hundred and sixty thousand dollars."

"Nine hundred and . . . ?"

"Yes."

"You are aware—"

"I'm aware that I'm not worth it. But if your client is as wealthy and as innocent as you say, then the truth is worth that to him. So my suggestion is that I work for free, have my expenses covered and only receive payment if I solve the case."

"But—"

"It's not that much. But, Krohn, I'll need an answer within the next five minutes. In English, on an email from your address and with your signature. Understand?"

"Yes, but Christ, Harry, that's—"

"There are people here who need to make a decision right this minute. So I sort of have a gun to my head."

"But two hundred thousand dollars ought to be more than—"

"Sorry, it's the amount I said or nothing at all, Krohn."

Krohn sighed. "It's an insane sum, Harry, but all right, I'll call my client. I'll get back to you."

"Five minutes," came the hoarse reply. Krohn heard another voice say something in the background.

"Four and a half," Harry said,

"I'll do my best to get hold of him," Krohn said.

Harry put the phone on the kitchen table and looked up at the man with the shotgun, which was still pointed at him. The other man was speaking Spanish into another cell phone.

"It's going to be all right," whispered Lucille, sitting next to Harry.

Harry patted her hand. "That's my line."

"No, it's mine," she said. "I'm the one who got you mixed up in this. And anyway, it's not true, is it? It won't be all right."

"Define all right," Harry said.

Lucille smiled faintly. "Well, at least I had a wonderful final evening yesterday, that's something. You know, everybody at Dan Tana's was convinced we were a couple."

"You think?"

"Oh, I saw it in their faces when you walked in with me on your arm. There's Lucille Owens with a tall, blond and much younger man, they thought. And wished they were movie stars themselves. And then you took my coat and gave me a kiss on the cheek. Thank you, Harry."

Harry was about to point out that he had only done as he had been instructed beforehand, including removing his wedding ring, but refrained.

"*Dos minutos,*" the man with the phone said, and Harry felt Lucille's hand squeeze harder on his.

"What's *el jefe* in the car saying?" Harry asked.

The man with the shotgun didn't answer.

"Has he killed as many people as you?"

The man gave a brief laugh. "No one knows how many he's killed. All I know is that if you don't pay you'll be the next two on his list. He likes to take care of things personally. And I mean *likes.*"

Harry nodded. "He the one who gave her the loan or did he just buy the debt?"

"We don't loan money, we just collect it. And he's the best. He can spot the losers, the ones in debt." He hesitated for a moment, then leaned forward a little and lowered his voice: "He says it's in their eyes and in the way they carry themselves, but mostly in their body odor. You can see it when you get onto a bus—the ones weighed down by debt are the ones with a seat free next to them. He said you're in debt too, *el rubio.*"

"Me?"

"He was in that bar looking for the lady one day and saw you sitting there."

"He's wrong, I'm not in debt."

"He's never wrong. You owe somebody something. That was how he found my father."

"Your father?"

The man nodded. Harry looked at him. Swallowed. Tried to picture the man in the car. Harry's phone had been lying on the kitchen table on speaker while Harry had put forward his proposal, but the man on the other end had not uttered a single word.

"*Un minuto.*" The man with the cell phone released the safety catch on the pistol.

"Our Father," Lucille mumbled, "who art in heaven . . ."

"How could you spend so much money on a movie that never materialized?" Harry asked.

Lucille looked at him in surprise at first. Before perhaps realizing that he was offering her some distraction prior to their stepping over the threshold.

"You know," she said, "that's the most frequently asked question in this town."

"*Cinco segundos.*"

Harry stared at his phone. "And the most frequent answer given?"

"Bad luck and lousy scripts."

"Mm. Sounds like my life."

The display lit up. Krohn's number. Harry pressed "Accept."

"Talk to me. Quickly, and just the conclusion."

"Røed says yes."

"You're going to get the email address." Harry handed the phone to the guy who was talking to *el jefe*. The guy stuck the pistol in the shoulder holster inside his bomber jacket and put the two phones against one another. Harry heard the low buzz of voices. When it went quiet, he gave the phone back to Harry. Krohn had hung up. The guy put his own phone to his ear and listened. Lowered it.

"You're lucky, *rubio*. You have ten days. From now." He pointed to his watch. "After that, we shoot her." He pointed to Lucille. "And then we come for you. She's coming with us now, and you shouldn't try to contact her. If you tell anyone about this, you die, along with whoever you talked to. That's the way we do things here, how we do things in Mexico and how we'll do things where you're going. Don't think you're beyond our reach."

"OK," Harry said, and swallowed. "Anything else I should know?"

The guy rubbed his scorpion tattoo and smiled. "That we won't shoot you. We'll strip the skin from your back and leave you lying in the sun. It'll only take a few hours before you're parched and die of thirst. Believe me, you'll be grateful it doesn't take longer."

Harry felt like saying something about Norway and the sun in September but held back. The clock was already ticking. Not just on the ten days, but on the flight he had a ticket for. He checked his watch. One and a half hours. It was Saturday and not many miles from here to LAX, but this was Los Angeles. He was already behind schedule. Hopelessly behind.

He looked one last time at Lucille. Yes, that was how she would have looked, his own mother, had she lived longer.

Harry Hole leaned over, kissed Lucille on the forehead, stood up and strode towards the door.

7

SUNDAY

HARRY WAS SITTING IN THE passenger seat of a 1970 Volvo Amazon. Bjørn was next to him and they were singing along to a Hank Williams song playing at an irregular speed on Bjørn's cassette player. Every time they stopped singing, a soft whimpering could be heard from a child in the back seat. The car began to shake. Odd, seeing as they were parked.

Harry opened his eyes and looked up at the flight attendant who was shaking him gently on his shoulder.

"We'll be landing soon, sir," she said from behind the face mask. "Please fasten your seat belt."

She removed the empty glass from in front of him, maneuvered the table to the side and down into the armrest. Business class. He had, at the last moment, decided to put on his suit and leave everything else, not even taking hand luggage along. Harry yawned and looked out the window. Forest passed below. Lakes. And then: city. More city. Oslo. Then forest again. He thought about the quick phone call he had made before they took off from LAX. To Ståle Aune, the psychologist who had been his regular collaborator on murder cases. Thought about his voice, which had sounded so different. About him telling Harry he had tried to reach him several times over the past few months. Harry's answer, that he'd had the phone switched off. Ståle saying it wasn't that important, he had only wanted to tell him that he was ill. Pancreatic cancer.

The flight from LA should, according to the schedule, take thirteen hours. Harry looked at his watch. Converted it into Norwegian time. Sunday 8.55. Sunday was a day of abstinence, but if he defined himself as still being on LA time, it was Saturday for another five minutes. He looked up at the ceiling for the call button before remembering that in business class it was on the remote control. He located it wedged into the console. He pressed, and a sonar ping sounded at the same time as a light came on above him.

She was there in under ten seconds. "Yes, sir?"

But within those ten seconds Harry had sufficient time to count the number of drinks he'd had in the course of his LA Saturday. Full quota. Shit.

"Sorry," he said, trying to smile. "Nothing."

Harry was standing in the duty-free in front of the shelf of whiskey bottles when a text pinged to let him know the car Krohn had arranged was waiting for him outside the arrivals hall. Harry answered OK, and—while he had the phone out—tapped on K.

Rakel sometimes joked about the fact he had so few friends, colleagues and contacts that one initial was all he needed for each.

"Katrine Bratt." Her voice sounded tired, drowsy.

"Hi, it's Harry."

"Harry? Really?" It sounded like she had sat up in bed. "I saw it was an American number, so I—"

"I'm in Norway now. Just landed. Did I wake you?"

"No. Or yeah, sort of. We have a possible double homicide, so I was working late. My mother-in-law is here looking after Gert, so I'm catching up on some sleep. Jesus, you're alive."

"Apparently. How are things?"

"OK. Not too bad, actually, considering the circumstances. I was just talking about you last Friday. What are you doing in Oslo?"

"A couple of things. I'm going to visit Ståle Aune."

"Shit, yeah, I heard. Cancer of the pancreas, isn't it?"

"I don't have the details. Have you time for a coffee?"

He noticed there was a moment's hesitation before she replied: "Why don't you come over here instead and have dinner?"

"At your place, you mean?"

"Yeah, sure. My mother-in-law is a terrific cook."

"Well. If it's OK, then . . ."

"Six o'clock? Then you'll get to say hello to Gert too."

Harry shut his eyes. Tried to recall the dream. Volvo Amazon. The whimpering child. She knew. Of course she knew. Had she realized that he knew as well? Did she *want* him to know?

"Six o'clock is great," he said.

They hung up, and he looked at the shelf of whiskey bottles again.

There was a shelf of cuddly toy animals right behind it.

The car moved slowly through the mostly pedestrianized streets of Tjuvholmen, Oslo's most expensive twelve acres, situated on two islands jutting out into the fjord. It was teeming with people visiting the stores, restaurants and galleries or just out for a Sunday stroll. At the Thief, the receptionist greeted Harry as though he were a guest they had genuinely been looking forward to putting up.

The room had a double bed of perfect softness, hip art on the walls and luxury-brand shower gel. Everything expected of a five-star hotel, Harry assumed. He had a view of the rust-red tower of City Hall and Akershus Fortress. Nothing seemed changed in the year he had been away. Yet it felt different. Perhaps because this—Tjuvholmen with all its designer stores, galleries, luxury apartments and mostly sleek facades—was not the Oslo he knew. He had grown up on the east side at a time when Oslo was a quiet, boring and rather gray little capital on the outskirts of Europe. The language you heard in the streets was mostly unaccented Norwegian, and people were for the most part white. But the city had slowly opened up. As a youth, Harry had first noticed this when the number of clubs grew, when more of the cool bands—not just those who played for 30,000 people at Valle Hovin—began including Oslo on their tours. And restaurants opened, a whole bunch of them, serving food from every corner of the world. This transformation into an international, open and multicultural city had naturally brought about an increase in organized crime, but there was still so few murders that they could barely keep a department of detectives employed. True, the city had already, for various reasons, in the 1970s become—and later remained—a graveyard for young people hooked on heroin. But it was a city without a Skid Row, a city where even women could in general feel safe, a sentiment also expressed by ninety-three per cent of the inhabitants when they were asked. And although the media did their best to paint another picture, the number of rapes over the past fifteen years had been consistently low compared with other cities, and street violence and other crime also low and still decreasing.

So one murdered and one missing woman with a possible link to each other was not a commonplace occurrence. Not so odd then that the Norwegian newspaper articles Harry had had time to Google were numerous and the headlines large. Nor was it strange that Markus Røed's name was mentioned in several of them. Firstly, everyone knew that the media, even the previously so-called broadsheets, survived on creating ongoing narratives about well-known names, and Røed was apparently a celebrity on account of his wealth. Secondly, the perpetrator in eighty per cent of all the murders Harry had investigated was a person closely linked to the victim. Therefore it was not strange that his prime suspect—for the time being—was the man who had hired him.

Harry showered. Stood in front of the mirror while he buttoned the only other shirt in his possession, which he had bought at Gardermoen. Heard the ticking of his wristwatch as he fastened the top button. Tried not to think about it.

*

It was less than a five-minute stroll from the Thief to Barbell's offices at Haakon VII's gate.

Harry walked up to the almost ten-foot high door and made eye contact with a young man in the lobby inside. He rushed over to open up, having obviously been assigned to wait for Harry. He let Harry through the glass airlocks and—following some momentary confusion when Harry explained he didn't take elevators—up the stairs. On the sixth and top floor, he walked ahead of Harry through weekend empty office space to an open door where he stopped, allowing Harry to pass by him and enter.

It was a corner office, which looked to be almost a thousand square feet, with a view over City Hall Square and the Oslo Fjord. At one end stood a desk with a large iMac screen, a pair of Gucci sunglasses and an Apple iPhone on it, but no papers.

At the other end there were two people sitting at a conference table. He knew one of them as Johan Krohn. The other he recognized from the newspaper articles. Markus Røed let Krohn get to his feet first and approach Harry with hand outstretched. Harry gave Krohn a quick smile without taking his eye off the man behind. Saw Markus Røed fasten a button on his suit jacket with an automatic movement, but remain standing at the table. After shaking Krohn's hand, Harry walked over to the table and did the same with Røed. Noticed they were probably much the same height. Estimated Røed had at least forty extra pounds to wrestle with. Now, close up, Røed's sixty-six years showed behind the artificially smooth skin, the white teeth and the thick, black hair. But OK, he had at least used better surgeons than some of the people he had seen in LA. Harry noticed a slight twitch in the large pupils in Røed's narrow blue irises, as though he had a fascicular condition.

"Have a seat, Harry."

"Thanks, Markus," Harry said, unbuttoning his jacket and sitting down. If Røed disliked the form of address or registered the riposte, his facial expression didn't reveal it.

"Thanks for coming at such short notice," Røed said, gesturing something to the young man in the doorway.

"A certain momentum suits me fine." Harry let his gaze wander over the portraits of the three serious-looking men on the wall. Two paintings and a photograph, all with gold plaques at the bottom of the frame, all with the surname Røed.

"Yes, well, of course things move at a different pace *over there*," Krohn said, the last two words in English, in what sounded to Harry like a slightly stressed diplomat's small talk.

"I don't know," Harry said. "I think Los Angeles is laid-back compared to New York and Chicago. But you're on it here too, I see. Office hours on a Sunday. Impressive."

"It does a man good to take a little time away from the hell of home life and the family," Røed said, and grinned at Krohn. "*Especially* on a Sunday."

"You have children?" Harry asked. He hadn't gotten that impression from the newspaper articles.

"Yes," Røed replied, looking at Krohn as if he was the one who had asked. "My wife."

Røed laughed, and Krohn joined dutifully in. Harry pulled the corners of his mouth up slightly so as not to appear undemonstrative. He thought about the pictures of Helene Røed he had seen in the newspapers. How big was the age difference? Had to be at least thirty years. In all the pictures the couple were photographed against backdrops with logos, in other words at premieres, fashion shows and the like. Helene Røed was of course dressed up and dolled up, but she looked more self-aware, less ridiculous than some of the women—and the men—you saw posing for the camera at similar events. She was beautiful, but there was something faded about her beauty, a youthful luster that seemed to have disappeared a tad too early. A little too much work? A little too much alcohol or other things? A little too little happiness? Or a little of all three?

"Well," Krohn said, "knowing my client as I do, I'd say he'd spend a lot of time here no matter. You don't get to where he is without hard work."

Røed shrugged, but offered no objection. "What about you, Harry? Do you have children?"

Harry was looking at the portraits. All three men were pictured in front of large buildings. Erected or owned by themselves, Harry presumed.

"Combined with a solid family fortune, perhaps," he said.

"Excuse me?".

"Along with the hard work. It makes it that bit easier, doesn't it?"

Røed raised a well-groomed eyebrow below his shiny black hair and looked inquiringly at Krohn, as though to demand an explanation for what kind of guy Krohn had gotten hold of. Then he raised his head to lift the onset of a double chin over his shirt collar and fixed his eyes on Harry.

"Fortunes don't take care of themselves, Hole. But perhaps you know that?"

"Me? What makes you think that?"

"No? You certainly dress like a man of means. Unless I'm very much mistaken, that suit of yours was sewn by Garth Alexander of Savile Row. I have two of them myself."

"I don't remember the name of the tailor," Harry said. "I got it from a lady for agreeing to be her escort."

"Bloody hell. Was she so ugly?"

"No."

"No? A looker, then?"

"Yeah, I'll say. For a septuagenarian."

Markus Røed put his hands behind his head and leaned back. His eyes became narrow slits.

"You know what, Harry, you and my wife have something in common there. You only take your clothes off to change into something more expensive."

Markus Røed's laughter was deafening. He slapped his thighs and turned to Krohn, who again quickly managed to supply a laugh. Røed's laughter turned into a fit of sneezing. The young man—who had just walked in with a tray of water glasses—offered him a napkin, but Røed waved him away, drew a large, light blue handkerchief with the initials M.R. on it, in lettering almost as large as the handkerchief itself from the inside pocket of his suit and blew his nose loudly.

"Relax, it's just my allergies." Røed said, stuffing the handkerchief back in his pocket. "You been vaccinated, Harry?"

"Yes."

"Me too. Been safe the whole time. Helene and I went to Saudi Arabia and took the first vaccine long before it came to Norway. Anyway, let's make a start. Johan?"

Harry listened to Johan Krohn's presentation of the case, which was more or less a repetition of what he had heard on the phone twenty-four hours earlier.

"Two women, Susanne Andersen and Bertine Bertilsen, disappeared on consecutive Tuesdays, three and two weeks ago respectively. Susanne Andersen was found dead two days ago. Police haven't released anything about the cause of death but say they're investigating it as a murder. Markus has been interviewed by the police for one reason and one reason only. That the two girls were at the same party four days prior to Susanne's disappearance, a rooftop party for the residents of the apartment building where Markus and Helene live. And the only connection between the two girls the police have found so far is that they both know Markus and both were invited by him. Markus has an alibi for the two Tuesdays the girls went missing, he was at home with Helene, and the police have cleared him of any suspicion in that respect. Unfortunately, the press are not as logical in their reasoning. That is to say, they have other motives than the desire for the case to be solved. They have, therefore, been running with all kinds of speculative headlines about Markus's relationship with the girls, implying that they were trying to extort money from him by threatening to tell their 'story' to a newspaper which was offering the two girls a large sum for this. And they've also drawn into doubt the value of an alibi provided by a spouse, even though they're well aware that it's common and completely legal tender in a criminal case. It is, of course, all to do with the sensational mix of celebrity and murder, not the truth. Should that come to light, the people in the media are no doubt hoping it's later rather than sooner, so they can continue with their sales-friendly speculation for as long as possible."

Harry nodded briefly, his face impassive.

"In the meantime, my client's business interests are suffering because he has not—according to the media's version at least—been cleared of all accusations. Naturally, there is the personal strain involved."

"First and foremost on the family," Røed interjected.

"Naturally," the lawyer continued. "This would be a temporary problem we could have lived with if the police had shown themselves equal to the task. But they have had almost three weeks and have found neither the perpetrator nor any lead that might have caused the media to call off their witch hunt against the only person in Oslo who has actually provided an alibi in the case. In short, we wish for the case to be solved as quickly as possible, and that's where you come in."

Krohn and Røed looked at Harry.

"Mm. Now that the police have a body, there's the chance they've found DNA traces from a perpetrator. Have the police taken a DNA sample from you?" Harry looked directly at Markus Røed.

Without replying, Røed turned to Krohn.

"We've said no to that," Krohn said. "Until the police produce a court order."

"Why?"

"Because we have nothing to gain by submitting to such a test. And because by accepting that sort of intrusive investigation we would be acknowledging indirectly that we can see the case from the perspective of the police, that is to say, that there could be grounds for suspicion."

"But you don't see any grounds?"

"No. But I have told the police that if they are able to establish any link whatsoever between the missing persons cases and my client, he'll be more than happy to submit to a DNA test. We haven't heard any more from them."

"Mm."

Røed clapped his hands together. "There you have it, Harry. In broad strokes. Can we hear what your battle plan is?"

"Battle plan?"

Røed smiled. "In broad strokes, anyway."

"In broad strokes," Harry said, stifling a jet-lag yawn, "it's to find the killer as quickly as possible."

Røed grinned and looked over at Krohn. "Now that was very broad, Harry. Can you say anything else?"

"Well. I'll investigate this case the same way I would as a policeman. Meaning without obligation or regard for anything other than the truth. In other words, if the evidence leads me to you, Røed, I'll take you down like I would any other murderer. And claim the bonus."

In the silence that followed the bells of City Hall began to chime.

Markus Røed chuckled. "You talk tough, Harry. How many years would it take you to scrape together that kind of bonus as a policeman? Ten? Twenty? What do you people even earn down there at the station actually?"

Harry made no reply. The bells continued to chime.

"Well," Krohn said, flashing a rushed smile, "essentially, what you're saying is what we want done, Harry. Like I said on the phone: an independent investigation. So although you're putting it in rather a rough way, we are on the same page. What you're expressing is the very reason we want you. An individual with that kind of integrity."

"Are you?" Røed asked, stroking his chin with his thumb and forefinger while looking at Harry. "A man with that kind of integrity?"

Harry again noticed the twitching in Røed's eyes. He shook his head. Røed leaned forward, smiled cheerfully and said in a low voice: "Not even a little?"

Harry smiled as well. "Only to the extent a horse wearing blinkers can be accused of having integrity. A creature of limited intelligence just doing what it's trained to: running straight ahead without allowing itself to be distracted."

Markus Røed laughed. "That's good, Harry. That's good. We'll buy that. What I want you to do first is put together a team of top people. Preferably with names people are aware of. That we can announce to the media. So they can see that we mean business, you get me?"

"I have an idea of who I could use."

"Good, good. How long before you get an answer from them, do you think?"

"By four o'clock tomorrow."

"As early as tomorrow?"

Røed laughed again when he realized Harry was serious. "I like your style, Harry. Let's sign the contract."

Røed nodded to Krohn, who reached into his briefcase and placed a one-page document in front of Harry.

"The contract states that the assignment is to be regarded as complete when there is an agreement of guilt among at least three lawyers in the legal department of the police," Krohn said. "Should the accused be acquitted in a court case, however, the fee will have to be repaid. That is to say it's a 'no cure no pay' agreement."

"But with a bonus an executive would envy you, myself included," Røed said.

"I'd like one additional clause in there," Harry said. "My fee is to be paid should the police—with or without my assistance—find the presumed guilty party within the next nine days."

Røed and Krohn exchanged glances.

Røed nodded before leaning towards Harry. "You're a tough negotiator. But don't think I don't understand why you have such exact numbers on the sum to be paid and the number of days."

Harry raised an eyebrow. "Really?"

"Come on. It gives the other guy the feeling that there's a true figure. A magic number where everything falls into place. You can't teach your dad to fuck, Harry, I use that negotiation ploy myself."

Harry nodded slowly. "You got me, Røed."

"And now I'm going to teach you a trick, Harry." Røed leaned back, grinning broadly. "I want to give you a million dollars. That's nearly four hundred thousand Norwegian kroner more than you're asking for, enough for a decent car. You know why?"

Harry didn't reply.

"Because people put in a lot more effort if you give them a little more than they expected. It's a psychologically proven fact."

"Then I'm willing to test it," Harry said drily. "But there is one more thing."

Røed's smile disappeared. "And that is?"

"I'll need permission from someone in the police."

Krohn cleared his throat. "You are aware that in Norway you don't need authorization or a license to undertake private investigations?"

"Yes. But I said *someone* in the police."

Harry explained the problem, and after a while Røed nodded and reluctantly agreed. After Harry and Røed had shaken hands, Krohn escorted Harry down to the exit. He held the door onto the street open for Harry.

"Might I ask you a question, Harry?"

"Shoot."

"Why did I have to send a copy of our contract in English to a Mexican email address?"

"That was for my agent."

Krohn's face remained expressionless. Harry figured that as a defense lawyer he was so used to being lied to that he was probably more inclined to bat an eyelid when his clients told the truth. And that Krohn also understood that such an obvious lie was a no-trespassing sign.

"Have a nice Sunday, Harry."

"You too."

Harry walked down to Aker Brygge. Sat down on a bench. Watched the ferry from the Nesoddtangen peninsula glide to the quay in the sunshine. Closed his eyes. He and Rakel had taken a day off in the middle of the week on occasion, brought their bikes aboard the boat and, after twenty-five minutes among the small islets and sailing boats, docked at Nesoddtangen. From there they had cycled straight into a rural landscape with country roads, trails and secluded, deserted bathing spots where they dived in and afterwards warmed themselves up on the smooth rock slabs, and the only sounds to be heard were the buzz of insects and Rakel's intense but low moaning as she dug her nails into his back. Harry forced himself to let go of the image and opened his eyes. Looked at his watch. Looked at the staccato progression of the second hand. In a few hours he was to meet Katrine. And Gert. He walked on, with long strides, towards the Thief.

"Your uncle seems on form today," said the nurse, taking leave of Prim at the open door of the small room.

Prim nodded. Looked at the elderly man in the bathrobe sitting up in the bed staring at the turned-off TV screen. He had been a handsome man at one time. A highly respected man accustomed to being listened to, both in his private life and his professional one. Prim thought it was still visible in his features, in his uncle's high, smooth forehead, his deep-set, clear blue eyes on either side of his aquiline nose. In the determined set to his tightly closed mouth with the surprisingly full lips.

Prim called him Uncle Fredric. Because that's what he was. Among other things.

His uncle looked up as Prim stepped into the room, and Prim, as usual, wondered which Uncle Fredric was at home today. If any.

"Who are you? Get out." His face was flushed with a mixture of contempt and amusement, and his voice lay in that deep register he used that made it impossible to be sure whether Uncle Fredric was joking or furious. He suffered from dementia with Lewy bodies, a brain disorder which brought about not only hallucinations and nightmares, but—as in his uncle's case—occasionally aggressive behavior. Mostly verbal, but also physical, rendering the limitations the muscle rigidity caused almost an advantage.

"I'm Prim, Molle's son." And before any possible response from his uncle, added: "Your sister."

Prim looked at the only decoration on the wall, a framed diploma hanging over the bed. He had once hung up a framed photo of his uncle, his mother and himself as a boy smiling by a swimming pool in Spain, a holiday his uncle had treated his sister and nephew to after his stepfather had left them.

But his uncle had taken the picture down after a few months, saying he couldn't stand looking at so many rabbit teeth. He was obviously refer-ring to the two large front teeth with a gap that Prim had inherited from his mother. But the diploma conferring the doctorate still hung there, with the name Fredric Steiner on it. He had changed the surname he shared with Prim's mother because—as he had plainly told Prim—a Jew-ish surname held more weight and authority in scientific circles. Especially in his own field, microbiology, where there were few who could be bothered to pretend that it was not the case that Jews—particularly Ashkenazi Jews—had genes which granted them superior intellectual capabilities. While it might be sensible in terms of decorum and for polit-ical reasons to deny—or at least ignore—such a fact was all well and good, but a fact was a fact. So if Fredric had a mind that was as brilliant and highly functioning as a Jewish one, why humbly join the back of the line with a staid, Norwegian peasant name?

"I have a sister?" his uncle asked.

"You had a sister, don't you remember?"

"Goddamnit, boy, I have dementia, can't you get that into your little pea brain? That nurse you came with . . . pretty nice, eh?"

"So her you remember?"

"My short-term memory is excellent. You want to bet some money on my fucking her before the weekend? Actually hang on, you probably don't have any money either, you loser. When you were a little boy I had hopes for you. But now. You're not even a disappointment, you're just nothing."

His uncle paused. Looked as though he were thinking carefully. "Or did you make anything of yourself? What is it you do?"

"I'm not planning on telling you."

"Why not? I remember you were interested in music. Our family wasn't musical in the slightest, but didn't you have ideas about becoming a musician?"

"No."

"So what . . . ?"

"Firstly you'll have forgotten it by the next time, and secondly you wouldn't believe it."

"What about a family? Don't look at me like that!"

"I'm single. For the time being. But I have met one woman."

"One? Did you say one?"

"Yes."

"Christ. Do you know how many women I've fucked?"

"Yes."

"Six hundred and forty-three. Six hundred and forty-three! And these were good-looking women. Apart from a few at the beginning before I knew what I could get hold of. Started when I was seventeen. You'll have to work hard to match your uncle, boy. This woman, does she have a tight cunt?"

"I don't know."

"You don't know? What happened to that other one?"

"Other one?"

"I distinctly remember you had a couple of kids and a little dark-skinned woman with big tits. Did I ever fuck her? Ha ha! I did, I can see it in your face! Why did you turn out to be the type of man no one could love? Was it those rabbit teeth you got from your mother?"

"Uncle—"

"Don't uncle me, you fucking freak! You were born ugly and stupid, you're an embarrassment to me, to your mother and to the entire family."

"All right. Why did you call me Prim then?"

"Ah, Prim, yes! Why do you think I did it?"

"You said it was because I was special. An exception among numbers."

"Special, yes, but as in an anomaly. A mistake. The type no one wants to be with, an outcast, one that can only be divided by one and itself. That's you, *primtallet*, the prime number. One and yourself. We all long for what we cannot have, and for you that meant being loved. That was always your weakness, and you inherited it from your mother."

"Did you know, Uncle, that one day soon I shall be more famous than you and the entire family. Put together."

His uncle's face lit up, as though Prim had finally provided him with something that made sense, or was at least entertaining.

"Let me tell you, the only thing that's going to happen to you is that one day you'll be just as demented as me, and you'll be only too happy to be! You know why? Because then you'll have forgotten that your life was one long series of humiliating defeats. That there—" he pointed at the diploma on the wall—"is the only thing I want to remember. But I can't even manage that. And the six hundred and forty-three . . ." His voice grew thick, and large tears welled up in his blue eyes. "I can't remember a single fucking one. Not one! So what's the point?"

His uncle was crying as Prim left. It happened more and more often. Prim had read that when Robin Williams took his own life, it was because he had been diagnosed with Lewy body dementia. That he wished to spare himself and his family the torture. Prim was surprised his uncle had not done the same.

The nursing home was situated in the heart of Vinderen on Oslo's west side. On his way to the car he passed the jeweler's he had been into several times recently. As it was Sunday, the store was closed, but pressing his nose against the window he could see the diamond ring in the glass display case inside. It was not large but it was so beautiful. Perfect for Her. He had to buy it this week, otherwise he risked someone else beating him to it.

He took a detour past his childhood home in Gaustad. The fire-damaged villa ought to have been torn down years ago, but he'd had the demolition postponed time and time again despite the council's orders and the neighbors' complaints. On some occasions he had claimed plans were underway for renovation, on others he had documents to prove that the demolition was booked but had been arranged with companies which later went bankrupt or where business had been suspended. Why exactly he had engaged in these stalling tactics he did not know. After all, he could have sold the plot for a good price. It was only recently that it had dawned on him. And that the plan—what the house would be used for—was something that must have been lying there, like a tiny worm egg in his mind.

8

SUNDAY

Tetris

"YOU LOOK GOOD," HARRY SAID.

"You look . . . tanned," Katrine replied.

Both of them laughed, she opened the door fully and they hugged. The smell of mutton and cabbage stew filled the apartment. He handed her the bouquet of flowers he had purchased at the Narvesen kiosk on the way.

"Have *you* begun buying flowers now?" Katrine asked, accepting them with a grimace.

"Was mostly to impress your mother-in-law."

"Well, the suit certainly will."

Katrine went into the kitchen to put the flowers in water, and Harry walked towards the living room. He saw the toys on the parquet floor and heard the child's voice before he saw the boy. He was sitting with his back to Harry, talking sternly to a teddy bear.

"You have to do wike me, you know. You have to go aweep."

Harry tiptoed in and crouched down. The boy began to sing in a low voice while tilting his head with airy, fair curls from side to side. "Bueman, Bueman, my buck . . ."

He must have heard something, perhaps a creaking in the floor, because the boy suddenly turned around, a smile already on his face. A child who still thinks all surprises are good surprises, Harry thought.

"Hi!" the boy said loudly and warmly, seemingly unalarmed that a large man with a gray beard, who was a complete stranger, had snuck up on him from behind.

"Hi," Harry said, reaching into his suit pocket. Pulled out a teddy bear. "This is for you."

He held it out, but the boy took no notice of the teddy, just stared wide-eyed at Harry.

"Aw you Santa Cwaus?"

Harry had to laugh, but that didn't faze the boy either, who happily laughed along with him. He took hold of the teddy bear. "What's his name?"

"He doesn't have a name yet, so you need to give him one."

"Then I wi caw him . . . what's you name?"

"Harry."

"Hawny."

"No. Eh . . ."

"Yeah, then he's cawed Hawny."

Harry turned and saw Katrine standing with her arms folded in the doorway looking at them.

Perhaps it was her Toten dialect, perhaps it was the red hair and the slightly bulging eyes. In any case, every time Harry glanced up from his plate on the kitchen table and looked at Bjørn's mother, he also saw his late colleague, Forensics Officer Bjørn Holm.

"Not so strange that he likes you, Harry," she said, nodding in the direction of the boy, who had been allowed to leave the table and was now pulling at Harry's hand to take him into the living room and play some more with the teddy bears. "You and Bjørn were such good friends. That's kindred chemistry, you know. But you need to eat more, Harry, you're skinny as a needle."

After a dessert of prune compote, Katrine's mother-in-law left them to put Gert to bed.

"That's a fine boy you've produced," Harry said.

"Yes," Katrine said, resting her chin on her hands. "I didn't know you had a way with children."

"Me neither."

"Didn't you notice it with Oleg, when he was little?"

"He was at the computer-game stage when I came into his life. Probably didn't mind someone coming between him and his mother."

"But you did become good friends."

"Rakel maintained it was because we hated the same bands. And both loved Tetris. On the phone you said that things were going OK. Anything new?"

"At work?"

"Anything at all."

"Well, yes and no. I've actually started to go out and meet people again—I suppose it's been a while since Bjørn died."

"Really? Anything serious?"

"No, I wouldn't say that. I have been out with one guy a few times lately, and it's nice enough, but I don't know. You and I were both weird to start off with, and neither of us is improving with the years. What about you?"

Harry shook his head.

"No, I see you're still wearing your wedding ring," Katrine said. "You had met the love of your life, so to speak. It was a bit different with Bjørn and me."

"Maybe it was."

"The nicest man in the world. Too nice." She raised her teacup. "And too vulnerable to be with a bitch like me."

"That's not true, Katrine."

"No? What do you call a woman who sleeps with one of her husband's best friends? OK, maybe whore is more precise."

"It just happened, Katrine. I was drunk and you . . ."

"I what? I wish I could say I was in love with you at least, Harry. And once, in the first couple of years we worked together, maybe I was. But after that? After that you were just the guy I never got. The guy that brown-eyed beauty up in Holmenkollen snatched."

"Mm. I don't think Rakel viewed it as her snatching me, exactly."

"You certainly weren't the one who snatched her."

"Why not?"

"Harry Hole! You don't realize a woman is interested until they spell it out. And even then you sit on that skinny butt of yours and wait."

Harry laughed quietly. He could ask now. Now would be a good time. There was no reason to put it off. It was so obvious. The blond curls. The eyes. The mouth. Of course, she didn't know that he had found it out one night while with Alexandra Sturdza from the Forensic Medical Institute. That Alexandra, courtesy of some unfortunate wording, had indirectly let it slip that Bjørn had checked the paternity of the child and her DNA analysis had revealed that it was Harry and not he who was Gert's father.

Harry cleared his throat. "I know that . . ."

Katrine gave him a questioning look.

"I know that Truls Berntsen got into some trouble. Has he been suspended?"

She raised an eyebrow. "Yes. He and two others are suspected of stealing from a drugs seizure at Gardermoen. You're hardly surprised—Truls Berntsen is notoriously corrupt and has gambling debts, apparently. It was only a question of time."

"No, not surprised maybe. Still, I'm sorry to hear it."

"Thought you couldn't stand the sight of each other."

"He may not be easy to like but he does have some qualities that are easy to overlook. Qualities he himself has overlooked, perhaps."

"If you say so. Why are you interested in him?"

Harry shrugged. "Bellman is still Minister of Justice, I read."

"God, yeah. Those power games suit him. Was always a better politician than a policeman, if you ask me. How are things with your people?"

"Well, my sister's still in Kristiansand, living with a guy, things are going well. Oleg is at the sheriff's office in Lakselv. He's living with his girlfriend. And Øystein Eikeland, if you remember him—"

"The taxi driver?"

"Yes, I spoke to him on the phone yesterday. He's changed careers. Making more money, he says. And I'm paying Aune a visit tomorrow. And, yeah, that's about it."

"You don't have many people left, Harry."

"No." He was doing his best not to check the time. To see how long was left of this damn Sunday. Monday was a drinking day. Only three units, but a drinking day, and there were no rules governing when on the Monday the permitted amount could be consumed, it could take place right after midnight, all in one go. He hadn't bought the bottle of whiskey at Gardermoen, had plumped for the teddy bear instead, but he had checked the minibar in his room, and it contained what he needed.

"What about you?" Harry said, lifting his coffee cup. "Who have you got left?"

Katrine thought about it. "Well. I don't have any family left on my side, so the closest are Gert's grandmother and grandfather. They're incredibly helpful. Toten is two hours away, but they still come here as often as they're able. And sometimes—when I ask—when they aren't really able, I think. They're so attached to the boy, he's all they have now as well. So . . ."

She paused. Stared over her teacup at the wall next to Harry. He could see it, how she was readying herself to take the plunge, as it were.

"I don't want them to know. And I don't want Gert to know. Understand, Harry?"

So she knew. And had realized that he knew.

He nodded. It wasn't hard to understand why she wouldn't want her son growing up knowing he was the product of infidelity, of his mother's one-night stand with an alcoholic. That she didn't want to break the hearts of two loving grandparents. Or lose the sorely needed support they could offer a single mother and her child.

"His father's name is Bjørn," Katrine whispered, shifting her gaze so her eyes fixed on Harry's. "End of story."

"I understand," Harry said in a low voice, his eyes not leaving hers. "I think what you're doing is right. All I ask is that you come to me if you need help. Whatever it might be. I won't be looking for anything in return."

He could see Katrine's eyes were moist. "Thanks, Harry. That's generous."

"Not really," he said. "I'm poor as a church mouse."

She laughed, sniffled and pulled a sheet of paper towel from the roll on the table. "You're a good man," she said.

The grandmother came in to say that Mama's presence was required as a song had been requested, and while Katrine disappeared into the child's room, Harry told Bjørn's mother about how Bjørn had taken charge the time he, Harry and Øystein had compiled playlists for the theme nights at the Jealousy Bar. There had been Hank Williams Thursdays, an Elvis week and—perhaps most memorably—Songs-at-least-forty-years-old-by-artists-and-bands-from-American-states-starting-with-M night. Even though the names of Bjørn's preferred choice of bands and artists didn't appear to ring any bells with his mother, her tear-glazed eyes expressed gratitude to Harry for recounting something, probably any-thing at all, about her son.

Katrine returned to the kitchen, and her mother-in-law withdrew to the living room and switched on the TV.

"The guy you're seeing?" Harry said.

Katrine waved the subject aside.

"Come on," Harry said.

"He's younger than me. And no, I didn't hook up with him on Tinder. I met him out in the real world. It was right after everything opened up again, so there was a bit of a euphoric atmosphere in town. So . . . yeah, he's kept in touch."

"He has, not you?"

"He's probably a little more serious than me. It's not that he isn't a nice, solid guy. He has a steady job, his own apartment and seems to have his life in order."

Harry smiled.

"All right, all right!" she said, making to give him a slap. "When you're a single mom, you automatically start taking these things into account, OK? But there has to be some *passion* there as well, and . . ."

"And there isn't?"

She paused. "He knows about the sort of stuff I don't, and I really like that. He teaches me things, you know? He's interested in music, like Bjørn. He's no problem with me being a weirdo. And he—" a broad smile spread across her face—"loves me. You know what? I'd nearly forgotten how good that feels. Being loved, like, to the core. Like Bjørn." She shook her head. "Maybe I've unconsciously been on the lookout for a new Bjørn. More than for *passion*, I'm afraid."

"Mm. Does Bjørn's mother know?"

"No, no!" She waved a dismissive hand. "No one knows. And I'm not planning on introducing him to anyone either."

"Not *anyone*?"

She shook her head. "When you know it's likely to end and you're probably going to have to see the guy around afterwards, then you involve as few people as possible, right? You don't want people looking at you and, like, *knowing*, as it were. But I don't want to tell you any more about him." She put her teacup down firmly. "Now you. Tell me about LA."

Harry smiled. "Some other time, maybe, when I'm not in such a hurry. I should probably tell you why I called you instead."

"Oh? I thought it was . . ." She tilted her head in the direction of the child's room.

"No," Harry said. "It had been on my mind of course. But figured it was your choice if you wanted to let me know."

"My choice? You've been impossible to get hold of."

"Mm. I had my phone turned off."

"For six months?"

"Something like that. Anyway. I called to tell you that Markus Røed wants to hire me as a private investigator on the case of these two girls."

Katrine stared at him in disbelief. "You're kidding."

Harry didn't respond.

She cleared her throat. "You're telling me that you, Harry Hole, have sold yourself like some whore to . . . whoremonger Markus Røed?"

Harry looked up at the ceiling as though considering the question. "That's putting it pretty much exactly how it is, yeah."

"For Christ's sake, Harry."

"Except that I haven't agreed to it yet."

"Why not? Isn't the whoremonger paying enough?"

"Because I had to speak to you first. You have a veto."

"Veto?" She snorted. "Why? You're both free to do as you please. Especially Røed—after all he has enough money to buy whatever he wants. Although, that said, I didn't think he had enough money to buy your ass."

"Take a few seconds and think about the pros and cons," Harry said, lifting the coffee cup to his mouth.

He saw the fire in her eyes die down, saw her bite her lower lip like she usually did when her brain was at work. Expected it to draw some of the same conclusions as he had.

"Are you going to work alone?"

He shook his head.

"Are you planning on stealing someone working for us or Kripos?"

"Nope."

Katrine nodded thoughtfully. "You know I don't give a shit about prestige and ego, Harry. I leave the pissing competitions to all you little boys. What I'm interested in, for example, is that girls can walk around in this city without fear of being raped or killed. And at the moment they can't. Meaning it's better that you're on the case than not." She shook her head as though not liking the advantages she could see. "And as a private investigator you can also do certain things we can't permit ourselves."

"Yep. How does the case stand, as you see it?"

Katrine looked down at her palms. "You know full well I can't share any details from the investigation with you, but I presume you read the papers, so I'm not revealing too much when I tell you that we and Kripos have been working round the clock for three weeks on this case, and that prior to finding the body we had nada. And I mean nada. We had footage of Susanne at Skullerud metro station at nine on Tuesday night, not far from where she was found. We had Bertine's car parked up by the hiking trails in Grefsenkollen. But no one knows what these women were doing in those places. Neither of them was a walker, and as far as we know they didn't have any acquaintances in either Grefsen or Skullerud. We had search teams with dogs in both areas, but they didn't find anything. And then a jogger and his dog stumbled over the body. Which makes us look like idiots. It's the usual story. The chance occurrences that crop up outstrip what little we manage to cover by systematic searching. But people don't understand that. Or journalists. Or—" she groaned resignedly—"bosses."

"Mm. What about this party at Røed's. Anything there?"

"Nothing other than it seems to be the only time Susanne and Bertine met one another. We've tried to get an overview of who attended the party, as someone could have talked to both girls there. But it's like contact tracing last year. We have most of the names, eighty-odd, but since it was a residents' party with a fairly free flow of guests in and out, nobody knew everyone. In any case, none of the names we have stand out as suspects, neither based on criminal records nor opportunity-wise. So we went back to what you always repeated over and over, until you bored holes in our ears."

"Mm. *Why.*"

"Yeah, why. Susanne and Bertine were I suppose what you'd call two normal girls. Similar in some ways, different in others. Both came from comfortable enough backgrounds, neither had any higher education— well, Susanne studied marketing but dropped out after six months. Both had had numerous jobs in retail, Bertine worked as a hairdresser. Both of them were interested in clothes, makeup, themselves and babes they competed with on the town or on Instagram, and yeah, I know I sound prejudiced—correction: *am* prejudiced. They spent a lot, were out a lot, friends characterize them as party girls. One difference was that Bertine pretty much paid her own way, while Susanne lived with and lived off her parents. Another difference is that while Bertine had a relatively high turnover of partners, Susanne was apparently more moderate in that regard."

"Because she lived with her parents?"

"Not just that. Apart from some brief relationships she had a reputation for being a bit of a prude. With the possible exception of Markus Røed."

"Sugar daddy?"

"We have lists of the girls' phone calls and texts. They show extensive contact with Røed over the last three years."

"Messages of a sexual character?"

"Not as much as you might think. A few risqué pictures from the girls but nothing obscene. It's more along the lines of invitations to parties and things they want. Røed has regularly transferred money to them both on Venmo. Not large amounts, a couple of thousand, ten thousand in one go tops. But enough to render the term sugar daddy not wholly inappropriate. In one of the last messages Bertine wrote, she told Røed that she'd been contacted by a journalist looking to confirm a rumor and he'd asked her to do an interview for ten thousand kroner. She ended the message with something like *Of course I said no. Even though ten thousand happens to be exactly what I owe the line man."*

"Mm. Lines. Cocaine or amphetamines."

"And sending something that *could* be construed as a threat."

"And you're thinking you've got your *why* right there?"

"I know it sounds like we're grasping at straws. But we've turned every stone without finding anyone in the girls' social circles with an obvious motive, so now we're only left with two. One is that Markus Røed may have wanted to rid himself of two girls threatening him with scandal. The other is that his wife, Helene Røed, was motivated by jealousy. The problem is the two of them give each other an alibi for both nights the girls disappeared."

"So I've gathered. What about the most obvious motive?"

"As in?"

"As in what you touched upon. A psychopath or a predator is at the party, happens to talk to both girls and gets their contact details."

"Like I said, none of the people we know were there fit the profile. And it's highly possible that party is a dead end. Oslo is a small town, it's not that unlikely for two girls the same age to both be at the same party."

"A little less likely that they both share the same sugar daddy."

"Maybe. According to the people we've spoken with, Susanne and Bertine weren't the only ones."

"Mm. Have you checked that?"

"Checked what?"

"Who else apart from Røed's wife could have had motive for getting rid of the competition."

Katrine smiled wearily. "You and your why. I've missed you. Crime Squad has missed you."

"I doubt that."

"Yeah, there are a couple of other girls Røed has had sporadic contact with, but they've been eliminated from our inquiries. You see, Harry? Everyone we have a name for has been ruled out. So that just leaves the remainder of the world's population." She rested her head against her fingertips as she massaged her temples. "Anyway, now we've got the newspapers and the rest of media on our back. The Chief of Police and the Chief Superintendent are on our back. Even Bellman has gotten in touch telling us to pull out all the stops. So in my book you're welcome to try, Harry. Just remember that we never had this conversation. Naturally, we can't cooperate, not even unofficially, and I can't give you any information other than what I'm also going public with. Apart from what I've already told you."

"Understood."

"I'm sure you understand too that there are those at Police HQ who won't look kindly on competition from the private sector. Especially when the competition has been bought and paid for by a potential suspect. You can imagine what a defeat it would be for the Chief Superintendent and Kripos if you solve the case before us. For all I know there may be legal grounds for stopping you, and if there is my guess is they'll use them."

"I presume Johan Krohn has examined that angle."

"Oh yeah, Røed has him on the team, I'd forgotten that."

"Anything you can tell me about the crime scene?"

"Two sets of footprints on the way in, one on the way out. I think he cleaned up after himself."

"Has a post-mortem been conducted on Susanne Andersen?"

"Just a forensic one yesterday."

"They find anything?"

"A slit throat."

Harry nodded. "Rape?"

"No visible signs."

"Anything else?"

"What do you mean?"

"You look like you found out something more."

Katrine didn't answer.

"I get it," Harry said. "Information you can't go public with."

"I've told you too much already, Harry."

"I hear you. But I assume you won't turn your nose up at information flowing in the opposite direction should we uncover something?"

She shrugged. "The police can't very well deny the public calling with any information they might have. But there's no reward being offered."

"Understood." Harry checked the time. Three and a half hours to midnight.

As though by tacit agreement they dropped the topic. Harry asked about Gert. Katrine talked about him, but Harry still had the sense she was holding something back. Eventually there was a lull in the conversation. It was ten o'clock when Katrine accompanied him down the steps to the back garden to throw two bags into the trash. When he opened the gate and stepped out onto the street she followed, giving him a long hug. He felt her warmth. Like he had that night. But knew that would be the one and only time. There had once been an attraction, physical chemistry neither of them had been in denial about, but which they both knew would be a foolish reason to destroy what they had with their respective partners. But now, even though those relationships were destroyed, so was this destroyed. And there was no way back to that sweet, forbidden excitement.

Katrine flinched, letting go of Harry. He saw her stare down the street.

"Something wrong?"

"Oh, nah."

She folded her arms, looked like she shuddered, even though it was a mild evening.

"Listen, Harry."

"Yeah?"

"If you want . . ." She paused, drew a breath. "You can babysit Gert one day."

Harry looked at her. Nodded slowly. "Goodnight."

"Goodnight," she said, and closed the gate hastily behind her.

Harry took the long way home. Through Bislett and Sofies gate, where he had once lived. Past Schrøder's, the brown cafe which at one time had been his place of refuge. Up to the top of St Hanshaugen, where he could see out over the city and the Oslo Fjord. Nothing had changed. Everything had changed. There was no way back. And there was no way that didn't lead back.

He thought about the conversation he'd had with Røed and Krohn. Where he had told them not to inform the media about the deal they had signed before he had spoken to Katrine Bratt. Explained to them that the chances of a good climate of cooperation would be increased if Bratt was under the impression she had the power of veto on whether Harry would work for Røed. Harry had described how he envisioned the conversation with Katrine was likely to go, how she would be the one to find the good arguments for him taking the case prior to agreeing. They had nodded, and he had signed. Harry heard a church bell in the distance chime the time. Tasted the lie in his mouth. He knew already it would not be the last.

Prim checked the time. Soon midnight. He brushed his teeth while tapping one foot along to the beat of "Oh! You Pretty Things" and looking at the two photos he had taped to the mirror.

One was of the Woman, beautiful, even though she was out of focus, but it was still only a pale imitation. Because her beauty was not such that a frozen moment could capture it. There was something she radiated, in the very movement of her body, in the sum of how one facial expression, word or laugh followed the next. A picture was like extracting one single note from a work by Bach or Bowie, it made no sense. Nevertheless it was better than nothing. But loving a woman, no matter how much, did not mean that you owned her. He had therefore made a promise to himself to stop watching her, stop surveying her private life as though she were his property. He had to learn to trust her, without trust there would be too much pain.

The other photo was of the woman he would fuck before the weekend. Or to be more precise, the woman who would get to fuck him. After that he would kill her. Not because he wanted to, but because he must.

He rinsed his mouth out and sang along with Bowie, about how all the nightmares came today and it looks as though they're here to stay.

Then he went into the living room and opened the fridge. He saw the bag with the thiabendazole. He knew he had taken too little today, but that if he took too much in one go, he would get stomach pains and throw up, possibly on account of it inhibiting the citric acid cycle. The trick was to take small doses at regular intervals. He decided not to take any now, offered himself the excuse that he had already brushed his teeth. Instead he took out the open tin with "Bloodworms" written on it and went over to the aquarium. Sprinkled half a teaspoon of the contents—mosquito larvae for the most part—into it, where it lay on the surface of the water like dandruff before beginning to sink.

With a couple of rapid beats of his tailfin Boss swiftly arrived. Prim switched on the flashlight and bent down so he could shine the light right into Boss's mouth as he opened wide. And he could see it in there. It looked like a little cockroach or a shrimp. He shuddered at the same time as he took delight. Boss and Lisa. It was probably how men—and women too perhaps—often felt when faced with the ultimate marriage. A certain . . . ambivalence. But he knew that once you found your intended, there was no way back. Because to the extent humans and animals had a moral duty, it was to follow their nature, the role appointed to them in order to maintain harmony, uphold the delicate balance. That was why everything in nature—even what at first glance seemed grotesque, hideous and cruel—was beautiful in all its perfect functionality. Sin entered the world on the day mankind partook of the tree of knowledge and achieved a level of reflection that enabled him *not* to choose what was intended by nature. Yes, that was how it was.

Prim switched off the stereo and the lights.

9

MONDAY

HARRY WALKED TOWARDS THE ENTRANCE of the large building in Montebello on Oslo's fashionable west side. It was nine in the morning and the sun was shining defiantly. All the same, Harry had a knot in his stomach. He had been here before. The Radium Hospital. Over a century ago, when the plans to build a dedicated hospital for cancer treatment became known, the neighbors had protested. They feared having this sinister, mysterious disease so close to them—some believed it was infectious—and that their properties would fall in value. While others gave support and made donations—over thirty million kroner in today's money—to buy the four grams of radium needed to irradiate and kill cancer cells before they killed their hosts.

Harry walked inside and stood in front of the elevator.

Not because he intended on taking it, but in order to try to remember.

He had been fifteen years old when he and his little sister Sis had visited their mother here at the Radium, as they began calling it after a while. She had lain here for four months, growing thinner and more pale each time they came, like a photograph fading in the sunlight, her mild, always smiling face seeming to disappear into the pillowcase. On the particular day he now called to mind, he'd had a fit of rage which in turn left him in tears.

"Things are how they are, and it's not your responsibility to take care of me, Harry," his mother had said while holding on to him and stroking his hair. "Your job is to look after your little sister, that's what you'll do."

On their way down after the visit, Sis had stood leaning against the wall, and when the elevator began to move, her long hair had caught between the open back of the elevator and the brick wall. Harry had stood rooted to the spot as Sis was lifted up from the floor, screaming for help. She'd had a clump of hair and a big patch of skin from her scalp ripped off, but had survived and quickly forgotten about it. Quicker than Harry, who could still feel the pang of horror and shame when he thought about how soon after his mother's earnest request he had seized on the first opportunity to let her down.

The elevator doors slid open, and two nurses wheeled a bed out past him.

Harry stood motionless as the elevator doors slid shut again.

Then he turned and began walking up the stairs to the sixth floor.

There was a smell of hospital; that had not changed since his mother had been here. He located the door with 618 on it and knocked gently. Heard a voice and opened. There were two beds inside, one was empty.

"I'm looking for Ståle Aune," Harry said.

"He's gone for a little stroll," the man in the occupied bed said. He was bald, looked to be of Pakistani or Indian extraction and around the same age as Aune, somewhere in his sixties. But Harry knew from experience that judging the age of cancer patients could be difficult.

Harry turned, saw Ståle Aune approaching him on shuffling feet, dressed in a Radium Hospital robe, and realized it was the same man he had passed on his way down the corridor.

The once pot-bellied psychologist now had folds of skin to spare. Aune waved with one hand at chest height and gave a pained smile without showing any teeth.

"Been on a diet?" Harry asked, after they'd hugged.

"You won't believe it, but even my head had shrunk." Ståle demonstrated by poking his small, round Freud glasses back up his nose. "This is Jibran Sethi. Dr Sethi, this is Inspector Hole."

The man in the other bed smiled and nodded, then put on his headphones.

"He's a vet," Aune said in a lower voice. "Nice fellow, but the adage about us becoming like our patients may be true. He hardly says a word and I can barely keep my mouth shut." Aune kicked off his slippers and eased himself onto the bed.

"Didn't know you had such an athletic physique underneath the padding," Harry said, sitting down on a chair.

Aune chuckled. "You've always been adept in the art of flattery, Harry. I was actually quite a useful rower at one time. But what about yourself? You need to eat for God's sake, or you'll disappear completely."

Harry didn't respond.

"Ah, I see," Aune said. "You're wondering which of us is going to disappear first? That would be me, Harry. This is what I shall die from."

Harry nodded. "What are the doctors saying about . . . ?"

"About how long I have left? Nothing. Because I don't ask. The value of staring the truth—and particularly that of your own mortality—in the face is, in my experience, greatly overestimated. And my experience is, as you know, long and deep. At the end of the day, people only want to be comfortable, and for as long as possible, preferably right up to a sudden final curtain. This comes as a partial disappointment to me, of course, to find that in that regard I am no different from anyone else, that I am incapable of dying with the courage and dignity I would wish. But I suppose I lack a good enough reason to die with greater bravura. My wife and daughter cry, and there's no solace for them in seeing me more afraid of death than necessary, so I avoid grim realities and shy away from the truth instead."

"Mm."

"Well, OK, I can't help but read the doctors, by what they say and their facial expressions. And judging by that I don't have much time left. But . . ." Aune threw his arms out, smiling with sad eyes. "There's always the hope I'm wrong. After all, I've gone through my professional life being more often wrong than right."

Harry smiled. "Maybe."

"Maybe. But you understand the way the wind is blowing when they give you a morphine pump, which you administer yourself, without any attendant warnings about overdose."

"Mm. So, pain then?"

"Pain is an interesting interlocutor. But enough about me. Tell me about LA."

Harry shook his head and thought it must be the jet lag, because his body had begun shaking with laughter.

"Cut that out," Aune said. "Death is no laughing matter. Come on, tell me."

"Mm. Doctor–patient confidentiality?"

"Harry, every secret will be taken to the grave here and the clock is ticking, so for the last time, tell me!"

Harry told him. Not everything. Not about what *actually* happened right before he left, when Bjørn shot himself. Not about Lucille and his own ticking clock. But everything else. About running to escape the memories. About the plan to drink himself to death someplace far away. When he had finished, Harry could see Ståle's eyes were glazed. Throughout the many murder cases Ståle Aune had assisted the detectives of Crime Squad with, the psychologist's stamina and powers of concentration when the days were long always impressed Harry. Now he read weariness, pain—and morphine—in his eyes.

"What about Rakel?" Aune asked in a weak voice. "Do you think about her a lot?"

"All the time."

"The past is never dead. It's not even past."

"That a Paul McCartney quote?"

"Close," Aune smiled. "Do you think about her in a good way, or does it just hurt?"

"It hurts in a good way, I suppose. Or the other way around. Like . . .

well, the booze. The worst are the days I wake up having dreamed about her and for a moment I think she's still alive, and that what happened is the dream. And then I have to go through the fucking thing all over again."

"Remember when you came to me in order to address the drinking, and I asked you if in the periods you were dry you wished that liquor didn't exist in the world. And you said you wanted liquor to exist, that even though you didn't want to drink, you wanted another option to be there. The thought of having a drink. That without that everything would be gray and meaning-less, and there would be no adversary in the struggle. Is it . . . ?"

"Yes," Harry said. "That's what it's like with Rakel as well. I'd rather have the wound than not have had her in my life."

They sat in silence. Harry glanced down at his hands. Around the room. Heard the sounds of a low phone conversation coming from the other bed. Ståle rolled onto his side.

"I'm a little tired, Harry. Some days are better, but today's not one of them. Thank you for coming."

"How much better?"

"What do you mean?"

"Good enough that you can work? From here, I mean."

Aune looked at him in surprise.

Harry pulled his chair closer to the bed.

In the conference room on the sixth floor of Police HQ, Katrine was about to wrap up the morning meeting of the investigative team. There were sixteen people sitting in front of her, eleven from Crime Squad and five from Kripos. Of the sixteen, ten were detectives, four were analysts, and two worked in Krimteknisk, the Forensics Unit. Katrine Bratt had gone through the findings of the Crime Scene Unit and the Forensic Medical Institute's preliminary post-mortem, showing photos from both. Watched her audience stare at the bright screen while shifting uneasily on hard chairs. The Crime Scene Unit hadn't found much, something they regarded as a discovery in itself.

"It seems he might know what we're looking for," one of the forensics officers said. "Either he's cleaned up after himself or he's just been very lucky."

The only concrete evidence they had were shoeprints on the soft ground from two people, one matching the shoes Susanne was wearing, the other made by a heavier individual wearing a size 42, probably a male. The tracks indicated they had been walking close to one another.

"As though he's forced Susanne with him into the woods?" asked Magnus Skarre, one of the veterans of Crime Squad.

"Could be, yes," the forensics expert confirmed.

"The Forensic Medical Institute did a preliminary post-mortem over the weekend," Katrine said, "and there's good and bad news. The good news is that they found a tiny amount of residue from spit or mucus on one of Susanne's breasts. The bad news is we can't be certain it came from the killer, given that Susanne's upper body was clothed when we found her. So if he did assault her, he must have dressed her again, which would be unusual. Anyway, Sturdza was kind enough to run an express DNA analysis on the residue, and the even worse news is that there was no match with any profile in the database of known offenders. So if it didn't come from the killer, we're talking . . ."

"A needle in a haystack," Skarre said.

No one laughed. No one groaned. Just silence. After three weeks in the proverbial wilderness, late nights, threatened cancellation of fall breaks and friction on domestic fronts, the discovery of a body had extinguished one hope and sparked another. Of leads. Of solving the case. This was now officially a murder investigation, and it was Monday, a new week, with new opportunities. But the faces staring back at Katrine were drained, drawn and tired.

She had been expecting that. And had therefore saved the last slide in order to wake them up.

"This was discovered when they were concluding the preliminary post-mortem," she said, as the next photo came up on the screen. When she had received it from Alexandra on Saturday, Katrine's first association had been with the monster from the film *Mary Shelley's Frankenstein*.

95

Everyone in the room stared in silence at the head with the rough stitches. That was the extent of the reaction. Katrine cleared her throat.

"Sturdza writes that it appears as though Susanne Andersen has recently received a cut to the head from just above the hairline over the forehead all the way around. And that the wound has been sewn shut again. We don't know if that might have occurred prior to her disappearance, but Sung-min spoke to Susanne's parents yesterday."

"As well as to a friend who met Susanne the night before she went missing," Sung-min said. "None of them had any knowledge of her having received stitches to her head."

"So we can assume this is the work of her killer. The pathologist will be performing a full clinical autopsy today, so hopefully we'll find out more." She checked the time. "Anyone want to add something before we get started on today's assignments?"

A female detective spoke up. "Now we know that one of the girls was forced off the path and into the forest, shouldn't we intensify our search for Bertine in the woody areas along the footpaths around Grefsenkollen."

"Yes," Katrine said. "That's already under way. Anything else?"

The faces looking back at her resembled those of fed-up schoolkids just looking forward to break time. If that. Last year someone had suggested they hire a former world champion cross-country skier who gave so-called inspirational speeches aimed at the business sector, about how to get over the mental hump everyone meets sooner or later in a 30-mile race. For his services, the national hero in question quoted a fee only a private sector company could pay. Katrine had said they could just as well have a single mother in full-time employment give the talk, and that it was the worst suggestion she had heard about how to waste the departmental budget. Now she wasn't quite so sure.

10

MONDAY

Horses

THE YOUNG TAXI DRIVER LOOKED in confusion at the pieces of paper Harry was holding out.

"It's called money," Harry said.

The taxi driver took the bills and studied the numbers on them. "I don't have . . . like . . . eh . . ."

"Change." Harry sighed. "That's all right."

Harry began making his way towards the entrance of Bjerke Racecourse as he stuffed the receipt in his back pocket. The twenty minutes from the Radium Hospital had cost as much as a plane ticket to Malaga. He needed a car, preferably one with a driver, as soon as possible. But first and foremost he needed a policeman. A corrupt one.

He found Truls Berntsen in Pegasus. The large restaurant had space for a thousand patrons, but today—the weekly lunchtime race day—only the tables with a view of the track were filled to capacity. There was one table with a customer seated alone, as though he exuded a smell. But a closer look might reveal the reason was in his eyes and also his bearing. Harry pulled out one of the empty chairs and looked out at the racetrack where horses trotted around pulling sulkies with drivers atop, while from the loudspeakers information was spat out in a continuous, monotone voice.

"That was quick," Truls said.

"Taxi," Harry replied.

"Must be flush then. We could have done this over the phone."

"No," Harry said, sitting down. They had exchanged exactly twelve words when Harry called. *Yes? Harry Hole here, where are you? Bjerke Racecourse. On my way.*

"Is that so, Harry? Have *you* gotten involved in shady business?" Truls let out his grunting laughter, which along with his weak chin, protruding brow and general passive-aggressive demeanor had earned him the nickname Beavis. He and the cartoon character also shared a nihilistic outlook and an almost admirable absence of any sense of social responsibility or morality. The subtext of his question was of course if Harry had *also* gotten involved in shady business.

"I might have an offer for you."

"The kind I can't refuse?" Truls said, casting a dissatisfied glance out at the track, where the announcer was listing the order of finishers.

"Unless your betting selection comes in, yeah. You're out of work, I hear. And have gambling debts."

"Gambling debts? Says who?"

"It's not important. You're unemployed, in any case."

"I'm not *that* unemployed. I'm receiving a salary without doing shit. So as far as I'm concerned they can take as long as they like trying to find some evidence, I couldn't give a rat's ass."

"Mm. I heard it was something to do with the skimming of a cocaine seizure at Gardermoen?"

Truls snorted. "Me and two others from Narcotics picked up the stuff. This weird, green cocaine. Customs reckoned it was green because it was so pure, as if they were like walking crime labs or something. We delivered it to Seizures who discovered there was a small anomaly in the weight in relation to what Gardermoen had reported. So they sent it for analysis. And the analysis showed that the cocaine, which was just as green as before, had been adulterated. So then they think we cut some of the cocaine with something else green, but screwed up by getting the weight slightly wrong. Or rather me, as I was the only one alone with the dope for a few minutes."

"So not only do you risk being fired but prison time?"

"Are you stupid, or something?" Truls grunted. "They don't have anything close to proof. A few morons from Customs who think the green stuff *looked* and *tasted* like pure cocaine? A difference of a milligram or two in weight that everyone knows could be due to all sorts of things? They'll go on about it for a while, and then the case will be dismissed."

"Mm. So you're ruling out them finding another guilty party?"

Truls leaned his head back slightly, looked at Harry as though taking aim at him. "I've got some stuff involving horses to take care of here, Harry, so if there was something you wanted to talk about?"

"Markus Røed has hired me to investigate the case of the two girls. I want you on the team."

"Bloody hell," Truls stared at Harry in surprise.

"What do you say?"

"Why are you asking me?"

"Why do you think?"

"No idea. I'm a bad cop, and you know that better than most."

"All the same, we've saved each other's lives on at least one occasion. According to an old Chinese proverb that means we have a responsibility for one another for the rest of our lives."

"Really?" Truls sounded unsure.

"Plus," Harry said, "if you're only suspended, then you still have full access to BL96?"

Harry noticed Truls flinch when he heard mention of the makeshift, antiquated system for investigation reports in use since 1996.

"So?"

"We need access to all the reports. Tactical, technical, forensics."

"Right. So this is . . . ?"

"Yep, shady business."

"The kind of thing that can get cops kicked off the force."

"If it's discovered, definitely. And that's why it well paid."

"Yeah? How well?"

"Give me a number and I'll pass it along."

Truls looked at Harry for a long time, thoughtfully. Lowered his gaze to the betting slip on the table in front of him. Crumbled it up in his hand.

It was lunchtime at Danielle's, and the bar and the tables were beginning to fill up. Although situated a few hundred yards from the city center and the hell of office complexes, it never ceased to surprise Helene that a restaurant located in a residential area got so many patrons on their lunch break.

She cast a glance around, scanning the large, open-plan premises from her small round table in the center. Found no one of interest. Then turned her attention back to the screen of her laptop. She had found a site with equestrian equipment. There appeared to be no limit to the amount of products available for horses and riders, or the prices demanded for them. After all, most people involved with horses were well-to-do, and riding was an opportunity to flaunt that. The drawback for most people was of course that the bar to impress in this milieu was set so high that most people had already lost before they even got started. But was importing equestrian equipment really what she wanted to do? Or would she be better off trying her hand at arranging riding tours in Valdres, Vassfaret, Vågå or other scenic shitholes beginning with V? She slammed the laptop shut, sighed deeply and looked around again.

Yes, there they were, sitting perched along the bar that ran the length of the establishment. The young men in whatever suit they were flogging to real estate agents at the moment. The young women wearing skirts and jackets or something else to make them look "professional." Some of the women actually had jobs, but Helene could point out the others, the ones who were a bit too pretty, wearing skirts which were a bit too short, who were more interested in what made a job superfluous—in short a man with money. She didn't know why she continued to come here. Ten years ago, the Monday lunches at Danielle's had been legendary. There had been something so deliciously decadent and couldn't-give-a-fuck about getting drunk and dancing on the tables in the middle of the first day of the working week. But, of course, it had also been a statement about status; an excess only the rich and privileged could allow themselves. These days it was quieter. Now the former fire station was a combination of bar and Michelin-starred gourmet restaurant, a place where the elite of Oslo's west side ate, drank, talked business, discussed family matters, built relationships and entered alliances that drew the distinction between those allowed within and those who would remain outside.

It was here, during a wild Monday lunch, that Helene had met Markus. She had been twenty-three years old, he was over fifty and filthy rich. So rich that people moved aside when he walked to the bar, everyone seemed to know what the Røed family were good for. And bad for. She had not been as innocent as she made out, of course, something Markus could probably tell after the first couple of times she stayed the night at his villa in Skillebekk. Could tell by her soundtrack to lovemaking, which was akin to something lifted straight from Pornhub, could tell by the pings from incoming messages on her phone all night and could tell by the way she arranged the cocaine in such even lines that he never knew which he should take. But he didn't seem to mind. Innocence wasn't something that turned him on, he claimed. She didn't know if that was true, but it wasn't so important. What was important, or one of the things that was important, was that he could facilitate the lifestyle she had always dreamed about. That dream was not about being a stay-at-home trophy wife investing all her time on the upkeep and improvement of the house, holiday home, social network and her own body and face. Helene left that sort of thing to the other parasitic bimbos on the hunt for a suitable host at Danielle's. Helene had a brain and was interested in things. In art and culture, especially theater and the visual arts. In architecture—she had long considered studying that. But her big dream was to run the best riding school in the country. It wasn't a pipe dream indulged in by a stupid, fanciful girl, but a realistic plan drawn up at a young age by an academically capable and hard-working girl who had mucked out at more than one stable, progressed through the ranks, and eventually become a riding school instructor, a girl who despised the term "horse mad" and knew what was required in terms of effort, money and expertise.

And still it had all gone to shit.

It hadn't been Markus's fault. Well, yes, it had, he had cut off the money just as some horses at the riding school got sick, which combined with unexpected competition and unforeseen expenses made the hurdle too high. She'd had to close down the school, and it was time to find something new.

In more ways than one. She and Markus were not going to last much longer either.

Some say that when a couple start having sex less than once a week, it's only a question of time before it's over. Nonsense of course, it had been years since she and Markus had had sex more than once every six months.

Not that it bothered her. But the possible consequences bothered her. She had gone all out on this, on a life with Markus, on the riding school, to the extent that she had abandoned all her plan Bs and Cs. She hadn't taken any of the educational paths so open to someone with her school grades. Hadn't saved up money, but had in a sense made herself dependent on his. Not in a sense, she *was* dependent on his money. Not in order to survive, maybe, but . . . yes, in order to survive. In fact.

When was it she had lost her hold on him? Or to be more precise: when was it he had lost interest for her in bed? It could of course have to do with the reduced production of testosterone in a man who was over sixty, but she believed it had started when she began expressing a desire for children. She knew that for a man there was hardly a bigger turn-off than duty sex. But when he had informed her that children were out of the question, the celibacy merely continued. Given that her own appetite for sex with Markus, which had never been voracious, had also waned, it was no big problem. Even though she suspected he had begun to look other places to satisfy his needs. As long as he was discreet and didn't make her a laughing stock, it was all right.

No, the problem was the two girls from the party. One had been found dead, and the other was still missing. And both of them could be connected to Markus. Their Sugar daddy. The words had even appeared in print. The idiot—she could have ripped his head off! She wasn't Hillary Clinton and this wasn't the nineties, she couldn't just "forgive" her husband. Because these days women weren't allowed to let the bastards get away with that sort of thing, it had to do with respect for yourself, your gender and the zeitgeist. Just her bloody luck not to be born a generation previous.

But even if she was "permitted" to forgive him, would Markus have let her? Was this not what he had been waiting for, an exit from her that was neither particularly shameful nor honorable given there were both positive and negative associations about a man over sixty who screws around? For someone like Markus Røed there were definitely worse things to be labelled than a virile bastard and womanizer. So shouldn't she get a move on and leave before he did? *That*, after all, would be the ultimate defeat.

So she was on the lookout. It was unconscious, but she had caught herself doing it. Getting an overview of the men among the clientele. Determining which of them could—in a notional future situation—be of interest. People think they can hide behind their secrets, but the truth of course is that we all exhibit what we think and feel, and those that pay close attention will take it in.

So perhaps she shouldn't have been surprised when a waiter stopped in front of her and placed a cocktail glass on the table.

"Dirty martini," he said in Norrland-accented Swedish. "From him over there . . ." He pointed towards a man sitting alone at the bar. He was looking out the window so she saw him in profile. The quality of his suit was perhaps a notch above the other male patrons, and he was a handsome man, no doubt about it. But young, probably around her own age, which was thirty-two. Though, it goes without saying, an enterprising man could have accomplished much in that time. She didn't know why he wasn't looking at her, maybe he was shy, or maybe it had been a while since he had ordered the drink and he didn't think he could stare at her the whole time. Charming, if that was the case.

"Were you the one who told him I usually drink a martini at the Monday lunch?" she asked.

The waiter shook his head, but something in his smile made her doubt he was being completely sincere.

She nodded to the waiter that she accepted the drink, and he departed from her table. As things stood she was likely to be accepting several such drinks from admirers in the future, so why not start with someone that seemed appealing?

She raised the glass to her lips and noticed that it tasted different. Presumably it was the two olives at the bottom of the glass, the ingredients in making the drink "dirty." Perhaps that was something she would also have to get used to, a different, dirtier taste to everything.

The man at the bar let his gaze drift over the room, as if he didn't know where she was sitting. Helene raised her hand, caught his eye. Lifted the glass in a toast. He lifted his own, a plain glass of water, in response. But without smiling. Yes, he was probably the shy type. But then he got to his feet. Looked around as though making sure there were no others involved before approaching her.

Because of course he approached her. All men did sooner or later if Helene wanted them to. But as he drew closer, she felt that she didn't want this, not yet. She had never been unfaithful to Markus, hadn't even flirted with other men, and neither would she, not before everything was settled, finalized. She was upfront like that, a one-man woman, and always had been. Even if Markus was far from being a one-woman man. Because it wasn't about what he thought of her, but about what she thought of herself.

The man stopped at her table, began to pull out the other chair.

"Please don't sit down." Helene looked up at him with a wide smile. "I just wanted to thank you for the drink."

"The drink?" He smiled back, but looked confused.

"This. Which you sent over. Yes?"

He shook his head with a laugh. "But shall we pretend as if I did? My name's Filip."

She laughed in return, and shook her head as well. He already looked a tiny bit smitten, poor guy. "Have a nice day, Filip."

He gave a gentlemanly bow and left her. He would still be there the day it ended with Markus too. And hopefully without that wedding ring he had tried to conceal. Helene gestured to the waiter. He stood beside the table with his head bowed and a guilty smile.

"You tricked me. Who really sent the drink over?"

"Sorry, fru Røed. I thought it was a joke being played on you by someone you knew." He pointed to an empty table by the wall a little behind her. "He just left. I served him two martinis, but then he waved me over and asked me to give one to you and pointed out who I was to say it came from. The good-looking gentlemen at the bar, that is. I hope I didn't go too far?"

"It's fine," she said, shaking her head. "I hope he tipped you well."

"Of course, fru Røed. Of course." The waiter grinned, black snus showing between his teeth.

Helene picked out the olives before drinking the last of the martini, but the taste lingered.

It was on the way down towards Gyldenløves gate that the anger descended, and it struck her. That it was madness, utter insanity that she, an intelligent, grown woman, should accept that her existence was controlled by men, men she neither liked nor respected. What was it she was actually afraid of? Being alone? She was alone, for fuck's sake, every one of us was alone! And it was Markus who had most reason to be afraid. If she told the truth, told what she knew . . . she shuddered at the thought, the same way presidents hopefully shuddered at the thought of pushing the button. While naturally at the same time the thought they *could* do it thrilled them. There was something so sexy about power! Most women sought it indirectly, by going after men with power. But why do that if you have a nuclear button? And why hadn't the thought ever crossed her mind before now? Simple: because the boat had hit the rocks and was taking on water.

Helene Røed decided there and then that from now on she would be in control of her own life, and that in that life there would be very little space for men. And because Helene Røed was well aware that when she set her mind to something, she saw it through, she knew that was how it was going to be. Now it just a matter of drawing up a plan. Then, when this was all behind her, she would send a drink over to a man she liked the look of.

11

MONDAY

Naked

AS HARRY ENTERED THE SQUARE in front of Oslo Central Station, he caught sight of Øystein Eikeland standing by the tiger statue, stamping his feet on the flagstones. Øystein was wearing a Vålerenga top, but the rest was pure Keith Richards. The hair, the wrinkles, scarf, eyeliner, cigarette, the emaciated frame.

As with Aune, Harry didn't hug his childhood friend too hard, as though afraid even more of the people in his life would go to pieces.

"Wow," Øystein said. "Nice suit. What were you doing over there? Running prostitutes? Selling coke?"

"No, but I can see you are," Harry said, looking around. The people on the square were mostly commuters, tourists and office workers, but there were few places in Oslo where the sale of drugs took place as openly as here. "I have to admit I didn't see that coming."

"No?" Øystein said, adjusting his sunglasses, the hug having knocked them out of position. "I did. Should have started years ago. Not only does it pay better than driving a cab, it's healthier too."

"Healthier?"

"Gets me closer to the source. Everything going into this body now is high-quality stuff." He ran this hands down his sides.

"Mm. And in moderate doses too?"

"Course. How 'bout you?"

Harry shrugged. "At the moment, I'm trying out your Moderation Management program. Not sure it'll work out in the long run, but we'll see."

Øystein tapped a finger to his temple.

"Yeah, yeah," Harry said, and saw a young man in a parka standing a little farther off staring at him. Even at this distance Harry could see that his eyes were blue and so wide open that the whites were visible all the way around his irises. He had both hands stuffed down in the deep pockets as though holding something.

"Who's that guy?" Harry asked.

"Oh, that's Al. He can see you're a cop."

"Dealer?"

"Yeah. Nice guy, but odd. Bit like yourself."

"Me?"

"Better looking than you of course. And smarter."

"Really?"

"Oh, you're smart in your own way, Harry, but that guy he's like nerd smart. You start talking about something and he knows everything about it, like he's studied it or something, you know. What you got in common is both of you have that thing the ladies fall for. That whole charismatic loneliness schtick. And he's a creature of habit, just like you."

Harry saw Al turn away as though he didn't want to show Harry his face.

"Stands here from nine to five, off on weekends," Øystein continued. "As if he had, like, a regular job. Likeable, as I said, but cautious, almost paranoid. Happy to talk shop, but won't say anything about himself, exactly like you. Except this guy won't even tell you his name."

"So Al is . . ."

"I gave him the name from the Paul Simon song. You Can Call Me Al, y'know?"

Harry grinned.

"You seem a bit jumpy and all yourself," Øystein said. "You OK?"

Harry shrugged. "I might've gotten a little paranoid myself over there."

"Yo," a voice sounded. "Got any coke?"

Harry turned and saw a boy in a hoodie.

"You think I'm a dealer?" Øystein hissed, "Get off home and do your homework!"

"Aren't you?" Harry asked, as they watched the boy wander towards the guy in the parka.

"Yeah, but not for kids that young. I leave that to Al and the West Africans on Torggata. Besides, I'm like a high-class hooker, mostly call-out." Øystein grinned, revealing a row of rotten teeth, and flashed a new, shiny Samsung phone. "Deliveries to the door."

"Does that mean you have a car?"

"Sure do. Bought that old merc I was driving. Got it cheap from the taxi company owner. He said the customers were complaining about the smell of smoke, that he couldn't get rid of it, and told me it was my fault. Hehe. I also forgot to remove the taxi sign from the roof, so I can drive in the bus lane. Speaking of the smell of smoke, you got a cig?"

"I quit. And it looks to me like you have your own anyway."

"Yours always tasted better, Harry."

"Well. That's over now."

"Yeah, I gather that's the kind of thing California can do to a man."

"The car parked far away?"

From the sprung, worn-out front seats of the Mercedes they looked out over the seaward approach into Bjørvika, the attractive new urban quarter comprising Oslobukta and Sørenga, but where the newly built Munch Museum, a thirteen-story mental patient in a straitjacket, blocked the view.

"Christ, that's ugly," Øystein said.

"So what do you say?" Harry asked.

"Driver and general dogsbody?"

"Yes. And if it turns out to have anything to do with the case, we may need an insider who can follow the cocaine trail to and from Markus Røed."

"So you're sure he uses the marching powder?"

"Sneezes. Has large, dilated pupils and sunglasses lying on the desk. His eyes dart all over the place."

"Nystagmus. But follow the trail from Røed, you say. Isn't he, like, your client?"

"My job is to solve a murder, probably two. Not to defend that man's interests."

"And you think it's about coke? If you said heroin, I might—"

"I don't think anything, Øystein, but when addiction is in the picture, it always plays a part. And I think at least one of the girls was a little too fond of blow too. She owed her dealer ten thousand kroner. So, are you in?"

Øystein studied the glow on his cigarette. "Why are you actually taking on this job, Harry?"

"I told you, money."

"Y'know, that was what Dylan said when he was asked why he started with folk music and protest songs."

"And you think he was lying?"

"I think it was one of the few times Dylan was telling the truth, but I think *you're* lying. If I'm going to be part of this madness, I want to know why you're in on it. So spit it out."

Harry shook his head. "OK, Øystein, I'm not going to tell you everything, for your sake and for my own. You're just going to have to trust me here."

"When was the last time that paid off?"

"Don't remember. Never?"

Øystein laughed. Pushed a CD into the player and turned up the volume. "Heard the latest from Talking Heads?"

"*Naked*, 1987?"

"'88."

Øystein lit up cigarettes for both of them as "Blind" streamed out of the speakers. They smoked without rolling down the windows while David

Byrne sang about signs being lost and signs disappearing. The smoke lay like a sea fog inside the car.

"Have you ever had the feeling that you know you're going to do something stupid, but do it all the same?" Øystein asked, taking one last drag on the cigarette.

Harry stubbed his cigarette out in the ashtray. "The other day I saw a mouse walk right up to cat and get killed. What was that all about, you think?"

"I dunno, you tell me. A lack of instinct for self-preservation?"

"Some sort of urge, anyway. We're drawn—some of us, at least—towards the edge of the precipice. They say it's because the closeness to death intensifies the feeling of being alive. But fuck it, I don't know."

"Well said," Øystein said.

They gazed at the Munch Museum.

"I agree," Harry said. "Absolutely horrible."

"OK," Øystein said.

"OK what?"

"OK, I'll take the job." Øystein stubbed his cigarette out on top of Harry's. "It's bound to be more fun than selling coke. Which is fucking boring, actually."

"Røed pays well."

"That's all right, I'll still take it."

Harry smiled and took out his phone, which was vibrating. Saw a "T" on the display.

"Yes, Truls."

"I've checked that report from the Forensic Medical Institute you asked about. Susanne Andersen had stitches to her head. And they found saliva and mucus on one of her breasts. They ran an express DNA analysis but got no hits on the database of registered offenders."

"OK. Thanks."

Harry hung up. That was it, what Katrine didn't want to—or thought she couldn't—tell him. Saliva. Mucus.

"So where to, boss?" Øystein asked, turning the key in the ignition.

12

MONDAY

Wegner Swivel Chair

"IS THIS A JOKE?" THE pathologist asked from behind her face mask.

Alexandra stared in disbelief at the open cranium of the corpse on the table in front of them. It was usual during a full autopsy for the pathologist to saw a round incision in the skull and examine the brain. And beside them, on the table of instruments, lay the usual tools: the manual and the electric bone saws, along with the T-shaped skull key that they used to remove the top of the skull. What was unusual was that none of these instruments had been used on Susanne Andersen. It had not been necessary. Because after they had cut the stitches, removed the scalp and placed the toupee of Susanne's long, blonde hair on another table, it had become clear that someone had beaten them to it. The skull had already been sawn open. The pathologist had tilted back the top of the skull, like a hinged lid. And now she was asking if it was supposed to be a joke.

"No," Alexandra whispered.

*

"You're kidding," Katrine said into the phone as she looked out the window of her office, at Botsparken, with the avenue of linden trees leading up to the old part of Oslo Prison, the almost picturesque Botsfengselet. The sky was clear, and although people were no longer lying on the grass in just their underwear, they were sitting on the benches with faces turned towards the sun in the knowledge that this might be the last day of the year with summer temperatures.

She listened and realized that Alexandra Sturdza was not kidding. She had never actually believed she was. Because wasn't this something she half expected on Saturday, when Alexandra had told her about the stitches? That they weren't dealing with a rational murderer, but a crazy person, one they could not find by answering Harry's *why*. Because there was no *why*, at least not that a normal person could understand.

"Thanks," Katrine said, hanging up, getting to her feet and making her way through the open-plan office. To the windowless office that had once been Harry's and which he had turned down exchanging for a larger, brighter one when he was promoted to inspector. Perhaps that was why Sung-min had chosen precisely this office as a base while working on the case, or perhaps he just thought it was better than the other two available offices she had shown him. The door was open, so she knocked on it as she entered.

Sung-min's suit jacket hung on the coat stand on a hanger she realized he must have brought with him. His shirt was so white it seemed to glow in the gloomy room. She found herself automatically looking around for the items that had been here when it was Harry's cave. Like the framed Dead Policemen's Society picture, with the photo of all the colleagues Harry had lost in service. But everything was gone, even the coat stand was new.

"Bad news," she said.

"Oh?"

"We'll get the preliminary results of the autopsy in an hour, but Sturdza gave me a heads-up. Susanne Andersen is missing her brain."

Sung-min raised an eyebrow. "Literally?"

"There's only so much a post-mortem can uncover, so yes, I mean literally. Someone's opened up Susanne's cranium and . . ."

"And?"

"Removed her entire brain."

Sung-min leaned back in the office chair. She recognized the drawn-out, plaintive creak. The chair. That worn-out wreck. So they hadn't replaced that.

Johan Krohn watched as Markus Røed sneezed, wiped his nose on one of his light blue handkerchiefs, put it back into his inside pocket and leaned back in the Wegner swivel chair behind his desk. Krohn knew it was a Wegner because he had wanted one just like it himself. But the listed price was close to thirteen thousand kroner, and he didn't feel he could justify that to the partners, his wife or the clients. It was a simple chair. Elegant, but in no way ostentatious, and thus untypical for Markus Røed. He presumed that someone, perhaps Helene, had advised him that the previous office chair, a high-backed Vitra Grand Executive in black leather, was too vulgar. Not that he thought the other two people in the room cared. Harry Hole had pulled out a chair from the conference table and sat down in front of Røed's desk, while the other individual—a highly dubious Captain Hook-like figure Harry had introduced as a driver and general factotum on his team—had sat down by the door. So at least he knew his place.

"Tell me, Hole," Røed sniffled, "is this a joke?"

"Nope," said Harry, who had sunk into the chair, placed his hands behind his head, stretched out his long legs and was now turning his shoes at angles to examine them as if he hadn't noticed them before. They looked like a pair of John Lobb shoes to Krohn, but it was hard to imagine someone like Hole could afford that.

"Seriously, Hole, you're thinking our team should consist of a hospitalized cancer patient, a policeman under investigation for corruption and a man who drives a taxi?"

"I said *drove* a taxi. He's in the retail business now. And it's not *our* team, Røed, it's mine."

Røed's face darkened. "The problem, Hole, is that there isn't a team, it's a . . . theater troupe. And I'd be made to look like a clown if I was foolish enough to announce that these . . . these are the best I could find."

"You're not going to announce it."

"But for Christ's sake, man, that's half the point, didn't we make that clear?" Røed's voice boomed in the large room. "I want the public to see that I've hired some of the best people to solve this case, only then will they realize that I actually mean it. This is about me and my firm's reputation."

"Last time you said it was because the suspicion was a strain on the family," said Harry, who as opposed to Røed had lowered his voice. "And we can't publicize who's on the team because the policeman will be immediately dismissed, automatically losing access to the police reports. Which is the very reason he's on the team."

Røed looked at Krohn.

The lawyer shrugged. "The important name on the press release is Harry Hole, renowned murder detective. We can write that he wants a team around him—that should suffice. As long as the man in the main role is good, people will just assume the rest of the team is good."

"And one more thing," Harry said. "Aune and Eikeland get the same hourly rate as Krohn. And Berntsen gets double."

"Are you insane, man?" Røed threw his arms wide. "Your bonus is one thing. That's fine as long as you're not taking pay but risking everything on success, that's gutsy. But to pay double what a lawyer makes to a . . . a *nobody* of a fraudster? Can you explain to me how in the world he deserves that?"

"I don't know if he *deserves* it, exactly," Harry said. "But he is worth it. Isn't that what business people such as yourself base payment on?"

"Worth it?"

"Let me say it again," Harry said, stifling a yawn. "Truls Berntsen has access to BL96, that means all the police reports in this case, including from Krimteknisk and the Forensic Medical Institute. There are currently somewhere between twelve and twenty people on the investigative team alone. Berntsen's password and irises are worth the combined work of all of these. In addition, there's the risk he's taking. Should it be discovered he's passing classified information to an outside party, he won't merely be fired, he'll be facing prison time."

Røed shut his eyes and shook his head. When he opened them again, he was smiling.

"You know what, Harry? We could use a bastard like you in the contract negotiations Barbell are involved in at the minute."

"Good," Harry said. "There is one more condition."

"Oh?"

"I want to question you."

Røed exchanged glances with Krohn again.

"Fine."

"With a lie detector," Harry said.

13

MONDAY

The Aune group

MONA DAA WAS SITTING AT her desk reading a piece by a blogger named Hedina about social pressure and beauty standards. The language was poor and clunky at times, but it had a direct quality which made it easy to digest, like sitting at a cafe table listening to a friend babble on about everyday problems. The blogger's "sage" thoughts and advice were so banal and predictable that Mona didn't know whether to yawn or snarl.

Using hackneyed phrases drawn from similar blogs, as though they were her own watchwords and ideas, Hedina employed them with sincerity and indignation to describe the frustration of living in a world where looks were regarded as paramount, and bemoaned how that created so many insecurities in young women. It was of course a paradox that Hedina herself posted soft-porn pictures of beautiful, slim, breast-augmented Hedina, but that discussion had come up time and time again, and eventually—after winning every battle—exhausted reason had lost the war to stupidity. And speaking of stupidity, the reason Mona Daa had now wasted half an hour of her life reading Hedina's blog was that Julia, the editor, had, due to people out sick and a lull in the Susanne case, assigned Mona to comment on the comments on Hedina's comments. Julia had, without a hint of irony, told Mona to count which comments there were most of, the positive or the negative, and let that determine whether the heading for the article should begin with "praised for" or "criticized for." With a slightly—but not too—sexy picture of Hedina as clickbait below.

Mona was mortified.

Hedina wrote that all women are beautiful, it was just a matter of each and every one finding their own unique beauty and trusting in it. Only in this way would you stop comparing yourself with others and succumb to the belief of losing in the beauty stakes, to eating disorders, depression and destroyed lives. Mona wanted to write what was obvious, that if everyone is beautiful, then no one is beautiful, because beauty is what stands out in a positive way, And that when she was growing up, a few movies stars and perhaps a classmate were privileged to be beautiful in the original meaning of the word, and it didn't bother her or her friends significantly to be in the large majority of the ordinary and non-beautiful. There were other more important things to focus on and an ordinary appearance didn't ruin any-one's life. It was people like Hedina who accepted the premise that all women wanted and *should* want to be "beautiful" as unquestionably true that created losers. If seventy per cent of the women around you have, through surgery, diet, makeup and exercise, achieved an appearance the other thirty per cent aren't able to achieve, it's these ordinary women, who previously managed just fine, who are suddenly in a minority and have been given a *reason* to suffer from ever so slight depression.

Mona sighed. Would she have thought and felt this way if she herself had been born with the looks of a Hedina? Even though Hedina hadn't been born the way she looked in pictures either? Perhaps not. She didn't know. She only knew there was nothing she hated more than having to give column inches to a blogger with no brain and half a million followers.

A breaking news notification popped up on her screen.

And Mona Daa realized that there was one thing she hated more. Being overtaken and left in the dust by Terry Våge.

"*Susanne Andersen's brain removed,*" Julia read aloud from *Dagbladet's* website, before fixing her eyes on Mona, who was standing in front of her desk. "And we have nothing on this?"

"No," Mona said. "Not us or any of the others."

"I don't know about the others, but we're *VG*, Mona. We're the biggest and the best."

Mona thought Julia may as well say what they were both thinking. *Were* the best.

"Someone in the police must be leaking this," Mona said.

"In that case they're obviously only leaking it to Våge, and then it's called a source, Mona. And our job is to cultivate sources, isn't it?"

Mona had never experienced Julia speaking to her in so patronizing a manner. As though she were a junior, and not one of the newspaper's most high-profile and respected journalists. But Mona also knew that if she herself had been the editor, the journalist wouldn't have gotten off lightly either, rather the opposite.

"Sources are one thing." Mona said. "But you don't get that type of information out of someone in the police unless you have information to give in exchange. Or pay very well. Or . . ."

"Yeah?"

"Or have a hold over the person concerned."

"You think that's the case here?"

"I've no idea."

Julia rolled her chair back, looked out the window and down at the building site in front of the government buildings. "But maybe you also have someone at Police HQ you . . . have a hold over?"

"If you're thinking of Anders, forget about it, Julia."

"A crime journalist with a partner in the police is going to be suspected of getting inside information anyway. So why not—"

"I said, forget it! We're not that desperate, Julia,"

Julia cocked her head to the side. "Aren't we, Mona? Ask management," she said, pointing towards the ceiling. "This is the biggest story we've had in months, in a year where more newspapers than ever have had to fold. Think about it, at least."

"Honestly, Julia, I don't need to. I'd sooner write about that fucking Hedina woman for all eternity than foul my own nest as you're suggesting."

Julia gave her a brief smile before placing her forefinger thoughtfully to her bottom lip and looking at Mona.

"Of course. You're right. That was desperate of me. And wrong. There are certain boundaries you don't cross."

When she returned to her desk, Mona quickly read through the websites of the other newspapers, which could only do the same as her: write about the missing brain by referring to *Dagbladet* and wait for the press conference later that day.

After sending a 200-word piece to the online editor, who promptly put it out, she sat thinking about what Julia had said. Source. Have a hold over. She had once spoken to a journalist from a local paper who had called the metropolitan newspapers "skuas" because they skimmed through the smaller newspapers, stole what they wanted and presented it as their own article, with the briefest possible reference to the local paper on the last line so no one could point a finger at them for breaking the rules of the game. Mona had googled "skua" afterwards and discovered on Wikipedia that it was a bird, a so-called kleptoparasite, which stole prey from smaller birds by flying after them until they let go of their quarry.

Was it conceivable for something similar to be done with Terry Våge? She could do a little digging around the rumors about the attempted rape of Genie; that shouldn't require more than a day's work. Then she could approach Våge and tell him she would put it in print if he didn't share his source in the Susanne case. Get him to let go of his prey. She thought about it. It did mean she would have to get in touch with the creep.

And—if he did go along with it—*refrain* from putting something in print about attempted rape although she had proof.

Then it was as if Mona Daa woke up, and she shuddered. What was she contemplating? Her, self-appointed judge of the ethical standards of some poor blogger, a young girl who had only stumbled onto a way to obtain attention, money and fame. Weren't these perhaps things she herself might like?

Yes, but not like that, not by cheating.

Mona resolved to punish herself that afternoon with three extra sets of biceps curls after the deadlift sets.

Evening darkness had descended on Oslo. From the sixth floor of the Radium Hospital, Harry could gaze down on the freeway. Here, at the road's most low-lying point, he could see the cars moving like a glow-worm at an angle up the hill, towards the freeway's most elevated point, three miles away, where the Rikshospital and the Forensic Medical Institute lay.

"Sorry, Mona," he said, "I have no comment, the press release says what needs to be said. No, you can't get the names of the others on the team, we prefer to work under the radar. No, I can't speak about that, you'll have to ask the police what they think themselves. I hear you, Mona, but, again, I have nothing further to add and I'm going to hang up now, OK? Give Anders my best."

Harry slipped the newly purchased phone into the inside pocket of his suit jacket and sat down again.

"Sorry, it was a mistake saying yes to keeping my old Norwegian number." He placed his palms together. "But everyone present has been introduced and the case has been roughly outlined. Before we go any further, I suggest we name this team the Aune group."

"No, it's not going to be named after me," Ståle Aune protested, pushing himself higher up in bed.

"Apologies for the imprecise language," Harry said, "I've *decided* it will be called the Aune group."

"Because?" asked Øystein, sitting on a chair on the other side of the bed, facing Harry and Truls Berntsen.

"Because this is our office from now on," Harry said. "The police are called the police because they're located at Police HQ, aren't they?" No oneresponded. Harry glanced over at the other bed to make sure the vet hadn't returned after leaving the room unprompted. Then he handed out three copies of stapled sheets from the printer in the business center at the Thief.

"This is a summary of the most important reports in the case so far, including the autopsy today. Everyone has a responsibility to make sure these papers don't go astray. If they do, this guy is in trouble."

He nodded in the direction of Truls, whose grunted laugh didn't reach his eyes or any other part of his face.

"Today, we're not going to work systematically," Harry said. "I just want to hear your thoughts on the case. What kind of murder is it? And if you don't have any thoughts, I'd like to hear them too."

"Bloody hell." Øystein grinned. "Is that what I've joined? A think tank?"

"That's where we're starting anyway," Harry said. "Ståle?"

The psychologist folded two thin hands on top of the duvet. "Well. This makes for an entirely arbitrary gambit, but—"

"Huh?" Øystein said, looking pointedly at Harry.

"To start at a random place," Aune said. "But my first thought is that when a woman dies, we can, with quite a high degree of probability, say that it involves someone with close ties, a husband or boyfriend, and that the motive is jealousy or another form of humiliating rejection. When, as is highly likely in this case, there are two murdered women involved, then the chances are the perpetrator has no close ties to either of them, and the motive is sexual. What sets this case apart is that the two victims were at the same place just before they disappeared. On the other hand, if the theory about there being six degrees of separation between everyone on the planet is correct, then it's not so peculiar after all. Also, we have the fact that a brain and an eye have been removed. That can indicate a killer who takes trophies. So, until we know more, I think we're looking for a—pardon the cliché—psychopathic sexual murderer."

"You sure that's not just the guy with the hammer?" Øystein said.

"I beg your pardon?" Aune adjusted his glasses as though to take a closer look at the man with the bad teeth.

"Y'know, when you've got a hammer, then all problems look like nails. You're a psychologist, so you think the solution to every mystery comes down to psycho stuff."

"Maybe so," Aune said. "Eyes are useless when the mind is blind. So, what kind of murder do you think it is, Eikeland?"

Harry could see Øystein chewing on it, because as usual he was actually chewing; his thin, protruding jawbone working back and forth. He cleared his throat as though he was going to spit on Aune and grinned.

"I think we say that I'm of the same opinion as you, doctor. And since I don't have a psycho hammer, I actually think we should place a little more weight on what I think."

Aune smiled back. "Then it's agreed."

"Truls?" Harry said.

As Harry had half expected, Truls Berntsen—who had only grunted three sentences during the round of introductions—shrugged mutely. Harry did not prolong the policeman's discomfort and spoke himself.

"I think there's a connection between the victims, and that the connection goes through the killer. The removing of body parts may have been done in order to make the police believe they're dealing with a classic serial killer and trophy hunter, so that they won't look too closely at other people with more rational motives. I've seen this type of diversionary maneuver before. I read somewhere that statistically speaking you'll pass a serial killer on the street seven times during your entire life. Personally, I think that number is too high."

Harry didn't particularly believe what he himself had said. He didn't believe anything. No matter what the opinions of the others were, he would have advanced an alternative hypothesis, just to show them that there were alternatives. It was a matter of training to keep the mind open, not consciously or unconsciously lock on to one specific idea. If that happened, an investigator ran the risk of new information being misinterpreted as confirmation of what the investigator already believed, so-called *confirmation bias*, instead of looking at the possibility that new information actually pointed in another direction. Information on a man you already suspected of murder having talked in a friendly manner to the female victim the day before would for example be interpreted as him lusting after her, as opposed to viewing it as him not being aggressive towards her.

Ståle Aune had seemed in relatively good form when they had arrived, but now Harry could see his eyes were becoming glazed, and his wife and daughter were due to visit at eight o'clock. In exactly twenty minutes.

"When we meet again tomorrow, Truls and I will have questioned Markus Røed. What we find out—or don't find out—will probably decide how we move forward. OK, gentlemen, the office is closed for the night."

14

MONDAY

Snuff bullet

IT WAS NINE THIRTY WHEN Harry walked into the bar on the top floor of the Thief.

He sat down at the counter. Tried to moisten his tongue enough to order. It was the anticipation of this drink that had kept him going until now. It was only supposed to be the one, but at the same time he knew that this plan too would soon unravel.

He looked at the cocktail menu the bartender had put down in front of him. Some of the drinks were named after films, and he assumed that actors or directors from those films had been guests here.

"Do you—" he began in Norwegian.

"Sorry, English."

"Do you have Jim Beam?" he asked in English.

"Certainly, sir, but might I recommend our own specially made—"

"No."

The bartender looked at him. "Jim Beam it is."

Harry looked at the clientele and at the city outside. At the new Oslo. Not the rich Oslo, but the *filthy rich* Oslo. Only the suit and shoes he was wearing belonged here. Or maybe not. A couple of years ago he had come by to check out this place, and before backing out the door, he had seen the lead singer from Turbonegro sitting at a table. He had looked as lonely as Harry was feeling now. He took out his phone. She was listed as A. He tapped in a message.

I'm in town. Can we meet?

Then he put the phone down on the bar, noticed a figure slipping in beside him and heard a soft American voice order ginger beer in an accent he couldn't quite place. He glanced at the mirror behind the bar. The bottles on the shelf hid the man's face, but Harry managed to see something bright white around his neck. A clerical collar of the sort visible all the way around, and which they called a dog collar in the USA. The priest was served his beer and disappeared.

Harry was halfway through his drink when the reply from Alexandra Sturdza came.

Yeah, I saw in the paper that you were back. Depends what you mean by meet.

A coffee at the Forensic Med, he typed. *After 12 tomorrow for instance.*

He had to wait a long time. She probably understood this wasn't an attempt to get back into the warmth of her bed, which she had so generously offered after Rakel had kicked him out. Generosity he had been unable to reciprocate in the end, despite how uncomplicated things had been between them. It had been all the rest, everything outside of Alexandra's bed, he hadn't been able to handle. *Depends what you mean by meet.* The worst part was that he wasn't entirely sure if the answer was that it was solely about the job in hand. Because he *was* lonely. He knew of no one who needed to be alone as much as he did, Rakel had called it "limited social capacity" and she had also been the only person he could—and wanted to—spend time with without picturing a finish line up ahead, knowing that he would be set free at some point. You could of course be alone without being lonely, and lonely without being alone, but now he was lonely. And alone.

Maybe that was why he had been hoping for an unequivocal yes instead of this *depends*. Had she gotten a boyfriend? Why not? Would make sense, really. Although the guy would be in for a wild ride.

Only when he had paid for the drink and was on the way down to his room did the phone vibrate again.

1 p.m.

Prim opened the freezer

Next to a large freezer bag, there lay several small ziplock bags, of the type drug dealers used. Two of them contained strands of hair, one some bloody skin fragments, and another pieces of a cloth he had cut up. Items he might one day have use for. He took out a ziplock bag containing moss and made his way past the dining table and the aquarium. Stooped down in front of the glass box on top of the desk. Checked the humidity sensor, removed the lid, opened the ziplock bag and sprinkled moss down onto the black soil. Studied the animal inside, a bright pink slug, almost eight inches in length. Prim never tired of watching it. Not that it was like an action film exactly; if the slug moved at all, it was only a matter of a few centimeters an hour. And neither was there much visible emotional drama or theatrics. The slug's only way of expressing itself—or of obtaining impressions—was its antennae, which you usually had to observe for a while to register movement. And it was that aspect of the slug that was comparable to looking at Her, even the slightest movement or gesture was a reward. Only by patience could he win Her favor, make Her understand.

It was a Mount Kaputar slug. He had brought two of them all the way home from the mountain in New South Wales in Australia. The pink slug was only found there, in a forested area of four square miles at the foot of Mount Kaputar. As the seller had told him: one single bushfire could at any time wipe out the entire species. Therefore, Prim had no pangs of conscience at sidestepping all export and import bans. Slugs were generally host to so many unpleasant parasite microbes that smuggling them over borders was as legal as smuggling radioactive material. So Prim was fairly certain that these were the only two specimens of the pink slug in all of Norway. And should Australia and the rest of the world burn, that might prove to be the salvation of the species. Yes, for that day humans no longer existed. It was simply a question of time. Because nature only retains that which serves nature. Bowie was right when he sang that *Homo sapiens* had outgrown their use.

The slug's feelers moved. It had caught the smell of its favorite dish; the thawed moss Prim had also smuggled from the foot of Mount Kaputar. Now the slug was moving, almost imperceptibly, its smooth, pink surface glistening. Advancing millimeter by millimeter towards its dinner, while laying a trail of slime behind it on the black soil. Closing in on its target, as slowly and surely as Prim was closing in on his. There were cannibal snails in Australia, blind predators which used the slime trail of the Mount Kaputar slug to hunt for it. They were only marginally faster, but slowly, ever so slowly, they closed in on their prey. They would eat the beautiful pink slug alive, scraping it up with a plate of tiny teeth and suck it in, layer by layer. Was the pink slug aware of them coming? Did it experience fear in the long wait until it was caught? Did it have any solution, any means of escape? Did it, for instance, ever consider crossing the slime trail of another Mount Kaputar slug in the hope the pursuers changed course? That, at least, was his own plan when they came for him.

Prim went back to the kitchen and put the ziplock bag back. Stood for a moment looking at the large freezer bag. At the human brain inside. Shuddered. It made him nauseous. He was dreading it.

After brushing his teeth and going to bed, he switched on the police radio and listened to the messages going back and forth. Sometimes it seemed reassuring and was sleep-inducing to listen to these calm voices expressing, in such sober brevity, what was going wrong out there in the city. Because so little occurred and what did was rarely dramatic enough to keep Prim from falling asleep after a short while. But not tonight. They had ended the search in Grefsenkollen for the missing woman and were now using the police radio to arrange times and rendezvous points for the different search parties early tomorrow morning. Prim opened the drawer of the bedside table and took out the cocaine holder. It was partially made of gold, he thought. Two inches long and shaped like a bullet. A snuff bullet. If you twisted the grooved area slightly, the bullet "loaded" with an appropriate dose you could then sniff through the hole at the tip. Truly elegant. It had belonged to the woman the police were now looking for, it even had her initials on the side, B.B. A gift no doubt. Prim ran his fingers across the grooves, rolled the bullet against his cheek. Then he placed it back in the drawer, switched off the radio and stared at the ceiling for a while. There was so much to think about. He tried to masturbate but gave up. Then he began to cry.

It was almost two in the morning when he finally fell asleep.

15

TUESDAY

TRULS LOOKED AT HIS WATCH. Ten past nine. Markus Røed should have arrived ten minutes ago.

Truls and Harry had pushed the bed against the wall in order to move the desk into the middle of Harry's hotel room and were now sitting on chairs on one side of the desk looking at the empty chair awaiting the third person. Truls scratched under his arm.

"Arrogant prick," he said.

"Mm," Harry said. "Just think about what he's paying you per hour and that you're on the clock. That feel better?"

Truls straightened out a forefinger and tapped aimlessly on the laptop in front of him. Thought about it. "A bit," he grunted.

They had gone carefully through the procedure.

The division of responsibilities was simple. Harry would ask the questions, and Truls would keep his mouth shut and concentrate on the screen without giving away what he saw. That suited Truls just fine, it was after all pretty much what he had been doing at Police HQ for the last three years. Playing solitaire, online poker, watching old episodes of *The*

Shield and looking at pictures of Megan Fox. But Truls was also supposed to attach the wires with the electrodes to Røed. Two blue and one red on the chest around the area of his heart, one red at the arteries on each wrist. The wires ran to a box which was in turn was connected to the laptop by a single cable.

"Planning on using the good cop/bad cop tactic?" Truls asked, nodding at the paper towel Harry had placed on the table. The routine was that after making the interviewee cry, the bad cop would march out angrily, whereupon the good cop would immediately proffer the paper towels, say a few compassionate words and then just wait for the interviewee to confide in him. Or in her. People thought women were kinder, they were stupid like that. But Truls knew better. Knew better now.

"Maybe," Harry said.

Truls looked at him. Tried to picture Harry in the good cop role but gave up. Years ago, back when Truls and Mikael Bellman had been partners on the force, Bellman had always been the good cop. He was bloody good at it too, and not just in interviews, the smart, sneaky bastard. So good he was now Minister of Justice. It was unbelievable, considering all the shit the two of them had gotten up to. On the other hand, it almost made perfect sense. No one had Mikael Bellman's ability to bury their hands so deep in shit without getting them dirty.

There was a knock at the door.

They had given word to reception to send Røed up when he arrived.

As agreed beforehand, Truls opened.

Røed was smiling, but seemed nervous, Truls thought. His skin and eyes were shiny. Truls showed him in without introducing himself or shaking his hand. Harry took care of the pleasantries, saying they wouldn't take up much of Røed's time, asking him to remove his jacket and unbutton his shirt. He held out his hand until Røed passed him his jacket, which Harry hung in the wardrobe. Truls started to attach the electrodes. Placing them to avoid the stripes of scabs above and below both nipples. There were also a couple of bruises. Either Røed had taken a beating from someone, or else that wife of his was a real savage in bed. Or maybe it was one of the girls he provided for.

After Truls had attached the last electrodes to the wrists, he went around to Harry's side of the desk, sat down, pressed the enter key, and looked at the screen of the laptop.

"Does it look all right?" Harry asked.

Truls nodded.

Harry turned to Røed. "The questions will be mainly yes or no; polygraph tests are best suited to the analysis of short answers. Ready?"

Røed's smile appeared a little forced. "Fire away, guys, I've got to leave in half an hour."

"Is your name Markus Røed?"

"Yes."

There was a pause, while they looked at Truls, who was looking at the screen. He gave a short nod.

"Are you a man or a woman?" Harry asked.

Røed smiled. "A man."

"Can I hear you say you're a woman?"

"I'm a woman."

Harry looked at Truls, who nodded again.

Harry cleared his throat. "Did you kill Susanne Anderson?"

"No."

"Did you kill Bertine Bertilsen?"

"No."

"Have you had sex with one or both of these women?"

The room went silent. Truls saw Markus Røed beginning to blush. Saw him gasp. And sneeze. Twice. Three times. Harry tore off a square of paper towel and held it out. Markus Røed reached to the back of the chair as though for his jacket—no doubt he had a handkerchief there—before he accepted the paper towel and wiped his nose on it.

"Yes, I have," he said, throwing the square in the wastebasket Harry lifted up. "With both of them. But it was consensual for all parties involved."

"At the same time?"

"No, I'm not into that sort of thing."

"Did Susanne and Bertine know each other?"

"Not to my knowledge. No, I'm fairly sure they didn't."

"Because you made sure that they didn't meet?"

Røed let out a brief laugh. "No, I never hid the fact I was seeing other women. And I invited them both to the party, didn't I?"

"Did you?"

"Yes."

"Did either of these women extort you for money?"

"No."

"Did they threaten to expose your relationship?"

Røed shook his head.

"Please respond verbally," Harry said.

"No. My relationships were not so secret as to matter. Not that I wanted them to be public knowledge, but I didn't make much effort to hide them either. Even Helene was aware of them."

"Do you think she might have been jealous and killed them?"

"No."

"Why not?"

"Helene is a rational woman. She wouldn't consider the risk of getting caught as being worth the upside."

"The upside?"

"Well. Revenge."

"Or killing them to keep you."

"No. She knows I'd never leave her for a bimbo. Or two. But that I might if she tried to curtail my freedom."

"When did you last meet Susanne or Bertine?"

"At the party."

"And prior to that?"

"Prior to that it had been a long time since I'd seen them."

"Why did you stop seeing them?"

"I lost interest, I suppose." Røed shrugged. "The physical aspect is always enticing, but the shelf life of girls like Susanne and Bertine isn't the same as Helene Røed, if you follow me."

"Mm. Did you and or the girls take any controlled substances at the party?"

"Drugs? Not me, anyway."

Harry looked at Truls. Truls gave a small shake of his head.

"You sure?" Harry said. "What about cocaine?"

Truls could feel Markus Røed's eyes on him but didn't lift his own gaze from the screen.

"All right," Røed said. "The girls had a couple of lines."

"Their own cocaine or yours?"

"There was a guy who brought some."

"Who was he?"

"I don't know. A friend of one of the neighbors or a guy they buy off, maybe, I don't know about that sort of thing. If it's cocaine dealers you're after, I can't give you a description either unfortunately, as he was wearing a face mask and sunglasses." Røed allowed himself a wry grin, but Truls could see he was irritated. Alpha males tended to be under questioning.

"But was he white, Norwegian or—"

"Yes, white. Sounded Norwegian."

"Did he speak to Susanne or Bertine?"

"Yes, I suppose he must have done if they were snorting his stuff."

"Mm. So you don't use cocaine yourself."

"No."

Harry leaned over to Truls, who responded by discreetly pointing at a place on the screen.

"Mm. Looks like the polygraph thinks you're not telling the truth."

Røed stared back at them like a defiant teenager at his parents. Before giving up with a groan of irritation.

"I don't understand what this has to do with the case. Yes, I used to enjoy myself on the weekends. But I made a deal with Helene about not taking anything, and that night I didn't. OK? And now I must be on my way."

"Just one last question. Have you hired or cooperated with anyone in order to kill Susanne Andersen or Bertine Bertilsen?"

"For fuck's sake, Hole, why would I do that?" Røed threw his arms in the air in exasperation, and Truls saw with concern that one of the electrodes was about to come loose from his wrist. "Don't you understand that when you're in your mid-sixties and have an understanding wife, you're not exactly afraid of the fact that you're still able to pick up and fuck girls in their twenties coming out? In the circles I move and do business in, it's in fact something which instils respect. It's proof there's still enough man left in you to be reckoned with." The level of Røed's voice rose. "Enough for people to understand they can't pull out of handshake deals they've made without there being consequences. Do you understand, Hole?"

"*I* understand," Harry said, leaning back in his chair. "But the polygraph test here responds best to yes/no answers. So allow me to repeat the ques—"

"No! The answer is no, I haven't ordered any—" Røed began to laugh as though at the absurdity of the thought—"killings."

"Right. Thank you for your time." Harry said. "You should make your next meeting. Truls?"

Truls stood up, walked around the table and removed the electrodes from Røed.

"By the way, I'll be asking to talk to your wife," Harry said while Røed was buttoning up his shirt.

"That's fine."

"Asking *her*, I meant." Harry quickly shut the laptop as Røed came around the table. "I just wanted to inform you."

"Do what you like. But don't make me regret hiring you, Harry."

"Think of it as going to the dentist," Harry said, getting to his feet. "You don't regret it after you've been there." He walked to the wardrobe and held up Røed's jacket while he slipped into it.

"That," Truls grunted after they had closed the door behind their employer, "depends on what you think when you see the bill."

16

TUESDAY

Seamaster

"SHE'S SITTING THERE," THE OLD lady in the white coat said, pointing into the laboratory. Harry saw a back, also in a white coat, sitting on a high stool hunched over a microscope.

He walked over, stood behind the back and coughed quietly.

The woman turned impatiently, and Harry saw a face that was hard, closed, still concentrated on work. But it changed to a sudden sunrise when she saw it was him.

"Harry!" She stood up and threw her arms around his neck.

"Alexandra," Harry said, slightly perplexed; he'd been unsure what sort of reception he could expect.

"How did you get all the way in here?"

"I was here a little early, and Lilly at reception remembered me, so she—"

"Well, what do you think?" Alexandra proudly stood up straight, even twirled a little.

Harry smiled. "You still look fantastic. Like a cross between a Lamborghini—"

"Not me, you idiot! The laboratory."

"Oh. Yeah, it's new, I see."

"Isn't it amazing? Now we can do everything here that we used to have to send abroad. DNA, chemistry, biology, we cover so much that when Krimteknisk lack analysis capacity, they just send it up here. We're allowed to use the lab for personal research as well. I'm working on my doctoral thesis on DNA analysis at the moment."

"Impressive," Harry said, letting his gaze sweep over trays of test tubes, flasks, computer screens, microscopes and machines whose functions he had no clue about.

"Helge, say hello to Harry!" Alexandra called out, and the other person in the room turned on his stool, smiled and waved before returning to his microscope.

"We're competing to see who gets their doctorate first," Alexandra whispered.

"Mm. Sure you have time for a coffee in the cafeteria?"

She slipped her hand under his arm. "I know a better place. Come on."

"So, Katrine knows that you know," Alexandra summed up. "And now she's offered to let you babysit the boy at some stage." She put down her empty cup on the roofing felt in front of the chairs they had taken out from inside the roof door. "That's a start. Are you scared?"

"Scared stiff," Harry said. "Besides, I don't have the time right now."

"Fathers have probably been saying that since time began."

"Yeah. But I need to solve this case in the next seven days."

"Did Røed only give you seven days? That's a bit optimistic, isn't it?" Harry didn't answer.

"Do you think Katrine would like you and her . . . ?"

"No," Harry said firmly.

"Those kinds of feelings never die completely, you know."

"Yes, they do actually."

Alexandra looked at him without saying anything, just pulled away a black corkscrew of hair which had blown across her face.

"Anyway," Harry said. "She knows what's in the boy's and in her own best interests."

"And that is?"

"That I'm not worth having around."

"Who else knows you're the father?"

"Just you," Harry said. "And Katrine doesn't want anyone else to know Bjørn wasn't."

"Don't worry," Alexandra said. "I only know because I did the DNA analysis, and I have an oath of confidentiality. Got a cig we can share?"

"I quit."

"You? Really?"

Harry nodded and looked up at the sky. Clouds had appeared. Leaden gray on the underside, white where they grew upward and the sunlight hit them.

"So you're single," Harry said. "Happy with that?"

"No," Alexandra said. "But I probably wouldn't be happy if I was with someone either." She laughed that husky laugh of hers. And Harry could feel that it had the same effect now as then. So perhaps it was true. Perhaps those kinds of feelings never quite died, no matter how fleeting they had seemed.

Harry cleared his throat.

"Here it comes," she said.

"What?"

"The reason you wanted to have a coffee."

"Maybe," Harry said, pulling out the plastic box with the square of paper towel inside. "Could you analyze this for me?"

"I *knew* it!" she snorted.

"Mm. And yet you still agreed to meet me for coffee?"

"I suppose I was hoping to be wrong. That you'd been thinking about me."

"I can see that telling you now that I have thought about you isn't going to look good, but actually I have."

"Say it anyway."

Harry gave a crooked smile. "I've thought about you."

She took the box from him. "What is it?"

"Mucus and saliva. I just want to know if it originates from the same person as the samples you lifted from Susanne's breast."

"How do you know about that? No, I don't want to know. What you're asking for might be within the law, but you know I'll still be in trouble if anyone finds out?"

"Yes."

"So why should I do it?"

"You tell me."

"OK, I will. Because you're going to take me to the spa at that snooty hotel you're staying at. And after that you're going to treat me to a bloody nice dinner. And you're going to dress up."

Harry pinched the lapels of his suit jacket. "You don't think I'm presentable?"

"A tie. You're going to wear a tie as well."

Harry laughed. "Deal."

"A *nice* tie."

"A millionaire like Røed setting up his own investigation is contrary to our democratic traditions and idea of equality," Chief Superintendent Bodil Melling said.

"Aside from the purely practical inconvenience of having an outside party treading on our toes," said Ole Winter, Kripos's senior inspector. "It simply makes our job more difficult. Now, I'm aware you can't prohibit Røed's investigation based on paragraphs in the penal code, but the department must have some way of stopping this."

Mikael Bellman stood looking out the window. He had a nice office. Large, new and modern. Impressive. But it was located in Nydalen. Far from the other departments in government buildings downtown. Nydalen was a sort of business park on the outskirts of the city; continue farther north and you wound up in dense forest after just a few minutes. He hoped the new government quarter would soon be finished, that his Labour Party would still be in power and that he would still hold the post of Minister of Justice. There was nothing to suggest otherwise. Mikael Bellman was popular. Some had even hinted that he should already begin to position himself, because the day the Prime Minister suddenly decided to step down could be upon us. And at one morning meeting, the day after one political journalist had written that someone in government, Bellman for example, should seize the highest office in the land in a coup, the Prime Minister had, to everyone's laughter, asked if someone could check Mikael's briefcase, a reference to Bellman's eyepatch and resemblance to Claus von Stauffenberg, the Wehrmacht colonel who attempted to assassinate Hitler with a bomb. But the Prime Minister had nothing to fear. Mikael simply didn't want the job. Of course, being Minister of Justice meant you were exposed, but being Prime Minister—numero uno—was something else entirely. The pressure was one thing, but it was the light he feared. Too many stones being turned and too much of the past being uncovered, even he didn't know what they might find.

He turned to face Melling and Winter. Many levels of hierarchy separated him from them, but the two must have believed they could go straight to Bellman on account of him being a former police detective in Oslo, meaning he was one of them.

"Obviously, as a Labour Party man I'm all in favor of equality," Bellman said. "And of course the Department of Justice wants the police to have as good working conditions as possible. But I'm not so sure we can expect a very sympathetic response among . . ." he searched for a different word to the giveaway "voters"—"the public in general if we impede one of the few renowned investigators we have. Especially when he wants to tackle a case in which your departments have made so little headway. And, yes, you're right, Winter. There are no laws which proscribe what Røed and Hole are doing. But you can always hope that Hole does what he eventually always did in my time."

He looked at the bemused expressions on the faces of Melling and Winter.

"Break the rules," Bellman said. "All you need to do is watch him closely, then I'm fairly certain you'll see it happen. Send me a report when it does, and I'll personally make sure he's frozen out." He glanced at his Omega Seamaster watch. Not because he had another meeting, but to show that this one was over. "Does that sound OK?"

On their way out they shook his hand as though he had gone along with their suggestion and not the other way around. Mikael had that effect. He smiled and held eye contact with Bodil Melling a half-second longer than necessary. Not because he was interested, more out of habit. And noticed that she'd finally gotten a bit of color in her face.

17

TUESDAY

The more interesting portion of humanity

"WE LEARN TO LIE AS children between the ages of two and four, and by the time we've reached adulthood, we've become experts," Aune said, adjusting his pillow. "Believe me."

Harry saw Øystein grin and Truls frown in confusion. Aune went on.

"A psychologist called Richard Wiseman believes most of us tell a lie or two each day. Proper lies, that is, not just white, your-hair-looks-lovely lies. What are the chances of us being found out? Well, Freud contended that no mortal could keep a secret, that if the lips are sealed, then the fingertips chatter. But he was wrong. Or rather, the listener isn't capable of sorting through the different ways a liar gives themselves away, because they vary from person to person. That's why a lie detector was needed. They had one in China three thousand years ago. The suspected criminal had his mouth filled with grains of rice and was asked if he was guilty. If he shook his head, he was asked to spit out the rice, and if any grains remained in his mouth, the logic was that it was dry due to his being nervous, and therefore guilty. Useless, of course, because you could, after all, be nervous due to fear of becoming nervous. And similarly useless is the polygraph which John Larson invented in 1921, and is, in principle, the lie detector in use to this very day, even though everyone knows it's a piece of junk. Even Larson regretted inventing it in the end, calling it his Frankenstein monster. Because it *lives* . . ." Aune raised his hands and clawed at the air with his fingers. "But it lives due to so many people *believing* it works. Because its fear of the lie detector which can sometimes actually force a confession, whether true or false. Once, in Detroit, the police captured a suspect, put his hand on the photocopier they'd convinced him was a lie detector and asked him questions as the machine spat out A4 sheets with HE IS LYING written on them, until the man became so terrified he confessed everything."

Truls snorted.

"But God knows if he was guilty," Aune said. "That's why I prefer the method they used in ancient India."

The door opened, and Sethi and his bed were wheeled in by two nurses.

"Listen, Jibran, you'll like this too," Aune said.

Harry had to smile, Aune, the most popular lecturer at Police College, holding forth again.

"The suspects were admitted one by one into a room that was pitch-dark, and told to feel their way in the darkness until they found a donkey which was standing in there and then to pull it by the tail. If they'd lied under questioning the donkey would shriek or bray or whatever it is donkeys do. Because this particular donkey was, the priest informed them, a holy donkey. What he didn't tell them was that the tail was smeared with soot. So when the suspects came back out and said that, yes, they had pulled the donkey's tail, all they needed to do was check their hands. If they were clean, it meant the person had been afraid the donkey would expose the fact he had lied, and he was sent to the gallows or whatever they used in India at the time."

Aune glanced over at Sethi, who had taken out a book, but nodded ever so slightly.

"And if he had soot on his hands," Øystein said, "then all it meant was the guy wasn't a complete moron."

Truls grunted and slapped his thighs.

"The question," Aune said, "is whether Røed walked out of there with soot on his hands or not."

"Well," Harry said, "what we carried out was probably more of a cross between the old photocopier trick and the holy donkey. I'm pretty certain Røed believed this was a lie detector." He pointed at the table with Truls's laptop and the wires and electrodes they had borrowed from down on the third floor, where they were used for ECG monitoring. "So, I do think he was wary of lying. But he passed the donkey test in my opinion. He showed up and took what he believed to be a real test. That in itself indicates he doesn't have anything to hide."

"Or," Øystein said, "he knows how to fool a lie detector and wants to use that to mislead us."

"Mm. I don't think Røed is trying to deceive us. He didn't want Truls on the team. Understandably so, as the whole project would lose credibility if it became known. It was only when we convinced him about how much it meant to gain access to the police reports that he agreed. Yes, he wants some names to make his investigation appear serious on paper and in a press release, but finding out the truth is even more important to him."

"You think?" Øystein said. "Then why refuse to give a DNA sample to the police?"

"I don't know," Harry said. "As long as there's no reasonable suspicion, the police can't force anyone to take a DNA test, and Krohn says volunteering a test is tantamount to an implicit agreement that there is reasonable suspicion. Anyway, Alexandra has promised me an answer within days."

"And you're sure the profile won't match the saliva found on Susanne?" Aune asked.

"I'm never sure of anything, Ståle, but I crossed Røed off my list of suspects when he knocked on the door of my hotel room today."

"So what do you want with the DNA analysis?"

"To be sure. And have something we can give to the police."

"So they don't arrest him?" Truls asked.

"So we have information to offer them, and they might give us something in return. Something not in the reports."

Øystein smacked his lips loudly. "That's, like, smart."

"So with Røed out of the running and a brain that's been removed," Aune said, "do you still believe the killer is someone with a connection to the victims?"

Harry shook his head.

"Good," Aune said, rubbing his hands. "Then maybe we can finally start looking at psychopaths, sadists, narcissists and sociopaths. In short, the more interesting portion of humanity."

"No," Harry said.

"All right," Aune said, looking miffed. "You don't think the perpetrator is to be found within their ranks?"

"Yes, I do, but I don't think we'll find him there. We're going to look where *we* are best equipped to find something."

"Which is somewhere we assume he isn't?"

"Exactly."

The three men looked at Harry with incomprehension.

"It's pure mathematics," Harry said. "Serial killers pick their victims at random and cover their tracks. The probability of finding them in the space of a year is less than ten per cent, even for the FBI. For the four of us, with the resources we have? Let's just put it at two per cent, to be kind. If, on the other hand, the killer is to be found among the victims' acquaintances and there's an understandable motive, the chances are seventy-five per cent. Let's say there's an eighty per cent probability the killer is in the category Ståle wants us to look at, let's say it is a serial killer. If we focus on that category and exclude the victims' acquaintances, then the chances of us succeeding are . . ."

"One point six per cent," Øystein said. "And the probability of success if we concentrate on people the victim knew is fifteen per cent."

The others turned in surprise to Øystein, who flashed them a broad, brown grin. "Have to have a head for numbers in my job, you know."

"Pardon me," Aune said. "I hear the numbers, but to be honest it feels slightly counter-intuitive." He registered the look Øystein gave him. "Contrary to common sense. To look where we *don't* think he is, I mean."

"Welcome to police investigation," Harry said. "Try to think of it this way. If the four of us find the guilty party . . . fantastic, jackpot. If we don't then we've done what detectives do on most of their working days, we've contributed to the total investigation by eliminating some people from our inquiries."

"I don't believe you," Aune said. "What you're saying is rational, but *you* aren't so rational, Harry. You're not the type to do work based on per-centages. Yes, the professional side of you sees that all the circumstantial evidences points to a serial killer. So you're *of the opinion* it's a serial killer, but you *believe* something else. Because your gut tells you so. That's why you've come up with this calculation, you want to convince yourself and us that the right thing to do is follow the gut instincts of Harry Hole. Am I right?"

Harry looked at Aune. Nodded.

"My mother knew God didn't exist," Øystein said. "But she was still a Christian. So who are we going to, like, eliminate as suspects?"

"Helene Røed," Harry said. "And the guy selling coke at the party."

"Helene, I understand," Aune said, "but why the drug dealer?"

"Because he's one of the few people at the party who hasn't been iden-tified. And because he showed up in a face mask and sunglasses."

"So what? Maybe he hasn't been vaccinated. Or suffers from mysopho-bia. Sorry, Øystein, a fear of bacteria."

"Maybe he was sick and didn't want to infect people," Truls said. "But did all the same. The reports say both Susanne and Bertine had a high temperature a couple of days after the party and at any rate, felt unwell."

"But now we're overlooking the most obvious reason," Aune said. "A drug dealer is, after all, involved in something which is highly illegal, so it's hardly remarkable he should wear a mask."

"Øystein," Harry said. "Explain."

"OK. If you sell . . . let's say cocaine, then you're not that worried about being identified. The police know pretty much who is selling on the street anyway and they don't care, it's the men behind the scenes they want. And if the police bust you, it happens during the transaction, and then a mask isn't gonna be much use to you. So it's the other way around—if you're going to sell on the street, then you want the customers to recognize your face and remember that you sold them good shit the last time. And if you offer home deliveries, which it sounds like this guy does, then it's even more important that the customer sees and trusts your honest face."

Truls grunted a laugh.

"Do you think you can find out who the guy at the party was?" Harry asked.

Øystein shrugged. "I can try. There aren't many Norwegians at the home-delivery end of the business."

"Good."

Harry paused, closed his eyes before opening them again, as though he were keeping to a script and had mentally turned a page.

"Since we're going to stick with the hypothesis that the killer knew at least one of the victims, let's take a look at what might actually support this idea. Susanne Andersen heads right across the city, from the lively west side of the city center to a place where there's no evidence to suggest she knows anyone, where as far as anyone is aware she hasn't been before and where not much happens on a Tuesday night . . ."

"Some nights fuck all happens," Øystein said. "I grew up nearby."

"So what was she doing there?"

"Isn't it obvious?" Øystein said. "She was meeting the guy who did her in."

"OK, then we'll work based on that," Harry said.

"Cool," Øystein said. "The country's leading expert agrees with me."

Harry gave a crooked smile and rubbed the back of his neck. He would soon need the one drink he had left today; he had dispatched the other two on the way from the Forensic Medical Institute when he and Øystein had made a pit stop at Schrøder's.

"While I'm at it," Øystein said, "I was wondering about something. The guy took Susanne for a walk in Østmarka, and that worked for him, yeah? The, like, perfect murder. Isn't it bloody odd that he takes Bertine to Grefsenkollen? Never change a winning formula—wouldn't that go for murderers too?"

"It's probably true of serial killers," Aune said. "Unless repeating the approach means increasing the risk of being discovered. And Susanne had already been reported missing around Skullerud, so there were police and search parties in the area."

"Yeah, but they went home as soon as it was dark," Øystein said. "No one could have known another girl would disappear. No, the guy wouldn't have been taking much of a risk bringing her to Skullerud. And he obviously knew the area well."

"I don't know," Aune said. "Perhaps it was simply that Bertine agreed to take a walk with him, but she insisted on Grefsenkollen?"

"But it's further from where she lives to Grefsenkollen than to Skullerud, and in the reports it says that nobody the police spoke with had any knowledge of Bertine ever being in Grefsenkollen."

"Maybe she had *heard* good things about Grefsenkollen," Aune said. "It offers views at least. As opposed to Østmarka, where it's just forest and small hills."

Øystein nodded thoughtfully. "OK. But there is one other thing I don't get."

He focused on Aune, since Harry seemed to have dropped out of the conversation and was sitting with his fingers to his forehead, staring at the wall.

"Bertine could have walked only so far from the car, right? And they've been searching for two weeks now, so I don't understand why the dogs can't find her. Do you know how good dogs smell? I mean, what a good sense of smell they have? In one of the reports Truls got there's a tip-off from a farmer in Wenggården in Østmarka. He got in touch with the police a week ago to say that his lame old bulldog was lying in the living room barking like it only does when there's a carcass nearby. I know Østmarka, and that farm is at least three and a half miles away from where they found Susanne Andersen. If a dog can smell a corpse from that far away, why can't they find Bertine—"

"It can't."

All four men turned in the direction the voice was coming from.

Jibran Sethi lowered his book. "If it had been a bloodhound or an Alsatian, then yes. But a bulldog has a very poor sense of smell for a canine. They're actually at the bottom of the list. That's what happens when we breed dogs to fight bulls, and not to hunt as nature intended." The vet raised his book again. "Perverse, but that's the sort of thing we do."

"Thanks, Jibran," Aune said.

The vet gave him a brief nod.

"Maybe he's buried Bertine," Truls said.

"Or dumped her in one of the lakes up there," Øystein added.

Harry sat looking at the vet while the voices of the other three men sounded like they were fading out. Felt the hairs on the back of his neck stand up.

"Harry!"

"What?"

It was Aune. "We said: 'What do you think?' "

"I think . . . do you have the number of the farmer who sent in that tip-off, Øystein?"

"No. But we have his name, and Wenggården, so it's no problem to find it."

"Gabriel Weng."

"Good afternoon, Weng. This is Hansen, Oslo Police. Just a quick question regarding the information you called in with last week. You said your dog was barking, and that you thought there could be a carcass or a corpse nearby?"

"Yes, sometimes dead animals can lie out here rotting in the woods.

But I'd read about the girl who was missing, and Skullerud isn't so far away, so when the dog started barking and howling in that particular way, I called you. But I never heard anything back."

"Apologies, it takes time to follow up on all the leads we have on a case like this."

"Yes, yes, you found the girl of course, poor thing."

"What I was wondering," Harry said, "is whether your dog is still making those sorts of noises."

There was no reply but he could hear the farmer breathing.

"Weng?" Harry said.

"Was it Hansen you said your name was?"

"That's right. Hans Hansen. Constable."

Another pause.

"Yeah."

"Yeah?"

"Yes, he's still making those sorts of noises."

"OK, thank you, Weng."

Sung-min Larsen stood looking at Kasparov, who had positioned himself at the wall of a building with his hind leg raised. Sung-min already had the plastic bag in hand so passers-by would understand he had no intention of leaving dog poop lying among the expensive apartment buildings in Nobels gate.

He was thinking. Not so much about the brain being removed as about the fact the scalp had been sewn back up. What did it mean that the person who had taken the brain had tried to conceal the fact? Trophy hunters didn't usually care. And the killer must have realized it would be discovered, so why take the trouble? Was it to clean up after himself? A fastidious killer? It wasn't as far-fetched as it might sound—the rest of the crime scene had been cleansed of the evidence you usually found. Apart from the saliva on Susanne's breast. The killer had made a mistake there. Granted there were those on the investigative team who thought the spit had to have come from someone other than the killer, since Susanne's upper body had been clothed when they found her. But if the killer was neat enough to sew the scalp back on, why not put all the clothes back on the body too?

His phone rang. Sung-min looked in surprise at the display before he tapped "accept."

"Harry Hole? It's been a while."

"Yeah, time marches on."

"I read in *VG* that we're working on the same case."

"Yeah. I've tried calling Katrine a couple of times, but her phone is going straight to voicemail."

"Putting the child to bed, maybe."

"Maybe. Anyway, I have some information I thought you'd want as soon as possible."

"OK?"

"I just spoke with a farmer living out in the forest who says his bulldog smells a carcass in the vicinity. Or a corpse."

"A bulldog? Then it's not far off, bulldogs have—"

"A poor sense of smell, so I've been told."

"Yes. A carcass in the forest isn't unusual, so since you're calling I'm guessing this is in Grefsenkollen?"

"No. In Østmarka. Three or four miles from where Susanne was found. Doesn't have to mean anything of course. Like you say, large animals die in the woods all the time. But I wanted to let you know. As you haven't found Bertine in Grefsenkollen, I mean."

"Okey-dokey," Sung Min said. "I'll notify the team. Thanks for the tip-off, Harry."

"No problem. I'll forward you the number of the farmer now."

Sung-min hung up and wondered if he had managed to sound as calm as he had been trying to. His heart was beating wildly, and the thoughts and conclusions—which had obviously been lying in wait, but had not been given leeway before now—went sliding through his mind like an avalanche. Could the perpetrator have murdered Bertine on familiar territory, in the same area where he had killed Susanne? The thought had, of course, occurred to him before, but then it had been in the form of a question as to why the killer *hadn't* done that. And the answer had been obvious. Everything indicated that the killer had arranged to meet the girls—why else would they go all alone to places they'd never been to previously? And because the media had been writing page after page about the missing girl in Skullerud, the killer had invited Bertine to a totally different part of town so she wouldn't make the connection. What Sung-min had not thought, or at least not all the way through, was that the killer could have arranged to meet Bertine at Grefsenkollen, and then driven her in his car to Skullerud. Before setting off, he must have convinced her to leave her phone behind in the car in Grefsenkollen. Maybe presented it as a romantic notion, something along the lines of let's-be-all-on-our-own-without-anyone-disturbing-us. Yes, this could make sense. He checked the time. Half past nine. It would have to wait until tomorrow. Or? No, it was only a tip-off, and chasing after every fire engine in a murder inquiry soon tired you out. All the same. It wasn't only his own intuition telling him that rather too many pieces fit, Harry Hole himself had called him because he thought the same. Yes, the very same thoughts had gone through Harry's mind as had gone through his own.

Sung-min looked at Kasparov. He had taken in the retired police dog because it had outlived its previous owner. It had suffered from hip trouble in the past couple of years and didn't like to walk too far or uphill. But unlike bulldogs, Labrador retrievers had one of the keenest senses of smell in the canine world.

His cell vibrated. He looked at the screen. A phone number and the name Weng. Half past nine. If they got in the car now, they could probably be there in thirty minutes.

"Come, Kasparov!" Sung-min tugged at the leash, his palms already sweaty from adrenaline.

"Hey!" A voice boomed from a darkened balcony, the sound echoing between the fashionable facades. "We pick up the shit after us in this country!"

18

TUESDAY

Parasite

"PARASITES," PRIM SAID, LIFTING THE fork to his mouth. "We die *of* them and live *off* them." He chewed. The food had a spongy consistency and didn't taste of much, even with all the spices. He raised his glass of red wine to his guest before washing down the mouthful and swallowing hard. He placed his palm on his chest, waiting for the food to go down before continuing. "And we're all parasites. You. Me. Everyone out there. Without hosts like us the parasites would die, but without the parasites we would also die. Because there are good parasites and there are malign parasites. The good ones come from blowflies, for instance, which deposit their parasite eggs into a corpse so that the larvae eat it up in no time." With a grimace, Prim cut off another piece and commenced chewing on it. "If they didn't, we'd literally be wading in corpses and carcasses. No, I'm not joking! The maths is simple. We would, in the space of a few months, have died from the noxious gases from corpses if not for the blowfly. Then you have the interesting parasites which are neither particularly useful nor do any great harm. Among these you have, for example, *Cymothoa exigua*. The tongue-eating louse."

Prim stood up and walked over to the aquarium.

"It's such an interesting parasite that I deposited a few in Boss's tank here. What happens is that the louse attaches itself to the tongue of the fish and sucks blood from it until the tongue eventually decomposes and disappears. Then the louse attaches itself to the stub of the tongue, sucks more blood, grows and develops into a completely new tongue."

Prim's hand shot down into the water and grabbed the fish. He brought it over to the table, squeezed the fish's mouth so it was forced open, and held it up in front of her face.

"Do you see it? Do you see the louse? Can you see that it has eyes and a mouth of its own? Yes?"

He walked quickly back and released the fish back into the aquarium.

"The louse—which I've named Lisa—functions just fine as a tongue, so no need to feel *so* sorry for Boss. Life goes on, as they say, and he has company now. It's a lot worse to cross paths with the malign parasites. Ones like this one here are packed with . . ."

He pointed at the large pink slug he had placed on the dining table between them.

"The dog and I live alone," Weng said, hiking his jeans up under his paunch.

Sung-min looked at the bulldog lying in a basket in the corner of the kitchen. It only moved its head, and the only sound it made was a pant.

"I took over the farm from my father a couple of years back, but the wife refuses to live out here in the forest, so she's still in the apartment in Manglerud."

Sung-min nodded at the dog. "Bitch?"

"Yes. She had a habit of attacking cars, thought of them as bulls, maybe. Anyway, she got caught on one and broke her back. But she still makes a sound if anyone comes . . ."

"Yes, we heard it. And makes a sound when she smells dead animals, I understand."

"Yeah, as I told Hansen."

"Hansen?"

"The officer who called."

"Hansen, yeah. But she's not making any noise now."

"No, it's only when the wind is coming from the south-east she smells it." Weng pointed out into the darkness.

"Would you mind if my dog and I had a little search?"

"You've a dog with you?"

"He's in the car. A Labrador."

"Be my guest."

"So," Prim said and waited until he was sure he had her full attention. "This slug looks pretty innocent, doesn't it? Beautiful, even. Its color makes you want to suck on it, it almost looks like candy. But I would strongly advise against that. You see, both slug and slime are packed with rat lungworm, so we definitely won't be using it as any kind of dressing." Prim laughed. As usual, she did not laugh along, only smiled.

"As soon as the worm enters your body, it begins to follow the bloodstream. And where does it want to go?" Prim tapped his forefinger against his forehead. "Here. To the brain. Because it loves brain. Sure, yes, I understand that the brain is nutritious and a nice place for eggs to hatch. But the brain isn't particularly *good*." He looked down at his plate and smacked his lips disapprovingly. "What do you think?"

Kasparov tugged hard at the leash. There was no longer any path where they were walking. It had become cloudy earlier in the day, and now the only light came from the beam of Sung-min's flashlight. It stopped on a wall of tree trunks and low-hanging branches which he had to bend down to negotiate. He had lost any sense of where they were or how far they had walked. He heard Kasparov panting below the carpet of ferns, but couldn't see him and had the feeling of being pulled by an invisible force into increasingly deep darkness. This could have waited. It could have. So why? Because he alone wanted to get the credit for finding Bertine? No. No, it wasn't as banal as that. He had just always been like this, when he was wondering about something he *had* to find out about it at once, to wait was unbearable.

But now he was having second thoughts. Not only did he risk messing up a crime scene should he stumble over a body here in the darkness, it was also the fact he was afraid. Yes, he could admit it. Right now he was that little boy who was scared of the dark, who had arrived in Norway not knowing what he was afraid of, but had a feeling that other people, his adoptive parents, his teachers, the other children in the street, *they* knew. They knew something he didn't know about himself, about his past, about what had happened. He never found out what that was, if indeed there was anything. His adoptive parents had no dramatic story to relate about his biological parents or how he had been adopted. But ever since he had been consumed with a need to know. Know everything. Know something *they*, the others, did not.

The leash slackened. Kasparov had stopped.

Sung-min felt the beating of his heart as he pointed the flashlight at the ground and pushed the fern leaves aside.

Kasparov had his muzzle to the ground, and the light found what he was sniffing at.

Sung-min crouched down to take a look. At first he thought it was an empty chip bag, but then he recognized it and understood why Kasparov had stopped. It was a Hillman Pets bag, an anti-parasitic powder that Sung-min had bought in a pet store once when Kasparov had round-worm. There was a flavor added to the powder which dogs liked so much that Kasparov only to catch sight of a bag of the stuff and he would wag his tail so wildly that Sung-min thought he was going to take off. Sung-min picked up the bag, crumpled it up and put it in his pocket.

"Will we go home, Kasparov? Supper time?"

Kasparov looked up at him as if he understood the words and thought his owner insane. He turned, Sung-min felt a hard tug and knew he didn't have a prayer, they were going deeper in to where he no longer wanted to go.

"What's most amazing is that when some of these parasites reach your brain, they begin to take over," Prim said. "Control your thoughts. Your desires. And the parasite will command you to do what's necessary for it to continue its natural cycle. You become an obedient soldier, willing to die if that's what it takes." Prim sighed. "As so very often it does, unfortunately." He raised his eyebrows. "Oh, you think this sounds like a horror story or science fiction? But you should know that some of these parasites aren't even rare. Most hosts live and die without knowing the parasite is present, as is likely the case with Boss and Lisa. We believe we struggle, work, and sacrifice our lives for our family, our country, our own legacy. While in reality it's for the parasite, the bloodsucker ensconced in the headquarters of the brain deciding things."

Prim refilled their glasses with red wine.

"My stepfather accused my mother of being just such a parasite. Claimed she began turning down roles because he had wealth so she could just sit at home drinking up his money. Of course that wasn't true. Firstly, she didn't turn down parts, but they did stop offering them to her. Because she sat at home all day drinking and had begun to forget lines. My stepfather was a very wealthy man, so her drinking could never have rendered him destitute, to put it mildly. Besides, he was the parasite. He was the one inside my mother's brain, making her see things the way he wanted her to see them. So she didn't see what he was doing to me. I was only a child and thought a father had the right, could demand that sort of thing from his son. No, I didn't think every six-year-old was forced to lie naked in bed with their father and satisfy them, or face threats about their mother being killed if they said a word about it to anyone. But I was frightened. So I *said* nothing, but tried to show my mother what was going on. I had always been bullied at school because of my teeth and . . . yes, the way a victim of sexual assault behaves, I suppose. Rat, they called me. But now I began to lie and steal. I started skipping school, ran away from home, and began taking money from men to jerk them off in public bathrooms. I robbed one of them. Put simply, my stepfather was nestled in both my and my mother's brains, destroying us bit by bit. Speaking of which . . ."

Prim pronged the last piece on his plate. Sighed. "But now it's over, Bertine." He turned the fork while he studied the pale pink piece of meat. "Now I'm the one nestling in the brain and giving orders."

Sung-min had to run to keep up with Kasparov, who was straining even harder. The dog was making sort of hacking cough, as if he were trying to dislodge something stuck in his throat.

Sung-min did something he had learned as an investigator. When he was almost entirely sure of something he tested his own deduction by trying to turn everything on its head. Could it be that what he had thought was impossible was possible all the same? Could, for example, Bertine Bertilsen still be alive? She might have run off, gone abroad. She may have been abducted and was now sitting locked up in a basement or an apartment someplace, was perhaps together with the perpetrator at this very moment.

Suddenly they were out of the woods and in a clearing. The light from the flashlight glittered on water. They were by a small lake. Kasparov wanted to get to the water and pulled Sung-min with him. The light flickered over a birch tree standing bowed over the water, and Sung-min momentarily caught sight of something that looked like a thick branch reaching all the way down to the water, as though the tree were drinking. He pointed the light at the branch. Which was not a branch.

"No!" yelled Sung-min, yanking Kasparov back.

The shout echoed back from the other side of the lake.

It was a body.

It was hanging folded at the hips over the lowest branch of the birch tree.

The bare feet were just above the surface of the water. The woman— because he could see at once that it was a woman—had, like Susanne, no clothes on her lower body. Her stomach was also exposed, because her dress was pulled up, stopping underneath her bra, and was hanging down towards the water, covering her head, shoulders and arms. Only her wrists were visible below the inside-out hem of the dress, and her fingers were reaching down below the surface of the water. Sung-min's first thought was to hope there were no fish in the lake.

Kasparov sat still. Sung-min patted him on the head. "Good boy."

He took out his phone. The coverage at the farm had been poor, but up here the signal indicator was down to one bar. But the GPS was working, and as he registered his position, he noticed he was breathing through his mouth. Not that there was much of a smell, it was just something his brain—after a couple of unpleasant experiences—had begun to do automatically upon understanding it was at a crime scene. His brain had also worked out that in order to establish that this was Bertine Bertilsen, he would have to position the flashlight on the ground and hold on to the tree trunk with one hand while leaning out over the water to pull up the hem of her dress so he could see her face. The problem was he might then place a hand on the trunk in the same place as the perpetrator and spoil a fingerprint.

He remembered the tattoo. The Louis Vuitton logo. Shone the light on her ankles. They were so white in the glare, as though she were made of snow. But no Louis Vuitton logo.

An owl, at least he guessed it was an owl, hooted somewhere out in the darkness. He couldn't see the outside of her left ankle, maybe that's where the tattoo was. He moved along the bank until he was at the right angle and shone the light on her.

And there it was. Black on snow white. An L over a V.

It was her. Had to be her.

He took out his phone again and called Katrine Bratt. Straight to voicemail. Strange. Not taking Harry Hole's call might have been a choice, but the lead detective should always be available to those they're working with, that was an unwritten rule.

"So you see, Bertine, I have an important task to carry out."

Prim leaned across the table and laid his hand against her cheek.

"I'm just sorry you had to become part of that task. And I'm sorry that I must leave you now. That this will be our last night together. Because even though I know you want me, you aren't the one I love. There, I've said it. Tell me you forgive me. No? Please. Sweet girl." Prim chuckled quietly. "You can try to resist, Bertine Bertilsen, but you know that I can turn you on any time with the slightest touch."

He did it, she could not prevent him. And, of course, she lit up for him. For the last time, he thought, raising his glass in a farewell toast.

Sung-min had gotten hold of the Crime Scene Unit, they were on their way. All he could do was sit on a tree stump and wait. He scratched at his face and neck. Mosquitoes. No, gnats. Little mosquitoes that sucked blood, even from larger mosquitoes. He had switched off the flashlight to save the battery and could just discern the body out there in front of him.

It was her. Of course it was her.

Still.

He checked the time, was already impatient. And where was Katrine? Why didn't she call back?

Sung-min found a long, thin branch on the ground. Turning the flashlight on again and placing it on the ground, he stood by the shore and used the branch to snag the edge of the dress. Lifted it. Higher. And higher. Saw the bare upper arms now, waited to see her brown hair, it had been long and worn loose in the photos he had seen. Was it tied up? Was it . . . ?

Sung-min made a hooting sound. Like an owl. He simply lost control, the sound just came out, the branch fell in the water and the dress was back covering what had caused him to make the sound. Covering what was not there.

"Poor thing," Prim whispered. "You're so beautiful. And spurned all the same. It's not fair, is it?"

He hadn't straightened her head after striking the table two nights previously and the shaking had caused the head to tilt a little to one side. The head was mounted on top of a standard lamp he had placed in front of the chair on the other side of the table. When he pressed the switch on the cord lying across the table and the 60-watt bulb inside Bertine's head turned on and the light shone out of her eye sockets, coloring her teeth in the gaping mouth blue, an unimaginative man might say it resembled a pumpkin head at Halloween. While a man with just a little more imagination would see that the whole of Bertine—at least that part of her not by a lake in Østmarka—lit up, beamed with joy, yes, a man could easily imagine she loved him. And Bertine *had* loved him, desired him at any rate.

"If it's any consolation, I enjoyed the lovemaking with you more than with Susanne," Prim said. "You have a nicer body, and . . ." He licked at his fork. "I like your brain better. But . . ." He cocked his head to one side, looking at her ruefully. "I had to eat it for the sake of the life cycle. For the eggs. For the parasites. For revenge. It's the only way I can become whole. The only way I can be loved for who I am. Yes, I know that probably sounds pompous. But it's true. To be loved, that's all any of us want, isn't it?

He pressed his forefinger on the light switch. The light bulb in her head went off and the living room was left lying in semi-darkness.

Prim sighed. "Yes, I was afraid you'd take it like that."

19

TUESDAY

Chimes

KATRINE WAS LISTENING TO SUNG-MIN.

Closing her eyes, she pictured the crime scene while he spoke. Answered that, no, she didn't need to see it herself, she would dispatch a couple of detectives, then study photos of the scene. And, yes, she apologized for not being available by phone. She had switched it off while putting the child to bed and must have performed a very good rendition of "Blueman," because she had put herself to sleep too.

"Maybe you're working too hard," Sung-min said.

"You can scratch *maybe*," Katrine said. "But that goes for all of us. Let's call a press conference for tomorrow at ten. I'll get Forensics to prioritize this."

"All right. Goodnight."

"Goodnight, Sung-min."

Katrine hung up and sat staring at the phone.

Bertine Bertilsen was dead. That was as expected. Now she had been found. That was as hoped. The place and way she had been found confirmed the suspicion that it was the same killer. That was as feared. Because that meant there might be more murders.

Katrine heard a whimper from behind the open door to his bedroom. She told herself she would stay sitting where she was, but wasn't able, stood up from the kitchen chair and tiptoed over to the doorway. It was quiet in there, just the sound of Gert's steady slumberous breathing. She had lied to Sung-min. She had read that on average we hear two hundred lies every day, most of them white fortunately, the sort that keep the social wheels turning. This had been one of them. It was true she had switched off the phone to put the child to bed, but not about falling asleep herself. She hadn't switched it back on because Arne usually called right after Gert's bedtime, knowing that was when he would catch her. That was nice, of course it was. After all, he just wanted to hear how her day had been. Listen to her small joys and petty frustrations. Lately—with the missing girls—she had been mostly sharing her frustrations, naturally enough. But he had listened patiently, asked follow-up questions that showed he was interested, did everything a good, supportive friend and potential boyfriend should do. It was just that tonight she really wasn't in the mood, she needed to be alone with her thoughts. Had decided to serve up the same white lie about having fallen asleep when Arne asked tomorrow. She had been thinking about Harry and Gert. How she was going to solve it. Because she had seen it in Harry's eyes, the same helpless love she had seen in Bjørn's when they looked at their son. Bjørn's son and Harry's son. How much should and could she include Harry in things? For herself, she wanted to have as little as possible to do with Harry and Harry's life. But what about Gert? What right did she have to take yet another father from him? Hadn't she herself had an unstable drunkard for a father, one she had loved in her own way and would not have been without?

She had switched the cell back on before going to bed, hoping there wouldn't be any messages. But there were two. The first, from Arne, was a declaration of love of the kind the younger generation obviously had a lower threshold for:

Katrine Bratt, you are the Woman, and I am the Man who loves you. Goodnight.

The other was from Sung-min and conformed to a style she was more familiar with:

Bertine found. Call me.

Katrine went into the bathroom and picked up her toothbrush. Looked in the mirror. *You are the Woman,* yeah, right. But OK, on a good day it might be warranted. She squeezed the toothpaste out of the tube. Her thoughts returned to Bertine Bertilsen and Susanne Andersen. And the woman—without a name yet—who might be the next in line.

Sung-min was giving his tweed jacket the once-over with a clothes brush. It was a waterproof Alan Paine hunting jacket, which Chris had given him for Christmas. After his conversation with Katrine, he had tapped in a text to him to say goodnight. It had bothered him in the beginning that he was always the one sending goodnight messages while Chris just responded. But it was fine now, that was just how Chris was, he needed to believe he had the upper hand in the relationship. But Sung-min knew that if he skipped texting one night, Chris would be a drama queen on the phone the next day, nagging about something being wrong, about Sung-min having met someone else or losing interest.

Sung-min watched the pine needles fall to the floor. Yawned. Knew he would sleep. That he wouldn't have any nightmares about what he had experienced tonight. He never did. He wasn't quite sure what that said about his personality. A colleague at Kripos said this ability he had to shut off indicated a lack of empathy and had compared him to Harry Hole, who apparently suffered from something they called parosmia, a defect hindering the brain from registering the smell of human remains that meant Hole remained unaffected at crime scenes where other people's stomachs were turning. But Sung-min didn't regard himself as having any defect, he merely believed he had a healthy ability to compartmentalize, to keep his private and professional worlds away from each other. He brushed at the pockets sewn to the outside of the jacket, noticed there was something inside one of them and took it out. It was the empty Hillman Pets bag. He was about to throw it in the trash when he remembered that when Kasparov had gotten another bout of worms, the vet had recommended a different anti-parasitic cure because Hillman Pets contained a substance now prohibited to import and sell in Norway. That had to have been at least four years ago. Sung-min turned the bag around, examining it until he found what he was looking for. The best-before date and the date of manufacture.

The bag was marked as produced last year.

Sung-min turned the bag over again. So what? Someone had bought a box abroad and brought it home, probably without even knowing it was banned. He considered whether to throw it away. It had been lying several hundred yards from the crime scene, and it was extremely unlikely that the killer had had a dog with him. But there was something about breaches of the law; they were usually linked. A rule-breaker is a rule-breaker. The sadistic serial killer begins by killing small animals, like mice and rats. Starting small fires. Then torturing and killing slightly bigger animals. Setting fire to vacant houses . . .

Sung-min folded the bag.

"Satan's cunt!" Mona Daa yelled, staring at her phone.

"What is it?" Anders asked, from the open bathroom door, as he brushed his teeth.

"*Dagbladet!*"

"You don't need to shout. And Satan doesn't have a—"

"Cunt. Våge is saying that Bertine Bertilsen has been found dead. Wenggården in Østmarka, only a few miles from where they found Susanne."

"Oh."

"Yeah, oh. Oh as in why the fucking hell has *Dagbladet* that news and not *VG*."

"They probably don't fuck—"

"That much in hell? Yes, I think they do. I think whoever is down there gets fucked in the mouth, in the nose and the ear, and they can only think of one thing worse, and that's working at *VG* and getting fucked in the ass by Terry Våge. Satan's cunt!"

She tossed the phone on the bed as Anders slid under the duvet and snuggled up to her.

"Have I told you that it gets me a little horny when you—"

She gave him a shove. "I'm not in the mood, Anders."

"—aren't in the mood . . . ?"

She pushed away his probing hand, but couldn't help smiling a little as she picked up her phone. Began reading again. At least Våge didn't have any details from the crime scene, so it was unlikely he had talked to anyone who had been there. But how had he found out about the discovery of the body so fast? Did he have an illegal police radio, could it be that simple? That he deduced what was going on from listening to those brief, half-coded messages the police used because they knew interlopers were always eavesdropping? And then Våge merely made up the rest based on what he heard, so it became a suitable blend of fact and fiction which could just about pass for real journalism? It had up to now at any rate.

"Someone suggested I should ask you for a little inside information," she said.

"Really? Did you tell them that I'm not on that case unfortunately, but that I can be bought for uninhibited sex?"

"Stop it, Anders! This is my job."

"So you think I should give you free info and risk my own?"

"No! I just mean . . . it's so bloody unfair!" Mona folded her arms. "Våge has someone feeding him while I'm sitting here . . . starving to death."

"What's unfair," Anders said, sitting up in bed and his playful cheeriness dissipating, "is that girls in this city can't go out without running the risk of being raped and killed. It's unfair that Bertine Bertilsen is lying dead in Østmarka while two people sit here thinking the world is unfair

166

because another journalist was first on the case or because the clearance rate of the department will go down."

Mona swallowed.

And nodded.

He was right. Of course he was right. She swallowed again. Tried to suppress the question that was forcing its way up:

Can you make a call to someone and ask how it looked at the crime scene?

Helene Røed lay in bed staring at the ceiling.

Markus had wanted them to have a drop-shaped bed, ten feet long and eight feet at its widest. He had read that it was the drop we originated from, from water, that we unconsciously sought to return and so the shape offered us harmony and deeper sleep.

She had managed not to laugh but also to get him to agree to a rectangular luxury bed six feet wide by seven long. Enough for two. Too much for one.

Markus was sleeping at the penthouse in Frogner, as he did almost every night now. So she presumed anyway. Not that she missed having Markus in bed, it had been a long time since that had been exciting or even particularly desirable. The sneezing and sniffing had only gotten worse, and he got up at least four times a night to piss. Prostate enlargement, not necessarily cancer, but something affecting more than half of men over sixty by all accounts. And apparently it would only get worse. No, she didn't miss Markus, but she missed having *someone*. She didn't know who, only that the feeling was particularly strong tonight. There had to be someone for her as well, someone who would love her and she could love in return. It was that simple, wasn't it? Or was that just something she hoped?

She turned over onto her side. She had been nauseous and feeling sick since last night. Had thrown up and had a slight temperature. She had done a test for the virus, but it had been negative.

She looked out the window, at the rear of the recently finished Munch Museum. No one who had bought their apartment prior to construction in Oslobukta had thought it would be so massive and ugly. People had been fooled by the drawings where the museum had a glass facade and was shown from an angle, rendering it difficult to see that it looked like that wall in the north in *Game of Thrones*. But that's how it was, things didn't turn out as promised or expected, you'd only yourself to thank for being taken in. Now the building cast a shadow on all of them, and it was too late.

She felt a fresh wave of nausea and hurried to get out of bed. The bathroom was on the other side of the room, but still it was so far! She had only been in Markus's apartment in Frogner once. It was much smaller, but she'd rather have lived there. Together with . . . someone. She managed to make it to the toilet bowl before the contents of her stomach came up.

Harry was sitting at the bar in the Thief when the text message came.

Thanks for the tip-off. Yours sincerely, Sung-min.

Harry had already read *Dagbladet*. It was the only newspaper with the story, which could only mean one thing: that no press release had been put out yet, and that this journalist, Terry Våge, had a source in the police. Since it was impossible the leak could be a tactical maneuver on the part of the police, that meant someone was receiving money or other favors to inform Våge. It wasn't as unusual as people believed—he had in his time been offered money by journalists on numerous occasions. The reason such transactions seldom came to light was that journalists never printed information which pointed towards the informant, that would after all be like sawing through the branch both parties were sitting on. But Harry had read most of the articles on the case, and something told him that this Våge was a little too eager and that it would backfire sooner or later. That is, Våge would walk away from it, yes, even with his journalistic credentials intact. It would be worse for the source of the leak. But the source was obviously unaware of how exposed he or she was as they were continuing to feed Våge information.

"Another?" The bartender looked at Harry, and was standing ready with the bottle over the empty whiskey glass. Harry cleared his throat. Once. Twice.

Yes, please, it said in the script. The one for the bad movie he had been in so many times, playing the only role he actually could.

Then—as though the bartender had seen the plea for mercy in Harry's eyes—he turned to a customer signalling from the other end of the bar, took the bottle and left.

Out in the darkness the chiming of the bells of City Hall could be heard. It would soon be midnight and there would be six days left, plus the nine-hour time difference to Los Angeles. Not much time, but they had found Bertine, and finding a body meant new leads and the possibility of a crucial breakthrough. That was how he had to think. Positively. It didn't come naturally to him, especially not to think so unrealistically positively as circumstances required, but hopelessness and apathy were not what he needed now. Not what Lucille needed.

As Harry left the bar and stepped out into the darkened corridor, he could see there was light at the end, like in a tunnel. As he drew closer, he realized that the light was coming from an open elevator and could see a person standing half outside holding the doors. As though he were waiting for Harry. Or someone else—after all, he had already been standing there when Harry appeared in the corridor.

"Just go ahead," Harry called out, signaling with a wave of his hand. "I'm taking the stairs." The man backed into the elevator and out of the light. Harry had time to see the clerical collar but not the face before the doors slid shut.

Harry was soaked with sweat as he unlocked the door to his room. He hung up his suit and lay down on the bed. Tried to put thoughts of how Lucille was doing out of his head. He had made up his mind he was going to have a pleasant dream about Rakel tonight. One from the time they lived together and went to bed together every night. From the time he was walking over water, stepping on ice that lay thick and solid. Always listening out for cracks, always on the lookout for fissures, but also with the ability to live in the moment. They had done that. As though they had known the time they had together would run out. No, they didn't live every day as if it were the last, but as if it were the first. As though they had discovered each other over and over again. Was he exaggerating, embellishing the memory of what they'd had? Maybe. So what? What had realism ever done for him?

He closed his eyes. Tried to picture her, her golden skin against the white sheets. But instead all he could see was her pale skin against the pool of blood on the living-room floor. And he saw Bjørn Holm in the car staring at him while the baby cried in the back seat. Harry opened his eyes. Yes, honestly, what was he supposed to do with realism?

His phone buzzed again. A message from Alexandra this time.

Will have DNA analysis ready by Monday. Spa and dinner on Saturday would be nice. Terse Acto is a good restaurant.

20

WEDNESDAY

"WELL, IT OUGHT TO BE clear," Aune said, laying his copy of the police report on the duvet. "This is all textbook. It's a sexually motivated murder carried out by a killer who will most likely do it again if he's not stopped."

The three people around the bed nodded, still absorbed in their own copies.

Harry finished first and looked up, squinting in the harsh light of the morning sun outside.

Then Øystein finished and let his sunglasses slide down from his forehead in front of his eyes again.

"Come on, Berntsen," he said. "You must've read it before."

Truls grunted in response and put down the printout. "What do we do if it's a needle in a haystack?" he asked. "Close up shop and leave the rest to Bratt and Larsen?"

"Not quite yet," Harry said. "This doesn't really change anything, we assumed Bertine had been killed in a similar way as Susanne."

"But we have to be honest and say it doesn't back up your gut feeling about a rational murderer with a rational motive," Aune said. "You don't have to decapitate the victim or steal their brain to mislead the police into believing it's a sexually motivated murder with random victims. There are ways of mutilating which require less work and would leave pretty much the same impression of a murderer without any connection to the victims."

"Mm."

"Don't *mm* me, Harry. Listen. The killer must have spent a long time at the scene of the crime, and thus have run a much higher risk than he needed to if his aim was mere misdirection. The brains are trophies, and now we see the classic sign of him learning by cutting off the entire head of the victim and taking it with him instead of sawing and sewing back up while he's at the crime scene. Harry, this walks, talks, smells and looks like a ritual killing with a whole range of sexual undertones and overtones, and that's what it *is*."

Harry nodded slowly. Turned to Øystein, who emitted a "Hey!" as Harry snatched the sunglasses off him and put them on himself.

"I didn't want to say anything," Harry said, "but you nicked these from me. I left them in the office at the Jealousy Bar after that power-pop night when you refused to play R.E.M."

"What? We were supposed to play *classic* power pop. As for the shades, finders keepers."

"When they're in a drawer?"

"Children . . ." Aune said.

Øystein made a grab for the sunglasses, but Harry was too quick and pulled his head back.

"Relax, you'll get them afterwards, Øystein. Come on, tell us that news you said you had instead."

Øystein sighed. "OK. I talked to a colleague who sells cocaine—"

"Taxi drivers are selling cocaine?" Aune inquired with surprise.

Aune and Øystein looked at one another.

"Is there something you haven't told me?" Aune said, shifting his gaze to Harry.

"Yes," Harry said. "Go on, Øystein."

"Yeah, so he put me on to Røed's regular dealer. A guy we call Al. And he was actually at that party. But he said he was upstaged by a guy who had such primo blanco that he just had to pack his stuff away. I asked who he was, but Al didn't know him, he was wearing a face mask and sunglasses. The weird thing, Al said, was that even though the guy had the best, purest blow he had ever snorted in Oslo, the guy behaved like an amateur."

"How so?"

"It's something you notice straight away. The pros are relaxed because they know what they're doing, while at the same time they're constantly scanning their surroundings like antelopes at a watering hole. They know which pocket they have the stuff in should the cops show up and they need to get rid of it in two seconds. Al said this guy was jumpy, only looked at the person he was talking to and had to rummage through his pockets to find the bags. But the most amateurish was that he hadn't diluted the product more, if he'd done it at all. And that he gave out free samples."

"To everyone?"

"No, no. I mean, this was a fancy party. You know, people from nice backgrounds. Some of them do coke, but not in front of the neighbors, They went with Røed into his apartment, the guy with the face mask, two girls, plus Al. The guy arranged a few lines on the glass table in the living room, which apparently also looked like something he'd picked up on YouTube and said Røed had to test it. But Røed being, like, all gentlemanly, said the others had to have a taste first. Then Al went to do just that, I mean, he wanted to test this stuff out. But the guy grabbed hold of Al's arm and yanked him away from the table, scratched his arm so bad it bled, like, he totally panicked. Al had to calm the guy down. The guy said it was only for Røed, but Røed said that at his place people had to behave themselves and that the girls went first, otherwise he could get the hell out. And then the guy backed down."

"Did Al know the girls?"

"No. And yes, I asked if they were the two girls who were missing, but he hadn't even heard about them."

"Really?" Aune said. "It's been front-page news for weeks."

"Yeah, but people in the junkie community live in—how would you say it?—an alternative world. These guys don't know who the Prime Minister of Norway is, put it like that. But, believe me, they know the price per gram in every Norwegian city of every bloody drug Our Lord has blessed this planet with. So, I showed Al pictures of the girls, and he thought he recognized them, Susanne at least, who he thinks he sold some E and coke to before, but he wasn't sure. Anyway, the girls each did a line, and then it was Røed's turn. But then his wife walked in, starts roaring about how he's promised to quit. Røed doesn't give a shit, already has the straw in his nose, takes a breath, probably planning on snorting every line left in one go and then . . ." Øystein began to chortle. "Then . . ." He bent forward, unable to stop laughing, wiping away tears.

"And then?" Aune said impatiently.

"Then the idiot *sneezes*! Blows all the cocaine off the table, just tears and snot all over the glass. He looks in desperation at the guy in the face mask and asks for some fresh lines, right? But the guy doesn't have any more, that was the lot, and he's also desperate, and goes down on his knees to try and salvage what he can. But the balcony door is open, and there's a draught, and now the powder is here, there and everywhere. Can you believe that shit?"

Øystein put his head back and roared with laughter. Truls laughed his grunted laugh. Even Harry broke into a smile.

"So Al goes into the kitchen with Røed, where the wife can't see them, opens his bag, and Røed gets a few lines of blanco from there. Because, yeah, I forgot to say, the stuff the guy with the face mask had, it wasn't blanco, it was green cocaine."

"Green?"

"Yeah," Øystein said. "That's why Al was so eager to test it. I've heard it can show up on the street in the States, but no one's ever seen it in Oslo. On the street the purest blanco you get is max forty-five per cent, but they say green's a lot higher. Apparently it's to do with residue from the color of the coca leaves."

Harry turned to Truls. "Green cocaine, huh?"

"Don't look at me," Truls said, "I haven't a clue how it wound up there."

"Fucking hell, was it you?" Øystein asked. "Incognito in a face mask and sungla—"

"Shut up! You're the bloody dealer, not me."

"Why not?" Øystein said. "It's genius! You skim, then mix it with something, the same way we used to fill our dads' vodka bottles in the drinks cabinet with water. And then you sell direct so you cut out the—"

"I don't skim!" Truls forehead had turned dark red, his eyes were bulging. "And I don't cut. I don't even know what levamisole is, for fuck's sake!"

"Oh?" Øystein said, looking like he was enjoying himself. "Then how do you know it was mixed with levamisole?"

"Because it said so in the report, and the reports are on BL!" Truls bellowed.

"Excuse me."

They all turned to the door, where two nurses were standing.

"We think it's nice that Ståle gets so many visitors, but we can't allow him and Jibran to be disturbed by—"

"Apologies, Kari," Aune said. "Things can get a little heated when inheritance settlements are being discussed, you know. Don't you think, Jibran?"

Jibran looked up and removed his headphones. "What?"

"Are we disturbing you?"

"Not at all."

Aune smiled to the older nurse.

"Well, in that case . . ." she said, her lips pursed, as she looked reprovingly at Truls, Øystein and Harry before closing the door behind her.

Katrine looked down at the bodies of Susanne and Bertine. As always, it struck her how forsaken corpses looked when laid out like this, how it could make you believe in the existence of a soul. Something she definitely didn't believe in, but—which was after all the incentive behind all religions and mysticism—hoped for. The two women were naked, their skin shades of white, blue, and also black, due mainly to blood and bodily fluids having sunk to the lowest lying parts of the body. Decomposition had set in, and Bertine's lack of a head reinforced the feeling they were looking at statues, lifeless objects given form by something living. There were seven living people in the autopsy room: Katrine and the pathologist, Skarre from Crime Squad, Sung-min Larsen, a female detective from Kripos, Alexander Sturdza and another post-mortem technician.

"We haven't found any signs of violence or a struggle prior to death," the pathologist said. "Causes of death. Susanne received a cut across the throat, severing her carotid artery. Bertine was probably strangled. I say probably because without her head we can't do a full analysis. But the marks on the lower part of her neck indicate asphyxiation with a strap or cord resulting in hypoxia. There were no traces of any substances in their blood or urine to suggest they were drugged. Congealed spit and mucus was found on one of the victim's nipples."

She pointed to the body of Susanne.

"It has, as far as I know, already been analyzed . . ."

"Yes," Alexandra said.

"Beyond that, we haven't found DNA material on the victims. As there is a suspicion of rape, we've paid particular attention to looking for traces of that. There are no marks from fingers holding tightly on the arms, legs or throat, no bite marks or suction marks. No wounds or bruising to the wrists or ankles. One victim has no head, so we can't say anything about her auricle."

"Pardon?" the female detective from Kripos said.

"The outer ear," Alexandra said. "Wounding is common there with victims of violence."

"Or possible petechiae," the pathologist said, pointing at Susanne's head. "The first victim didn't exhibit it."

"Small, discolored spots around the eyes or the palate," Alexandra explained.

"Neither victim has visible injury to their labia minora," the pathologist continued.

"The inner pudenda," Alexandra translated.

"Nor were there any scratch marks from fingernails on the neck or grazing to the knees, hips or back. Otherwise, there are microscopic marks in Bertine's vagina, but they're of an order that may just have well occurred due to consensual sex. In short, there is no physical evidence on either of them pointing to rape."

"Which isn't to say that rape *can't* have taken place," Alexandra added.

The look the pathologist gave Alexandra made Katrine suspect she might be having words with her younger colleague about role under-standing after they had left.

"So, no injuries," Katrine said. "And no semen. What then makes you so sure they both had intercourse?"

"Prophylactic," said the other post-mortem technician, Helge something-or-other, a sweet guy who hadn't said anything so far, and who Katrine had instinctively understood was at the bottom of the pecking order out of the three.

"A condom?" Skarre said.

"Yes," Helge replied. "When we don't find semen, we look for signs of a condom. Primarily traces of nonoxynol 9, the substance in the lubricant, but evidently this was a type without lubricant. Instead, we found traces from the fine powder on the condom which prevents the latex from sticking to itself. The composition of the powder is unique to every manufacturer. The powder on this brand—Bodyful—was the same for Susanne and Bertine."

"Is that a common powder?" Sung-min asked.

"Neither common nor uncommon," Helge said. "Of course, it's entirely possible they didn't have intercourse with the same man, but . . ."

"I see," Sung-min said. "Thanks."

"Based on these findings, is there any way to tell when intercourse occurred?" Katrine asked.

"No," the pathologist said firmly. "Everything we've told you, minus the details about the condom powder, you can find in the report we placed in the case file on BL96 just before you arrived. OK?"

The ensuing pause was interrupted by Helge, his voice more cautious now.

"We might not be able to say *exactly* when, but—" he cast a quick glance at the pathologist, as if seeking permission, before continuing—"it seems safe to assume that in both cases intercourse occurred not long before they died. Possibly after."

"OK?"

"Had they been alive for some time after intercourse, their bodily functions would have disposed of traces of the condoms. A living body would do that over the course of a few days, perhaps three. But semen and condom powder would last longer in a dead body. It . . ." He swallowed, gave a small smile. "Yeah, that was all."

"Any more questions?" the pathologist asked. She waited a couple of seconds before clapping her hands together. "Well. Like the title of the movie: *If more bodies turn up, just give us a call.*"

Only Skarre laughed. Katrine wasn't sure if it was because he was the only one of them old enough to remember the movie, or if morbid humor worked best when there weren't corpses present.

She felt her phone vibrate and looked at the display.

21

WEDNESDAY

The thrill begins

KATRINE HAD TO PULL HARD on the steering wheel of the fifty-year-old Volvo Amazon as she swung up in front of the entrance to the Radium Hospital.

She drew up beside the tall man with the beard.

Saw Harry hesitate before opening the door and sitting down in the passenger seat.

"You kept the car," he said.

"Bjørn loved it so much," she said, patting the dashboard. "And he took good care of it. Runs like clockwork."

"It's a classic car," Harry said. "It's also dangerous."

She smiled. "You're thinking of Gert? Relax, I only use it in the city. My father-in-law comes by and tinkers on it, and . . . it smells of Bjørn."

She could tell what he was thinking. *This is the car Bjørn shot himself in.* Yes, it was. The car Bjørn had loved, and had driven out of the city, to a straight stretch of road alongside a field in Toten. A place he had fond memories of perhaps. It was night and he had moved to the back seat. Some believed it was because his idol, Hank Williams, had died in the back seat of a car, but she suspected it was because he didn't want to mess up the driver's seat. So that she could continue using it. So that she *had* to continue using it. Yes, she knew it was crazy. But if this was her self-imposed punishment for fooling a good man into believing that their child was his, a man who had always been good, way too good, then so what? He loved her like crazy and always doubted that she really loved him, he had even gone as far as asking her straight out why she hadn't chosen a man in her own league. No, this was a punishment she gladly accepted.

"Good you could get here so quick," he said.

"I was just up the road at the Forensic Medical Institute. So, what's up?"

"I just realized my usual driver isn't quite sober, and I need to go to a place where you can get me in."

"Doesn't sound very promising. Where were you thinking?"

"The crime scenes," he said. "I want to see them."

"Not a chance."

"Come on. We found Bertine for you."

"I realize that, but I made it clear we don't reward tip-offs."

"Yes, you did. Is it still cordoned off?"

"Yes, so no, you can't go there on your own either."

Harry looked at her with something like quiet desperation. She recognized that look, recognized those damned pale blue eyes, now a little wider than usual, the body he wasn't able to keep quite still in the seat. It was ants under his skin, it was the mania. Or was it something more? She had never seen him so worked up before, as though this case were a matter of life or death. Which of course it was, but not *his* life or death. Or? No, of course it was just the mania. Meaning he must—*must*—hunt.

"Mm. Drive me to Schrøder's then."

Or drink.

She sighed. Checked the time. "Suit yourself. All right if I collect Gert from kindergarten on the way?"

He raised an eyebrow. Gave her a look as if to say he suspected her of having an agenda. Which of course she might have, it was never wrong to remind a man he had a child. She put the car in gear and was letting the temperamental clutch out when her phone rang. She looked at the display and put the car back into neutral.

"Sorry, I have to take this, Harry. Yes, Bratt speaking."

"Have you read what *Dagbladet* have written now?" Compared to most people the Chief Superintendent didn't even sound annoyed. But Katrine was using the Bodil Melling yardstick and knew her boss was furious.

"If by now you mean—"

"It went up on their website six minutes ago, it's this Våge again. He's written that forensic examination has revealed that both girls had sex just prior to or after they were killed, and that a condom was used, probably so as not to leave any DNA behind. How does he know that, Bratt?"

"I don't know."

"Well, then let me tell you. We have someone leaking information to Våge."

"Sorry," Katrine said. "I was imprecise. *How* is obvious. What I mean is I don't know *who* the leak is."

"And when are you planning on finding out?"

"Hard to say, boss. At the moment my priority is finding a killer who, for all we know, may be looking for his next victim."

There was silence at the other end. Katrine closed her eyes and cursed herself. She would never learn.

"I've just had Winter on the phone, and he rules out anyone at Kripos. I'd be inclined to agree with him. So, you're the one who needs to find the person concerned and shut their mouth, Bratt. You hear me? This makes us all look like idiots. I'm calling the Police Chief now before he calls me to ask about it. Keep me informed."

Melling hung up. Katrine shifted her gaze to Harry's phone, which he was holding up for her. It was *Dagbladet*'s website. She skimmed Våge's comments.

The discovery of Bertine indicated a sexually motivated murder, but today's examinations at the Forensic Medical Unit do not strengthen that theory and do not clear Markus Røed of suspicion. The real estate mogul had sexual relationships with both Susanne Andersen and Bertine Bertilsen and is—as far as the police know—the only person tying the two women together. Sources say investigators have speculated whether Røed could have ordered contract killings tailored to look like sexually motivated murder and not hits.

"The guy really has it in for Røed," she said.

"Have you?" Harry asked.

"Have we what?"

"Speculated if the murders were arranged so as to look like they were a sexually motivated murder?"

She shrugged. "Not that I've heard. I bet it's Våge's own speculation, and he's attributing it to a source because he knows it can never be checked."

"Mm."

They drove down towards the freeway.

"What do you guys think?" she asked.

"Well. Most of the team think it's a rapist and serial killer, and that the link between the two victims is coincidental."

"Because?"

"Because Markus Røed has an alibi and contract killers don't have sex with their victims. What do your lot think?"

Katrine checked the traffic in the mirror. "OK, Harry, I'll give you something. What Våge didn't write is that one of the post-mortem technicians found the same type of condom powder in both girls. So it's the same perpetrator."

"Interesting."

"What he also didn't write is that the medical examiners aren't ruling out that the girls were raped, even though they didn't find any clear physical indicators. They only do in one in three cases. Minor injuries in just half the rapes. The remainder they find nothing."

"Do you think that's what's happened here?"

"No. I think it's because the victims were dead before intercourse took place."

"Mm. The thrill begins with death."

"What?"

"Something Aune says. With sadists, their sexual excitement begins with the suffering and ceases when the victim dies. With necrophiliacs their excitement begins when the victim is dead."

"OK, but then you were rewarded a little all the same."

"Thanks. What do you make of the boot prints at the scenes?"

"Who said there were boot prints?"

Harry shrugged. "The crime scenes are in the forest, so I presume the ground is soft. It's hardly rained over the past few weeks, so obviously there'll be boot prints."

"They have the same pattern," Katrine said, after some hesitation. "The victim and the suspected perpetrator's footprints are close to one another, as if he was holding her or was threatening her with a weapon."

"Mm. Or just the opposite."

"What do you mean?"

"Maybe they walked with their arms around each other. Like a couple. Or two people about to engage in mutual, consensual sex."

"Are you serious?"

"If I was threatening someone, I'd walk behind them."

"You believe the girls knew their killer?"

"Maybe. Maybe not. What I don't believe in are coincidences. Susanne went missing four days after the party at Røed's building, and Bertine one week after that. They met the perpetrator there. There was a man at the party I'm guessing you don't have on that guest list."

"Oh?"

"A guy in a face mask and sunglasses selling cocaine?"

"No one's mentioned anyone like that to us, no. Not so strange, perhaps, if he was selling cocaine to the guests."

"Or because you soon forget faceless people. He wasn't selling to the guests; he was handing out samples of something we think was close to pure cocaine to a few guests."

"How do you know?"

"That's not important. What is important is that he was in contact with both Susanne and Bertine. Do you know of anyone else at the party who talked to both girls?"

"Just Markus Røed." Katrine put the indicator on and checked the mirror again. "You think this guy chatted up both of them at the party and arranged to go for a walk in the woods with them?"

"Why not?"

"I don't know, but I can't see how it makes sense. It's one thing Susanne heading off with a guy she's just met at a party for an adventure in the forest. One who's been dealing coke into the bargain. But that Bertine a week later voluntarily accompanies a man like that, one she barely knows, into the forest at Skullerud when it's been in the newspapers that Susanne was last seen in Skullerud? At that stage Bertine would also have been aware that the three of them had been at the same party. No, Harry, I don't buy it."

"OK. So what do you think?"

"I think we're looking at a serial rapist."

"Serial killer."

"Absolutely. Quick murders, necrophilia. A brain cut out, a head cut off, a body hung up like a slaughtered animal. That's what I'd call a ritual murder carried out by a serial killer."

"Mm." Harry said. "Why condom powder?"

"What?"

"In these kinds of sexual offense cases you look for lubricant, not powder, when you're trying to identify the condom, isn't that right?"

"Yes, but there wasn't any lubricant used here."

"Exactly. You've worked in Vice. Don't serial rapists—those of them smart enough to use a condom—use lubricant?"

"Yes, but these are criminal maniacs, Harry, they don't have a set script, and you're just splitting hairs."

"You're right," Harry said. "But I've yet to see or hear anything that means we can rule out that Bertine and Susanne had consensual sex with the perpetrator right before he killed them."

"Apart from it being . . . highly unusual. No? You're the expert on serial killers here."

Harry rubbed the back of his neck. "Yeah, it's unusual. Murder after rape isn't so unusual, either as part of the killer's sexual fantasy or to avoid being identified. But murder after consensual sex only occurs in exceptional cases. A narcissist could kill if he's been humiliated in relation to the act, if he's unable to perform, for instance."

"The traces of a condom indicate that he managed to perform, Harry. I'll be right back."

Harry nodded. They had stopped on lower Hegdehaugsveien, and he watched Katrine as she walked quickly towards the gate where children in snowsuits hung over the fence waiting to be collected.

She disappeared beyond the gate, but after a few minutes she and Gert appeared, walking hand in hand. He heard the sound of an eager child's voice. He had been a quiet child himself, apparently.

The car door opened.

"Hi Hawny." Gert leaned forward from the back seat and gave Harry a hug from behind before Katrine pulled him back into the child seat.

"Hello, old chap," Harry said.

"Old chap?" Gert said, looking at his mother.

"He's messing with you," Katrine said.

"You messing, Hawny!" Gert laughed heartily, and glancing in the mirror Harry gave a start as he glimpsed something familiar. Not himself. Not his father. But his mother. He had Harry's mother's smile.

Katrine got in behind the wheel.

"Schrøder's?" she said.

Harry shook his head. "I'll get out at your place, then walk."

"To Schrøder's?"

Harry didn't answer.

"I've been thinking," she said. "I want to ask you for a favor."

"OK?"

"You know these cross-country skiers and people who walk to the South Pole and charge a ton of money to give talks and inspire people?"

A wave caused the Nesodden ferry to rock slightly.

Harry looked around. The passengers in the seats nearby were gazing at their phones, wearing headsets, reading books or looking out at the Oslo Fjord. On their way home from work, college, a shopping trip in town. No one looked like they were on an outing with their partner.

Harry looked down at his own phone, at the latest forensic report Truls had taken a screenshot of and mailed to all of them. He had read it while eating in the cafeteria at the Radium Hospital, after texting Katrine to ask if she could come and pick him up. Had he felt guilty pretending not to know about it when she told him about her visit to the Forensic Medical Institute? Not really. Besides, he hadn't needed to act like he wasn't aware of the information about the condom powder and necrophilia, it hadn't been in the report. Neither had it appeared in Våge's article. In other words, Våge's informant was not one of those who had been present at the institute, otherwise he would have had what wasn't in the report in his story too. But Våge had included that some of the investigators believed the murder was made to look like the work of a serial killer to hide what it actually was.

Condom powder.

Harry thought about it.

Then tapped T.

"Yeah?"

"Hi, Truls, it's Harry."

"Yeah?"

"I won't take up much of your time. I've spoken to Katrine Bratt, and it turns out that not everything the Forensic Medical Institute has found is winding up in the reports."

"Oh?"

"Yeah. She shared one detail with me which the investigative team at Police HQ are sure to be discussing but we don't have."

"Which is?"

Harry hesitated. Condom powder.

"The tattoo," he said. "The killer cut off the Louis Vuitton tattoo Bertine had on her ankle and sewed it back on again."

"Like Susanne Andersen's scalp?"

"Yep," Harry said. "But that's not important. What is important is whether you have some way we can get hold of that kind of thing in the future."

"Stuff not in the reports? I'll have to talk to people then."

"Mm. We don't want to chance that. I wasn't expecting any suggestions off the top of your head but have a think about it and we'll talk tomorrow."

Truls grunted. "All right."

They hung up.

When the boat docked, Harry remained seated, watching the other passengers stream out and go ashore.

"Not getting off?" asked a ticket inspector, making a sweep of the empty lounge.

"Not today," Harry said.

"Same again," Harry said, pointing at the glass.

The bartender raised an eyebrow, but took down the Jim Beam bottle and poured.

Harry knocked that one back too. "And another."

"Rough day?" the bartender asked.

"Not yet," Harry said, before picking up the glass and walking towards the same table where he had seen the Turbonegro vocalist sitting. Noticed he was already slightly unsteady on his feet. On his way he passed a man sitting with his back to him and smelled a perfume that reminded him of Lucille. He slid into the sofa. It was early in the evening, not many guests yet. Lucille, where was she right now? Instead of drinking more he could go to his room and reread the reports, search for the mistake, the lead. He looked at the glass. The hourglass. Five days plus a few hours until he let someone down again. Yes, that was the story of his life. What the hell, soon he'd have nobody left to let down anyway. He raised the glass.

A man had entered the bar and was looking around. Caught sight of Harry. They exchanged brief nods before the man headed in Harry's direction, and sat down in the chair on the other side of the low glass table.

"Evening, Krohn."

"Good evening, Harry. How's it going?"

"With the investigation? Going well."

"Good. Does that mean you have a lead?"

"No. What brings you here?"

The lawyer looked like he had planned on asking a follow-up question but dropped it. "I heard you called Helene Røed today. That the two of you are going to talk."

"That's right."

"I just wanted to draw your attention to a couple of things prior to you having that conversation. First of all, her and Markus's relationship isn't the best at the moment. There could be several reasons for that. Like—"

"Markus's cocaine addiction?"

"I don't know anything about that."

"Yes, you do."

"I was thinking about the fact they've drifted apart over time. And that all the public attention Markus has received regarding this case, especially in *Dagbladet*, hasn't improved matters."

"What are you trying to say?"

"Helene is under a lot of stress, and I wouldn't rule out that she might say things which put her husband in a bad light. Both with regard to his person in general and his involvement with Miss Andersen and Miss Bertilsen in particular. Not something that changes the facts of the case, but should the press, *Dagbladet*, get hold of it then it would be unfortunate for my . . . or rather *our* client."

"So you came to tell me not to leak possible gossip?"

Krohn smiled briefly. "I'm just saying that this Terry Våge will use everything he can get his hands on to smear Markus."

"Because?"

Krohn shrugged. "It's ancient history. It was in the days Markus was just investing a little here and there for fun. At the time he was also chairman of the board for the free newspaper Våge wrote for. When the Press Complaints Commission found the newspaper had broken the code of practice for the stories Våge had made up, the board fired him. That had big repercussions on his life and career thereafter, and he's obviously never forgiven Markus."

"Mm. I'll keep it in mind."

"Good."

Krohn remained sitting.

"Yes?" Harry said.

"I understand if it's something you don't want to dredge up, but we do have a secret binding us together."

"You're right," Harry said, taking a swig of his drink. "I don't want to dredge it up."

"Of course. I just wanted to say that I still believe we did the right thing."

Harry looked at him.

"We made sure the world was rid of an evil, evil man," Krohn said. "He was, admittedly, my client—"

"And innocent," Harry slurred.

"Of your wife's murder, perhaps. But he was guilty of ruining the lives of many others. Far too many. Young people. Innocent people."

Harry studied Krohn. The two of them had seen to it that Svein Finne, a man with multiple convictions for rape, was killed and that Rakel's murder was pinned on him. Krohn's motive had been the threats Finne had made against him and his family, while Harry's had been the desire for who had actually killed Rakel, and their reason for doing it, never coming to light.

"While Bjørn Holm," Johan Krohn said, "he had only been a good man. A good friend, a good husband. Isn't that right?"

"Yes," Harry said, feeling his throat tighten. He signaled to the bar by raising the empty glass.

Krohn took a deep breath. "The reason Bjørn Holm killed the woman you loved instead of you was because it was the only way he could make you suffer like he was suffering."

"That's enough now, Krohn."

"What I'm trying to say, Harry, is that this is the same thing. Terry Våge wants to disgrace Markus Røed, just like he was disgraced. Let him feel the social condemnation. It can break people, you know? They take their own lives. I myself have had clients who have done that."

"Markus Røed is no Bjørn Holm, he's not a good man."

"Maybe not. But he is innocent. In this case anyway."

Harry closed his eyes. *In this case anyway.*

"Goodnight, Harry."

When Harry opened his eyes, Johan Krohn was gone from the chair, and the drink had arrived on the table.

He tried to drink slowly, but that felt meaningless, so he threw it back. He was soon there, just one more.

A woman came in. Slim, red dress, dark hair, her back was even willowy. There was a time when he saw Rakel everywhere. Not any longer. Yes, he missed it, even the nightmares. As though she felt his eyes on the bare small of her back, the woman at the bar turned and glanced in his direction. Only for the briefest moment, before turning back around. But he had seen it. A look devoid of interest, only slight pity. A look registering that the occupant of the sofa was a very lonely soul. The sort you didn't want rubbing off on you.

Harry couldn't remember how he had gotten to his room as he crawled into bed. As soon as he shut his eyes the same two sentences began churning around in his head.

Make you suffer the way he did.

Innocent—in this case anyway.

The phone buzzed and lit up in the darkness. He turned over and picked it up from the nightstand. It was an MMS from a number prefixed with +52. He didn't need to guess that was Mexico, because the picture showed Lucille's face against a background of a wall with peeling paint. She looked older without makeup. She had turned one side of her face to the camera, the one she claimed was prettier. Although pale, she was smiling, as if to comfort the person she knew would receive the picture. And it occurred to him that it was the same kindly regret as in his mother's face that time she had stood in the classroom doorway with his lunch box.

The text below was short.

5 days, counting.

22

THURSDAY

Debt

IT WAS FIVE MINUTES TO ten and Katrine and Sung-min were standing outside the conference room, each with a cup of coffee in their hands. Others on the investigation team mumbled morning greetings as they passed on their way into the morning meeting.

"Right," Sung-min said. "So, Hole thinks the perpetrator is a cocaine dealer who was at the party?"

"Sounds like that," Katrine said, checking her watch. He had said he would be there early, now it was four minutes to.

"If the cocaine was so pure, maybe he smuggled it in himself. Along with other things."

"What do you mean?"

Sung-min shook his head. "Just an association. There was an empty bag of anti-parasitic powder lying not far from the scene. It must have been smuggled in as well."

"Oh?"

"The powder's banned. Contains powerful toxins against a whole range of intestinal worms, including the serious types."

"Serious?"

"Parasites that can kill dogs and are transmissible to humans. I've heard of a couple of dog owners who have contracted it. Attacks the liver, very unpleasant."

"You're saying the killer could be a dog owner?"

"Who feeds his pet an anti-parasitic cure in the great outdoors before killing and raping his victim? No."

"So why . . . ?"

"Yeah, why. Because we're grasping at straws. You've seen the videos where American traffic cops stop motorists for being a little over the speed limit or having a broken tail light? How cautiously they approach the car, as though someone violating a traffic regulation dramatically increases the likelihood of them being hardened criminals?"

"Yes, and I know why. Because it does dramatically increase the likelihood of them being hardened criminals. Lots of research on that."

Sung-min smiled. "Exactly. Rule-breakers. That's all."

"OK," Katrine said, checking the time again. What had happened? She had seen in Harry's eyes that there was a danger of him falling completely off the wagon. But he usually still stuck to his word. "If you've got the bag, you should drop it in to Krimteknisk."

"I found it far from the scene," Sung-min said. "We could've picked up a thousand things within that radius which, with a little imagination, might be connected to the murder."

One minute to ten.

She spotted the officer she had sent down to reception to meet him. And—towering a head taller behind him—Harry Hole. He looked more rumpled than his suit, and it was as if she could see the alcohol on his breath before she smelled it. Katrine noticed how Sung-min automatically straightened up next to her.

Katrine drained the rest of the coffee cup. "Shall we get started?"

*

"As you can see, we have a visitor," Katrine said.

The first part of the plan was working. It was as though the weariness and apathy on the faces in front of her had been washed away.

"He needs no introduction, but for those of you are very new, Harry Hole began as a detective here at Crime Squad in . . ." She looked at Harry.

He grimaced behind the beard. "The Stone Age."

Chuckling.

"The Stone Age," Katrine said. "He's played a major part in solving some of our biggest cases. He's been a lecturer at Police College. He is, as far as I'm aware, the only Norwegian who has attended the FBI's course on serial homicides in Chicago. I wanted to bring him into this investigative team but wasn't allowed." Katrine looked out at the people present. It was only a question of time before Melling got wind that she had brought Harry into the inner sanctum. "So, all the better that Markus Røed has hired him to investigate the murders of Susanne and Bertine, which means more expertise is being brought to bear, if not by our superiors." She saw Sung-min's mildly admonitory glance and Magnus Skarre's furious glare. "I've invited Harry to speak about these murders in general terms, and so we can ask questions."

"First question!" It was Skarre. His voice shaking with indignation. "Why should we listen to a guy talk about serial killers? This is TV show stuff, and two murders by the same hand doesn't mean—"

"It does." Harry got to his feet from a chair on the front row, but without turning to face the audience. For a moment he seemed to sway, as though the drop in blood pressure would make him tip over, before he stood more firmly. "Yes, it does mean it's a serial killing."

There was complete silence in the conference room as Harry took two long, slow strides towards the board before he pivoted around. The words came slowly at first, then gradually a little faster, as if his mouth needed to get up to speed. "The term serial homicide is an invention of the FBI, and their official definition is 'a series of two or more murders, committed by the same offender as separate events', simple as that." He fixed his eyes on Skarre. "But although this case is by definition a serial homicide, it doesn't mean the offender necessarily conforms to your ideas of a serial killer from TV shows. He doesn't need to be a psychopath, a sadist or a sex maniac. He could be a relatively normal person like you or me with an utterly banal motive, like money, for example. In fact, the second most common motive for serial killers in the USA is just that. So, a serial killer doesn't need to be the type driven by voices in his head or an uncontrollable urge to kill again and again. But he can be. I say 'he' because serial killers are, with few exceptions, men. The question is whether what we're looking at can be that type of serial killer."

"The question," Skarre said, "is what you're doing here when you work in the private sector. Why should we believe you want to help us?"

"Well, why wouldn't I help you, Skarre? I've been assigned to make sure—or at least increase the likelihood—that this case is solved. Not that I'm the one who solves it, necessarily. I can see that that concept is a little difficult for you to take in just like that, Skarre, so allow me to illustrate. If I'm tasked with saving people from burning to death in a building but the place is already ablaze, what do I do? Use my bucket or call the fire station located around the corner?"

Katrine suppressed a smile but noticed Sung-min did not.

"So, you're the fire brigade, and I'm on the phone. My job is to tell you what I know about where it's burning. And as I happen to know a little about fires, I'll tell you what I think is special about this particular fire. OK?"

Katrine saw some nodding of heads. Others glanced at one another, but no one objected.

"Getting right to the point about what's special," Harry said. "The heads. Or to be more precise, the missing brains. And the question—as always—is why? Why cut open or cut off the victims' heads and remove the brains? Well, in some circumstances the answer is simple. In the Old Testament, there's the story of Judith, a poor Jewish widow, who saves her city when it's under siege by seducing the enemy general and cutting off his head. The point wasn't to kill him, but to show his head to everyone, as a display of power, to frighten his troops, who, sure enough, run away. So, a rational act, with a motive recognizable throughout the history of warfare and which we see to this day when political terrorists spread video recordings of beheadings. But it's difficult to see that our man needs to frighten anyone, so why? In tribes of headhunters—or at least in the myths about them—they often want the victims' heads for themselves, as trophies, or to drive out evil spirits. Or to keep the spirits. Tribes in New Guinea believed you took possession of the victims' souls when you took their heads. And that might bring us closer to what we're looking at here."

Katrine noticed that even though Harry was speaking in a neutral, almost flat tone and without facial expressions or dramatic gestures, he had the full attention of the room.

"The history of serial killers is full of decapitations. Ed Gein severed the heads of his victims and placed them on bedposts. Ed Kemper cut the head off his mother and had sex with it. But perhaps our case has more parallels with Jeffrey Dahmer, who killed seventeen men and boys in the eighties. He met them at parties or clubs, got them drunk or gave them drugs. Something I'll come back to that may have occurred in our case too. Dahmer then took his victims home. Murdered them, usually by strangling them while they were drugged. Had sex with the corpses. Dismembered them. Drilled holes in the head, poured in various fluids, like acid. Cut off the head. Ate selected parts of the bodies. He told his psychologist he was keeping the heads because he feared rejection, and in that way ensured they could never leave him. Hence the parallel to the soul collectors of New Guinea. But Dahmer went further, He made sure the victims remained with him by eating part of them. Incidentally, psychologists believed that Dahmer wasn't insane in the criminal sense, they thought he only suffered from some personality disorders. Like most of us can and still function. In other words, Dahmer was a person who could have sat among us now, and we wouldn't necessarily suspect him of anything. Yes, Larsen?"

"Our perpetrator didn't take Susanne's head, but her brain. With Bertine he took both the head and the brain. So, is it brains he's after? And in that case, do the brains serve as trophies?"

"Mm. We differentiate between trophies and souvenirs. Trophies are symbols of you having defeated your victim, and in such cases, heads are much used. Souvenirs are used as mementoes of the sexual act and for sexual gratification afterwards. I don't know if brains stand out in that regard. But if you were to draw conclusions based on what we know about sexually motivated, psychopathic serial killers, there are all manner of reasons for them doing what they do, just like there is for everyone. And that's why there're no common patterns of behavior, at least not to a level of detail that allows us to easily predict their next move. Except for one thing, which we can assume with a large degree of probability."

Katrine knew that this wasn't a dramatic pause, it was simply that Harry had to draw breath and at the same time take an almost imperceptible step to the side to gain balance.

"That they will strike again."

In the silence that followed, Katrine heard hard, fast-approaching footsteps in the corridor outside. And she recognized their sound and knew who it was. Perhaps Harry heard them too and guessed his time was about to run out. At any rate, he sped up.

"I don't think this person is after heads, but rather the brains of the victims. Cutting Bertine's head off only means he's refining his method, also a typical feature of the classic, psychopathic serial killer. He's learned from the last time that removing the brain at the scene of the crime requires time and is therefore risky. In addition, when he saw the result of sewing the scalp back on and knew it would be discovered, he realized that in order to hide the fact it was the brain he really wanted, it would be better to take the entire head. I don't think he choked Bertine to death in an attempt to mislead the police into thinking Susanne was killed by someone else. If that was important, he wouldn't have chosen Skullerud both times, and he wouldn't have left both bodies naked from the waist down. The reason for the change in method of killing was practical. He got blood on himself when he cut Susanne's throat, you can see that by the traces of blood spray. Blood on his hands, face and clothes meant he'd be noticed if he met anyone on the way back. And he'd have needed to throw away the clothes, wash the car and so on."

The door opened. Sure enough it was Bodil Melling. She took up position in the doorway with arms folded, fixing Katrine with a gaze promising a gloomy outlook.

"That was also the reason he brought her to a lake. There he could minimize the blood spill by holding her head underwater while cutting it off. In that sense, this serial killer is like most of us. The more often we do something the better we get. In this case that's bad news for what may come." Harry looked at Bodil Melling. "Don't you think, Chief Superintendent?"

The corners of her mouth turned up in the affectation of a smile. "What's coming, Hole, is you leaving this building at once. Then we'll discuss internally how we interpret the guidelines regarding access to information for individuals without clearance."

Katrine felt her throat tighten in a mixture of shame and anger and was aware her voice didn't mask it. "I understand your concern, Bodil. But it goes without saying, Harry hasn't been given access to—"

"As I said, we'll deal with this internally. Would someone other than Bratt escort Hole down to reception? And, Bratt, you come with me."

Katrine sent a despairing look to Harry, who shrugged in response, then she followed Bodil Melling while listening to the staccato strike of heels on the corridor floor.

"Honestly, Katrine," Melling said when they were in the elevator, "I warned you. Don't involve Hole. Yet you did it anyway."

"I wasn't allowed to bring him in as part of the group, but this was as a consultant, someone sharing their experience and imparting information without getting anything in return. Neither money nor info. I consider it within my area of responsibility to do that."

The elevator pinged to announce their floor.

"Is that so?" Melling said, walking out.

Katrine hurried after. "Did someone text you from the conference room?"

Melling smiled sourly. "If only it were that type of conscientious leak we needed to worry about."

Melling walked into her office. Ole Winter and Head of Information Kedzierski were at the small meeting table, each sitting with a cup of coffee and a copy of *Dagbladet* in front of them.

"Good morning, Bratt," the head of Kripos said.

"We're sitting here discussing the leaks in the double murder case," Melling said.

"Without me?" Katrine said.

Melling sighed, sat down and motioned to Katrine to follow suit. "Without any of those who theoretically could be behind the leaks being present. No reason to take it personally. Now we might as well take it up with you directly. I presume you've seen what Våge has written today?"

Katrine nodded.

"It's a scandal," Winter said, shaking his head. "Nothing less. Våge had details from the investigation that can only have come from one place, and that's here. I've checked my people who are on the case, and none of them are behind it."

"How have you *checked* them?" Katrine asked.

Winter ignored that, just continued shaking his head. "And now, Bratt, you invite the competition in as well?"

"You may be in competition with Hole, but I'm not," Katrine said. "Is there coffee for me too?"

Melling looked at her in surprise.

"But back to the leaks," Katrine said. "Give me a few pointers on how to *check* my colleagues, Winter. Surveillance? Reading emails? Interrogation by Chinese water torture?"

Winter looked at Melling as though appealing to common sense.

"But I have checked something else," Katrine said. "I've gone back and checked what Våge has and doesn't have. And it turns out that everything he seems to have obtained from our investigators has appeared in print *after* it's been logged in reports filed in BL. Which means that the leak could come from anybody in Police HQ with access to those files. Unfortunately, the system doesn't register who has been in looking at which files."

"That's not true!" Winter said.

"It is," Katrine said. "I've spoken to our IT people."

"I meant the part about everything Våge writing having been in the reports." He grabbed the newspaper from the table and read aloud: *"The police have declined to make public several grotesque details, such as Bertine Bertilsen's ankle tattoo being cut off and sewn back on again."* He threw the newspaper back on the table. "That has *not* appeared in any reports!"

"I should hope not," Katrine said. "Because it's simply not the case. Våge is making things up. And surely that's beyond the bounds of what we can be blamed for, Winter?"

"Thanks, Anita," Harry said, his eyes fixed on the beer the elderly waitress had just put down in front of him."

"Anyway." Anita sighed, as a continuation of something she had thought but not said. "It's nice to see you again."

"What's up with her?" asked Truls, who had already been sitting at the window table in Schrøder's when Harry arrived at the agreed time.

"She doesn't like serving me," Harry said.

"Then Schrøder's isn't the right place to work," Truls grunt-laughed.

"Maybe not." Harry lifted the beer. "Maybe she just needs the money." He brought the glass to his lips and drank while holding Truls's gaze.

"What was it you wanted?" Truls asked, and Harry saw a twitching below one eye.

"What do you think?"

"Dunno. Brainstorm again?

"Maybe. What do you think about this?" Harry drew *Dagbladet* from his jacket pocket and placed it in front of Truls.

"About what?"

"About what Våge writes about Bertine's tattoo. That it was cut off and sewn back on."

"Think? I think he seems well informed. But that's his job, I guess."

Harry sighed. "I'm not asking so I can drag this out, Truls. It's to give you the chance to say it before I do."

Truls had his hands on the worn tablecloth, one either side of a paper napkin. He hadn't ordered anything. Didn't want anything. His hands were red against the white of the napkin, and looked bloated, swollen. As though they would shrink to a pair of gloves if Harry were to stick a pin in them. His forehead had taken on a dark red hue, the color the devil had in comics.

"No idea what you're talking about," Truls said.

"It's you. You're the one who's been feeding Terry Våge."

"Me? Are you stupid? I'm not even on the investigation team."

"You're feeding Våge the same as us, you're reading the reports as soon as they're on BL96. You were already doing it when I contacted you, so not so strange you said yes to my offer. You're getting paid double for the same job. And Våge is probably paying you even more now that you're giving him updates on the Aune group as well."

"What the fuck? I haven't—"

"Shut up, Truls."

"Fuck off! I'm not going to—"

"Shut up! And sit down!"

The few tables where there were customers had gone quiet. They weren't staring openly, but looking down into their beer glasses, using their peripheral vision. Harry had placed his hand on Truls's and was pressing it so hard on the tabletop that Truls was forced to sit back down. Harry leaned forward and continued in a low voice.

"Like I said, I'm not going to drag this out, so here it is. I got suspicious when Våge wrote about the investigators speculating if Røed had ordered the killings to look like sex attacks. That was something we'd discussed in the Aune group and is so outside the box that I checked with Katrine if anyone on their team had suggested it. They hadn't. So I came up with that story about Bertine's tattoo being sewn back on and told you and only you. Said it was common knowledge at Police HQ, so you'd feel comfortable passing it on without it pointing back to you. And sure enough, Våge had it in print a few hours later. So there you have it, Truls."

Truls Berntsen stared straight ahead, his face expressionless. Took hold of the paper napkin and crumbled it up, the same way Harry had seen him do with the losing ticket at the racetrack.

"All right," Truls said. "So I sold a little info. And you all can just fuck off, because no damage has been done. Våge has never gotten anything that could wreck the investigation."

"That's your assessment, Truls, but we'll drop that discussion for now."

"Yes, we will, because I'm off, adios. And you can take that money from Røed and wipe your ass with it."

"I told you to sit." Harry allowed himself a wry smile. "And thanks, but the toilet paper at the Thief is excellent. So soft in fact it makes you want to take a second shit. Have you ever felt it?"

Truls Berntsen didn't look like he understood the question but remained seated.

"So here's your chance to shit on things one more time," Harry said. "You're going to tell Våge that your access to BL96 has been taken away, and he's going to have to manage for himself. From now on you're also not going to say jackshit about what's going on in the Aune group. And you're going to tell me how big your gambling debts are."

Truls stared in bewilderment at Harry. Swallowed. Blinked a couple of times.

"Three hundred thousand," he said eventually. "Give or take."

"Mm. That's a lot. When's payment due?"

"Due ages ago. Interest is accruing, you might say."

"They're eager to collect?"

Truls snorted. "It's not just pliers, they threaten you with all kinds of shit. I'm walking around looking over my shoulder the whole time, if you only knew."

"Yeah, if I only knew," Harry said, closing his eyes. Last night he had dreamed about scorpions. They seeped into the room from under the door and the baseboards, through cracks in the windows and wall sockets. He opened his eyes and gazed at his beer. He had been both looking forward to and dreading the next couple of hours. He had been wasted yesterday, and he was going to get wasted today. This was now officially a relapse. "OK, Truls, I'll get you the money. Tomorrow, all right? Pay me back when you can."

Truls Berntsen continued to blink. His eyes were moist now.

"Why . . . ?" he began.

"Don't get confused," Harry said. "It's not because I like you. It's because I have use for you."

Truls fixed his eyes on Harry as though trying to work out whether he was joking or not.

Harry lifted the beer. "You don't have to sit any longer now, Berntsen."

It was eight in the evening.

Harry's head was drooping. He registered that he was sitting on a chair and had vomit on his suit trousers. Someone had said something. And now the voice was saying something else.

"Harry?"

He raised his head. The room was spinning and the faces around him were blurred. But he still recognized them. Had known them for years. Safe faces. The Aune group.

"Being sober at these meetings isn't a requirement," the voice said, "but speaking clearly is advantageous. Are you able to do that, Harry?"

Harry swallowed. The last few hours came back to him. He had wanted to drink and drink until there was nothing left, no liquor, no pain, no Harry Hole. No voices in his head calling for help that he was unable to give. This clock ticking louder and louder. Could he not drown them in alcohol and let everything go, let time run out? Letting people down, failing. That was all he knew how to do. So why had he taken out his phone, called this number and come here?

No, it wasn't the Aune group sitting in the chairs in the circle he was a part of.

"Hi," he said, in a voice so gravelly it sounded like a train derailing. "My name's Harry, and I'm an alcoholic."

23

FRIDAY

The yellow log

"ROUGH NIGHT?" THE WOMAN ASKED, holding the door open for Harry.

Helene Røed was smaller than he had expected. She was wearing a pair of tight jeans and a black turtleneck. Her blonde hair was held in place by a simple hairband. He concluded she was as pretty as the photographs.

"Is it that obvious?" he said, stepping inside.

"Sunglasses at ten in the morning?" she said, showing him into what he already could make out to be a huge apartment. "And that suit is too nice to look like that," she said over her shoulder.

"Thanks," Harry said.

She laughed, led him into a large room with a living area and an open kitchen with an island.

Daylight flooded in from every side. Concrete, wood, glass, he assumed everything was of the highest quality.

"Coffee?"

"Please."

"I was going to ask what kind, but you look like the sort who'll drink anything."

"Anything," Harry said with a crooked smile.

She pressed a button on the shiny metal espresso machine which began to grind the beans as she rinsed a filter holder under the tap. Harry let his gaze drift over the items attached by magnets to the double-doored fridge. A calendar. Two pictures of horses. A ticket bearing the logo of the National Theater.

"You're going to see *Romeo and Juliet* tomorrow?" he said.

"Yes. It's a fantastic production! I was at the first night with Markus. Not that he's interested in the theater, but he's a sponsor so we get a lot of tickets. I handed out loads of the tickets for that production at the party, I think people simply *must* see it, but I still have two or three lying around. Have you ever seen *Romeo and Juliet*?"

"Yeah, sort of. A film version."

"Then you have to see this."

"I . . ."

"You do! Just a sec."

Helene Røed disappeared, and Harry let his eyes wander over the rest of the fridge door.

Pictures of two children with their parents, taken on holiday it looked like. Harry guessed Helene was the children's aunt. No pictures of Helene herself or Markus, together or on their own. He walked over to the windows which went from floor to ceiling. A view over the whole of Bjørvika and the Oslo Fjord, the Munch Museum being the only obstruction. He heard Helene approaching with brisk steps.

"Apologies for the museum," she said, handing Harry two tickets. "We call it Chernobyl. Not every architect is able to ruin an entire city district with a single building, but Estudio Herreros was, I'll give them that."

"Mm."

"Just go ahead with what you came for, Hole, I'm good at multitasking."

"OK. For the most part, I'd like you to tell me about the party. About

Susanne and Bertine, of course, but in particular the man who brought the cocaine."

"Right," she said. "So you know about him."

"Yes."

"I presume no one is going to jail because of a little coke on the table?"

"No. Anyway, I'm not a policeman."

"That's right. You're Markus's boy."

"I'm not that either."

"Sure, Krohn told me you've been given carte blanche. But you know how it is. The person paying the bills is the person in control at the end of the day." She smiled, with a hint of contempt which Harry wasn't sure was directed at him or at the man paying. Or perhaps at herself.

Helene Røed told him about the party while she made coffee. Harry noted that what she said matched both her husband's and Øystein's accounts. The man with the green cocaine had shown up pretty much out of nowhere and approached her and Markus on the roof terrace. Might have gatecrashed the party, but if so, he wasn't the only one.

"He was wearing a face mask, sunglasses and a baseball cap, so he did look rather sketchy in that gathering. He insisted Markus and I test his powder, but I told him that wasn't going to happen, that Markus and I had promised each other never to touch the stuff again. Then, after just a few minutes, I noticed Markus and a few of the others were missing. I was already a little suspicious, because one of the people who'd popped up at the party was the guy Markus usually buys his blow from. I walked into the apartment. And it was so pathetic . . ."

She closed her eyes and placed her palm on her forehead. "Markus was leaning over the table with a straw already up his nose. Breaking his promise right there in front of me. And then that cocaine nose of his causes him to sneeze and ruin it for him." She opened her eyes and looked at Harry. "I wish I could laugh about it."

"The dealer with the face mask, he tried to gather together enough powder from the floor to make a line for Markus, I understand."

"Yeah. Or maybe he was just trying to tidy up. He even wiped Markus's snot off the table." She nodded towards the large glass table in front of the sofa in the living area. "He probably wanted to make a good impression, have Markus as a regular customer, who doesn't? You may have noticed that Markus isn't exactly the type to haggle. He prefers to overpay than underpay, it gives him a sense of power. Or rather, it gives him power."

"You mean power is important to him?"

"Isn't it important to everyone?"

"Well. Not to me. Granted, that's just self-analysis."

They had sat down at the dining table, across from each other. Helene Røed was looking at Harry in a way that made him think she was assessing the situation. Assessing how much she should say. Assessing *him*.

"Why do you have a metal finger?" she asked, nodding towards his hand.

"Because a man cut off the finger I had. It's a long story."

Her gaze didn't flinch. "You smell of stale alcohol," she said. "And vomit."

"Sorry. I had a rough night and haven't had a chance to change."

She smiled vaguely, as though to herself. "Do you know the difference between a handsome man and an attractive man, Harry?"

"No. What is it?"

"I'm asking because I don't know."

Harry met her eyes. Was she flirting?

She shifted her gaze to the wall behind him. "Do you know what I found attractive about Markus? I mean, apart from his surname and his money."

"No."

"That he seemed attractive to other people as well. Isn't that strange? How that sort of thing is self-reinforcing?"

"I know what you mean."

She shook her head as though in resignation. "Markus has no talents apart from one. He can send out the signal that he's in charge. He's like that boy or girl in school who, without anyone understanding why, takes the lead and decides who is in and who is out. When, like Markus, you're sitting on that social throne, then you have power, and power begets power. And there is nothing, absolutely nothing more attractive than power. You understand, Harry? It isn't calculated opportunism that makes women fall for power, it's biology. Power is sexy, full stop."

"OK," Harry said. She probably wasn't flirting.

"And when, like Markus, you've learned to like that power, then you're terrified of losing it. Markus is good with people, but because he and his family have power, he's probably more feared than liked. And that bothers him. Because it's important for him to be liked. Not by the people who don't matter, he couldn't care less about them, but by those he wants to identify with, those he sees as his equals. He went to BI Norwegian Business School because he wanted to take over the family's real estate business, but there was more partying than studying, and in the end, he had to go abroad to get a degree. People think he's good at his job because money has been accumulated, but if you've been in real estate for the last fifty years, it's been impossible not to make money. Markus was actually one of the few who almost managed to run his company into the ground all the same, but the bank bailed him out at least twice. And money tells the only success story people are capable of hearing. Myself included." She sighed. "He had a regular table at a club where men with money pick up girls who like men with money and do as they're told. It sounds banal, and it is. I knew that Markus had a marriage behind him, but it had been years ago, and that he'd been single since. I figured he hadn't met the right woman. And that was me."

"Was it?"

She shrugged. "I was right for him, I suppose. A bombshell thirty years his junior to be shown off, capable of conversing with people his age without it becoming embarrassing, and keeping things in order at home. The question was probably more if he was the right one for me. It took a long time before I asked myself that question."

"And?"

"And now I live here, and he lives in a man cave in Frogner."

"Mm. Yet the two of you were together on both of the Tuesdays the girls went missing."

"Were we?"

Harry thought he saw something challenging in her eyes. "That's what you told the police."

She smiled briefly. "Yes, then I suppose we were."

"Are you trying to let me know you weren't telling the truth?"

She shook her head with a resigned expression.

"Is it you or Markus that is most in need of an alibi?" Harry asked, and followed her reaction closely.

"Me? You think I could have . . ." The look of astonishment on her face disappeared and her laughter resounded in the room.

"You have a motive."

"No," she said, "I don't have a motive. I've let Markus run around, the only condition I set was that he doesn't embarrass me. Or let them take my money."

"Your money?"

"His, ours, mine, whatever. I don't think those two girls had any plans like that. And they weren't exactly high-maintenance either. Anyway, you'll realize soon enough that I really don't have any motive. My lawyer sent a letter to Krohn this morning stating that I want a divorce, and that I want half of everything. You see? I don't want him, they can take Markus, whoever is so inclined. I just want my riding school." She laughed coldly. "You look surprised, Harry?"

"Mm. A movie producer in Los Angeles told me that your first marriage is the most expensive college. That it's where you learn to ensure there's a prenuptial agreement in your next marriage."

"Oh, Markus has a prenup. Both with me and his ex, he's not stupid. But because of what I know, he'll give me what I ask for."

"And what is it you know?"

She smiled broadly. "That's my leverage, Harry, so I can't tell you that. The chances are I'll sign a non-disclosure agreement. I hope to God someone finds out what he's done, but if they do it'll be without my help. I know that sounds cynical, but right now I need to save myself not the world. Sorry."

Harry was about to say something but thought better of it. She wasn't going to be manipulated or persuaded.

"Why did you agree to this meeting?" he asked instead. "If you knew you weren't going to tell me anything?"

She thrust out her bottom lip, nodded. "Good question. You tell me. That suit of yours will have to go to the dry cleaner's, by the way. I'll give you one of Markus's, you're around the same size."

"Sorry?"

Helene had already gotten to her feet and was walking farther into the apartment. "I've put aside a few suits he's too fat to fit into any more, which I was going to give to the Salvation Army," she called out.

While she was gone, he stood up and went over to the fridge. He saw now that there was a photo of Helene after all; she was holding the bridle of one of the horses. The theater ticket was for the following day. He looked at the calendar. Noticed "horse ride Valdres" written in for next Thursday. Helene returned with a black suit and a garment bag.

"Thank you for the thought but I prefer to buy my own clothes," Harry said.

"The world needs more reusing," she said. "And this is a Brioni Vanquish II, it'd be a crime to throw it away. Come on, do the planet a favor."

Harry looked at her. He hesitated. But something told him to humor her. He took off his jacket and put on the other one.

"Well, you're slimmer than he was, even back then," Helene said, her head cocked to one side. "But you're the same height and your shoulders are just as broad, so it works."

She held out the trousers. Didn't turn around as he changed.

"Perfect," she said, threading the garment bag over the hanger with the other suit. "I thank you on behalf of future generations. If there's nothing else, I have a Zoom meeting now."

Harry nodded as he accepted the garment bag.

Helene walked him out to the hall and held the door open for him. "Actually, I just remembered the one good thing about the Munch Museum," she said. "Which is Edvard Munch. Go take a look at *The Yellow Log*. And have a nice day."

*

Thanh maneuvered herself and the sidewalk sign out the door of Mons Pet Shop. She spread the legs of the sign, placing it to be clearly visible beside the display window, but not so as to obscure anything. She didn't want to test Jonathan's goodwill; after all, the sign was advertising her own business within the store—dog sitting by appointment.

She looked up from the sign and saw her reflection in the display window. She was twenty-three now, but still didn't quite know where she was going. She knew what she *wanted* to be: a vet. But the entry requirements for veterinary studies in Norway were through the roof; you needed better grades than for medical school, and her parents couldn't afford to send her to veterinary school abroad. But she and her mother had looked at courses in Slovakia and Hungary, and they might be feasible if Thanh worked at Mons for a couple of years and looked after dogs before and after work.

"Excuse me, are you the manager?" a voice said from behind her.

She turned. The man was Asian in appearance but was not from Vietnam.

"He's tidying behind the counter," she said, pointing to the door.

She inhaled the autumn air and looked around. Vestkanttorget. The fine old apartment buildings, the trees, the park. This was the place to live. But you had to choose, becoming a vet wouldn't make you rich. And she wanted to be a vet.

She entered the small pet store. Sometimes people—especially children—would express disappointment when they came in and saw the shelves of animal feed, assorted cages, dog leashes and other equipment. "Where are all the animals?"

Then she sometimes took them around to show them what they had. The fish in the aquariums, the cages with hamsters, gerbils and rabbits, and the glass terrariums with insects.

Thanh walked over to the aquariums with the *Ancistrus* fish. They loved vegetables, and she had brought some dinner leftovers of peas and cucumber from home. She heard the man tell the owner he was from the police, that they had found a Hillman Pets bag dated from after it was banned and asking whether this was something he had any knowledge of since Mons had been the import agent and the sole vendor.

She saw the owner just shake his head mutely. Knew that the policeman had his work cut out if he wanted Jonathan to talk. Because her boss was the introverted, quiet sort. When he did speak it was in short sentences, a little bit like the text messages from her ex-boyfriend, all lower case without punctuation or emojis. And he could come across as ill-tempered or annoyed, as though words were unnecessary encumbrances. In her first few months working here she'd wondered if he didn't like her. Perhaps it was because she herself came from a family where everyone spoke all at once. Gradually she'd understood it that wasn't her but him. And that it wasn't because he didn't like her. But might be the opposite.

"I see online that a lot of dog owners think it's a shame about the importation ban, that Hillman Pets is a lot more effective than the other products on the market."

"It is."

"Then it's possible to imagine someone could make a tidy profit by circumventing the ban and selling it under the counter."

"I don't know."

"Really?" She saw the policeman waiting, but nothing more came. "And you yourself haven't . . . ?" the policeman asked tentatively.

Silence.

"Brought any in?" the policeman concluded.

When Jonathan answered, it was in such a low and deep tone of voice that it was more like a vibration in the air. "Are you asking if I've smuggled goods?"

"Have you?"

"No."

"And you don't know anything you think might help me find out who could have managed to get hold of a Hillman Pets bag with a best-before date for next year?"

"No."

"No," the policeman repeated, rocked on his heels and looked around.

Looked around as though he had no intention of giving up, Thanh thought. As though merely pondering his next move.

Jonathan cleared his throat. "I can check in the office if I have a note of who ordered it last. Wait here."

"Thank you."

Jonathan squeezed past Thanh in the narrow aisle between the aquariums and the rabbit hutches. She could see something in his eyes she hadn't seen before, unease, yes, anxiety. And he smelled of sweat more than usual. He went into the office, but the door was left ajar, and from where she was standing, she could see him lay a blanket over the glass cage he had in there. She knew exactly what was in the glass cage. The one and only time she had brought some children into the office and shown it to them, he had been furious and told her customers had no business being in the office, but she knew that wasn't the reason. It was the animal. He didn't want anyone to see it. Jonathan was a decent enough boss. She was allowed time off when she needed, and he had even given her a raise without her having asked. But to work so closely with another person—there was only the two of them—and still not know anything about that person was strange. Sometimes it seemed he liked her a little too much, and other times not at all. He was older than her, but not by so much; she figured he was around thirty, so they ought to have things in common to talk about. Yet any efforts she made to get a conversation going elicited only terse replies. But occasionally he would gaze at her when he thought she wouldn't notice. Was he interested in her? Was that sullen manner of his bad temper, shyness, or an attempt to conceal what he felt for her? Maybe she was just imagining it, a flight of fancy you come up when you're bored, when the days drag out and the alternatives are few. Sometimes she thought his behavior was like the boys back in primary school, throwing snowballs at the girls they liked. Only that he was an adult. It was weird. *He* was weird. But there wasn't much she could do about it, apart from take him for what he was; after all, she needed the job.

Jonathan was walking back towards her. She moved aside, standing as close to the aquarium as she could, and still his body brushed against hers.

"Sorry, I don't have anything," Jonathan said. "It's too long ago."

"Right," the policeman said. "What was it you covered in the office?"

"What?"

"I think you heard what I said. May I take a look?"

Jonathan had a slender, white neck with black stubble which Thanh found herself sometimes wishing he shaved a little closer. And now she could see his Adam's apple rise and fall in his throat. She felt almost sorry for him.

"Sure," Jonathan said. "You can look at what you like in here." Again, he used that low, deep voice. "All you have to do is show me a search warrant."

The policeman took a step back and tilted his head slightly to the side, as though taking a closer look at Jonathan. Reassessing him, as it were.

"Then I'll make a mental note of it," the policeman said. "Thank you for your help thus far."

He turned and walked towards the door. Thanh gave him a smile but got nothing in return.

Jonathan opened the box of fish feed and began hanging the bags up behind the counter. She made her way to the bathroom, located beyond the office, and when she was coming out, Jonathan was standing waiting just outside.

He was holding something in his hand and slipped in behind her without shutting the door.

Her eyes fell automatically on the glass cage. The blanket had been removed and the cage was empty.

She heard Jonathan pull the chain above the old toilet and the water flush.

She turned around and saw him standing at the little sink soaping his hands thoroughly. Then he turned on the hot-water tap. He rubbed his hands together under the jet of water, which was so hot steam rose to his face. She knew why. The parasites.

Thanh swallowed. She loved animals, all animals. Even those—yes, maybe especially those—other people thought were hideous. Many people found slugs disgusting, but she remembered the disbelieving, excited children's faces when she had shown them the big bright pink slug and tried to convince them that no, it hadn't been painted, it was as nature made it.

Perhaps that was the reason a sudden wave of hate swept through her. Hate for this man who did not love animals. She thought about the sweet wild fox cub someone had brought in, which he had taken payment for, hadn't he? She had nursed and fussed over it, loved the lonely, abandoned pup. Even given it a name. Nhi, meaning small. But then one day when she came to work, he wasn't in his cage. Or anywhere to be seen. And when she asked Jonathan, he had only answered in that gruff way of his: "Gone." And she hadn't asked any more, because she didn't want confirmation of what she had already understood.

Jonathan turned off the tap, came out and looked with a little surprise at Thanh who was standing in the middle of the office with her arms folded.

"Gone?" she asked.

"Gone," he said, sitting down at the desk, which was always cluttered with piles of papers they never got through.

"Drowned?" she asked.

He looked at her as if she had finally asked a question that interested him.

"Possibly. Some slugs have gills, but Mount Kaputar slugs have lungs. On the other hand, I know some slugs with lungs can survive under water for up to twenty-four hours before they drown. You're hoping it survives?"

"Of course. Aren't you?"

Jonathan shrugged. "I think the best thing for something that's separated from its species and ends up in a strange environment is death."

"Really?"

"Loneliness is worse than death, Thanh."

He stared at her with something in his eyes she couldn't interpret.

"On the other hand," he said, scratching at his bearded throat thoughtfully, "this particular slug might not be lonely, it's actually a hermaphrodite. And it will find nourishment in the sewers. Reproduce . . ." He looked down at his newly scrubbed hands. "Poison everything else living down there with rat lungworm and eventually take over the whole of Oslo's sewer system."

Thanh could hear Jonathan's laughter from the office as she walked back to the aquariums. It was a laugh she had heard so seldom that it sounded unfamiliar, strange, yes, almost unpleasant.

Harry stood looking at the painting in front of him. It showed a felled log lying with the yellow end towards him and the rest of it stretching back into a wooded landscape. He read the plaque next to the painting: *"The Yellow Log," Edvard Munch, 1912.*

"Why were you asking about this painting in particular?" asked the boy in the red T-shirt, which denoted him as one of the staff.

"Well," Harry said, glancing at the Japanese couple standing next to them, "why do people want to see this painting in particular?"

"Because of the optical illusion," the boy said.

"OK?"

"Let's move a little. Excuse me!"

The couple smilingly made room for them both by stepping to the side.

"See?" the boy said. "The end of the log appears to be pointing directly at us no matter where we view the picture from."

"Mm. So the message is . . . ?"

"You tell me," the boy said. "Perhaps that things aren't always how they look."

"Yes," Harry said. "Or that you need to move and look at things from a different angle in order to see the whole picture. Anyway, thank you."

"You're welcome," the boy said, and walked away.

Harry remained looking at the picture. Mostly to rest his eyes on something beautiful after riding escalators through a building that even on the inside made Police HQ appear human and warm.

He took out his phone and called Krohn.

While waiting for him to pick up, he grew aware of the pulse in his temple throbbing, as was normal the day after he had been drinking. And it occurred to him that his resting heart rate was around 60. That if he remained standing here looking at art, he could, in other words, expect his heart to beat slightly under four hundred thousand times before Lucille was killed. Considerably fewer if he panicked and raised the alarm in the hope the police could find her . . . where? In Mexico someplace?

"Krohn."

"Harry here. I need an advance of three hundred thousand."

"For what?"

"Unforeseen expenses."

"Can you be more specific?"

"No."

The line went quiet.

"All right. Come by the office."

As Harry put the phone back in the pocket of the jacket, he noticed something was already in there. He took it out. It was a mask. A half-mask depicting a cat, it looked like, which must have been from a masquerade ball Markus Røed had attended. He felt in the other pocket, and sure enough, there was something in there too. He pulled out a laminated card. It seemed to be a membership card for something called Villa Dante, but instead of *Name* it read *Alias*. The alias on the card was "Catman."

Harry looked at the picture again.

See things from another angle.

I hope to God someone finds out what he's done.

Helene Røed hadn't forgotten to empty the contents of the pockets. She may even have put the items there.

24

FRIDAY

Cannibal

"I CAN ONLY ISSUE YOU with a warrant if there is probable cause for suspicion."

"I know that," Sung-min said, quietly cursing section 192 of the Criminal Procedure Act, as he held the phone to his ear and stared at the wall of the windowless office. How had Hole endured working in here all those years? "But I think there's more than a fifty per cent chance of us finding something illegal there. He was sweating, wouldn't look me in the eye, and then he put a blanket over something he most definitely wanted hidden in the office."

"I understand, but your suspicion alone is not enough. The section states there must be concrete evidence."

"But—"

"You also know that as a prosecutor I can only grant you a search warrant if there is a danger in delaying. Is there? And will you be able to explain why it was urgent afterwards?"

Sung-min sighed heavily. "No."

"Any evidence of other offenses which could be used as a pretext?"

"None."

"Does the person concerned have previous convictions?"

"No."

"Have you anything at all?"

"Listen. The word 'smuggling' appears both in connection with the party at Røed's and at the crime scene where I found that bag. You know me and you know I don't believe in coincidences. I have a strong feeling in my gut here. Do you want the request in writing?"

"I'll save you the work and tell you no here and now. But you called first, so you were probably aware what the outcome would be? This isn't like you. You say you've got nothing at all? Just a gut feeling?"

"Gut feeling."

"When did you start getting those?"

"I'm trying to learn."

"Imitate us ordinary mortals, you mean?"

"Autism and autistic traits are two different things, Chris."

The police lawyer laughed. "Fine. Are you coming over to eat tomorrow?"

"I've bought a bottle of Château Cantemerle 2009."

"Your taste is too elevated and your habits too exclusive for me, darling."

"But you can also learn, dear."

They hung up. Sung-min noticed he had received a text message from Katrine with a link to *Dagbladet*. He tapped on the link and leaned back in the chair while he waited for it to download. The walls of the office were so thick they affected the coverage. And why hadn't Hole replaced this broken chair? His back was already sore.

Cannibal.

According to a source, there is clear evidence that the killer has consumed the brains and eyes of his victims, Susanne Andersen and Bertine Bertilsen.

Sung-min felt the need to swear and thought it a shame he wasn't in the habit of it. That he should consider starting.

Satan's cunt!

Mona Daa was on the treadmill.

She hated running on the treadmill.

And right now that was the very reason she was running on the treadmill. She could feel the sweat dripping down her back and see her reddened cheeks in the gym's mirrored wall. Carcass was coming through the earphones, from a playlist Anders had compiled, and according to him it was from their early period when they played grindcore, not that melodious shit that came later. It just sounded like raging noise to her and, at the moment, that was exactly what she needed. Her feet pounded upon the rubber belt rotating beneath, which kept coming and coming, the same shit over and over.

Våge had done it again. A cannibal. Jesus Christ! Jesus fucking Christ!

She saw someone approaching from behind.

"Hello, Daa."

It was Magnus Skarre. The detective from Crime Squad.

Mona switched off the machine and pulled out her earphones.

"How might I help the police?"

"Help?" Skarre threw out his arms. "Can't I just be popping in?"

"Never seen you in here before, and you're not wearing gym gear. Was there something you wanted to know or something you wanted to plant?"

"Hey, hey, take it easy." Skarre laughed. "I just thought I'd update you. Always pays to have a good relationship with the press, right? Give and take and all that."

Mona remained standing up on the treadmill, she liked the height difference. "In that case, I'd like to know what you want to take before you give, Skarre."

"Nothing, this time. But we might have use for something further down the line."

"Thanks, but in that case the the answer's no. Anything else?"

Skarre looked like a little boy who'd had his toy gun taken away. Mona realized she was playing a high-stakes game. Or rather: that she was so angry she wasn't thinking clearly.

"Sorry," she said. "Bad day. What is it?"

"Harry Hole," he said. "He called up a witness, gave a false name and claimed to work for the Oslo Police."

"Oh." She changed her mind and stepped down from the treadmill. "How do you know?"

"I took the witness's statement. It was the guy with the dog that caught the scent of Bertine's corpse. He said that prior to our visit, someone had called to check a tip, an officer Hans Hansen. Only thing is we don't have anyone by that name. So, I got the number the farmer still had on his phone and checked. And you know what, I didn't even have to contact the phone company, it was Harry Hole's number. Talk about being caught with your pants down, eh?" Skarre grinned.

"And I can quote you on that?"

"No, are you crazy?" He laughed again. "I'm a 'reliable source', isn't that what you call it?"

Yes, Mona thought. Except you're neither reliable nor a source. Mona was aware that Skarre didn't harbor warm feelings for Harry Hole. According to Anders the reason for this wasn't particularly complicated. Skarre had always worked in Hole's shadow, and Hole had never tried to conceal the fact he thought Skarre was a jerk. But it seemed like a long way from there to a personal vendetta like this.

Skarre shifted his weight, cast a glance towards the girls in the spin class in the room next door. "But if you want confirmation on what you've dug up, you could contact the Chief Superintendent."

"Bodil Melling?"

"Precisely. I'm guessing she'd give you a comment too."

Mona Daa nodded. This was good. Good and dirty. But whatever, she finally had something Våge didn't have, and she couldn't afford to be fussy. Not now.

Skarre was grinning. Like a customer in a whorehouse, Mona thought. And tried to block out what that made her.

25

FRIDAY

Cocaine blues

THE AUNE GROUP HAD GATHERED, but Aune himself had given word that his family were coming at three, so everyone needed to be gone by then. Harry had been filling them in on his visit to Helene Røed.

"So now you're walking around in your boss's suit," Øystein said. "And your mate's sunglasses."

"Plus, I have this," Harry said, holding up the cat mask. "And you still can't find anything about Villa Dante online?"

Truls stared at his phone, grunted and shook his head. With the same minimal expression as when he had accepted the brown envelope of cash Harry had handed discreetly to him when he arrived.

"What I'm wondering, is where Våge has gotten this cannibalism stuff from," Aune said.

Harry saw Truls look up, meet his eyes and give him an imperceptible shake of his head.

"Was wondering that myself," Øystein said. "Doesn't say jackshit about eating human flesh in the reports."

"I have a feeling Våge has lost his source," Harry said. "And has begun making things up. Like that business about Bertine having had her tattoo cut off and sewn back on—that wasn't true."

"Maybe," Aune said. "Våge did resort to fabrications previously in his career, and it is strange how consistent we humans are. Even though we're punished for a pattern of behavior and should learn, we still tend to employ the same poor solutions when problems arise. It's not unlikely that Våge has found the attention he's received of late so intoxicating that he's unwilling to let go of it and is resorting to something that has worked in the past. Or worked for a while, at least. Although I'm not discounting the possibility Våge may be right about the cannibalism. But given the circumstances, it's obvious he's making things up and has been familiarizing himself with the literature on serial killers."

"Isn't he implying . . ." Øystein began, as his eyes scanned down through Våge's article on the screen of his phone again.

The others looked at him.

"Isn't he actually implying that the killer himself is the source?"

"That's a bold but interesting interpretation," Aune said. "But our work for the day is done and the weekend awaits, gentlemen. My wife and daughter will be here soon."

"What will we do over the weekend, boss?" Øystein asked.

"I don't have any particular work for you," Harry said. "But I've borrowed Truls's laptop and I'm going to go through police reports."

"Thought you'd already read them."

"Skimmed them. Now I'm going to study them. Come on, let's go."

Aune asked Harry to wait and he remained standing by the bed while the others went out.

"Those reports," he said. "They're the work of how many people? Forty, fifty? Who have all been on the case for over three weeks. How many pages? A thousand? Are you going to read all those pages because you think the solution is to be found in there?"

Harry shrugged. "It's got to be found somewhere."

"The mind also needs rest, Harry. I've noticed from the get-go that you're more stressed. You seem . . . can I use the word desperate?"

"Apparently."

"Is there something you're not saying?"

Harry lowered his head and rubbed his hand back and forth across the nape of his neck. "Yeah."

"You want to tell me what it is?"

"Yeah." He lifted his head straight. "But I can't."

Aune and Harry held each other's gaze. Then Aune closed his eyes and nodded.

"Thanks," Harry said. "We'll talk on Monday."

Aune moistened his lips, and Harry could tell by the tired cheeriness in his eyes that he was about to formulate a witty response. But that he changed his mind and merely nodded.

Harry was on the way out of the Radium Hospital when he realized what Aune had considered replying. *If I'm alive on Monday.*

Øystein drove in the bus lane towards the city center with Harry in the passenger seat.

"Pretty cool in rush-hour traffic on a Friday, eh?" Øystein grinned in the mirror.

Truls grunted from the back seat.

Harry's phone rang. It was Katrine.

"Yeah?"

"Hi, Harry, just a long shot here. Arne and I have a date tonight at that restaurant that he finally managed to get a table at. But my mother-in-law is sick and . . ."

"Babysitting?"

"Just say the word if it's inconvenient, then I can drop going out, I am a little tired. But at least then I can tell him I tried to get someone."

"But I can. And I want to. When?"

"Fuck you, Harry. Seven o'clock."

"OK. Make sure there's a Grandiosa frozen pizza in the oven."

Harry hung up, but the phone rang immediately afterwards.

"Doesn't have to be a Grandiosa," Harry said.

"It's Mona Daa from *VG*."

"Oops . . ."

Harry understood by the full presentation that it wasn't Mona, Anders' girlfriend, calling, but the journalist. Which meant everything he said could and would be used against him.

"We're working on a piece about . . ." she began. This was the introduction used to signal that the wheels were already in motion, could not be stopped, and the plural first-person pronoun slightly diminished the responsibility this single journalist had for the unpleasant questions she was about to ask. Harry looked out at the traffic, grasped that it was about Weng, and about Harry posing as a policeman. That they would be quoting Chief Superintendent Bodil Melling when she said there was up to a six-month sentence for impersonating an officer of the law, and that she hoped the Minister of Justice in the wake of this case could put a stop to dubious and unauthorized private investigations and how, furthermore, it was of the utmost importance that this be done with immediate effect in regard to this murder inquiry.

Mona was calling to offer him the opportunity to respond, in line with the code of press ethics. Mona Daa was pushy and tough but had always been fair in that regard.

"No comment," Harry said.

"No? Does that mean you don't dispute the facts of the story as presented?"

"I'm pretty sure it means that I'm not commenting on it, doesn't it?"

"All right, Harry, but then we need to print 'no comment'." He heard the tap of rapid keystrokes in the background.

"Do you all still say *print*?"

"It's the kind of thing that lingers."

"True. Which is why I call what I'm about to do *hanging up*. OK?"

He heard Mona Daa sigh. "OK. Have a nice weekend, Harry."

"Likewise. And—"

"Yes, I'll say hi to Anders."

Harry put the phone in the inside pocket of Røed's slightly too baggy suit jacket.

"Trouble?"

"Yeah," Harry said.

A new grunt from the back seat, louder and angrier this time.

Harry half turned, saw the light of the phone display and realized Mona had been sitting with her finger on the publish trigger. "What did they write?"

"That you're deceitful."

"Fair enough, it is true after all, and I don't have a reputation to protect." Harry shook his head. "What's worse is that they'll close us down."

"No," Truls said.

"No?"

"What's worse is that they'll arrest you."

Harry raised an eyebrow. "For helping them locate a body they'd been trying to find for over three weeks?"

"It's not about that," Truls said. "You don't know Melling. Battleaxe wants to get ahead. And you're in the way, aren't you?"

"Me?"

"If we solve this case first it'll make her look like an amateur, won't it?"

"Mm. OK. But arresting me sounds a bit drastic."

"That's the way they play their power games, that's why those scheming bastards are where they are. That's how you become . . . well, Minister of Justice, for example,"

Harry glanced once more at Truls. His forehead was as red as the traffic light they had stopped for.

"I'm getting out here," Harry said. "Get some rest over the weekend, but don't switch off your phones, and don't leave town."

At seven o'clock, Katrine opened the front door for Harry.

"Yes, I've read *VG*," she said, walking back to the dresser in the hallway to put on a pair of earrings.

"Mm. How do you think Melling would like it if she found out the enemy was babysitting for the lead detective?"

"Oh, you probably won't be much of a threat any more come Monday."

"You seem awfully sure of that?"

"Melling hasn't given the Minister of Justice much of a choice with her comments about dubious private investigations."

"No, maybe not."

"Shame, we could've used you. Everybody knew you'd cut some corners, but screwing up over something so unnecessary."

"Got overeager and made a bad judgment call."

"It's like you're so predictably unpredictable. What have you got there?" She pointed at the plastic bag he had placed on top of the shoes he had removed.

"Laptop. I need to do a bit of work after he falls asleep. Is he . . . ?"

"Yeah."

Harry went into the living room.

"Mama smell na-ice," said Gert, sitting on the floor with two cuddly toys.

"Perfume," Harry said.

Na-ice," said Gert.

"Look what I've got." Harry carefully took a chocolate bar out of his pocket.

"Shoco-ha."

"Sugar high?" Harry smiled. "We'll keep it a secret then."

"Mama! Uncle Hawny has shoco-ha!"

After Katrine had gone, Harry entered a virtual world where he did his best to keep pace with a three-year-old's imaginative transitions in thought and contribute with some of his own in between.

"You aw good at pwaying," Gert commended him. "Whew is de dwagon?"

"In the cave, of course," Harry said, pointing underneath the sofa.

"Uhhoo," Gert said.

"Double-uhhoo," Harry said.

"Shoco-ha?"

"OK," Harry said, and put his hand in the pocket of the jacket he had draped over the chair.

"What is dat?" Gert asked, pointing at the mask Harry was holding.

"A cat," Harry said, placing the half-mask over his face.

Gert's face contorted and his voice was suddenly tear-choked.

"No, Uncle Hawny! Scawey!"

Harry quickly removed the mask. "OK, no cat. Just dragons. All right?"

But the tears had already begun to flow, and Gert sobbed. Harry cursed himself, another bad judgment call. Scary cats. No Mama. A little past bedtime. What *wasn't* there to cry about?

Gert stretched his arms out towards Harry, and before he'd had time to think had pulled the boy close. Patting him on the head while he felt Gert's chin against his shoulder and his warm tears through his shirt.

"A little shoco-ha, brush our teeth and a lullaby?"

"Yeah-eh!" Gert sobbed.

Following a toothbrushing session Harry suspected Katrine would not have given her full approval, he got Gert into his pyjamas and under the duvet.

"Bueman," Gert commanded.

"I don't know it," Harry said. His phone vibrated and he saw he'd received an MMS from Alexandra.

Gert regarded him with ill-concealed disapproval.

"But I know some other good songs."

"Sing," Gert said.

Harry understood it would have to be something slow and swaying and tried the Rolling Stones's "Wild Horses." He was stopped after one verse.

"A diffwant song."

Hank Williams's "Your Cheatin' Heart" got the thumbs down after two verses.

Harry thought for a long time.

"OK. Close your eyes."

He began to sing. If it could be called singing. It was more a low, slow chanting in a rough voice that now and then hit the notes of an old blues song about the perils of cocaine. When he had finished, Gert's breathing had become deeper and more regular.

Harry opened the MMS, which was accompanied by some text. The picture had been taken in the hall mirror in her apartment. Alexandra was posing in a creamy-yellow dress which managed the feat expensive clothes often did; display the body in such a good light that you don't for a moment think it has anything to do with the dress. At the same time he could see that Alexandra hadn't needed the dress. And that she knew it.

This cost half a month's salary. Looking forward to tomorrow!

Harry closed the message and looked up. Into Gert's wide-open eyes.

"Mow."

"More . . . of the last one?"

"Yeah-eh."

26

FRIDAY

Cement

IT WAS NINE O'CLOCK WHEN Mikael Bellman unlocked the door to his house in Høyenhall. It was a nice house; he had built it on the edge of a hill so that he, Ulla and their three children had a view over the city all the way to Bjørvika and the fjord.

"Hi!" Ulla called from the living room. Mikael hung up his new coat and walked into the living room where his petite, beautiful wife, his sweetheart since childhood, was sitting with their youngest boy watching TV.

"Sorry, that meeting dragged on." He hadn't heard any suspicion in her voice, neither was there any in her eyes, as far as he could see. Nor was there any reason to be; right now Ulla was actually the only woman in his life. If you disregarded that young TV2 reporter, but that was something he had more or less discontinued. He wasn't ruling out future indiscretions, but if so they needed to be something he was guaranteed to get away with. A married woman with power. Someone with as much to lose

231

as himself. They say power corrupts, but it had only made him more cautious.

"Truls is here."

"What?"

"He came by to talk to you. He's out on the terrace."

Mikael closed his eyes and sighed. As he had risen through the ranks, from head of Orgkrim to Chief of Police and on to Minister of Justice, he had gradually ensured there was more and more distance between him and his friend and former co-conspirator. He was, again, more cautious.

Mikael went out to the large terrace and closed the sliding door behind him.

"Quite a view you've got from here," Truls said. His face was red in the light from the heat lamps. He raised a bottle of beer to his mouth.

Mikael sat down next to him and accepted the bottle Truls opened and handed to him.

"How's the investigation going?"

"The one into me?" Truls asked. "Or the one I'm on?"

"You're working on an investigation?"

"You didn't know? Good, means we don't have a leak at least. I'm working with Harry Hole."

Mikael let it sink in. "You are aware that if it comes out you're taking advantage of your position as a police officer to assist—"

"Yeah, yeah. But that's not going to matter much if someone does close us down. Which would be a shame, by the way. Hole is good. You know the chances of this nutcase getting caught are greater if Hole is allowed continue." Truls stamped his shoes on the concrete floor of the terrace.

Mikael didn't know if his friend's feet were cold or if it was an unintentional reminder of their shared past and shared secrets.

"Did Hole send you?"

"No, he has no idea I'm here."

Mikael nodded. It was unusual for Truls to take the initiative himself; Mikael had always been the one who decided what they would do, but he could hear by Truls's voice he was telling the truth.

"This is about something bigger than apprehending one individual criminal, Truls. This has to do with politics. With the big picture. Principles, you know?"

"People like me don't get politics," Truls said, belching discreetly. "Don't get why the Minister of Justice would rather let a bloody serial killer run free than allow Norway's best-known detective to get away with lying about being Officer Hans fucking Hansen. Especially when it was that very lie that led to Bertine Bertilsen being found."

Mikael took a sip of the bottle. He may have liked beer at one time, but he didn't any longer, not really. But those in the Labour Party and the Labour movement were generally skeptical of people who didn't drink beer.

"Do you know how you become Minister of Justice and retain that position, Truls?" Mikael continued without waiting for an answer. "You listen. You listen to those you know are looking out for your best interests. Listen to those who have the experience you do not. I have good people who will present this in the right way. They'll make it look like the Minister of Justice's office stopped a millionaire from forming his own private army of investigators and lawyers. It will show that we don't allow American-style conditions where the wealthy enjoy all manner of privileges, where only the most expensive lawyers win, where the claim that everyone is equal before the law is just some patriotic tripe. Here, in Norway, we don't have equality just on paper, and that's something we're going to keep working for." Mikael made a mental note of a couple of the points, perhaps they could be used in a future speech, albeit in a more sublime form.

Truls laughed that grunted laugh that always put Mikael in mind of a pig.

"What?" Mikael could hear he sounded more annoyed than he had intended. It had been a long day. Serial killers and Harry Hole might get column inches, but they weren't the only things a Minister of Justice had on his plate.

"I'm just thinking how great it is we have that whole equality before the law," Truls said. "Imagine, in this country even a Minister of Justice couldn't prevent the police from investigating him if they were to get a tip-off. And it might come out that there was a body encased in the concrete on his terrace. Not anyone society really missed, just a member of a biker gang who smuggled heroin and was connected to two dirty cops. Equality before the law would mean the investigation would reveal that the Minister of Justice was once a young policeman more concerned with money than power. That he had a slightly naive childhood friend who one night helped him cover up the evidence in the much smarter friend's new house." Truls stamped his foot on the cement again.

"Truls," Mikael said slowly. "Are you threatening me?"

"Not at all," Truls said, putting the empty beer bottle down next to the chair and getting to his feet. "I just think what you said about listening sounded like a good idea. Listening to those who have your best interests at heart. Thanks for the beer."

Katrine stood in the doorway of the nursery looking at them.

Gert asleep in his bed and Harry asleep on a chair with his forehead against the headboard. She squatted down so she could see Harry's face too. And concluded that the resemblance was even more pronounced when they slept. She shook Harry gently. He smacked his lips, blinked and looked at his watch before getting to his feet and following her out into the kitchen, where she put the kettle on.

"You're home early," he said, sitting down at the kitchen table. "Weren't you having a good time?"

"Yeah. He'd picked the restaurant because it had a Montrachet wine which, apparently, I'd said I liked the first time we went on a date. But a meal can only last so long."

"But you could have gone on someplace else. Had a drink."

"Or gone back to his place for a quickie," she said.

"Yeah?"

She shrugged. "He is sweet. He still hasn't invited me back to his home. He wants to wait with the sex until we know for sure that the two of us are meant for one another."

"But you . . ."

"Want to fuck as much as possible before we realize we're *not* meant for one another."

Harry laughed.

"At first I thought he was playing hard to get." She sighed. "And that does work on me."

"Mm. Even when you know it's a tactic?"

"Sure. I'm turned on by anything I can't have. Like you that time."

"I was married. Do all married man turn you on?"

"Only the ones I can't have. There aren't many of those. You were annoyingly faithful."

"Could have been even more faithful."

She made instant coffee for Harry and tea for herself. "I seduced you when you were drunk and in despair. You were at your weakest, and that's something I'll never forgive myself for."

"No!"

It had come so quickly and sharply it gave her a start and the tea sloshed and spilled.

"No?"

"No," he said. "I won't let you take that guilt away from me. It's—" he took a sip, grimacing as though he had scalded himself—"all I have left."

"All *you* have?" She felt tears and anger well up at the same time. "Bjørn didn't take his life because you let him down, Harry, but because I did." She had been almost shouting, and stopped, listening for sounds from the nursery. Lowered her voice. "He and I lived together, he thought he was the happy father of our child. Yes, he knew how I felt about you. It wasn't something we spoke about, but he knew. He also knew—or thought he knew—that he could trust me. Thanks for the offer of division of guilt, Harry, but this is mine alone. All right?"

Harry stared down into his cup. He obviously wasn't planning on having this argument. Good. At the same time something wasn't right. *Guilt is all I have left.* Was there something she had misunderstood here? Or something he wasn't saying?

"Isn't it tragic?" he said. "That love is what kills those we care about."

She nodded slowly. "Shakespearean," she said, studying his face. *Those we care about.* Why the plural form?

"Listen, I better go back to the hotel and get some work done," he said, the chair leg scraping the floor. "Thanks for letting me . . ." He nodded in the direction of the nursery.

"Thank you," she said quietly, pensively.

Prim lay underneath the duvet staring at the ceiling.

It was close to midnight, and on the police scanner the messages went back and forth in a regular, reassuring buzz. All the same, he couldn't sleep. Partly because he was dreading tomorrow, but mostly because he was wound up. He had been together with Her. And he was almost certain now. She loved him too. They had talked about music. She was interested in that. And also in his writing, she had said. But they had avoided talking about the two dead girls. That was a topic the others around them had probably been discussing. But not with the insight the two of them could have brought to bear on it, of course, if they only knew! If *she* only knew that he knew more than her. At one point he had actually been tempted to tell her everything, tempted in the same way as when you feel that pull to launch yourself into the abyss when standing by the railing on a bridge. Like, for instance, the bridge from the mainland over to Nesøya at three in the morning on a Saturday in May when you had just realized the one you thought was Her did not want you. But that was a long time ago, he had gotten over that, had moved on. Further than her; last he checked everything she had been involved in had hit a wall, her marriage included. Perhaps she would read about him soon, about all those who lauded him, and then maybe she would think that he, he could have been mine. Yes, then she'd be sorry.

But there were things that needed doing before that.

Like what needed to be done tomorrow.

She would be the third.

No, he wasn't looking forward to it. Only an insane person would. But it needed to be done; he needed to overcome the doubt, the moral resistance any normal individual had to feel when faced with such a task. Speaking of feelings, he needed to keep in mind that revenge was not the objective. Losing sight of that could risk his being sidetracked and lead to failure. Revenge was merely the reward he would grant himself, a by-product of the real purpose. And when it was completed, they would kiss his feet. Finally.

27

SATURDAY

"SO, THE POLICE WORK AT weekends too," Weng said, studying the empty bag.

"Some of us," Sung-min said, crouching by the basket in the corner, scratching the bulldog behind one ear.

"*Hillman Pets*," the farmer read aloud. "No, can't say it's something I give my dog."

"All right." Sung-min sighed, rising to his feet. "I just had to check."

Chris had suggested they take a walk around Sognsvann today and was peeved when Sung-min had said he needed to work. Because Chris knew that it wasn't true, he didn't *need* to work. Sometimes that sort of thing was hard to explain to other people. Weng handed the bag back to Sung-min.

"But I have seen that bag before," Weng said.

"You have?" Sung-min said in surprise.

"Yes. A few weeks ago. There was a guy sitting on a fallen tree trunk in the woods at the end of the field there." He pointed towards the kitchen window. "He was holding a bag like that." Sung-min peered out. It had to be at least a hundred yards to the edge of the woods.

"I was using these," said Weng, clearly noticing Sung-min's skepticism, and picked up a pair of Zeiss binoculars which had been lying on a stack of car magazines on the kitchen table.

"Magnifies twenty times. Like standing right next to the guy. I remember it now because of the Airedale terrier on the bag, but at the time I didn't think it was an anti-parasitic. I mean, the guy was eating it."

"He was *eating* it? Are you sure?"

"Oh yeah. What was left, obviously, because he crumpled up the bag and threw it on the ground afterwards. Bastard. I went out to give him a piece of my mind, but he got up and made off the moment I went outside. I walked over to the spot but there was a brisk north wind that day, so it must have already been blown into the woods."

Sung-min could feel his pulse beating faster. This was the sort of police work that paid off one out of a hundred times, but when it did it could mean hitting the jackpot, solving an entire case where hitherto they hadn't had a single lead. He swallowed.

"Does that mean, Weng, that you can give me a description of the man?"

The farmer looked at Sung-min. Then smiled sadly and shook his head.

"But you said it was like standing right next to him." Sung-min could hear the frustration in his own voice.

"Ye-es. But the bag was directly in my line of sight, and when he threw it away, he put on a face mask before I had a chance to take a good look at him."

"He wore a face mask?"

"Yeah. And sunglasses and a baseball cap. Didn't really see much of his face at all."

"You didn't think it strange that a man alone in the forest was wearing a face mask long after everyone else has stopped?"

"Yes. But there are a lot of strange people out here in the forest, aren't there?"

Sung-mi understood that Weng was being self-deprecating, but he wasn't in the mood to smile.

*

Harry stood in front of the headstone and could feel the rainwater in the soft ground seep into his shoes. Gray morning light filtered through the clouds. He had stayed up until five o'clock reading reports. Slept for three hours, then continued reading. And understood now why the investigation had come to a standstill. The work that had been done seemed good, seemed thorough, but there was nothing there. Absolutely nothing. He had come out here to clear his head. He wasn't even a third of the way through the reports.

Her name was carved in white on the gray stone. Rakel Fauke. He didn't quite know why, but right now he was glad she hadn't taken his surname as well.

He looked around. There were some people by other graves, probably more than usual since it was a Saturday, but they were so far away that he presumed he could speak out loud without them hearing him. He told her he had spoken to Oleg on the phone. That he was well, liked it there up north, but was considering applying for a position at Police HQ.

"PST," Harry said. "He wants to follow in his mom's footsteps."

Harry told her he had called Sis. She'd had some health problems but was better now and back at work at the supermarket. Wanted him to come visit her and her boyfriend in Kristiansand.

"I said I'd see if I could make it down before . . . before it's too late. I'm having a bit of bother with some Mexicans. They're going to kill me and a woman who looks like my mother unless I, or the police, solve this murder case within the next three days." Harry chuckled. "I've got a fungal nail infection, otherwise I'm doing fine. So there you go, all is well with your people. That was always what was most important to you. You yourself were less important. You wouldn't even have wanted to be avenged if it'd been up to you. But it wasn't. And I wanted revenge. That no doubt makes me a worse human being than you, but I'd be that even without the fucking thirst for revenge. It's like sexual desire. Even though you're disappointed every time you exact revenge, even though you *know* you're going to be disappointed the next time as well, you just need to go on. And when I feel it, feel that fucking urge, I think now I'm standing in the shoes of a serial killer. Because that feeling of avenging something that's been taken from me is so good that sometimes I want to lose something, something I love. Just so I can take my revenge. You understand?"

Harry felt a lump in his throat. Of course she understood. That was what he missed the most. His woman, Rakel, who understood and accepted most things about her weird husband. Not everything. But a lot. A hell of a lot.

"The problem," Harry said, clearing his throat, "is of course that after you I have nothing left to lose. There's nothing more to avenge, Rakel."

Harry stood motionless. Looked down at his shoes, sunken down in the grass, the leather growing darker where the water had soaked in. He raised his eyes. Up by the church, on the steps, he saw a figure, just standing there watching. There was something familiar about the figure, and he realized it was a priest. He seemed to be looking in Harry's direction.

The phone rang. It was Johan Krohn.

"Talk to me," Harry said.

"I've just been on another call. And not with just anyone. The Minister of Justice himself."

"It is a small country so don't tell me you were *that* starstruck. Well, we're finished then?"

"That's what I thought he was ringing to tell me, after that article in *VG*. But naturally I was surprised over Bellman delivering the message personally. This sort of thing is usually communicated via formal channels. That is to say, the people I expected to get in touch—"

"Not that I'm unduly busy here on a Saturday morning, Krohn, but can we fast-forward to what Bellman said?"

"Right. He said he couldn't see that the Department of Justice had any legal argument for closing down our investigation, and they would not therefore be taking any action regarding this case. However, in light of the transgression that appears to have occurred, they would be watching us closely and the next time something of a similar nature took place, the police *would* take action."

"Mm."

"Yes, that's not overstating it. Very surprising—I was certain they'd put a stop to us. Politically, it's almost incomprehensible, Bellman will now have his own people and the media to deal with. Do you have any explanation for it?"

Harry pondered the question. Offhand he could only think of one person on their side who could possibly pressure Bellman.

"No," he said.

"Well, in any case, now you know we're still in the game," Krohn said.

"Thanks."

Harry hung up. Reflected. They were able to continue. He had three more days and no good leads. How did that saying go? *He who is born to be hanged will never drown?*

"Your mother had talent, you see."

Uncle Fredric made his way along the narrow footpath on Slemdalsveien, seemingly oblivious to the fact people coming in the opposite direction had to step out onto the road to let them pass. Apart from that, he appeared lucid today.

"That's why it was so sad to see her throw away her career and jump into the arms of the first patron who came her way. Well, I say patron, but he abhorred the theater, your stepfather, he went only went once in a blue moon to put in an appearance, it was a family tradition for the Røeds to sponsor the National Theater. No, he saw Molle onstage only the one time. In the title role of *Hedda Gabler*, ironically. Molle was a fine-looking woman and quite the little celebrity at that time. Perfect for a man to show off to the outside world."

Prim had heard the story before but had asked his uncle to tell it all the same. Not so much to check if it was still lodged in the memory of his uncle's diseased mind, but because he needed to hear it to be further reassured that the decision he had taken was the right one. He didn't know why he had suddenly wavered in faith the night before, but apparently it was quite common ahead of big moments in life. Like when your wedding day was approaching. And this—revenge—was, after all, something he had thought about, dreamed about, since he was a boy, so not so strange his thoughts and emotions should play tricks on him as it drew closer.

"That was how their relationship was," his uncle said. "She lived off him. And he lived off her. She was a beautiful young single mother who didn't demand much. He was an unscrupulous fellow with enough money to give her everything except the one thing she needed. Love. That was why she became an actress, above all she wanted, as all actors do, to be loved. And when she didn't get that love, neither from him nor, as time went on, from any audience, she fell apart. Of course, it didn't help matters that you were an overactive, spoilt little shit. When her patron eventually left you both, your mother was a depressed, worn-out alcoholic who no longer got the parts her talent warranted. I don't think she loved him. It was being left by someone—anybody at all—that was the final nail in the coffin. Your mother's psyche had always been fragile, but I must admit I hadn't expected she would set fire to the house."

"You don't know if she did," Prim said.

His uncle stopped, straightened up and smiled broadly to a young woman coming towards them. "Bigger!" he shouted, pointing at his own chest to illustrate. "You should have bought bigger ones!"

The woman looked at him aghast and hurried past.

"Oh yes," his uncle said. "She started the fire. Yes, yes, it started in her bedroom and they found a high concentration of alcohol in her blood—the report said that the cause of the fire was probably smoking in bed while intoxicated. But believe me, she set the fire with the desire to burn both of you alive. When parents take their children with them into death it's usually to spare them from life as orphans, and I know this is painful for you to hear, but in your mother's case the reason was she thought you were both worthless."

"That's not true," Prim said. "She did it so I wouldn't be entrusted to him."

"To your stepfather?" His uncle laughed. "Are you a fool? He didn't want you, he was happy to be rid of you both."

"He did," Prim said, in a voice so low it was drowned by the noise of the metro train passing next to them. "He did want me. Just not in the way you think."

"Did he ever give you any presents, for instance?"

"Yes," Prim said. "One Christmas when I was ten, he gave me a book about the torture methods of the Comanches. They were the most proficient. For example, they would hang their victims upside down from trees and light fires beneath them, so eventually their brains boiled."

His uncle laughed. "Not bad. Anyway, my moral indignation has limits, both when it comes to Comanches and your stepfather. Your mother should have treated him better, he was her patron, after all. Just like the parasite that is humanity should treat this planet better. Well, no reason to be sorry about that either. People think we biologists wish to preserve nature unchanged, like an organic museum. But we seem to be the only ones who understand and accept that nature is in flux, that everything dies and disappears, *that* is what's natural. Not the continued existence of the species, but its destruction."

"Shall we turn and go back?"

"Go back? Back where?"

Prim sighed. His uncle's mind was obviously clouding over again. "To the nursing home."

"I'm just messing with you." His uncle grinned. "That nurse who showed you up to my room. Bet you a thousand-krone note I fuck her by Monday. What do you say?"

"Every time we make a bet and you lose, you claim not to remember we made a bet. When you win, however . . ."

"Now don't be unreasonable, Prim. Suffering from dementia must have its advantages."

After they had rounded off their short walk and Prim had delivered his uncle back into the care of the nurse in question, he walked back the same way. He crossed Slemdalsveien, continuing east, before coming to a residential area with villas on spacious plots. The houses were expensive in this area, but the ones located next to the Ring 3 freeway

244

were more reasonably priced due to the noise. That was where the ruins lay.

He lifted the latch on the rusty iron gate and walked up the gravelly incline to the grove of birch trees. On the other side of the rise, obscured behind trees, stood a burnt-out villa. The fact the house lay so hidden from the neighbors had been a help to him over the years in his stalling tactics with the council, who wanted the ruins demolished. He unlocked the door and went inside. The staircase up to the first floor had collapsed. Mother's bedroom had been up there. His had been on the ground floor. Perhaps that was what had made it possible. The distance. Not that she hadn't known, but it had made it possible for her to *pretend* she didn't know. All the non-load-bearing internal walls had also burnt down, the entire ground floor was one big room covered in a carpet of ash. Here and there vegetation sprouted and grew in the ash. A bush. A seedling that would perhaps grow into a tree. He walked over to the burnt-out iron bed in what had been his room. A homeless Bulgarian had broken in and lived here for a while. If it wasn't for the fact his presence would have inevitably led to complaints from the neighbors and more hassle about demolition, Prim would have let the poor wretch stay. He had given the Bulgarian some cash, and the man had left peacefully with what few possessions he had, apart from a pair of damp wool socks with holes in them and the mattress on the bed. Prim had changed the lock on the front door and nailed new boards over the windows.

The metal springs creaked as he sat his full weight down on the dirty mattress. He shuddered. It was the sound of a childhood, a sound that was stuck in his mind, as undeniable as the parasites he had bred.

Yet ironically, this bed had been his salvation when he crept under it during the fire.

Though there had been days he had cursed that salvation.

The loneliness at the institutions. The loneliness at the different homes of foster parents he had run away from. Not because they weren't good, well-meaning people, but because in those years he was unable to sleep in a strange room, but always lay awake, listening. And waiting. For fire.

For the father in the house. And eventually couldn't stand it any longer and would run. Soon he would be placed in a new institution where Uncle Fredric would visit him now and again, pretty much how he now visited Uncle Fredric. His uncle, who had made it clear that he was just an uncle after all and, as he lived alone, was in no position to take the boy in. The liar. Yet he was in a position to look after the boy's modest inheritance from his mother. So Prim had seen precious little of that. Apart from this, the property. It was just one of the reasons he had been opposed to selling it, he knew all the proceeds would disappear into his uncle's pocket.

Prim bobbed up and down on the bed. The springs screeched in protest, and he shut his eyes. Returned to the sounds, the smells, the pain and the shame. Needed those sounds now, needed them in order to be sure. After all, he had crossed all the lines, come so far, so why this recurring hesitation? They say taking a life is worst the first time, but he wasn't so sure of that any more. He rocked back and forth on the bed. Reflected. Then finally the memories came, the sensations as clear as if it was all happening here and now. Yes, he was sure.

He opened his eyes and checked his watch.

He was going to go home and shower, get changed. Apply his own perfume. Then he was going to the theater.

28

SATURDAY

The final act

THE ONLY SOURCE OF LIGHT was the lamps in the bottom of the swimming pool, and in the semi-darkness of the room, the light flickered across the walls and ceiling. Harry's brain eventually stopped dwelling on details in the reports when he saw her. Alexandra's one-piece swimsuit seemed to show more of her body than if she had been stark naked. He rested on his elbows on the edge of the pool as she stepped down into the water, which according to the receptionist at the Thief Spa was heated to exactly thirty-five degrees. Alexandra observed him observing her while she smiled that enigmatic smile women display when they know—and like—that men like what they see.

She swam over to him. Apart from a couple sitting half submerged at the far end, they had the pool to themselves. Harry lifted the champagne bottle out of the cooler by the pool, poured a glass and handed it to her.

"Thanks," she said.

"Thanks as in we're even?" he said, watching as she drank.

"Far from it," she said. "After what was in *VG*, it would be very unfortunate if it came out that I'm running secret DNA analyses for you. So I want you to tell me something secret."

"Mm. Like what?"

"That's up to you." She slipped close to him. "But it has to be something from the darkest depths."

Harry looked at her. She had a look in her eyes not unlike Gert's when he demanded the "Blueman" lullaby. Alexandra was aware that Harry was Gert's father, and now he was struck by a crazy thought. That he would tell her the rest. He looked at the champagne bottle. Had already realized when he ordered it—albeit with one glass—that it was a bad idea. Just as it would be a bad idea to tell her what only he and Johan Krohn knew. He cleared his throat.

"I crushed a guy's throat in Los Angeles," Harry said. "I felt it against my knuckles, felt it give. And I liked it."

Alexandra stared at him wide-eyed. "Were you fighting?"

"Yeah."

"Why?"

Harry shrugged. "A bar brawl. Over a woman. I was drunk."

"What about you? Were you OK?"

"I was fine. I only hit him once, then it was over."

"You hit him in the throat?"

"Yeah. Chisel fist." He held up his hand to demonstrate. "A specialist in close-combat who trained FSK in Afghanistan taught me. The point is to hit your opponent on a specific area of the throat, then all opposition will cease immediately because our brain can only think of one thing, and that's getting air."

"Like this?" she asked, squeezing the middle joints and the tips of her fingers together.

"And like this," Harry said, straightening her thumb and pushing it in towards her forefinger. "And then you aim here, at the larynx." He tapped her forefinger against his own throat.

"Hey!" he shouted as without any warning she jabbed him.

"Stand still!" she laughed, hitting him again.

Harry jinked away. "I don't think you understand. You risk killing someone if you hit them right. Let's say this is the larynx." He pointed to one of his nipples. "And then you need to utilize these . . ." He took hold of her hips under the water and showed her how to rotate in order to generate power in the punch. "Ready?"

"Ready."

After four attempts she had landed two punches hard enough to make Harry groan.

The couple at the other end of the pool had gone quiet and were watching them with anxious expressions.

"How do you know you didn't kill him?" Alexandra said, as she got in position to strike again.

"I don't know for sure. But if he had died, I don't think his friends would have let me live afterwards."

"Have you also considered that if you had killed him it would put you in the same boat as those you've hunted down throughout your entire career?"

Harry wrinkled his nose. "Maybe."

"Maybe? Arguing over a woman—you think that's a more noble motive?"

"Let's call it self-defense."

"There're a lot of things that can be classed as self-defense, Harry. Honor killings are self-defense. Crimes of passion are self-defense. People kill to defend their self-respect and their dignity. You yourself have experience of people killing in order to save themselves from humiliation, don't you?"

Harry nodded. Looked at her. Had she understood? Had she realized that it wasn't just his own life that Bjørn had taken? No, her gaze was inward, this was about her own experience. Harry was about to say something when her hand shot out. He didn't move. Just stood there as a triumphant smile spread across her face. Her hand—clenched to a chisel—was barely touching the skin on his throat.

"Could have killed you that time," she said.

"Yeah."

"You didn't have time to react?"

"No."

"Or were you banking on me not crushing your larynx?"

He smiled a little, didn't answer.

"Or . . ." She frowned. "Don't you give a shit?"

Harry's smile widened. He gripped the bottle behind him, filled up her glass. Eyed the bottle, pictured bringing the end of it to his mouth, putting his head back and hearing the low gurgling sound as the alcohol filled him, lowering the bottle, now empty, wiping his mouth with the back of his hand while she stared wide-eyed at him. Instead, he placed the almost full bottle back in the cooler. Cleared his throat.

"What do you say we go into the sauna?"

Instead of Shakespeare's five acts, The National Theater's production of *Romeo and Juliet* consisted of two long acts with a fifteen-minute intermission at around the hour mark.

When the house lights came up for the intermission, the audience swarmed out, filling the foyers and the lounge, where light refreshments were available. Helene joined the line at the bar, while listening with half an ear to the conversations around her. Oddly enough none of them were about the play, as though that would be pretentious or vulgar. She became aware of something, a fragrance that made her think of Markus, and she half turned. A man was standing behind her, and he just managed to give her a smile before she quickly faced forward again. His smile had been . . . yes, what had it been? Her heart was beating faster in any case. She almost had to laugh; it must be the play, psychological priming that guaranteed it was not only her who suddenly thought they saw their Romeo in every other man's face. Because the man behind her was by no means attractive. Not downright ugly, perhaps—his smile had revealed he had nice teeth at least—but uninteresting. Still, her heart continued to beat, and she felt a desire—a desire she couldn't remember having felt in years—to turn around again. Look at him. See what it was that made her want to turn.

She managed to restrain herself, ordered a plastic glass of white wine and took it to one of the small round tables along the walls of the lounge. Watched the man, who was now trying to pay cash for a bottle of water while the woman behind the counter was pointing at a sign which read CARD ONLY. To her surprise she found herself considering going up and paying for him. But he had given up his attempted purchase and turned towards Helene. Their eyes met and he smiled again. Then he began walking in the direction of her table. Her heart pounded. What was this? It wasn't as if it were her first time experiencing a man being so direct. "May I?" he asked, placing a hand on the empty chair by the table.

She shot him a brief and—she assumed—dismissive smile, as her brain commanded her mouth to say, "I'd rather you didn't."

"By all means."

"Thank you." He sat down and leaned across the table as though they were in the middle of a long conversation.

"I don't mean to spoil it," he said, almost in a whisper. "But she's drunk poison and is going to die."

His face was so close she could smell his cologne. No, it was quite different from the one Markus had used, more raw. "As far as I'm aware she doesn't drink the poison before the last act," Helene said.

"That's what everyone thinks, but she's already poisoned. Believe me." He smiled. White teeth. Predator-like. She was tempted to offer herself, feel them bite through her skin as she buried her nails in his back. Jesus, what was this? Part of her wanted to run, another part to throw herself on him. She recrossed her legs the other way, noticing—was it possible?— that she was wet.

"Imagine I wasn't familiar with the play," she said. "Then why would you want to ruin the ending for me?"

"Because I want you to be prepared. It's an unpleasant thing, death."

"Yes, it is," she said, her eyes not leaving his. "But isn't the sum of that unpleasantness only greater when you have to prepare for death in addition?"

"Not necessarily." He leaned back in the chair. "Not if the joy of living is increased by the knowledge of its not lasting forever."

There was something vaguely familiar about him. Had he been at the party on the roof terrace? Or at Danielle's?

"Memento mori," she said.

"Yes. But now I must have some water."

"So I noticed."

"What's your name?"

"Helene. And yours?"

"Call me Prim. Helene?"

"Yes, Prim?" She smiled.

"Would you like to accompany me to somewhere they serve water?"

She laughed. Sipped at the glass of wine. Was going to say they had water here, that she could pay. Or even better, that he could borrow her glass and get some from the tap in the restroom, that Oslo tap water was better than anything you got in a bottle, and more environmentally friendly to boot.

"Where did you have in mind?" she asked.

"Does it matter?"

"No." She couldn't believe her own ears.

"Good." He pressed his palms together. "Then let's go."

"Now? I thought you meant after the final act."

"We already know how it ends."

Terse Acto was located in Vika, was obviously newly opened and served tapas at the upper end of upmarket prices.

"Good?" Alexandra asked.

"Very," Harry said, patting his mouth with the napkin while trying not to look at her wine glass.

"I like to think I know Oslo, but I hadn't heard of this place. It was Helge who recommended we book a table here. Gay men always know best."

"Gay? I didn't pick up those kinds of vibes."

"That's because you've lost your mojo."

"You mean at one stage I had it?"

"You? Big time. Didn't work on everyone, of course. Not that many, truth be told." She tilted her head to the side, thoughtfully. "Now that I think about it, probably only worked on a few of us." She laughed, lifted her wine and clinked his glass of water.

"So, you think Terry Våge has lost his source, grown desperate and begun making things up?"

Harry nodded. "The only way he could know what he professes to know is if he's in direct contact with the killer. And I don't see that."

"What if he's his own source?"

"Mm. That Våge is the killer, you mean?"

"I read about a Chinese author who murdered four people, wrote about it in several books and was convicted more than twenty years later."

"Liu Yongbiao," Harry said. "And then you've got Richard Klinkhamer. His wife disappeared, and shortly afterwards he writes a novel about a man killing his wife and burying her in the garden. And that was where they found her. Both those guys didn't kill *in order* to write about it, which I presume is what you're suggesting here?"

"Yes, but Våge could have done it. Heads of states start wars in order to be re-elected or go down in history. Why shouldn't a journalist do the same so he can be king of the hill? You ought to check if he has an alibi."

"OK. Speaking of checking things out. You said you know Oslo. Heard of a place called Villa Dante?"

Alexandra began to laugh. "Yeah, Sure. You want to head over there to see if you've still got it? Although I doubt they'd let you in. Even with those suits you wear these days."

"What do you mean?"

"It's a . . . how shall I put it . . . a very exclusive gay club."

"You've been?"

"No, are you mad, but I have a gay friend, Peter. He's actually one of Røed's neighbors, and invited me to the roof party."

"You were invited to that?"

"Not formally, it was more the type of party people just come along to. I was planning on taking Helge to fix him up with Peter, but I had to work that night. I have gone with Peter to SLM a few times, though."

"SLM?"

"You're so not with it, Harry. Scandinavian Leather Man. A gay club for the masses. You need to conform to a dress code there too, and there are dark rooms and whatnot in the basement. A little vulgar for the clientele who are members of Villa Dante, I imagine. Peter told me he'd tried to obtain membership there, but that it was impossible. You had to belong to the inner of the inner circle, a sort of gay Opus Dei. It's stylish there apparently. Think *Eyes Wide Shut.* Open just one night a week, a masquerade ball for gay men in expensive suits. Everyone walks around in animal masks and has accompanying monikers, total anonymity all round. All kinds of escapades and waiters who are . . . let's call them *young men.*"

"Above legal age?"

"Now they probably are. That was why the club had to shut down back when it was called Tuesdays. A fourteen-year-old who was working there accused one of the guests of rape. We got a sperm sample, but no match on the database, of course."

"Of course?"

"The clientele of Tuesdays weren't the kind to have previous convictions. Anyway, now it's reopened as Villa Dante."

"Which no one seems to have heard of."

"They operate under the radar, they don't need the publicity. That's the reason people like Peter are so obsessed with gaining admittance."

"You said it used to be called Tuesdays."

"Yeah, they had the club night on a Tuesday."

"And they still do?"

"I can ask Peter, if you like."

"Mm. What would it take for me to gain access, you think?"

She laughed. "A court order, a search warrant, probably. Which, incidentally, I hereby grant you with regard to myself tonight."

It took Harry a moment before he understood what she meant. He raised an eyebrow.

"Yep," she said, lifting her glass. "As in order."

"Do you live out here?" Helene asked.

"No," said the man, who'd called himself Prim. He steered the car between new, modern commercial buildings dotting the flat, open landscape on both sides of the road towards the tip of Snarøya. "I live in the city center, but I used to walk my dog here in the evenings after the airport closed. There was no one here then, and I could let my dog run free. Out there." He pointed towards the sea in the west and ate some more from the bag of chips or whatever it was; he hadn't offered any to her at any rate.

"But that's the marshlands preserve," Helene said. "You weren't afraid the dog would attack birds nesting there?"

"Sure, and it happened a couple of times. I tried to find comfort by telling myself it was the natural order of things and that we can't stand in the way of that. But of course, that's not true."

"It's not?"

"No. Mankind is also a product of nature, and we aren't the only organism doing our utmost to destroy the planet as we know it. But just as Mother Nature has granted us the intelligence to commit collective suicide, she has also gifted us self-reflection. Perhaps that can save us. I hope so. In any case, I stood in the way of nature and began to use this."

He pointed towards the grab handle above her door, and Helene became aware of a retractable dog leash with a collar dangling from the end.

"He was a good dog," he said. "I could sit in the car reading with the courtesy light on and the window open while he ran free, fifty yards in every direction. Dogs—and people—don't need more. Many people don't *want* more.

Helene nodded. "All the same, some day they might want more and want to get away. What does the dog owner do then?"

"I've no idea. My dog never wanted more." He had swung off the main road and onto a forest path. "What would you have done?"

"Set it free," Helene said.

"Even if you knew it wouldn't survive alone out there?"

"None of us survive."

"True," he said.

He slowed down. The road had ended. He switched off the engine and the headlights, and it turned pitch-black around them. She could hear the wind rustling through reeds, and between the trees they could see the sea and lights from the islands and headland farther out.

"Where are we?"

"Just by the marshlands," he said. "That foreland there is Høvikodden, and the two islands are Borøya and Ostøya. Since they built houses out here this has become a popular place to walk. In the daytime it's swarming with families. But at the moment, you and I have it completely to ourselves, Helene."

He released his seat belt and turned to her.

Helene took a deep breath, closed her eyes and waited. "This is crazy," she said.

"Crazy?"

"I'm a married woman. This . . . is extremely bad timing."

"Why?"

"Because I'm in the process of leaving my husband."

"Sounds to me like excellent timing."

"No." She shook her head without opening her eyes. "No, you don't understand. If Markus found out about this before we discuss terms . . ."

"Then you'll get a few million less from him."

"Yes. What I'm doing now is plain stupid."

"So why are you doing it, do you think?"

"I don't know." She pressed her palms to her temples. "It's like someone or something has taken over my mind." Just then she was struck by another thought. "What makes you think he has millions?" She opened her eyes and looked at him. Yes, there was something familiar about him. Something in his eyes. "Were you at the party? Do you know him?"

He didn't answer. Just smiled a little as he turned up the music. A theatrical vibrato singing something about scary monsters; she'd heard the song before but wasn't able to place it.

"The martini," she said with sudden certainty. "You were at Danielle's. It was you who sent over that drink, wasn't it?"

"And what makes you think that?"

"Standing behind me in the line, coming over and sitting down, that's not something you do during the intermission at a play. That wasn't by chance."

He ran a hand through his hair and glanced in the mirror.

"I confess," he said. "I've been watching you for a while. I've wanted to be alone with you. And now I am. So, what will we do?"

She drew a deep breath and unbuckled her own seat belt. "We'll fuck," she said.

"Unfair, isn't it?" Alexandra said. They had finished their meal and withdrawn to the restaurant bar. "I've always wanted a child but never had one. While you, who never wanted one . . ." She snapped her fingers over her White Russian cocktail.

Harry took a sip of his water. "Life is rarely fair."

"And so *random*," she added. "Bjørn Holm sent in DNA to check if he was the father of . . . what's the name of the boy again?"

"Gert."

Alexandra could see by Harry's face this was not something he wanted to talk about. Nevertheless—perhaps because she had drunk a little more than she should—she continued.

"Turns out he *isn't*. And right afterwards I run a DNA analysis of something which turns out to be your blood, check it by mistake against the entire database of paternity tests, and it emerges that *you're* Gert's father. If it hadn't been for me—"

"It's not your fault."

"What isn't my fault?"

"Nothing. Forget it."

"That Bjørn Holm killed himself?"

"That he . . ." Harry stopped.

Alexandra saw him grimace as though he were in pain somewhere. What was it he wasn't telling her? What was it he *couldn't* tell her?

"Harry?"

"Yeah?" His eyes seemed to be fixed on the row of bottles on the shelf behind the barman.

"It *was* that sex offender who killed your wife, right? Finne."

"Ask him."

"Finne is dead. If it wasn't him, then . . ."

"Then?"

"You were a suspect."

Harry nodded. "We always suspect the partner. And are usually right."

Alexandra took a gulp of her drink. "Was it you, Harry? Did you kill your wife?"

"A double of that there," Harry said, and it took a moment for Alexandra to realize he wasn't talking to her.

"This?" the barman asked, pointing to a square bottle hanging inverted in a bracket.

"Yes, please."

Harry remained silent until the glass with the golden-brown liquid was in front of him.

"Yes," he said, lifting the glass. Held it for a moment as though dreading it. "I killed her." Then he emptied the contents in a single go and had ordered a refill before the glass was back on the counter.

Helene got her breath back but remained sitting on top of him.

She had maneuvered him over to the passenger side, reclined the seat while he turned on the dome light and put on a condom. Then had rode him like one of her horses, although without the same feeling of control.

He had come without making a sound, but she had felt how his muscles had jerked and relaxed.

She had also come. Not because he had been an adept lover, but because she had been so horny before taking off her pants and underwear that anything would have sufficed.

She could feel him going soft inside her now.

"So why have you been stalking me?" she asked, looking down at him lying flat on the recumbent seat, as naked as she was.

"Why do you think?" he asked, putting his hands behind his head.

"You've fallen in love with me."

He smiled and shook his head. "I'm not in love with you, Helene."

"No?"

"I am in love, but with someone else."

Helene could feel herself getting annoyed. "Are you playing games?"

"No, I'm just telling you how it is."

"Then what are you doing here, with me?"

"I'm giving you what you want. Or rather, what your body and mind want. Which is me."

"You?" She snorted. "What makes you so sure that it couldn't have been any man?"

"Because I'm the one who's planted that desire in you. And now it's crawling and creeping inside your body and mind."

"The desire for you specifically?"

"Yes, for me. Or, to be more precise, what's creeping inside you desires to enter my intestinal tract."

"So sweet. You mean I want to take you with a strap-on? My husband once wanted me to do that when we started going out."

The man who called himself Prim shook his head. "I mean the small intestines and the large intestines. Bacterial flora. So they can multiply. As for your husband, it's news to me he wants to be penetrated from behind. When I was a little boy, he was the one who did the penetrating."

Helene stared down at him. In bewilderment, but she knew she hadn't misheard.

"What do you mean?"

"Didn't you know your husband fucks boys?"

"Boys?"

"Little boys."

She swallowed. It had of course crossed her mind that he liked men but she had never confronted him about it. Markus being bisexual or—more likely—a closet gay wasn't perverse. What was sick was that Markus Røed—one of the richest, most powerful men in the city, a man the press had accused of greed, tax evasion, bad taste and worse—didn't dare admit to the world the one human characteristic which could have helped him breathe more freely. Instead he had become a textbook case of a homosexual homophobe, a self-loathing narcissist and walking paradox. But little boys? Children. No. At the same time, now that the idea was presented to her and she reflected, it was all too logical. She shuddered. Another thought made its way into her mind: that this might come in useful as regards the divorce settlement.

"How do you know this?" she asked, without moving while she looked around for her underpants.

"He was my stepfather. He abused me from the time I was six years old. I say six because the earliest time I can recall him doing it was the same day he gave me a bicycle. Three times a week. Three times a week he screwed that little ass of mine. Year in. Year out."

Helene was breathing through her mouth. The air inside the car was thick with the smell of sex and that unusual musk scent. She swallowed. "Your mother, did she know about . . . ?"

"It was the usual. She suspected, I suppose, but did nothing to confirm it. She was an unemployed alcoholic who was afraid of losing him. Yet that's what happened."

"It's always the ones who are afraid that end up being left behind."

"Aren't you afraid?"

"Me? Why would I be?"

"Now that you understand the reason you and I are here."

Was she mistaken or was he growing hard inside her again?

"Susanne Andersen?" she asked at length. "Was it you?"

He nodded.

"And Bertine?"

He nodded again.

Maybe he was bluffing, maybe not. Either way Helene knew she ought to be afraid. So why wasn't she? Why instead did she begin moving her hips back and forth? Slowly at first, then more intensely.

"Don't . . ." he said, his face suddenly pale.

But she rode him again. It was as if her body had a will of its own, and she raised herself up on his cock and back down again with full vigor, Felt his stomach tighten, heard a muffled groan, thought he was about to come again. Then she saw a cascade of yellow-green vomit spew from his mouth. It went onto his chest, spilling onto the seat and down to his stomach, towards her. The smell was so acrid she felt her own stomach begin to turn, and she pinched her nose with her thumb and forefinger as she held her breath.

"No, no, no," he groaned, without moving while groping about on the floor beneath them. Found his shirt and began wiping himself with it. "It's that shit there," he said, pointing at the chip bag in the center console. Helene could see it said Hillman Pets on it.

"I need to eat it to regulate the population of parasites," he said, rubbing the shirt across his stomach. "But it's hard to find the balance. If I eat too much my stomach can't handle it. I hope you understand. Or can sympathize."

Helene neither understood nor sympathized she just concentrated on not breathing while she held her nose. And felt a strange change come over her. It was as though the desire and longing were gradually subsiding and being replaced by another emotion: fear.

Susanne. Then Bertine. And now it was her turn.

She needed to get out, get away, now!

He regarded her as if he sensed her fear. She made a concerted effort to smile. Her left hand was free, she could open the door with it, get out and run. Towards the terraced houses they had passed where the forest path began, it couldn't be more than three or four hundred yards there. Good, four hundred yards had been her best event, and she ran faster barefoot than in shoes. Furthermore, she guessed he would hesitate to follow her since they were both naked, enough to give her the head start she needed. He wouldn't have time to turn the car around and catch up her either, and if he tried, she could just cut into the woods. He just needed to be distracted a little while her left hand located the door handle. She was about to let go of her nose to place her right hand over his eyes in a pretense of affection when another thought entered her mind. That the change had occurred when she wasn't breathing and wasn't smelling. That there was a connection there.

"I understand," she whispered ingratiatingly. "These things happen. You're clean now. Let's have it a little dark again." She tried not to inhale the air and hoped he couldn't hear the quaver in her voice. "Where's the dome light?"

"Thanks," he said with a wan smile and pointed to the roof.

She found the switch and put out the light. In the darkness she clawed at the inside of the passenger door with her left hand. Found the door handle, eased it open and shoved the door wide. Felt the cold night air against her skin. Kicked off to get out. But he was too quick. His hands were around her throat, tightening their grip. She beat him on the chest with both hands, but the grip around her throat grew even tighter. She raised herself up on one knee in the seat and drove her other knee forward in the hope of striking his crotch. She had no sense of connecting, but he let go, and she got out, felt the gravel against her bare feet, fell over, but got back up and began to run. It was difficult to breathe, like he still had her in a stranglehold, but she had to ignore it, had to get away. And now she got a little air. She could see the lights down by the main road. Had to be less than four hundred yards away, surely? Yes, not even three hundred. This was going to be OK. She increased her pace, she really took off. There was no way he'd be able to catch up wi—

It was as if someone had appeared in the darkness in front of her and hit her so hard in the throat that she was knocked to the ground. She landed on her back, hitting her head on the gravel.

She must have been out for a few seconds, because on opening her eyes again she could hear footsteps approaching on the gravel.

She tried to scream but the stranglehold tightened again.

She brought her fingers to her throat and felt what it was.

The collar.

He had fastened the dog collar on her and allowed her to run, letting the retractable leash be drawn from the housing, waiting calmly until she had reached her fifty yards of freedom.

She no longer heard the footsteps as her fingers located the clasp. She squeezed it together and was free. From the collar. She didn't have time to scramble to her feet before she was pushed back down onto the gravel.

His naked body seemed shimmering white as he stood over her in the darkness with one foot on her chest. She stared at what he was holding in his right hand. What little light there was reflected on the shiny steel. It was a knife. A large knife. Still, she wasn't scared. At least not as scared as when she had held her breath in the car. It wasn't that she was unafraid to die, but it was as though her lust was stronger. She simply couldn't explain it any other way.

He crouched down, put the blade to her throat, leaned forward and whispered in her ear: "If you scream, I'll cut right away. Nod if you understand."

She nodded mutely. He leaned back, still on his haunches. And she could still feel the cold steel against her neck.

"I'm sorry, Helene." His voice sounded tearful. "It's not fair that you have to die. You haven't done anything, you're not the target. You just have the terrible misfortune to be a necessary means."

She coughed. "Ne . . . necessary for what?"

"To humiliate and destroy Markus Røed."

"Because he . . ."

"Yes, because he fucked me. And when he wasn't doing that, I had to suck on that ugly fucking cock of his for supper and breakfast and sometimes for lunch. Can you relate, Helene? The difference is that in my case there were no fringe benefits. Apart from the bike that one time. And that he stayed with my mother, of course. Sick, isn't it? That I was afraid that he would leave us. I don't know if it was me or my mother who grew too old for him, but he left us for a younger woman with a younger son. All this was long before your time, so I don't imagine you've heard about it."

Helene shook her head. She could see herself from outside, lying naked and freezing on a gravel path with a knife to her throat. She could feel the stones digging into her skin; she saw no way out, maybe this was where life ended. And yet she wanted to be here, yet she wanted him. Had she gone crazy?

"My mother disappeared into a depression," he said in a tremulous voice, and she could see that he too was freezing cold now. "It was only when she was emerging from it again that she had the energy to do what she'd promised me so many times when she was drunk. She took her own life and tried to take mine. The fire department classed it as an accident, smoking in bed. Neither I nor her brother, Uncle Fredric, saw any reason to inform them or the insurance company that she didn't smoke, that the pack they found had been Markus Røed's.

He fell silent. Something warm hit her breast. A tear.

"Are you going to kill me now?" she asked.

He drew a shaky breath. "As I've said, I'm sorry, but the life cycle of the parasites needs to be completed. So that they can reproduce, you see. I need new, fresh parasites when a new individual is to be infected. You understand?"

She shook her head. She wanted to stroke his cheek, it felt like she had taken ecstasy, the love was all-encompassing. But it wasn't love, it was lust, she was just so fucking horny.

"And, of course, there's the advantage that the dead tell no tales," he said.

"Of course," she said. She was breathing harder. As though she knew these were her final breaths.

"But tell me, Helene, while we had sex, did you feel loved for a little while?"

"I don't know," she said, smiling tiredly. "Yes, I think so."

"Good," he said, taking one of her hands in his free one. Squeezing it. "I wanted to give you that as a gift before you died. Because that's the only thing that matters, isn't it? To feel loved?"

"Maybe," she whispered, closing her eyes.

"Keep that in mind now, Helene. Say it to yourself: I am loved."

Prim looked down at her. Saw her lips moving. Forming the words. *I am loved.* Then he lifted the knife, pointed the tip towards her carotid artery, leaned forward, placing all his weight over it as he let the blade sink in. The warm spurt of blood on his ice-cold skin made him shudder with elation and horror.

He held on tightly to the knife handle. The vibrations letting him know that life was leaving her. After the blood spurted for a third time it began to flow. A few seconds later the knife told him Helene Røed was dead.

He pulled out the knife and sat down on the ground next to her. Wiped his tears. He shivered with cold, fear and the release of tension. It didn't get any easier, it got worse. But these were the innocent ones. The guilty one remained. That would be something entirely different. Taking the life of Markus Røed would be a joy. But first the bastard would suffer so much that death would come as a deliverance.

Prim felt something on his skin. Light rain. He looked up. Black. More rain was forecast tonight. It would wash away most of the traces, but he still had work to do. He looked at his watch, which was the only thing he hadn't taken off. Half past nine. If he was efficient, he could be back in the city center by half past ten.

29

SATURDAY

Tapetum lucidum

IT WAS AN HOUR TO midnight, and the wet pathways glistened under the lamplights in the Palace Gardens.

Harry was pleasantly anesthetized and reality appropriately distorted. He was, in short, in the sweet spot of intoxication, where he was conscious of the deception, yet still mentally pain-free. He and Alexandra were walking through the park. The faces they met drifting past. In order to support him, she had put his arm over her shoulder and her own arm around his waist. She was still angry.

"It's one thing to refuse to serve us," she hissed.

"Refuse to serve *me*," Harry said, his diction considerably steadier than his gait.

"Another thing throwing us out."

"Throwing *me* out," Harry said. "I've noticed barmen don't like customers going to sleep with their heads on the counter."

"Still. It was the *way* they did it."

"There're worse ways, Alexandra. Believe me."

"Oh yeah?"

"Oh yeah. That was one of the more tactful ways I've been thrown out. I think it might sneak into my top-five-most-pleasant-ejections-list."

She laughed, putting her head against his chest. With the result that Harry swerved off the pathway out onto the royal lawn, where an elderly man holding the retractable leash of his dog while it relieved itself glared disapprovingly at them.

She got Harry back on an even keel. "Let's stop at Lorry and get a coffee," she said.

"And a beer," Harry said.

"Coffee. Unless you want to get thrown out again."

Harry thought it over. "OK."

Lorry was crowded, but they got seats with two French-speaking men in the third booth to the left of the entrance door and were served large cups of steaming coffee.

"They're talking about the murders," Alexandra whispered.

"No," Harry said, "they're talking about the Spanish Civil War."

At midnight, they left Lorry after sticking to coffee, and were a little less drunk.

"Back to mine or back to yours?" Alexandra asked.

"Can I get some other alternatives?"

"No," she said. "Back to mine. And we're walking. Fresh air."

Alexandra's apartment was in a building on Marcus Thranes gate, halfway between St Hanshaugen and Alexander Kiellands plass.

"You've moved since the last time," Harry said as he stood lightly swaying in the bedroom while she tried to undress him. "But the bed is still the same, I see."

"Good memories?"

Harry paused to think.

"Idiot," Alexandra said, pushing him onto the bed and getting to her knees to unbutton his pants.

"Alexandra . . ." he said, placing a hand on hers.

She stopped and looked up at him.

"I can't," he said.

"Too drunk, you mean?"

"That too, probably. But I was at her grave today."

He waited for the anger of humiliation. Coldness. Contempt. Instead only tired resignation was detectable in her eyes. She pushed him under the duvet with his pants on, switched off the light and crawled in after him. Snuggled up to him.

"Does it still hurt?" she asked.

Harry tried to think of another way to describe the feeling. Emptiness. Loss. Loneliness. Fear. Panic, even. But she had actually hit the nail on the head, the overarching feeling was one of pain. He nodded.

"You're lucky," she said.

"Lucky?"

"To have loved someone so dearly that it can hurt so much."

"Mm."

"Sorry if that sounded banal."

"No, you're right. Our emotions are banal."

"I didn't mean it was banal to love somebody. Or to want to be loved."

"Me neither."

They held each other. Harry stared into the darkness. Then shut his eyes. He had half of the reports left. The answer might be in there. If not he would have to try the desperate plan he had discarded, but which had resurfaced again and again after the conversation with Truls at Schrøder's. He drifted off.

He was riding a mechanical bull. It flung his body this way and that while he held on tightly and tried to order a drink. He tried to focus on the barman behind the counter, but the jerks were too sharp, and the facial features in front of him blurred.

"What is it you'd like, Harry?" It was Rakel's voice. "Tell me what you want."

Was it really her? *I want the bull to stop. I want you and me to be together.* Harry tried to shout it, but he couldn't make a sound. He pressed the

268

buttons on the back of the bull's neck, but the tossing and rotations only grew in intensity and speed.

He heard a sound like a knife cutting through meat and then she screamed.

The bull began moving more slowly. Until it stopped completely.

He couldn't see anyone behind the bar, but blood was running down over the mirror shelves, the bottles and the glasses. He felt something hard being pressed against his temple.

"I can tell you're in debt," a voice whispered behind him. "Yes, you owe me a life."

He looked up at the mirror. In the cone of light coming from above he saw his own head, the barrel of a pistol and a hand holding a finger on the trigger. The face of the man holding the gun lay in darkness, but he could see something white shimmer. Was he naked? No, it was a white collar.

"Wait!" Harry said and turned around. It wasn't the man in the elevator. Or the man behind the tinted glass of the Camaro. It was Bjørn Holm. His red-haired colleague pressed the pistol to his own temple and pulled the trigger.

"No!"

Harry discovered he was sitting up in bed.

"Jesus!" a voice mumbled, and he saw black hair against the white pillow beside him. "What's going on?"

"Nothing," Harry said hoarsely. "I was just dreaming. I'm going to go now."

"Why?"

"I have reports to read. And I promised to go for a walk in the park with Gert early in the morning." He pushed himself out of bed, found his shirt on a chair, put it on and began to button it. Felt the nausea rising.

"Are you excited about seeing him?"

"I just want to be there on time." He bent down and kissed her on the forehead. "Sleep tight and thanks for a lovely evening. I'll let myself out."

When Harry made it down to the inner courtyard he had to throw up. He managed to push his way between two green dumpsters by a wall before his stomach knotted itself and the contents slapped on the dirty cobblestones. As he stood collecting himself, he saw something glowing red in the darkness at the wall on the other side of the yard. It was a cat's eyes. Tapetum lucidum, Lucille had explained to him, a layer at the back of the eye that was now reflecting the light from one of the windows on the ground floor. He could discern the cat as well, sitting quietly and look- ing at him. Or rather, when Harry's eyes adjusted to the darkness, he saw it was not him, but a mouse between them that had captured the cat's attention. The mouse moved slowly from the dumpsters towards the cat. It was like a déjà vu from that last morning in the bungalow on Doheny Drive. It dragged its long, glossy tail after itself, like a condemned man forced to lug his own rope to the gallows. The cat leaned forward slightly and with a swift maneuver sank its teeth in the back of the rodent's neck. Harry threw up again and supported himself against the wall as the cat dropped the already dead mouse on the ground in front of him. The glowing eyes looked at Harry again as though expecting applause. It's a theater, Harry thought. A fucking theater where, for a brief while, we just play the roles someone has written for us.

30

SUNDAY

THE MORNING SUN HAD YET to dry the rain-drenched streets when Thanh arrived at Mons.

She didn't have the keys to the pet store with her. It was Sunday, and this was just the meeting point for the handover of dogs she walked. The client was new; he had called the day before. It was unusual for people to avail themselves of her dog-sitting service on the weekends, generally that was when they had time to look after their pets themselves. Thanh was looking forward to taking a walk and had worn workout clothes in case the dog wanted to run a little. She and her mother had spent yesterday making food. Her father had come home from the hospital, and although the doctor had given him strict instructions not to eat too much and steer clear of spicy food, he had—to the delight of her mother—dug enthusiastically into all the dishes she served.

Thanh saw a man with a dog approaching across the gravel-covered park of Vestkanttorget. The dog was a Labrador, and judging by its gait, suffered from hip dysplasia. As they drew closer, she saw it was the policeman who had been in the store two days previously. Her first thought—perhaps because he was dressed in a suit—was that he was going to a Sunday service or a confirmation, and that was why he needed a dog sitter. But he had also been wearing a suit the first time she met him; maybe it was his work outfit. In which case, she was glad she hadn't brought the keys, in the event his plan had been to convince her to let him in.

"Hi," he said, smiling. "My name is Sung-min."

"Thanh," she said, and patted the dog, which was wagging its tail.

"Thanh. And his name is Kasparov. How do I pay?"

"Vipps. If you have the app. I can get a receipt if you want."

"You mean you won't work off the books for a policeman?" He laughed. "Sorry, bad joke," he said, when she didn't laugh along. "Do you mind if I walk with you some of the way?"

"By all means," she said, and took the lead, noting that Kasparov's collar was a William Walker. It was an expensive brand, but soft and gentle on a dog's neck. She wanted to stock them in the store, but Jonathan had refused.

"I usually walk in Frogner Park," she said.

"Fine."

They walked south and turned into Fuglehauggata in the direction of the park.

"I see you're wearing workout clothes, but I'm afraid Kasparov's running days are behind him."

"I've noticed. Have you considered an operation?"

"Yes," he said. "Several times. But the vet has advised against it. But I think he's on the right track, with proper food and—the periods it's bad—painkillers and anti-inflammatories."

"Sounds like you care about your dog."

"Oh yes. Have you a dog yourself?"

She shook her head. "I'm more into hook-ups. Like with Kasparov here."

Now they both laughed.

"I'm afraid I didn't hit it off so well with your boss the other day," he said. "Is he always so morose?"

"I don't know," Thanh said. The policeman was quiet, and she was aware that he was waiting for her to elaborate. She didn't need to, of course, but such silent pauses might serve to underscore an unwilling-ness to say more, as though there was something fishy going on.

"I don't know him that well," she said, hearing that now it sounded like she wanted to distance herself from Jonathan, which might put him in an unfavorable light, and that certainly wasn't her intention.

"That's odd," the policeman said. "You not knowing one another when the two of you are the only people in the store."

"Yeah," she said. They stopped for a red light by the pedestrian cross-ing over Kirkeveien. "It may be a little odd. But what you're wondering is if I know whether he's smuggled something into the country. And I don't."

In her peripheral vision she could see him looking at her, and when the light changed to green, she walked so quickly that he was left stand-ing on the sidewalk behind her.

Sung-min hurried after the girl from the pet store.

He was annoyed. Clearly, this wasn't leading anywhere, she had her guard up and wasn't going to talk. It was a waste of a day off, and his mood was not improved by the fact he and Chris had argued yesterday.

A flower seller was standing by the monumental main gate to Frogner Park, proffering his sad specimens to the tourists.

"A rose for the beautiful beloved."

The seller had taken a step forward so that he was blocking one of the smaller side gates which Sung-min and Thanh had headed towards.

"No thank you," Sung-min said.

The seller repeated his sales pitch in broken Norwegian, as though Sung-min must have misheard him.

"No," Sung-min said, and followed Thanh and Kasparov, who had skirted around the man and walked through the gate.

But the seller came after him.

"A rose for the beautiful—"

"No!"

The man obviously thought that Sung-min, judging by his attire, could afford it, and that Sung-min and Thanh were a couple since they both looked Asian. Not an unreasonable assumption, of course, and neither was it one that would have bothered Sung-min on another day. He rarely, if ever, allowed himself to be provoked by preconceptions, they were just a part of how people dealt with a complicated world. In fact, Sung-min was more often provoked by people who were so self-centered that they took offense every time they believed themselves the victim of even the most innocuous preconception. "A rose for—"

"I'm gay."

The seller stopped and stared blankly at Sung-min for a moment. Then he moistened his lips and held out one of the plastic-wrapped, pallid flowers.

"A rose for the beau—"

"I'm gay!" Sung-min roared. "Do you understand? Gay as gay can be!"

The flower seller backed away and Sung-min saw that people going in and out of the gates had turned to look at them. Thanh had come to a halt, a startled expression on her face, and Kasparov gave a brief bark and pulled at the lead to come to his owner's rescue.

"I'm sorry." Sung-min sighed. "Here." He took the flower and handed the seller a hundred-krone note.

"I don't have any . . ." the man began.

"It's fine." Sung-min walked over to Thanh and held out the rose to her.

At first she just looked at him in surprise. Then she began to laugh.

Sung-min hesitated a moment before seeing the funny side of the situation then laughed as well.

"My dad says it's largely a European tradition, giving flowers to your sweetheart," Thanh said. "The Greeks in antiquity, the French and English in the Middle Ages."

"Yes, but the rose is originally from the same continent as us," Sung-min said. "The place where I was born in South Korea, Samcheok, has a very well-known rose festival. And mugunghwa, the rose of Sharon, is the national symbol of Korea."

"Yes, but is mugunghwa strictly speaking a rose?"

Before they reached the Monolith, the conversation had moved on from flowers to pets.

"I don't know if Jonathan really likes animals that much," she said when they were standing at the top of the park looking down towards Skøyen. "I think he just ended up in this business. It could just as easily have been, like, a grocery or electronics store."

"But you don't know anything about him continuing to stock Hillman Pets after the import ban?"

"What makes you so sure he has?"

"He was very stressed when I came by the store."

"Maybe he was scared of . . ."

"Yes?"

"No, nothing."

Sung-min took a deep breath. "I'm not a customs officer. I'm not going to charge him with illegal importation. What I'm working on is following a lead, which in a roundabout way could maybe help us to apprehend the man who killed those two girls who disappeared. And prevent any more from dying."

Thanh nodded. Looked like she hesitated slightly before making up her mind. "The only illegal thing I've seen Jonathan do was when he agreed to take a fox cub someone had taken with them from London—apparently foxes live in the city there. It's an offense to bring foxes into the country, of course, and I think that when they found out they got scared. They couldn't face going to the vet to have it put down and they weren't able to do it themselves, so they gave the cub to Jonathan instead. Had to reimburse him generously to take the problem off their hands, no doubt."

"People do things like that?"

"You don't know the half of it. Twice I've had owners not bothering to pick up their dogs and vanish into thin air."

"So what did you do?"

"Took them home. But we don't have much space, so eventually I had to take them to the animal shelter. It's so sad."

"What happened to the fox cub?"

"I don't know, and I'm not sure I want to. I loved that cub." Sung-min

275

could feel her eyes becoming moist. "Suddenly one day it was gone. He probably flushed it down the toilet . . ."

"The toilet?"

"No, of course not. But like I said, I don't want to know how he got rid of Nhi." They continued walking while Thanh told him of her plans, about her dream of becoming a vet. Sung-min listened. It was hard not to like this girl. Besides she was bright, and there was no longer any reason to pretend he had gotten in touch to have his dog looked after, so he accompanied her the entire way. His questioning had proved fruitless, but he consoled himself with the fact that he had at least gotten to spend time with someone who appreciated a four-legged friend as much as he did.

"Oh," Thanh said as they approached Mons again. "There's Jonathan."

The door of the store was open, and a Volvo station wagon was parked outside. A man was leaning in the open door on the passenger side. He probably couldn't hear them due to the sound of the vacuum cleaner. By his feet was a bucket of water, suds spilling over the brim, and the car was wet and glistening. Water still trickled from the hose lying on the pavement.

Sung-min took Kasparov's lead and wondered whether he should slip away unnoticed and leave it up to Thanh to decide if she wanted to tell him about their meeting. But before he had a chance to make up his mind, the store owner straightened up and turned in their direction.

Sung-min saw the man's eyes blaze as he took in and undoubtedly interpreted the situation correctly.

"Isn't it unchristian to wash your car during church-service hours," Sung-min said before the others had a chance to say anything.

The man's eyes narrowed.

"We've just been for a walk in the park," Thanh added quickly. "Dog sitting."

Sung-min wished she hadn't sounded so anxious. As though they were the ones who had cause to be on the defensive and not him.

Without a word, the man carried the vacuum cleaner and hose into the store. Reappeared, picked up the bucket and emptied the contents out onto the sidewalk. Soapsuds and dirty water pooled around Sung-min's handmade shoes.

Sung-min didn't react, just concentrated on the man marching into the store with the empty bucket. The anger he saw, was that merely due to a policeman being a nuisance? Or was it because the man was scared? Sung-min didn't know exactly what nerve he had hit, but he had hit something, of that he was in no doubt. The man came back out and locked the door of the store, then walked towards the car without gracing them with a glance. Sung-min saw the remains of some clods of earth in the water that had run from the tires to the manhole cover.

"Been driving in the forest?" Sung-min asked.

"Been barking up the wrong tree?" the store owner asked, slipping into the driving seat, shutting the door and starting the engine.

Sung-min watched the Volvo as it accelerated down the Sunday calm of Neuberggata.

"What was it he had in the back?"

"A cage," Thanh said

"A cage," Sung-min repeated.

"Oh," Katrine whispered, withdrawing the arm she'd linked through Harry's.

"What's wrong?" he asked.

She didn't answer.

"What's wong, Mama?" asked Gert, who was holding Harry's hand.

"I just thought I saw someone," Katrine said, squinting up at the higher ground behind the Monolith.

"Sung-min again?" Harry said. Katrine had told him that while she and Gert were waiting at the gate, they had seen Sung-min enter the park with a girl.

Katrine hadn't tried to attract his attention; she wasn't eager for colleagues to see her in Harry's company. In that sense, Frogner Park on a sunny Sunday was a risky choice. There were already lots of people inside, some of them were even sitting on the grass, which had to be still damp after last night's rain.

"No, I thought it was . . ." She paused.

"Your date?" Harry asked, while a snowsuit-clad Gert pulled at his sleeve for Uncle Harry to lift him off the ground and swing him around once more.

"Maybe. You're thinking about someone, then suddenly you start seeing their face everywhere you go, you know?"

"You mean you saw him up there?"

"No, couldn't have been him, he was going to work today. But I can't walk arm in arm with you anyway, Harry. If we were to run into any colleagues and they saw the two of us . . ."

"I know," Harry said, checking the time. Two full days left. He had explained to Katrine that he only had a couple of hours to spare before he needed to get back to the hotel to work. But he knew it was only to give himself the feeling he was doing something, that it was unrealistic to think he would find anything there. That something needed to *happen*.

"Not dat way, dis way!" Gert said, pulling Harry off the path and onto the trail leading between the trees towards the playground and Frogner Castle, a wooden fortress in miniature that children climbed and played in.

"What did you say it was called again?" Harry asked innocently.

"Fwognaw Catal!"

Harry saw Katrine's warning glare as he tried his best not to laugh. What the hell was happening to him? He had heard that lack of sleep could make people psychotic—was he at that stage?

His phone rang and he checked the display. "I have to take this. You two go ahead."

"Thanks for a great night," he said into the phone when the other two were out of earshot.

"No, thank *you*," Alexandra said. "But that's not why I'm calling. I'm at work."

"On a Sunday?"

"When you leave the warmth of a girl in her bed in the middle of the night to read reports, then I have to be allowed to do a little work as well."

"Fair enough."

"I actually came in to catch up on my thesis, but it turns out the DNA analysis from the paper towel you asked for is ready, so I thought you'd like the results right away."

"Mm."

"It has the same DNA profile as the saliva we found around Susanne Andersen's nipple."

Harry's overtired brain took in the information bit by bit as his heart rate increased. He had just been wishing for something to *happen* and now it had. One could turn religious from less. But it also occurred to him that he shouldn't be so surprised. The suspicion about who the saliva on Susanne's breast came from had after all been strong enough for him to finagle DNA from Markus Røed.

"Thanks," he said, and ended the call.

When he got to the playground, he found Katrine on all fours in the sand in front of the castle. She was making neighing sounds while Gert—who was sitting on her back—was digging his heels into her sides. She explained—still on all fours—that Gert had seen a film about knights and had insisted on arriving at the castle on horseback.

"The saliva found on Susanne belongs to Markus Røed," Harry said.

"How do you know?"

"I got hold of Røed's DNA and sent it to Alexandra."

"Fuck."

"Mama . . ."

"Mama will mind her language, yes. But if it's been obtained in that way, it's not by the book, and then we can't use it in court."

"It wasn't done in the police prescribed manner, no, but this is exactly what we talked about. There's nothing to prevent you and your people from using information procured by others."

"Can you . . . ?" She nodded back in the direction of her rider. Harry lifted Gert off the horse despite his protests, and she got to her feet.

"Røed's wife still gives him an alibi; all the same this might be enough to arrest him," she said, brushing sand off the knees of her pants and

279

watching Gert, who had run over to the slide coming down from one of the towers.

"Mm. I think Helene Røed might waver slightly where that alibi is concerned."

"Oh?"

"I talked to her. The alibi is her bargaining chip in an upcoming divorce settlement."

Katrine frowned and took out her own ringing phone. Looked at the display.

"Bratt."

Her work voice, Harry thought. And going by the change in facial expression he could guess the rest.

"I'll be right there," she said and cut the connection. Looked up at Harry. "A body's been found. Lilløyplassen."

Harry thought for a moment. Wasn't that out on the tip of Snarøya, in the wetlands?

"OK," he said. "But what's the big hurry to get tactical investigators out there? Shouldn't you be concentrating on having Røed arrested?"

"It's the same case. A woman. And she's been decapitated."

"Shit."

"Can you play with him in the meantime?" She nodded towards Gert.

"You're going to be busy for the rest of the day," Harry said. "And tonight. Røed needs to—"

"These are to the gate and to the apartment." She slipped two keys off a set. "There's food in the fridge. And save me the skeptical look, you are the father after all."

"Mm. I'm the father when it suits you, apparently."

"Right. And now you sound like one of those police wives who are always complaining." She handed him the keys. "We'll get Røed afterwards. I'll keep you posted."

"Of course," Harry said and clenched his teeth.

He watched Katrine walk over to the slide, say a few words to Gert and hug him, and followed her with his eyes as she jog-trotted out of the park with the phone to her ear. He felt a tug on his hand and looked down into Gert's upturned face.

"Hawse."

Harry smiled and pretended he hadn't heard.

"Hawse!"

Harry's smile widened, and he looked down at his suit trousers and knew he was going to lose.

31

SUNDAY

Large mammals

IT WAS JUST AFTER ELEVEN in the morning. The sun warmed but as soon as it slid behind one of the clouds, Katrine shuddered. She was standing by a grove of trees looking out over a beach with tall yellow marram grass and, beyond that, the glittering sea where sailing boats crossed back and forth. She turned. The stretcher with the body of the woman was on its way to the ambulance up at the road from where Sung-min was walking towards her.

"Well?" he said.

"She was lying in the tall grass just by the beach." Katrine sighed heavily. "Pretty bad shape, worse than the other two. Out here it's mostly families with small children who are up walking early, so of course one of them had to find her."

"Oh dear." Sung-min shook his head. "Any idea about the identity?"

"She was naked, and her head was cut off. No one reported missing. As yet. But I'm guessing she was young and beautiful, so . . ."

She didn't finish the sentence. That it wouldn't be long. That from experience it was the young and beautiful who were reported missing earliest.

"No tracks, I presume."

"No, the perpetrator was lucky, it rained last night."

Sung-min shivered as a sudden cold gust of wind hit. "I don't think it's luck, Bratt."

"Me neither."

"Will we do something proactive to get an ID on the body?"

"Yeah. I was thinking of calling Mona Daa at *VG*. Give her this as an exclusive in return for them running hard with it and in the way we want. Not too much, not too little. Then the rest of them can quote from her piece and complain about preferential treatment afterwards."

"Not a bad idea. Daa will go for it just to have something Våge doesn't."

"My thoughts exactly."

They watched the crime scene technicians in silence, as they continued photographing and fine-combing the cordoned-off search area for evidence.

Sung-min rocked on his heels. "She was brought here in a car, just like Bertine, don't you think?"

Katrine nodded. "There're no buses out here, and the taxi companies we checked had no fares to the area last night, so yeah, in all likelihood."

"You know if there're any gravel or dirt roads around?"

Katrine looked at him closely. "Tire tracks, that what you're thinking? I've only seen paved roads around here. But any tire marks have probably been washed away by the rain now."

"Of course, I just . . ."

"You just?"

"Nothing," Sung-min said.

"Then I'll make that call to *VG*," Katrine said.

It was a quarter to twelve. Prim slowly unfolded the wax paper in front of him.

A fresh wave of anger washed over him. They had come at irregular intervals ever since he had seen the two of them together. Like two love-birds. Her, the Woman he loved, and that guy. When a man and a woman take a walk in the park like that, there's little doubt about what's going on. He was after her. A policeman as well! He hadn't yet had time to come up with a plan to get this unexpected rival out of the way, but he would soon enough.

The wax paper lay unfolded in front of him, and in the center of it: an eye.

Prim felt his mouth get dry.

But he must.

He held the eye between two fingers, felt nausea rising. He couldn't throw it up again, that would be a waste. He placed the eye back on the paper and tried to breathe deeply and calmly. Checked the online newspapers on his phone again. There it was, finally! In *VG*. It was at the top, with a large picture of the wetlands. Beneath Mona Daa's byline, he read that the body of an as yet unidentified woman had been found by Lilløyplassen on Snarøya. The body was without a head again, and *VG* urged the public to get in touch with the police if they had any information about who the murdered woman might be. As well as those who had been in the area the previous evening, irrespective of whether they had seen anything or not. Mona Daa wrote that the police were refusing to comment for the time being on whether this murder was connected to the murders of Susanne Andersen and Bertine Bertilsen, but that that would clearly turn out to be the case.

Prim gazed at the article. It was placed above several items about the politician who had cheated on her taxes, that day's decisive clash between Bodø/Glimt and Molde, and the war in the East.

He felt the odd intoxication at being there, center stage, in the main role. Was this how Mummy had felt in front of a spellbound, breathless theater audience as she brandished the magic wand of the narrator? Was this her genes and passion finally awakening within him?

He took out the other phone, the burner, which he had bought on eBay with a SIM card from Latvia registered under a fictive name. Tapped in the number for *VG*'s tip-off line. Said it concerned the dead woman by Lilløyplassen and asked to be put through to Mona Daa.

It sounded like an order when she came on the line.

"Daa."

Prim affected a deeper tone to his own voice, which from experience he knew no one was able to identify as his. "Who I am is of no importance, but I'm very worried. I was supposed to meet Helene Røed in Frogner Park today. She never showed up, she's not answering her phone, and she's not at home either."

"Who—"

Prim hung up. Looked down at the wax paper. Lifted the eye and studied it. Put it in his mouth. And chewed.

Just after half past twelve Johan Krohn called Harry Hole's number.

He had come in from the veranda, where his wife was still sitting with a cup of coffee and her face turned to the sun. She said she didn't trust the weather report which forecast there was more warm weather in store. He buttoned his coat while waiting for an answer. Finally, he heard Harry's breathless voice.

"Sorry, am I disturbing a workout?"

"No, I'm playing."

"Playing?"

"I'm a dragon attacking a castle."

"I see," Johan Krohn said. "I'm ringing because I just received a call from Markus. His assistant just informed him that the Forensic Medical Institute have been in touch. They want him to come and identify a body." He drew a deep breath. "They think it might be Helene."

"Mm."

Johan Krohn couldn't tell whether Hole sounded shocked or not.

"I thought you might want to accompany him. Then you can see the body. Whether it's Helene or not, the killer is probably the same."

"Good," Hole said. "Can you come over here and look after a three-year-old for a few minutes?"

"A three-year-old?"

"He's likes it if you pretend to be an animal. A large mammal, preferably."

Johan Krohn pressed the call button that said Forensic Medical Institute for a second time.

"It's Sunday—you sure there's anyone at work?"

"They said I was to come asap and buzz this door," Markus Røed said, glancing up at the building's facade.

Eventually they saw someone wearing green scrubs on the inside trotting towards the glass door, which he opened. "Apologies, my colleague has left for the day," he said from behind the surgical mask. "I'm Helge, post-mortem technician."

"Johan Krohn." The lawyer instinctively put his hand out, but the technician shook his head as he held up his gloved hands.

"Can the dead be infected?" Røed asked sarcastically from behind.

"No, but they can infect the living," the post-mortem technician said.

They followed him through an empty corridor to a room with a window facing into what Krohn assumed was the autopsy room.

"Which of you will be making the identification?"

"Him," Krohn said, nodding towards Markus Røed.

The man handed Røed a face mask, scrubs and a scrub cap like he himself was wearing.

"Can I ask what your relationship is to the individual who may be the deceased?"

Røed looked at a loss for a moment. "Husband," he said. The sarcastic tone was gone, as though the possibility of Helene really lying there was beginning to sink in.

"Before putting on your face mask, I'd like you to have a drink of water," the post-mortem technician said.

"Thank you, but that won't be necessary," Røed said.

"Experience suggests it can be a good idea to have fluid in the body when we're dealing with a case such as this." The post-mortem technician poured water from a carafe into a glass. "Believe me, you'll understand when we enter."

Røed looked at him, nodded briefly and drained the glass.

The post-mortem technician held the door open, and he and Røed went inside.

Krohn went over to the window. They stood on either side of a gurney where the outline of a female form lay in profile underneath a white sheet. Apart from the head. Evidently there were microphones inside, and he could hear their voices over a loudspeaker above the window.

"Are you ready?"

Røed nodded, and the post-mortem technician removed the sheet.

Krohn backed away from the window. He had seen corpses in his professional life but nothing like this. The post-mortem technician's voice sounded dry and matter-of-fact over the loudspeaker.

"I'm sorry, but it does appear as though the perpetrator has subjected her to extreme violence. One thing is what you see here, stab wounds over the entire body and the slashed stomach. But the worst is probably the area here around the anus, where we can see that the perpetrator must have used something other than a knife or his hands to cause so much damage. The entire rectum has been torn open and the mutilation continues upward, so he must have used a pipe, a thick branch or similar. I apologize if this is more information than you wish, but it's necessary to explain the level of violence inflicted so that you understand she is no longer the woman you knew or were used to seeing. So, take your time and try to look beyond the injuries."

Due to the face mask, Krohn couldn't see Røed's facial expression, but he did see the trembling of his body.

"Di-did he do this while . . . while she was alive?"

"I wish I could say that we knew for certain that she was dead, but I can't."

"Then she suffered?" Røed's voice sounded thin and tear-filled.

"Like I said, we don't know. We can determine that some of the injuries were inflicted after the heart had stopped beating, but not all. I am sorry."

A single whimper escaped from Røed. Johan Krohn had never at any point in their relationship felt sorry for Markus Røed. Not for one second—his client was too much of a bastard for it. But just now he felt compassion, perhaps because he had inevitably for a moment put his own wife on the gurney and himself in Røed's shoes.

"I know it's painful," the post-mortem technician said, "but I have to ask you to take your time. Look at her and do your best to confirm whether or not this is Helene Røed."

Krohn assumed it was the sound of her name in connection with the mutilated body that made Røed break down in convulsive sobbing.

Krohn heard the door behind him open.

It was Harry Hole accompanied by a dark-haired woman.

Hole gave a brief nod. "This is Alexandra Sturdza. She works here. We picked her up on the way."

"Johan Krohn, Røed's lawyer."

"I know," Alexandra said, as she walked to the sink and began washing her hands. "I was here earlier today, but I've obviously missed out on all the action. Has she been identified?"

"They're doing it now," Krohn said. "It's not an entirely . . . eh, straightforward task."

Hole had come to the window beside Krohn and was now looking in. "Rage," he said simply.

"Pardon?"

"What he's done to her. It's not the same as he did to the other two. This is rage and hatred."

Krohn tried to moisten his dry mouth. "You mean it's someone who hates Helene Røed?"

"Could be. Or he hates what she represents. Or he hates himself. Or he hates someone who loves her."

As a lawyer, Krohn had heard these statements before. They were the court psychologist's more or less customary description in cases involving violence and sexually motivated murder, except for the last one, about hating someone who loved the victim.

"It's her." Røed's whispered voice over the loudspeaker caused the three of them outside the autopsy room to go quiet.

The dark-haired woman turned off the tap and turned to the viewing window.

"I'm sorry, but I'm required to ask you if you are certain," the post-mortem technician said.

A new, shuddering sob escaped Røed. He nodded. Pointed to one shoulder.

"That scar. She got it when we were in Chennai and she was riding on the beach. I'd hired a racehorse; it was to run in a race the following day. They were so beautiful together. But the horse wasn't used to running on sand and didn't see the sinkhole left by the tide. They were so beautiful as they . . ." His voice didn't carry any longer and he hid his face in his hands.

"Must have been a bloody nice horse for him to take it so hard," the dark-haired woman said. Krohn turned to her in disbelief, met her cold gaze and swallowed the reprimand on the tip of his tongue. He turned to Harry in exasperation instead.

"She's analyzed DNA material from Røed," Harry said. "It matches the saliva found on Susanne Andersen's breast."

Harry studied Johan Krohn's face as he spoke the words. He thought he saw pure surprise, as though the lawyer had truly believed in his client's innocence. But what lawyers and policemen believed didn't really matter. Research showed that there was little or no difference in people's ability, irrespective of their occupations, to tell when someone was lying, or put another way: that we are all about as poor at it as John Larson's lie detector. All the same, Harry found it hard to believe that Krohn's surprise or Røed's tears were an act. Of course, a man could grieve over a woman he had killed, either by his own hand or by paying someone else, Harry had seen enough guilty husbands who had wept, probably out of a mixture of guilt, lost love, that same jealous frustration that had led to the murder and the sudden violence in the moment of realization. Christ, hadn't he himself believed for a time that he, in the midst of an alcohol fog, had killed Rakel? But Markus Røed *did not look* like a man who had murdered the woman lying in front of him, though Harry was at a loss to explain quite why or how. The tears were too pure somehow. Harry closed his eyes. *Tears too pure?* He sighed. Screw this esoteric bullshit; the evidence was there, and it told its own story. The miracle that would save both him and Lucille was about to take place, so why not welcome it with open arms?

A buzz sounded in the room.

"Someone at the main door," Alexandra said.

"Probably the police," Harry said.

Alexandra left the room.

Johan Krohn looked at him. "Was it you who called them?"

Harry nodded.

Røed entered and removed the coat, face mask and scrub cap. "When can we move her to a funeral home?" he asked, addressing Krohn, and taking no notice of Harry. "I hate seeing her this way." His voice was hoarse, and his eyes moist and red. "And the head. We need to make a head for her. We've tons of pictures. A sculptor. The best, Johan. It has to be the best." He began to cry again. Harry had withdrawn to a corner of the room where he observed Røed closely.

Observed the puzzled shock as the door opened, three policemen and one policewoman entered, two of them seizing Røed by each arm, the third placing handcuffs on him and the fourth explaining why he was under arrest.

On his way out the door, Røed turned his head as though to get one last glimpse of the body of the woman lying through the window behind him, but only managed to turn it enough to notice Harry.

The look he gave him reminded Harry of the summer he had worked at a foundry, when the molten metal was poured into a mold and turned in seconds from hot, red and runny to cold, gray and hard.

Then they were gone.

The post-mortem technician entered and removed his face mask. "Hi, Harry."

"Hi, Helge. Let me ask you something."

"Yeah?" He hung up his scrubs.

"Have you seen someone who was guilty cry like that?"

Helge puffed out his cheeks pensively and slowly let the air out. "The problem with empiricism is that we don't always get the answer about who is guilty and who isn't, do we?"

"Mm. Good point. May I . . . ?" He nodded in the direction of the autopsy room.

He saw Helge hesitate.

"Thirty seconds," Harry said. "And I won't tell a soul. At least, not anyone who can get you into trouble."

Helge smiled. "All right. Hurry up then, before anyone comes. And don't touch anything."

Harry went in. Looked down at what was left of the vivacious person he had spoken to only two days ago. He had liked her. And she had liked him, he wasn't wrong on the few occasions he noticed that sort of thing. In another life he might have asked her out for a coffee. He studied the wounds and the cut where decapitation had occurred. He breathed in a faint, barely discernible odor that reminded him of something. Since his parosmia rendered him unable to perceive the smell of a corpse, it wasn't that. Of course—it was the smell of musk, and it reminded him of Los Angeles. Harry straightened up. Time—for him and Helene Røed—was up.

Harry and Helge walked out together and just caught sight of the police cruiser driving away. Alexandra was leaning against the front of the building smoking a cigarette. "That's what I call two cute boys," she said.

"Thanks," Harry said.

"Not you two, those two." She nodded in the direction of the parking lot where there was an old Mercedes with a taxi sign and a Keith Richards clone standing in front of it with a three-year-old on his shoulders. The clone was holding up an arm as an extension of his nose while he made what Harry assumed were supposed to be elephant noises and staggered in a way Harry hoped was intentional.

"Yeah," he said, while trying to sort through the chaos of his thoughts, suspicions and impressions. "Cute."

"Øystein asked if I was going to join you at the Jealousy Bar tomorrow to celebrate solving the case," she said, handing the cigarette to Harry. "Will I?"

Harry took a long drag. "Will you?"

"Yes, I will," she said, snatching the cigarette back again.

32

SUNDAY

Orangotango

THE PRESS CONFERENCE BEGAN AT four o'clock.

Katrine looked out over the Parole Hall. It was packed and the atmosphere was electric. The names of the victim and the man in custody had obviously begun to circulate. She stifled a yawn as Kedzierski outlined to those present how the case had developed. It was already a long Sunday, and it was far from over. She had sent a text to Harry to ask how it was going and he had replied: *Gert and I have gone for a drink. Cocoa.* She had responded with *ha ha* and a stern-faced emoji and tried not to think about them, clearing space in her mind for what she needed to concentrate on. Kedzierski had finished and opened the floor for questions. They came thick and fast.

"NRK, please," the head of Information said, in an attempt to maintain order.

"How can you have DNA evidence against Markus Røed when we know he has refused to submit to a DNA test?"

"Because the police haven't taken a DNA test," Katrine said. "The DNA material was obtained by an individual outside the police who also had it analyzed and thus confirmed a match to the DNA at the crime scene."

"Who was this individual?" a voice asked, cutting through the buzz of the others in the hall.

"A private investigator," Katrine said.

The buzz of conversation abruptly ceased. And in that brief pocket of silence, she said his name. And enjoyed it. Because she knew Bodil Melling—however much she wished to have her head on a plate—couldn't come after her for telling it like it was, that Harry Hole had virtually solved the case for them.

"What was Røed's motive for killing Susanne Andersen and Bert—"

"We don't know," Sung-min said, interrupting the journalist.

Katrine glanced sideways at him. It was true they didn't know, but they had had time to discuss it, and it was Sung-min who had mentioned the old murder case—also a Harry Hole case—where a jealous husband had, in addition to killing his wife, also murdered random women and men to make it appear as part of a serial killing and focus attention away from himself.

"*VG,*" Kedzierski said.

"If Harry Hole has solved the case for you, why isn't he here?" Mona Daa asked.

"This is a press conference with spokespeople from the police," Kedzierski said. "You can talk to Hole yourselves."

"We've tried getting in touch with him but he's not answering."

"We can't—" Kedzierski began, but was interrupted by Katrine.

"He probably has his hands full with other matters, then. As have we, so if there're no more questions pertaining to the case . . ."

A furor of protests rang out around the hall.

It was six o'clock.

"A beer," Harry said.

The waiter nodded.

Gert looked up from the cup of cocoa and let go of the straw. "Gwanny says people who dwink bee don't go to heaven. And then they won't meet my daddy, because he's dead."

Harry looked at the boy, and a thought struck him. That if one beer sent him to hell, then that was where he would meet Bjørn Holm. He looked around. They were sitting at several of the tables, the lonely men with their beers as sole company and collocutor. They didn't remember him and he didn't remember them, even though they were as ingrained in Schrøder's as the tobacco smell he could still perceive in the walls and furniture, a generation after the introduction of the smoking ban. Back then they had been older than him, but it was as though the inscription above the skeletons in the Capuchin Crypt had been imprinted on their foreheads: *What you are now we used to be; what we are now you will be.* For Harry had of course always been aware of a line of alcoholism stretching back through his lineage, like a little demonic bloodsucker sitting within, screaming for sugar and spirits, that had to be fed, a damn parasite transmitted through the genes.

The phone rang. It was Krohn. He sounded more resigned than angry.

"Congratulations, Harry. I saw online that it was you who got Markus arrested."

"I gave both of you advance warning."

"With methods the police themselves couldn't use."

"That was the reason you hired me."

"Fine. The contract states that three police lawyers must consider it highly likely that Røed is convicted."

"We'll have that by tomorrow. And then the amount needs to be transferred too."

"Speaking of which. That account in the Cayman Islands that I've been provided with . . ."

"Don't ask me about it, Krohn."

There was a pause.

"I'm hanging up now, Harry. I hope you can sleep."

Harry dropped the phone back into the inside pocket of Røed's suit.

Turned his attention to Gert, who at that moment was primarily occupied with his cocoa and the large paintings of old Oslo covering the walls. When the waiter returned with the beer, Harry asked him to take it back and paid him. It obviously wasn't the waiter's first experience of an alcoholic who checked himself at the last moment, and he disappeared with the beer without a word or a raised eyebrow. Harry looked at Gert. Thought about the lineage.

"Granny is right," he said. "Beer isn't good for anyone. Remember that."

"OK."

Harry smiled. The boy had picked up this "OK" from Harry. He only hoped he wouldn't pick up much else. He had no desire for a descendant created in his own image, on the contrary. The almost automatic tenderness and love he felt for the boy on the other side of the table was just about his being happy, more than he himself had been. A scratching sound came from the straw, and at that moment Harry's phone vibrated.

A text from Katrine.

Home now. Where are you two?

"Time to go home to Mama," Harry said, tapping a message to say they were on the way.

"Whew aw you going?" Gert asked, kicking the table leg.

"I'm going to the hotel," Harry said.

"Nooo." The boy lay a small, warm hand upon his. "You aw going to sing dat song when I go to bed. About the dwink."

"The drink?"

"Coke-cane . . ." Gert sang.

Harry wanted to laugh but had to swallow the lump in his throat instead. Bloody hell. What was that exactly? Was it what Ståle called priming? Did Harry only feel this way because the certainty that he was the father of the child had been planted in him? Or was it something more physical or biological, something in the blood calling, pulling two people helplessly towards one another?

Harry got to his feet.

"Which animal ah you?" Gert asked.

"Orangotango," Harry said, and lifted Gert out of his chair and performed a pirouette that earned applause from one of the lonely guests. He put Gert down, and they walked hand in hand towards the door.

It was ten o'clock at night, and Prim had just fed Boss and Lisa. He sat down in front of the TV to watch the news again. To enjoy once again the results of what he had staged. Although the police didn't say it directly, he could tell by the platitudes they were spouting that they hadn't found any evidence at the scene. He had made the right decision when Helene got out of the car, and he'd had to kill her on the gravel road. Leaving behind DNA was unavoidable—a hair, a flake of skin or sweat—and seeing as he couldn't carry out such a thorough clean-up on a road where witnesses might show up, he'd had to ensure that the gravel road wasn't identified as the crime scene. So, he had taken the body in the car and deposited it at the end of the island, which he could be fairly certain was deserted late on an autumn night, leaving him to carry out his work behind the cover of the tall reeds. And be fairly certain also that Helene's body would be found when families and children descended on the area the next day. First, he had cut off her head, then gone over her body, washing and scraping off his own DNA from under the nails she had dug into his thighs when she had ridden him in the car. Care had to be taken, because although he had never been convicted of anything, the police had his DNA profile in their database.

The female news anchor on the TV was speaking via telephone to a male police lawyer, while a photo of him along with his name—Chris Hinnøy—appeared in the top right corner of the screen. They were talking about Røed being remanded in custody. It was no wonder they were beginning to run out of exciting angles, the news channels had largely focused on the arrest of Markus Røed and the murder of his wife all day, even Bodø/Glimt's narrow victory over Molde had received scant coverage. The same with the online papers, everything was about Markus Røed. Which, in an indirect way, meant that it was about him, Prim. Granted, now that the online editions had put up so many pictures of Markus Røed, pictures of Harry Hole had begun to crop up as well. They wrote that it had been he—the outsider, the private investigator—who had linked Markus Røed's DNA to the saliva on Susanne's breast. As if that was so amazing. As if the police shouldn't have found out something like that by themselves ages ago. He was actually beginning to get pretty annoying, this Harry Hole. What business did he have being in the limelight? The stage ought to be reserved for the case, the mystery, *his* mystery. They should dwell even more on the fact that Markus Røed, a man of privilege, a man who thought himself above the law, had now been wonderfully exposed and put in the stocks. People loved that sort of thing, Prim certainly did, it was sugar for the soul. Still, the public had received a hefty dose. He hoped his stepfather had access to the newspapers where he was, that he had ample opportunity to suffer, that this public humiliation was now the acid bath Prim had drawn for him. The confusion, desperation and fear Markus Røed must be feeling. Had the thought of taking his own life occurred to him yet? Prim wondered. No, the trigger for suicide, the factor that had pushed his mother to suicide, was hopelessness, and his stepfather still had hope. He had Johan Krohn himself acting on his behalf, and the only evidence the police had was some saliva. They were going to have to balance that against the false alibi Helene had given Markus for the nights Susanne and Bertine went missing. But what the police lawyer on TV had just said disturbed Prim.

This Chris Hinnøy had explained that there would be a preliminary hearing tomorrow where the judge would doubtless grant the police the usual four weeks of remand in custody, and—given the evidence and serious nature of the crime—further detention thereafter if required. That, in Norwegian law, there was no time limit on how long a person could be held in custody, so in principle years could pass. And it was of particular importance that the police were afforded generous access to the detention of people of advantage and means who could otherwise use their money or influence to have evidence destroyed, tamper with witnesses, yes, there were even examples of them attempting to influence investigators.

"Like Harry Hole?" the interviewer asked, as if that had anything to do with it!

"Hole is paid by Røed," the police lawyer said. "But Hole has been educated and trained within the Norwegian police and clearly possesses the integrity we expect of members of the force, both past and present."

"Thank you for joining us, Chris Hinnøy . . ."

Prim turned the volume down. Swore while he pondered matters. If the police lawyer was right, then Markus Røed could stay locked up indefinitely, safe in a cell where he couldn't be reached. That wasn't the plan.

He tried to think.

Did the plan—the grand plan—need changing?

He looked at the pink slug on the coffee table. At the slimy trail it had left behind after a half-hour's exertion. Where was it going? Did it have a plan? Was it hunting something? Or fleeing? Was it aware that sooner or later the cannibal slugs would find the trail and take up pursuit? That coming to a standstill was death?

Prim pressed his fingers against his temples.

Harry ran, felt his heart pump blood out to his body as he watched the news anchor thank Hinnøy.

Chris Hinnøy was one of the three police lawyers Harry and Johan Krohn had contacted a couple of hours ago to ask them to provide a subjective and unofficial assessment of the likelihood of Markus Røed being found guilty given the evidence in the case. Two of them had wanted to answer straight off, but Krohn had asked them to sleep on it until the morning.

The trainer of Bodø/Glimt was being interviewed on the news, and Harry shifted his gaze from the TV screen attached to the treadmill to the mirror in front of him.

He had the hotel's small gym to himself. He had left his suit hanging in his room and put on a hotel bathrobe, which was now hanging on a peg behind him. The mirror in front covered the entire wall. He was running in underwear, a T-shirt and his handmade John Lobb shoes, which functioned surprisingly well as running shoes. He looked ridiculous, of course, but didn't give a shit. On his way down he had even stopped by the reception in this outfit and said he had met an affable priest in the bar but forgotten his name. The black female receptionist had nodded and smiled. "He isn't a guest at the hotel, but I know who you mean, Mr Hole. Because he was here inquiring about you as well."

"Really? When?"

"Not long after you checked in, I don't remember exactly when. He asked for your room number. I told him we don't give out that information but that I could place a call to your room. He declined and left."

"Mm. Did he say what he wanted?"

"No, just that he was . . . curious." She'd said the last word in English. And smiled again. "People tend to speak English to me."

"But he's American, isn't he?"

"Maybe."

Harry turned up the speed on the treadmill. He still had the pace. But was he running well enough? Would he ultimately be able to outrun everything? Everything behind him? Those who were out after him? Interpol had access to the guest lists of every hotel in the world, as did every halfway decent hacker. Suppose the priest was there to keep an eye on him, suppose he was the one who, in two days, when the deadline expired without the debt being paid, was going to take care of Harry. So what? Debt collectors don't kill their debtors before all hope of getting their money is out, and then only as a warning to other debtors. And now Røed had been arrested. Saliva on the victim's nipple. You don't get better fucking forensic evidence than that. In the morning, the three police lawyers would say the same thing, the money would be transferred, the debt cleared, and he and Lucille would be free. So why was his mind still churning? Was it because it felt as though there was something else he was trying to run from, something that had to do with this case?

The phone, which Harry had placed in the bottle holder in the treadmill, rang. No initials appeared on the screen, but he recognized the number, and answered.

"Talk to me."

He heard laughter in response. Then a soft voice. "I can't believe you're still using that same expression from back when we worked together, Harry."

"Mm. I can't believe you're still using the same number."

Mikael Bellman laughed again. "Congratulations on Røed."

"Which part?"

"Oh, both on the job and the arrest."

"What do you want, Bellman?"

"Now now." He laughed again, that charming, hearty laughter so effective in making men and women believe that Mikael Bellman was a warm, sincere individual, someone they could trust. "I must admit, you become a little spoilt as Minster for Justice, you get used to being the one pressed for time, it's never the person you're talking with."

"I'm not pressed for time. Not any longer."

The pause that followed was a long one. When Bellman continued, the cordiality sounded slightly more forced.

"I called to say we appreciate what you've done on this case, it demonstrates integrity. We in the Labour Party care about equality before the law, and that's why I gave the green light for an arrest earlier today. It's important to send out the signal that in a functioning state governed by the rule of law there are no advantages in being wealthy and famous."

"Quite the opposite, perhaps," Harry said.

"Pardon?"

"I wasn't aware that the Minister for Justice had to authorize arrests."

"This isn't just any arrest, Harry."

"That's what I mean. Some are more important. And it doesn't exactly hurt the Labour Party to be seen going after a well-heeled sleazeball."

"My point, Harry, is that I've sweet-talked Melling and Winter, and they're willing to have you on board the investigation moving forward. There is some work remaining before we file charges. Now that your employer has been arrested, I assume you're out of a job. Your contribution is important to us, Harry."

Harry had slowed the treadmill to walking speed.

"They'd like you to be present when Røed is interviewed in the morning."

What's important to you is that it looks like the hero of the hour is on your team, Harry thought.

"Well, what do you say?"

Harry considered it. Felt the distaste and distrust Bellman always evoked in him. "Mm. I'll be there."

"Good. Bratt will keep you up to speed. I have to run. Goodnight."

Harry ran for another hour. When he realized he wasn't going to out-run what was bothering him, he sat down in one of the chairs, letting the sweat seep into the cushion cover as he called Alexandra.

"Have you missed me?" she cooed.

"Mm. That club, Tuesdays . . ."

"Yeah?"

"They had club nights every Tuesday. Didn't your friend say something about Villa Dante carrying on the tradition?"

33

MONDAY

EDITOR-IN-CHIEF OLE SOLSTAD SCRATCHED HIS cheek with one tip of his reading glasses. Looked across his desk, piled with coffee-stained stacks of paper, at Terry Våge. Våge was slouched in the visitor's chair, his wool coat and porkpie hat still on, as though he expected the meeting to take only a few moments. And hopefully it would. Because Solstad was dreading it. He should have listened to his colleague at the newspaper Våge had worked at before, who had quoted from the movie *Fargo* when he said, "I don't vouch for him."

Solstad and Våge had exchanged a few general words about Røed's arrest. Våge had grinned and said they had the wrong man. Solstad detected no lack of self-confidence, but that was likely the way with all con men, they were almost as adept at fooling themselves.

"So, we have decided not to commission any more content from you," Solstad said, aware he had to be careful not to use words like "let you go," "terminate" or "sack," either verbally or in writing. Although Våge was only on a freelancer contract, a good lawyer could use a de facto dismissal against them at an employment tribunal. The way Solstad had now phrased it only meant they would not be printing what Våge wrote, while at the same time he was not ruling out Våge being assigned other tasks covered by the contract, such as research for other journalists. But labor law was thorny, as *Dagbladet*'s lawyer had made clear to him.

"Why not?" Våge said.

"Because the events of the past few days have cast doubt on the veracity of your latest articles." And added, since someone had recently told him that a reprimand was always more effective if it included the name of the target, "Våge."

As soon as he had spoken, it struck Solstad that admonishment was hardly the appropriate tactic, given that the goal here wasn't for Våge to promise to mend his ways but to be rid of the guy with the least possible fuss. On the other hand, Våge needed to understand why they were taking such a drastic step, that it was about *Dagbladet*'s credibility.

"Can you prove that?" Våge said, without batting an eyelid, yes, even going so far as stifling a yawn. Demonstrative and puerile, but provocative nonetheless.

"The real question is if you can prove what you wrote. It looks like, smells like and sounds like fiction. Unless you can give me your source—"

"Christ, Solstad, as the editor of this rag you must know I have to protect—"

"I'm not saying you go public with it, just give it to me. Your editor-in-chief. The man responsible for what you write and we publish. Understand? If you tell me the source, then I'm obligated to protect it, same as you. As far, that is, as the law allows confidentiality of sources. Do you understand?"

Terry Våge let out a lengthy groan. "Do *you* understand, Solstad? Do you understand that then I'll go to another paper, let's say *VG* or *Aftenposten*, and do for them what I've been doing for *Dagbladet*? As in, turn them into the market leaders on crime reporting."

Ole Solstad and the other editors had of course taken that into consideration when they'd agreed on this decision. Våge had more readers than any of their other journalists—his click rates were simply enormous. And

Solstad would hate to see those numbers transferred to a competitor. But, like someone on the editorial staff had said, if they gave the discreet outward impression of having gotten rid of Terry Våge for similar reasons as the last time he was fired, Våge would be about as attractive to *Dagbladet*'s rivals as Lance Armstrong had been for US Postal's competitors after the doping scandal. It was a scorched earth policy, and it was Terry Våge they were burning, but in an era when respect for the truth was on the wane, old bastions like *Dagbladet* had to lead the way by example. They could always apologize if it turned out that Våge—against all odds—was in the clear.

Solstad adjusted his glasses. "I wish you all the best at our competitors, Våge. Either you're a man of exceptional integrity, or you're the very opposite, and we can't take a chance on the latter, I hope you understand." Solstad got to his feet behind the desk. "Along with payment for your last article, the editorial team wanted to give you a small bonus for your overall contribution."

Våge had also stood up, and Solstad tried to read the other man's body language to deduce whether he faced rejection if he proffered his hand. Våge flashed a white grin. "You can wipe you ass with your bonus, Solstad. And then you can wipe your glasses. Because everyone apart from you knows they're so caked in shit it's no wonder you see fuck all."

Ole Solstad remained standing for a few seconds staring at the door Våge had slammed behind him. Then he removed his glasses and studied them carefully. Shit?

Harry was standing in the room next to the small interview room staring at Markus Røed, who was sitting on the other side of the glass wall. Three other people were in there with him, the lead interviewer, his assistant and Johan Krohn.

It had been a busy morning. Harry had met up at Krohn's office in Rosenkrantz' gate at eight o'clock where they had called the three police lawyers, who in turn had declared it "highly likely" that Røed would be found guilty in court, with the proviso that other significant factors did not come into play. Krohn hadn't said a lot but had behaved in a professional manner. Without objection, he had immediately contacted the bank and, acting on the prior issued power of representation, had instructed them to transfer the contractual amount to the bank account on the Cayman Islands. According to the bank the recipient would see the money in their account the same day. They were saved. That is to say, he and Lucille were saved. So why was he standing here? Why wasn't he already at a bar getting on with what he had begun at Creatures? Well. Why do people finish books they've realized they don't like? Why do single people make up their beds? When he awoke that morning, he had realized it was the first night in weeks he hadn't dreamed about his mother, about her standing in the doorway of the classroom. He had made peace. Or had he? Instead, he had dreamed that he was still running, but that everything his feet landed on turned into treadmills, and that he wasn't able to flee from . . . from what?

"Responsibility." It was his grandfather's voice, the kind, alcoholic man who vomited in the dawn light before shoving the row boat out of the boat-shed, lifting Harry aboard while Harry asked why they were going to pull in the nets now when Grandad was sick. But Harry didn't have any bloody responsibilities left to run from. Or did he? Apparently, he thought he did. He was standing here in any case. Harry felt a headache coming on and pushed the thoughts away. He did so by concentrating on simple, concrete things he understood. Like trying to interpret Røed's facial expressions and body language as he sat answering questions. Harry tried, without listening to the answers, to decide if he thought Markus Røed was guilty or not. Sometimes it felt as though all the experience Harry had gathered throughout his life as a detective was useless, that his ability to read other people was mere illusion. While other times this—this gut feeling—was the only certainty, the only thing he could always count on. How many times had he been without physical proof or circumstantial evidence, but known, and been right in the end? Or was that just cognitive bias, confirmation bias? Had he thought he'd known just as often but been wrong and consigned it to oblivion? Why was he so sure Markus Røed hadn't killed the women—and was still so sure he wasn't innocent? Had he ordered the murders, ensured he had an alibi and been so confident his innocence would be proved that he had paid Harry and the others to do it? If that was the case, why not provide yourself with a better alibi than being at home alone with your wife when the first two murders were committed? And now he didn't even have an alibi, Markus Røed claimed he had been home on his own the night Helene was killed. Her—the witness who could save him if there was a trial. It didn't add up. And yet . . .

"Is he saying anything?" a voice whispered next to Harry. It was Katrine who had entered the semi-darkness of the room and stood between Harry and Sung-min.

"Yes," Sung-min whispered. "Don't know. Can't remember. No."

"Right. Picking up any vibes?"

"I'm trying," Harry said.

Sung-min didn't answer.

"Sung?" Katrine said.

"I might be wrong," Sung-min said, "but I think Markus Røed is a closet gay. With the emphasis on closet."

The other two looked at him.

"What makes you think that?" Katrine asked.

Sung-min gave a crooked smile. "That would be a long lecture, but let's just say it's the sum of a long series of subliminal details which I notice, and you don't. But I could be wrong of course."

"You're not wrong," Harry said.

Now the two others looked at him.

He cleared his throat. "Remember I asked if you'd heard of Villa Dante?"

Katrine nodded.

"It's actually a club called Tuesdays, just reopened under a different name."

"Sounds familiar," she said.

"Exclusive gay club a few years back," Sung-min said. "It was shut down when an underage boy was raped there. Then it was referred to as Studio 54, after the gay bar in New York, you know. Because it was open exactly as long, thirty-three months."

307

"Now I remember," Katrine said. "We called it the Butterfly case because the boy said the rapist was wearing a butterfly mask. But wasn't the reason they had to close because they had waiters under eighteen serving alcohol?"

"Technically, yes," Sung-min said. "The court wasn't willing to accept the club's activities fell under private function, and consequently ruled they'd broken licensing laws."

"I've reason to believe that Markus Røed frequented Villa Dante," Harry said. "I found a membership card and a cat mask in the pockets of this suit. Which is his."

Sung-min raised an eyebrow. "You're . . . eh, wearing his suit?"

"What are you getting at, Harry?" Katrine's voice was sharp, her stare hard.

Harry took a deep breath. He could still let it lie.

"It seems Villa Dante has continued to hold the club nights on Tuesdays. If Røed is as anxious to stay in the closet as you believe, he may have an alibi for the nights Susanne and Bertine were killed, just not the alibi he's given us."

"What you're saying," Katrine said slowly, while Harry felt as though her eyes were drilling into his head, "is that we have arrested a man with a better alibi than that he was with his wife. That he was at a gay club. But doesn't want anybody to know that?"

"I'm just saying it's a possibility."

"You're saying it's possible Røed would rather risk prison rather than have his sexual orientation revealed?" Her voice was monotone but quivered with something Harry could guess at. Sheer unadulterated anger.

Harry looked at Sung-min, who nodded.

"I've met men who would sooner be dead than be outed," Sung-min said. "We might believe things have moved forward for all in that regard, but unfortunately that's not the case. The shame, self-loathing, condemnation, it's not a thing of the past. Especially for those of Røed's generation."

"And with his family background," Harry added. "I've seen pictures of his forefathers. They didn't look like men who would hand over the reins of the business to someone who has sex with men."

Katrine still hadn't taken her eyes off Harry. "So tell me, what would you do?"

"Me?"

"Yes, you. There's a reason you're telling us this, right?"

"Well." He reached into his pocket and handed her a note. "I'd take the opportunity of this interview to ask him these two questions."

He watched Katrine read the note as they listened to Krohn's voice coming over the loudspeaker. ". . . over an hour, and my client has answered all your questions, most of them two or three times. Either we can stop here or I'd like my objection put on the record."

The lead interviewer and her colleague looked at each other.

"OK," the lead interviewer said, looked up at the clock on the wall and became aware of Katrine, who had opened the door of the interview room. She went over to her, took the note and listened. Harry could see Krohn's questioning look. Then the lead interviewer sat down and cleared her throat.

"Two final questions. Were you at the Villa Dante club at the times it's believed that Susanne and Bertine were killed?"

Røed exchanged a glance with Krohn before answering. "I've never heard of that club, and I will simply repeat that I was with my wife."

"Thank you. The other question is for you, Krohn."

"For me?"

"Yes. Were you aware that Helene Røed was seeking a divorce and that if her demands in the related settlement were not met, she was planning to retract the alibi she'd given her husband for the nights of the murders?"

Harry saw Krohn's face turn red. "I . . . I see no reason to answer that."

"Not even a simple no?"

"This is highly irregular, and I think we'll consider this interview over." Krohn got to his feet.

"That spoke volumes," Sung-min said, rocking on his heels.

Harry made to go but Katrine held him back.

"Don't try to tell me you didn't know all this before we arrested Røed," she whispered angrily. "OK?"

"He just lost his stated alibi," Harry said. "That was the only one he had. So let's just hope no one at Villa Dante can attest to his being there."

"And what exactly are you hoping for, Harry?"

"The same as always."

"Which is?"

"That the guiltiest get caught."

Harry had to take long strides to catch up with Johan Krohn on the hill down from Police HQ towards Grønlandsleiret.

"Was it you who gave them the idea of asking me that last question?" Krohn said, scowling.

"What makes you think that?"

"Because I know exactly what Helene Røed told the police, which wasn't much. And when I arranged for you to have your conversation with Helene, I was foolish enough to tell her she could trust you."

"Did you know she'd use the alibi to blackmail Markus?"

"No."

"But you did receive the letter from her lawyer where she demanded half of everything despite the prenup and managed to put two and two together."

"She may have had other leverage which bore no relation to this case."

"Like outing him?"

"It would seem we've nothing more to discuss, Harry." Krohn made an unsuccessful attempt to hail a passing taxi, but from across the street a parked taxi made a U-turn and glided up to the sidewalk beside them. The window on the driver's side was lowered and a face with a brown grin appeared.

"Can we offer you a lift?" Harry asked.

"No thank you," Krohn said and strode down Grønlandsleiret.

Øystein watched the lawyer stalk off. "Bit pissed off?"

It was six o'clock and beneath the low, dense cloud cover the lights in the houses were already coming on.

Harry stared at the ceiling. He was lying on his back on the floor next to Ståle Aune's bed. On the other side of the bed, Øystein was lying in a similar position.

"So, your gut is telling you that Markus Røed is both guilty and innocent," Aune said.

"Yeah," Harry said.

"How, for example?"

"Well, he orders both murders, but doesn't commit them. Or the first two murders are carried out by a sex attacker, and Røed spots his chance to kill his wife by copying the serial killer, so no one thinks he's guilty."

"Especially if he has an alibi for the first two murders," Øystein said.

"Do either of you believe in that theory?" Aune asked.

"No," Harry and Øystein said in unison.

"It's baffling," Harry said. "On the one hand Røed had motive to kill his wife if she was blackmailing him. On the other hand, his alibi is severely weakened now that she can't confirm her statement to the police under oath in a trial."

"Well, maybe Våge's right then," Øystein said, as the door opened. "Even though he's been given the boot. There's a cannibal and serial killer on the loose, full stop."

"No," Harry said. "The type of serial killer Våge is describing doesn't murder three people from the same party."

"Våge is making stuff up," Truls said, putting three large pizza boxes on the table and tearing off the lids. "*VG* have it up on their website now. They have sources saying Våge was fired from *Dagbladet* because he was concocting stories. I could've told them that."

"Could you?" Aune looked at him in surprise.

Truls just grinned.

"Ah, smells like pepperoni and human flesh," Øystein said, getting to his feet.

"Jibran, you have to help us eat this," Aune called over to the neighboring bed where the vet lay with his headphones on.

While the other four crowded around the table, Harry sat on the floor with his back against the wall reading *VG* 's webpage. And thinking.

"By the way, Harry," Øystein said, his mouth full of pizza, "I told that girl at the Forensic Medical Institute we'd meet in the Jealousy at nine tonight, all right?"

"OK. Sung-min Larsen from Kripos is coming as well."

"What about you, Truls?"

"What about me?"

"Come to the Jealousy. It's 1977 today."

"Huh?"

"1977. Only the best tunes from 1977."

Truls chewed while he scowled distrustfully at Øystein. As though he was unable to decide whether he was being made fun of or if somebody was actually inviting him to hang out.

"All right," he said finally.

"Excellent, we'll be the dream team. This pizza's going fast here, Harry. What are we doing anyway?"

"Pulling in the net," Harry said without looking up.

"Eh?"

"I'm wondering if I'm going to try getting Markus Røed that alibi he doesn't want."

Aune approached him. "You seem relieved, Harry."

"Relieved?"

"I won't ask but I'm guessing it has something to do with what you didn't want to talk about."

Harry looked up. Smiled. Nodded.

"Good," Aune said. "Good, then I'm a little relieved too." He shuffled towards the bed.

At seven o'clock Ingrid Aune arrived. Øystein and Truls were in the cafeteria, and when Ståle went to the bathroom, Ingrid and Harry were left sitting alone in the room.

"We're heading off now, so the two of you can get some peace," Harry said.

Ingrid, a small, stocky woman with steel-gray hair, a steady gaze and the residue of a Nordland accent straightened up in the chair and took a deep breath. "I've just come from the senior consultant's office. He's received a report expressing concern from the head nurse. About three men who tired Ståle Aune out with their numerous and lengthy visits. As the patients tend to find it difficult to say it themselves, he was wondering if I could urge you to curtail the visits from now on as Ståle is entering the final phase."

Harry nodded. "I understand. Is that what you want?"

"Absolutely not. I told the consultant that you need him. And . . ." She smiled. "That he needs you. We need something to live for, I said to him. And sometimes something to die for. The consultant said they were wise words, and I told him they weren't mine, but Ståle's."

Harry smiled back. "Did the senior consultant say anything else?"

She nodded. Turned her gaze to the window.

"Remember that time you saved Ståle's life, Harry?"

"No."

She gave a brief laugh. "Ståle has asked me to save his life. That's how he put it, the nitwit. He's asked me to get hold of a syringe. He suggested morphine."

In the ensuing silence, Jibran's steady breathing as he slept was the only sound in the room.

"Are you going to?"

"I am," she said. Her eyes filled with tears and her voice grew thick. "But I don't think I can manage it, Harry."

Harry placed a hand on her shoulder. Felt it tremble weakly. Her voice was only a whisper.

"And I know *that's* what I'm going to feel guilty about for the rest of my life."

34

MONDAY

Trans-Europe Express

PRIM READ THE ARTICLE ON *VG*'s website once more.

It didn't directly say that Våge had falsified his stories but that was the subtext. Nevertheless, if they weren't saying it directly that had to mean they had no proof. Only he, Prim, could prove it, tell them what *actually* happened. Once again, this instilled in him that warm, intoxicating sense of control which he hadn't anticipated, but was a pure bonus.

He had been thinking over and over ever since this morning, when he saw the small notice in *Dagbladet* about Terry Våge being taken off their crime cases. Prim had understood why right away. Not only why Våge had been removed, but why *Dagbladet* had drawn attention to it instead of just letting it happen quietly. They knew they had to actively distance themselves from Våge before the other newspapers confronted them with the lies they had published about cannibalism and resewn tattoos.

What was interesting was that Våge could now be used to solve the problem that had arisen. The problem of Markus Røed sitting safely in prison and beyond his reach indefinitely. This was time he didn't have, because biology runs its course, the natural cycle has its rhythm. But it was a major decision to take, a big deviation from the original plan, and past improvisation had already proved there was a price to pay. So he would have to think carefully. He went through the details yet again.

He looked down at the burner phone and at the note with Terry Våge's number, which he had found in directory inquiries. Felt the nervousness a chess player running out of time must feel when he decides on a move, in the knowledge it will either win or lose him the game but has yet to move the piece. Prim thought through the scenarios one more time, what could go wrong. And what must *not* go wrong. Reminded himself that he could retreat at any time without any trails leading back to him. *If* he did everything right.

Then he tapped in the number. He had a feeling of free fall, a wonderful shiver of excitement.

It was answered on the third ring.

"Terry."

Prim tried to hear if there was anything in Våge's voice to reveal the desperation he must be feeling. A man at rock bottom. A man nobody wanted. A man without alternatives. A man who had managed to make a comeback once before and was willing to do whatever it took to do so again, to win back his throne. To show them. Prim took a breath and put his voice in a deeper register.

"Susanne Andersen liked being slapped in the face when she had sex, I'd imagine you can get her ex-boyfriends to confirm that. Bertine Bertilsen smelled of sweat, like a man. Helene Røed had a scar on her shoulder."

Prim could hear Våge breathing in the pause that followed.

"Who is this?"

"This is the only person at large who could have this combined knowledge."

Another pause.

"What do you want?"

"To save an innocent person."

"Who's innocent?"

"Markus Røed, of course."

"Because?"

"Because I'm the one who killed the girls."

Terry Våge knew he should have tapped reject when *unknown caller* came up on the display, but as usual he couldn't help himself, it was that bloody curiosity of his. The belief that suddenly something good might occur, that one day the woman of his dreams might just ring him up, for instance. Why didn't he learn? The calls today had been from journalists looking for a comment on *Dagbladet* giving him the sack, and from a couple of die-hard fans letting him know how unfair they thought it was, among them a girl who sounded fit on the phone, but he had found her Facebook page and discovered she was much older than she sounded and pig ugly. And now this call, yet another nutter. Why couldn't normal people ring? Friends, for instance? Was it due to him no longer having any perhaps? His mother and sister got in touch, but his brother and father didn't. That's to say, his father had called once—he probably thought the success at *Dagbladet* compensated somewhat for the scandal that had brought shame to the family name. In the past year a couple of girls had contacted Terry. They always popped up when he attracted attention; it had been the same when he was a music journalist. Obviously the band members got more pussy, but he got more than the guys on the mixing desk. The best strategy was sticking close to the band—a couple of positive reviews were always rewarded with a backstage pass—and hope for trickle-down benefits. The next best was the opposite: slate the band and reap the cred. As a crime journalist he no longer had the gigs as a hunting ground, but he compensated with the gonzo style he had cultivated as a music journalist; he was *in* the story, he was the war correspondent of the streets. And with a byline and a photo there was always the occasional woman who'd call. It was for that very reason he had kept his number listed—not for people to call him up at all hours of the day with all manner of idiotic tips and stories.

Taking this anonymous call was one thing, not hanging up was something else entirely. Why hadn't he? Perhaps it wasn't what the man said, about him being the one who had killed the girls. It was the way he had said it. Without fanfare, just stated it calmly.

Terry Våge cleared his throat. "If you really killed those girls, shouldn't you be happy the police suspect someone else?"

"True, I've no desire to be caught, but it gives me no pleasure that an innocent man should atone for my sins."

"Sins?"

"Granted, choice of word's a tad biblical. The reason I'm calling is that I think we can help one another, Våge."

"Can we?"

"I want the police to realize they have the wrong man so that Røed is released immediately. You want to reclaim your place at the top after your attempts to fake your way there."

"What would you know about that?"

"You wanting to get back to the top is just guesswork on my part, but as for your last article, I know it's made up."

Våge thought for a moment while his eyes wandered around what with a measure of goodwill could be termed a bachelor pad, but without had to be termed a hole. In a year, with the level of income he was receiving from *Dagbladet*, he had imagined he could get someplace bigger, with more air and light. Less dirt. Dagnija, his Latvian girlfriend—she thought she was at any rate—was coming to stay for the weekend, she could give the place a clean then.

"I will of course have to check what you claimed to know about the girls at the outset," Våge said. "Assuming that's correct, what's your suggestion?"

"I'd prefer to call it an ultimatum, since it either happens in exactly the detail I want or not at all."

"Go on."

"Meet me on the south side of the roof of the Opera House tomorrow night. I'll provide you with proof that I was the one who killed the girls.

317

Nine on the dot. You're not to tell a soul we're meeting and naturally you've got to come alone. Understood?"

"Understood. Can you tell me a little about—"

Våge stared at the phone. The man had hung up.

What the fuck was that? It was too crazy to be the real thing. And he didn't have any number to find out who'd called either.

He checked the time. Five to eight. He felt like heading out for a beer. Not to Stopp Pressen! or anywhere like that, but someplace he wouldn't risk running into colleagues. He thought wistfully about the times he could go to release concerts where the record companies handed out beer bongs to the journalists in the hope of a favorable review, and it wasn't unheard of for a young female artist to seek his sympathy with the same aim in mind.

He looked at the phone again. Too crazy. Or was it?

It was half past nine, and Bob Marley and the Wailers' "Jamming" was streaming out of the loudspeakers at a packed Jealousy Bar. It looked like the entire population of middle-aged hipsters in Grünerløkka had turned out to drink beer and offer their opinions on the playlist. They alternated between cheers and boos each time a new song came on.

"I'm just saying that Harry's wrong!" Øystein shouted to Truls and Sung-min. "'Stayin' Alive' isn't better than 'Trans-Europe Express,' and it's as simple as that!"

"The Bee Gees versus Kraftwerk," Harry translated for Alexandra as the five of them worked their way through four beers and a mineral water. They were sitting in a booth they'd secured, where the sound level was lower.

"Nice to be on the same team as you all," Sung-min declared, holding up his glass for a toast. "And congratulations on the arrest yesterday."

"Which Harry's going to try and get reversed tomorrow," Øystein said, clinking his glass against the others."

"Pardon?"

"He said he's going to get Røed the alibi he doesn't want."

Sung-min looked across the table at Harry, who shrugged.

"I was going to try to get into Villa Dante and find witnesses who can confirm that Røed was there on the Tuesday nights Susanne and Bertine were killed. If I find them, they'll be worth a lot more than the statement of a dead wife."

"Why are you going there?" Alexandra asked. "Why can't the police just raid the place and make inquiries?"

"Because," Sung-min said, "for one thing, we'd need a court order, and we're not going to get that as there's no reason to suspect anything criminal is going on at the club. For another, we'd never get anyone there to come forward as a witness given that the whole point of Villa Dante is complete anonymity. What I'm wondering is how *you're* going to gain entry and get someone to talk, Harry."

"Well. Number one, I'm not a cop any more and I don't need to concern myself about court orders. Number two, I have these." Harry had reached inside his jacket pocket and was holding up a cat mask and a Villa Dante membership card. "Plus, I have Røed's suit, we're both the same height, same mask . . ."

Alexandra laughed. "Harry Hole intends to go to a gay sex club and pose as . . ." She snatched the card and read, "Catman? In that case you might need a few pointers first."

"I was actually wondering if you might consider coming along," Harry asked.

Alexandra shook her head. "You can't take a woman with you to a gay club, that's a deal breaker, no one will chat you up. The only way would be if I could pretend I was in drag."

"Not a chance, dear," Sung-min interjected.

"Listen, this is what's going to happen," Alexandra said, and her wicked grin made the others lean in closer to hear. While she elaborated, they alternated between gasping and laughing in disbelief. When Alexandra was finished, she looked at Sung-min for confirmation.

"I don't frequent those sorts of clubs, dear. What I'm wondering is how *you* know so much."

"You're allowed to bring women to Scandinavia Leather Man one night a year," she said.

"Still interested in going?" Øystein asked, poking Harry in the ribs. Truls grunted his laugh.

"More performance anxiety than penetration anxiety," Harry said. "I doubt I'll be raped."

"No one's going to get raped, certainly not a daddy over six feet tall," Alexandra said. "But there'll probably be twinks there who'll hit on you."

"Twinks?"

"Cute, skinny boys who want to be towered over. But like I said, watch out for bears, and take care in the dark rooms."

"Another round?" Øystein said. He counted three fingers being held up.

"I'll help you carry them," Harry said.

They squeezed their way to the bar and were standing in the line when the guitar riff of David Bowie's "Heroes" sounded to rousing cheers all around.

"Mick Ronson is God," Øystein said.

"Yeah, but that there is Robert Fripp," Harry said.

"Correct, Harry," a voice behind them said. They turned. The man had a flat cap, several days of stubble and warm, slightly sad eyes. "Everyone thinks Fripp used an EBow but it's just feedback from the studio monitors." He held out his hand. "Arne, Katrine's boyfriend." He had a nice smile. Like an old friend, Harry thought. Except that this guy had to be at least ten years younger than them.

"Aha," Harry said, and shook his hand.

"Big fan," Arne said.

"Us too," Øystein said as he tried in vain to attract the attention of the busy bartenders.

"I didn't mean of Bowie, but of you."

"Of me?" Harry said.

"Of him?" Øystein said.

Arne laughed. "Don't look so shocked. I was thinking of the incredible things you've done for the city as a policeman."

"Mm. Is it Katrine who's been telling you tales?"

"No, no, listen, I knew about Harry Hole long before I met her. I must have been in my late teens when I was reading about you in the papers. You know, I even applied to Police College because of you." Arne's laughter was happy, breezy.

"Mm. But you didn't get in?"

"I was called in to take the entrance exams. But in the meantime I'd been accepted by a course at university that I thought I could use to become an investigator later."

"I see. Is Katrine with you?"

"Is she here?"

"I don't know, she sent me a text saying she might stop by, but it's so crowded in here and she might have bumped into some other people she knows. How did you find her, by the way?"

"Has she said it was me who found her?"

"Wasn't it?"

"Is that a guess?"

"Educated guess."

Arne looked at Harry in mock seriousness for a moment. Then his face broke into a boyish smile. "You're right, of course. The first time I saw her was on TV, but don't tell her, please. And not long after that she happened to come by where I work. So, I approached her, said I'd seen her on TV, and that she seemed like a hell of a woman."

"So, kind of like you're doing now."

More breezy laughter. "I can see how you'd think I was a fanboy, Harry."

"Aren't you?"

Arne seemed to think it over. "Yeah, you're right again, I suppose I am. Although you and Katrine aren't my biggest idols."

"Comforting to hear. Who is your biggest idol then?"

"You wouldn't be interested, I'm afraid."

"Maybe not but try me."

"All right. *Salmonella typhimurium*." Arne pronounced it slowly and reverently with clear diction.

"Mm. Salmonella as in bacteria?"

"Exactly."

"And why is that?"

"Because *typhimurium* is outstanding. It can survive anything and anywhere, even out in space."

"And why are you interested in it?"

"It's part of my job."

"Which is?"

"I search for particles."

"The kind within us or out there?"

"It's the same, Harry. The stuff life is made of. And death."

"OK?"

"If I were to gather up all the microbes, bacteria and parasites within you, guess how much it would weigh?"

"Mm."

"Four and a half pounds." Øystein handed two beers to Harry. "Read it in *Science Illustrated*. Scary stuff."

"Yeah, but it'd be even scarier if they weren't present," Arne said. "Then we wouldn't be alive."

"Mm. And they survive in space?"

"Some microbes don't even need to be in proximity to a star or have access to oxygen. Quite the opposite, in fact. They've carried out research on it aboard the space stations and discovered that *typhimurium* is even more dangerous and more effective in those surroundings than on the earth's surface."

"Seeing as you sound like you know a lot about that kind of stuff . . ." Øystein sucked the froth off one of the beers he was holding. "Is it true that thunder can only occur when it rains?"

Arne looked slightly disorientated. "Eh . . . no."

"Exactly," Øystein said. "Listen."

They listened. Fleetwood Mac's "Dreams" had reached the chorus where Stevie Nicks was singing about thunder only happening when it rains.

The three of them laughed.

"Lindsey Buckingham's fault," Øystein said.

"No," Harry said. "It was actually Stevie Nicks who wrote that song."

"Well, it's the best two-chord song ever at any rate," Arne said.

"No, Nirvana have that," Øystein said quickly. " 'Something in the Way.' "

They looked at Harry. He shrugged. "Jane's Addiction. 'Jane Says.' "

"You're improving," Øystein said, smacking his lips. "And the worst two-chord song of all time?"

They looked at Arne. "Well," he said, " 'Born in the U.S.A.' might not be the worst, but it's definitely the most overrated."

Øystein and Harry nodded in acknowledgement.

"You coming over to our table?" Øystein asked.

"Thanks, but I have a pal over there I need to keep company. Another time."

With their hands full of beer glasses they exchanged careful knuckle bumps as they took their leave of one another, before Arne disappeared into the crowd and Harry and Øystein started on their way back to the booth.

"Nice guy," Øystein said. "I think Bratt might be onto a good thing there."

Harry nodded. His brain was searching for something, which it had registered, but had not paid attention to. They arrived at the table with four beers, and since the others were drinking so slowly, Harry took a sip of one. And then another.

When the Sex Pistols's "God Save the Queen" finally came on, they got to their feet in the booth and pogoed up and down along with the rest of the rabble.

By midnight the Jealousy Bar was still jam-packed and Harry was drunk.

"You're happy," Alexandra whispered in his ear.

"Am I?"

"Yes, I haven't seen you like this since you got home. And you smell good."

"Mm. Guess it's true then."

"What's true?"

"That you smell better when you're not in debt."

"I don't get it. But speaking of home, are you going to walk me?"

"Walk you home or come home with you?"

"We can figure that out along the way."

Harry realized how drunk he was when he hugged the others goodbye. Sung-min smelled of a distinctive fragrance, lavender, or something similar, and wished him luck at Villa Dante, but added that he would pretend not to have heard about Harry's improper plans.

Maybe it was the talk of the smell of debt and Sung-min's lavender that did it, but on the way out the door Harry realized what detail had eluded him. The smell. He had breathed it in at some point in the evening, here, in this bar. He shuddered, turned and let his gaze sweep over the crowd. A scent of musk. The same scent he had caught when he was in the autopsy room with Helene Røed.

"Harry?"

"I'm coming."

Prim traversed the streets of Oslo. The wheels of his mind were going around and around, as though trying to grind the painful thoughts into pieces.

He, the policeman, had been at the Jealousy Bar, and that had made his blood boil. He should have left straight away, avoided the policeman, but it was as though he had been drawn to him, as though he were the mouse and the policeman the cat. He had looked for Her too, and maybe she had been there, maybe not, it had been so packed that most people were standing, making it difficult to get an overview. He was meeting her tomorrow. Should he ask if she was there? No, she could bring it up if she wanted. He had too many things to think about at the moment, he needed to push this to the back of his mind, he needed to have a clear head for tomorrow. He continued walking. Nordahl Bruns gate. Thor Olsens gate. Fredenborgsveien. His heels struck the sidewalk in a rhythmic beat as he hummed the tune of "Heroes" by David Bowie.

35

TUESDAY

THE TEMPERATURE PLUMMETED ON TUESDAY. Along Operagata and Dronning Eufemias gate, the wind gathered speed, and sidewalk signs outside the restaurants and clothing stores were blown over in the gusts.

At five past nine, Harry picked up his suit from the dry cleaner's in Grønland and at the same time asked if they could press the suit he was wearing while he waited. The Asian woman behind the counter shook her head regretfully. Harry said that was a pity, as he was attending a masked ball that evening. He could see her hesitate slightly before she returned his smile and said he was sure to have a lovely time all the same.

"*Xièxiè*," Harry said, bowing slightly then turning to leave.

"That was good pronunciation," the woman said before he had managed to place his hand on the door handle. "Where did you learn Chinese?"

"In Hong Kong. I only know a little."

"Most foreigners in Hong Kong don't know any at all. Take off your suit, I can give it a quick press."

*

At a quarter past nine Prim was standing by the bus stop gazing across the road over at Jernbanetorget. Studying the people he saw there, those crossing the station square and those who loitered. Were any of them police? He was carrying cocaine and didn't dare set foot in the square before he felt sure. But you can never be sure, you just had to make a judgment and put your fear behind. It was that simple. And that impossible. He swallowed. Crossed the street, entered the square and walked over to the tiger statue. Scratched it behind the ear. That's it, caress the fear and make it your friend. He took a deep breath and fiddled with the cocaine in his pocket. A man over by the steps was staring at him. Prim recognized him and ambled over.

"Good morning, sir," he said. "I have something you might like to try."

The daylight faded early, and it already felt late at night as Terry Våge crossed Operagata and stepped upon the Carrara marble. The choice of the Italian slabs had generated heated debate while the building was being constructed at the seafront in Bjørvika, but criticism had died away and the inhabitants had taken it to their hearts. Even on a September evening it was teeming with visitors.

Våge checked the time. Six minutes to nine. As a music journalist he used to arrive at least half an hour later than the artists were supposed to go onstage. Occasionally some weird band might go on at the advertised time and he would miss the first few songs, but then he would just ask some people who looked like fans what the opening number was, how the crowd had responded, and then embellish a little. It had always gone fine. But he wasn't taking that chance tonight. Terry Våge had made up his mind. From now on there was no more arriving late or making stuff up.

He used the steps on the side instead of walking straight up the sloping, smooth marble roof like he saw most of the youngsters doing. Because Våge was no longer young, and he couldn't afford any more slips.

When he reached the top he walked to the south side, like the guy on the phone had told him to. Stood by the wall between two couples and looked out over the fjord, which the wind was whipping white farther out.

He looked around him. Shivered and checked the time. Became aware of a man approaching him out of the gloom. The man raised something and pointed it towards Terry Våge, who stiffened.

"Excuse me," the man said, in what sounded like a German accent, and Våge moved to give him a clear shot.

The man pressed the shutter button, the camera gave a low hum, and he thanked him and disappeared. Våge shivered again. Leaned over the edge and looked down at the people on the marble below him. Looked at his watch again. Two minutes past nine.

There was light in the villa windows and the wind rustled the chestnut trees along the side road off Drammensveien. Harry had instructed Øystein to drop him a little way off from Villa Dante, even though pulling up in a taxi would hardly be conspicuous. Parking your own car in front of the villa would after all be asking to be identified.

Harry shuddered, regretted not bringing a coat. When he was fifty yards from the villa, he put on the cat mask and the beret he had borrowed from Alexandra.

Two flashlights flickered in the wind by the entrance to the large, yellow-brick building.

"Neo-baroque with art nouveau windows," Aune had noted when they found pictures on Google. "Built around 1900, I'd say. Probably by a shipowner, a merchant or some such type."

Harry pushed open the door and stepped inside.

A young man in a dinner jacket standing behind a small counter smiled at him, and Harry showed him the membership card.

"Welcome, Catman. Miss Annabell will be performing at ten o'clock."

Harry nodded mutely and walked towards the open door at the end of the hall. Music was coming from there. Mahler.

Harry entered a room illuminated by two huge crystal chandeliers. The bar and furniture were in a light brown wood, perhaps Honduran mahogany. There were thirty to forty other men in the room, all with masks and dark suits or dinner jackets. Young, unmasked males wearing close-fitting waiters' outfits sashayed between the tables carrying trays of drinks. But there were no male go-go dancers, like Alexandra had described, nor any naked man, caged on the floor, huddled with hands tied behind his back whom the guests could prod, kick or humiliate at will in other ways. The guests' glasses suggested martinis or champagne were the tipple of choice. Harry moistened his mouth. He'd had a beer at Schrøder's on the way back from Alexandra's that morning but promised himself that would be the only alcohol today. A few of the guests had turned and taken brief notice of him before returning to their conversations. Except for one, a clearly young and effeminate man of slight build who continued to watch Harry as he steered towards an unoccupied part of the bar counter. Harry hoped it didn't mean his cover was already blown.

"The usual?" the bartender asked.

Harry felt the twink's eyes on his back. He nodded.

The bartender turned and Harry watched him take out a tall glass and pour in Absolut Vodka, add Tabasco and Worcestershire sauce, and something resembling tomato juice. Finally, he put a stick of celery in the glass and placed it in front of Harry.

"I only have cash today," Harry said, and saw the bartender grin as though he had made a wisecrack. And realized at the same moment that cash was likely the sole currency in a place like this, where anonymity was demanded and accorded.

Harry stiffened as he felt a hand glide across his backside. He had been prepared for this; Alexandra had said it usually began with eye contact, then continued with bodily contact, often prior to a single word being said. And from there the possibilities were legion.

"Long time no see, Catman. You didn't have a beard then, did you?"

It was the twink. His voice was high, so high that Harry wondered if he was putting it on. The animal his mask was meant to depict was not obvious, but it wasn't a mouse anyway. It was green, and the scaly pattern and narrow eyes pointed more in the direction of a snake.

"No," Harry said.

The twink raised his glass and looked questioningly at Harry when he hesitated.

"Tired of Caesar?"

Harry nodded slowly. The Caesar had been the number-one gay drink at Dan Tana's in LA; apparently it was a Canadian thing.

"Maybe we should have something that wakes us up, then?"

"Like what?" Harry asked.

The twink cocked his head to one side. "You're different, Catman. Not just the beard, but your voice and—"

"Throat cancer," Harry said. It had been Øystein's suggestion. "Radiation treatment."

"Oh dear," the twink said without any appreciable interest. "Well, then I get the ugly hat, and that you've gotten so thin. Certainly was aggressive, I must say."

"You're not wrong," Harry said. "How long has it been exactly, since we've seen each other?"

"You tell me. A month. Or is it two? Time flies, and you certainly haven't been here for a while."

"If I'm not mistaken, I was here on a Tuesday five weeks ago, wasn't I? And on the Tuesday before that?"

The twink drew his head back a little between his shoulders, as though to regard him at slightly more distance. "Why the interest?"

Harry heard the skepticism in his voice and realized he had gotten ahead of himself. "It's the tumor," he said. "The doctor says it pressed on the brain and is caused partial memory loss. Sorry, I'm just trying to reconstruct the last months."

"You sure you remember *me*?"

"A little," Harry said. "But not everything. Sorry."

The twink snorted at the affront.

"Can you help me?" Harry asked.

"If you help me."

"With what?"

"Let's say you pay a little more for my blow than usual." The twink drew something halfway up out of his jacket pocket, and Harry saw the little plastic bag with white powder. "Then I can give it to you the same way as last time."

Harry nodded. Alexandra had told him that drugs—cocaine, speed, poppers, emma—were bought and sold more or less openly at the gay clubs she had been to.

"How did you give it to me last time?" Harry asked.

"Jesus, I thought you would have remembered that. I blew it up your lovely, tight bear-hole with this . . ." The twink held up a short metal straw. "Shall we go downstairs?"

Harry considered Alexandra's warning about dark rooms. Rooms where anything and anyone were fair game.

"OK."

They stood up and moved through the room. Eyes watched them from behind animal masks. At the far end the twink opened a door and Harry followed him into the darkness and down a steep, narrow staircase. Already halfway down he heard the sounds. Moans and cries and—when he came down into the basement—the slapping of flesh on flesh. There were small blue lights on the walls and when his eyes eventually adjusted sufficiently to the semi-darkness, he could see in detail what was going on around him. Men having sex in all manner of ways, some naked, some half dressed and some with just their flies open. He heard the same sounds behind the doors to the cubicles. Harry's eyes met those of a man wearing a gold mask. He was big and muscular and thrusting in and out of a person bent over a bench. The pupils behind the gold mask were large and black in the wide-open eyes fixed on Harry who instinctively flinched when the man bared his teeth in a predatory leer. Harry let his eyes wander farther. There was a smell in the room almost making him gag. Something other than the mixture of bleach, sex and testosterone, an acrid odor resembling gasoline. He couldn't put his finger on what it was until he glimpsed a naked man open a small, stubby bright yellow bottle and sniff. Of course, it was the smell of poppers. The stimulant had been popular in the clubs Harry had frequented in Oslo in his early twenties. They had called it rush back then, probably because that was what it was, a rush of a few seconds where the heart beat like hell, increasing the blood circulation for a brief moment, heightening all the senses. It was only later he learned that gay men—receivers—used it to boost the anal pleasure.

"Hi." It was the man in the gold mask. He had sidled up next to Harry and placed a hand on his crotch. His predatory smile widened and he breathed on Harry's face.

"He's mine," the twink said in a sharp voice, grabbing Harry by the arm and pulling him along. Harry heard the beefcake laugh behind them.

"Seems all the cubicles are occupied," the twink said. "Shall we . . . ?"

"No," Harry said. "In private."

The twink sighed. "Might be some empty ones further in. Come on."

They passed the open door of a room with a splashing sound like that of a running shower coming from within. Harry looked in as they walked by. Two naked men were sitting in a bath with their mouths open as other men, some wearing clothes, stood around urinating on them.

They went through a large room with strobe lighting and Joy Division's "She's Lost Control" pounding in the background out of loudspeakers. In the center of the room was a swing, attached to the ceiling by chains. A man appeared to be flying like Peter Pan as he, with his body outstretched, swung back and forth within a circle of men. They took turns using him, like a joint being passed around.

Harry and the twink entered a corridor with several cubicles, and again the sounds indicated what was happening behind the sliding doors. Two men exited one cubicle and the twink hurried to claim it. Harry followed him in and the twink pushed the door closed. The room measured about six and a half feet square. Without preamble, the twink began unbuttoning Harry's shirt. "Maybe a little cancer isn't such a bad thing, Catman, you feel more like a jock than a bear now."

"Wait," Harry said. He put his back to him and reached into his suit pocket. When he turned around, he was holding a wallet in one hand and a phone in the other.

"You wanted to sell me some cocaine, right?"

The other man smiled. "If you pay the price."

"Then let's get the deal done first."

"Oh, now that's more like the old you, Catman. Cokeman." He laughed and produced the bag of powder.

Harry accepted the bag and handed him the wallet. "Now I've received cocaine from you, and you can take out what you're due for the cocaine from my wallet."

The twink's eyes fixed on him dubiously from behind the mask. "You're being awfully meticulous today." Then he opened the wallet, peered inside and pulled out two thousand-krone notes.

"That should do it for now," he said, put the wallet back in Harry's suit pocket and began unbuttoning Harry's trousers. "You want me to suck your bear-dick? Sorry, your *jock*-dick?"

"No thanks, I've got what I wanted," Harry said, placing the hand not holding the phone behind the other man's head as though to caress him, but instead pulling the snake mask off him with a tug.

"What the fuck, Catman! That's . . . yeah, yeah, no big deal for me." The twink made to continue opening Harry's trousers but Harry stopped him and buttoned them up again.

"Oh, I get it, coke first."

"Not exactly," Harry said, taking off the beret and his own mask.

"You're . . . blond," the twink said in surprise.

"More importantly," Harry said, "I'm a policeman who just made an audio and video recording of you selling me cocaine. Which carries a penalty of up to ten years."

It was impossible to make out in the blue light if the other man's face went pale, so Harry was unsure the bluff had been successful until he heard the sobbing in his voice.

"Fuck, I *knew* it wasn't you! You don't walk like him, you have an East Oslo accent, and I could feel you didn't have that doughy ass of his. I'm such an idiot. Fuck you! And Catman!"

The twink grabbed the sliding door to get out but Harry held him back.

"Am I under arrest?"

Something in the twink's tone of voice and in the way he looked up at him made Harry wonder if the guy was turned on by the predicament.

"Are you going to . . . handcuff me?"

"This isn't a game"—Harry pulled a cardholder from the man's inside pocket—"Filip Kessler."

Filip put his face in his hands and began to cry.

"However, there is a way we can work this out," Harry said.

"There is?" Filip looked up with tear-stained cheeks.

"We can walk out of here now, go someplace nice and quiet, and you can tell me everything you know about Catman. All right?"

Terry Våge checked the time again. Nine thirty-six. No one had tried to contact him. He reread the message he had gotten on his phone again and arrived at the same conclusion as before, neither the time nor the place had been unambiguous. He had given the guy an extra half-hour as a gesture to the half-hour he used to give himself. But forty minutes was too much. The guy wasn't coming. A bluff. A practical joke, perhaps. Maybe someone was standing among the tourists on the level below having a good snigger at him now. Laughing at the disgraced, despised charlatan of a journalist. Maybe this was the punishment. He pulled his woolen coat tighter around him and began walking towards the sloping roof. Fuck them, fuck all of them!

Prim moved among the tourists on the marble slabs at ground level. He had seen Terry Våge arrive, recognized him from the byline photo and other images he had found online. Watched him stand on the roof and wait. Prim hadn't seen anyone follow Våge, nor anyone who looked like police in position at the place beforehand. He had moved around, taken note of most of the people who were there, and after half an hour concluded he no longer saw any of the faces he had seen when he arrived. At twenty to ten he saw Våge make his way down from the roof, he had given up. But now Prim was certain. Terry Våge had come alone.

Prim cast one last glance around him. Then set off for home.

36

WEDNESDAY

"AND WHAT'S HE DOING HERE?" Markus Røed sputtered, pointing at Harry. "A guy I've paid a million dollars to send me to jail when I'm innocent to boot!"

"Like I told you," Krohn said, "he's here because he doesn't actually think you're guilty, he thinks you were—"

"I heard what he thinks! But I haven't been to any bloody . . . *gay club*."

He spat the last two words out. Harry felt a drop hit the back of his hand, shrugged and looked at Johan Krohn. The room the three of them had been allocated for their meeting was actually a visiting room for the inmates' families. It had a window where the morning sun shone in behind rose-patterned curtains and iron bars, a table with an embroidered tablecloth, four chairs and a sofa. Harry had avoided the sofa and noticed Krohn did the same. He probably knew it was marinated in the juices from desperate and fast sex.

"Could you explain?" Harry said.

"Yes," Krohn said. "Filip Kessler is saying that on the two Tuesdays

Susanne and Bertine were murdered, he was with a person wearing the mask you see here."

Krohn pointed at the cat mask lying on the table next to the membership card.

"This person had the nickname Catman. Both items were in your suit, Markus. And the rest of the physical description matches you as well."

"Really? Which distinguishing features did he tell you about, then? Tattoos or scars? Birthmarks? Any peculiar abnormalities?" Røed looked from one to the other.

Harry shook his head.

"What?" Røed laughed angrily. "Nothing?"

"He doesn't remember anything like that," Harry said. "But he's pretty sure he'd recognize you if he was to touch you."

"Oh, Jesus fucking Christ," Røed said, looking like he was going to retch.

"Markus," Krohn said, "this is an alibi. An alibi we can use to get you released immediately, and that we can enter as evidence to have you acquitted should they still decide to prosecute. I understand that you're worried what this alibi would mean to people's image of you, but—"

"You understand?" Røed roared. "*Understand?* No, you don't fucking *understand* what it's like to sit here suspected of killing your own wife. And then be accused of this filth on top of it. I haven't seen that mask before. You want to know what I think? I think Helene got that mask and the membership card from some queer who looks like me and gave it to you so she could use it against me in the divorce. As for this Filip guy, he's got nothing on me, he just sees the opportunity to make a quick buck. So find out how much he wants, pay him and make sure he keeps his mouth shut. That isn't a suggestion, Johan, it's an order." Røed sneezed hard before continuing. "And the two of you are contractually bound by confidentiality clauses. If either of you say a single word about this to anybody, I'll sue the shit out of you."

Harry cleared his throat. "This isn't about you, Røed."

"What was that?"

"There's a killer out there who can and will, in all likelihood, strike again. That will be made all the easier for him as long as the police are convinced they already have the guilty party, as in you, in custody. If we withhold information about you being at Villa Dante, it makes us complicit when he kills his next victim."

"*We?* You can't honestly believe you still work for me, Hole?"

"I intend to honor the contract and I don't regard the case as solved."

"Really? Then give me back my money!"

"Not as long as three police lawyers are of the opinion you face conviction. What's important now is to get the police to refocus their attention, and that means we have to give them this alibi."

"I wasn't at that place, I'm telling you! It's not my fucking responsibility if the police aren't able to do their job. I'm innocent, and they'll find that out in a straightforward fashion, not with these . . . gay lies. There's no reason for panic or rash actions here."

"You idiot," Harry said with a sigh, as though it were a sad fact he was merely stating. "There's every reason to panic." He got to his feet.

"Where are you going?" Krohn asked.

"To inform the police," Harry said.

"You wouldn't dare," Røed snarled. "You do that and I'll make sure you and everyone you care about rot in hell. Don't think I'm not capable of it. And another thing. You might be under the impression I can't reverse a wire transfer to the Cayman Islands two days after I've instructed my bank to pay it. Wrong."

Something snapped in Harry, a familiar feeling of free fall. He took a step towards Røed's chair, and before he knew it, his hand was around the real estate mogul's throat and he was squeezing. Røed jerked back in his chair, gripped Harry's forearm with both hands and tried to pull it away as his face turned red from lack of blood flow.

"You do that, and I'll kill you," Harry whispered. "Kill. You."

"Harry!" Krohn had also risen to his feet.

"Sit down, I'll let go," Harry hissed, staring into the bulging, imploring eyes of Markus Røed.

"Now, Harry!"

Røed gurgled and kicked, but Harry held him down in the chair. He squeezed even harder and felt the power, the thrill, that he could squeeze the juice out of this anti-human. Yes, thrill, and that same feeling of free fall as when he lifted the glass of his first drink after months of sobriety. But he could already feel the thrill subside, the power in his grip ebb. Because there was no reward for this free fall either, other than it was free for the briefest of moments, and only led one way. Down.

Harry let go, and Røed drew in air in a drawn-out wheeze before leaning forward in a fit of coughing.

Harry turned to Krohn. "I'm guessing that *now* I am fired?"

Krohn nodded. Harry smoothed his tie and left.

Mikael Bellman stood by the window gazing longingly down towards the city center, where he could make out the high-rise in the government quarter. Closer, down by Gullhaug Bridge, he could see the treetops waving. The wind speed was supposed to increase even further; there had been talk of strong gales overnight. Something else had been forecast too, something about a lunar eclipse on Friday; apparently the events weren't connected. He raised his arm and looked at his classic Omega Seamaster watch. One minute to two. He had spent much of the day discussing in his own mind the dilemma the Chief of Police had presented to him. In principle, an individual case like this had of course no business being on the desk of the Minister for Justice, but Bellman had made it his business by getting involved earlier, and now he couldn't just drop it. He cursed.

Vivian tapped gently on the door and opened it. When he hired her as his personal assistant, it wasn't just because she had a master's in political science, spoke French after two years as a model in Paris and was willing to do everything from making coffee to greeting visitors and transcribing his speeches. She was pretty. There was much to be said about the function of physical appearance in today's world, and much was said. So much that one thing was certain: it was as important as it had always been. He himself was a handsome man and was under no illusions as to it having played a part in his career advancement. Despite the modeling career, Vivian was not taller than him, and was therefore someone he could take into meetings and to dinners. She had a live-in boyfriend, but he saw that as more of a challenge than a drawback. Actually, it was an advantage. A visit to a couple of South American countries was planned for winter; the main issue on the agenda was human rights, a pure pleasure trip, in other words. And like he told himself, there're a lot less flashbulbs and shepherding of a Minister for Justice than a Prime Minister.

"It's the Chief of Police," Vivian said softly.

"Send him in."

"On Zoom," she said.

"Oh? I thought he was coming—"

"Yes, but he just called and said it was too far to get up to Nydalen because he has another meeting downtown afterwards. He sent a link—shall I . . . ?"

She went over to the desk and the PC. Quick fingers, so much quicker than his own, ran across the keyboard. "There." She smiled. And added, as though to ease his irritation, "He's sitting waiting for you."

"Thank you." Bellman remained standing by the window until Vivian left the room. And then waited some more. Until he tired of his own childishness, walked over and sat down in front of the PC. The Chief of Police looked tanned, probably a recent fall break abroad somewhere. But it didn't help much when the camera angle was so unfortunate that his double chin dominated. He had obviously placed the laptop on the desk that had been there when Bellman himself was Chief of Police, instead of on top of a stack of books.

"Compared to down where you are, there's hardly any traffic up here," Bellman said. "I get home to Høyenhall in twenty minutes. You should try it."

"Apologies, Mikael, I was called into an emergency meeting about the state visit next week."

"OK, let's get straight to business. Are you alone, by the way?"

"Completely alone, go for it."

Mikael felt the irritation rise again. Lax use of first names and invitations like "go for it" ought to be the prerogative of the Minister for Justice. Especially as the six-year term of the Chief of Police was soon up and it was no longer the National Police Commissioner but the King in Council—in effect, the Minister for Justice—who decided who would continue and who would not, and Bellman had little to lose politically by giving the keys to Bodil Melling. Firstly because she was a woman, and secondly because she understood politics, understood who was in charge.

Bellman took a deep breath. "Just so we understand each other. What you're seeking my advice on is whether you should release Markus Røed from custody or not. And you also feel sure that both options are open to you."

"Yes," the Chief of Police said. "Hole has a witness who says he was with Røed the nights the first two girls were killed."

"A credible witness?"

"Credible in that, as opposed to Helene Røed, the person concerned has no obvious motive in providing Røed with an alibi. Less credible because according to the Drug Squad, the person in question is on their list of people selling cocaine in Oslo."

"But not convicted?"

"A small-time dealer, one which would be replaced overnight."

Bellman nodded. They let those they had control over continue their activities. Better the devil you know.

"But?" Bellman said, glancing at his Omega watch. It was impractical and bulky but sent the right signals. At the moment, the signal was for the Chief of Police to hurry up, he wasn't the only one with a busy day.

"On the other hand, Susanne Andersen had saliva from Markus Røed on her breast."

"That's a pretty overwhelming argument for continuing to keep him in custody, I should imagine."

"Yes. It is of course a possibility he and Susanne met earlier that day and had sex—it hasn't been possible to retrace all her movements. But if they had, it's odd Røed made no mention of it in interviews. Instead he denies ever having been intimate with her and claims he never saw her after the party."

"In other words, he's lying."

"Yes."

Bellman drummed his fingers on the desk. Prime ministers were only re-elected if the harvest has been good, figuratively speaking. His advisers emphasized repeatedly that as Minister for Justice, he would always share some measure of blame or credit for what happened further down the system, no matter if the mistake or good decision was made by people who were in the same job under the previous government. If the voters felt that a wealthy, privileged slimeball like Røed was let off the hook easily it would indirectly affect Bellman no matter what. He made up his mind.

"We have more than enough to keep him in custody with the semen."

"Saliva."

"Yeah. And I'm sure you agree that it wouldn't look good if Harry Hole got to decide when Røed is to be arrested and when he's to be released."

"I don't disagree, no."

"Good. Then I think you have my advice . . ." Bellman waited for the name of the Chief of Police to come to him, but when for some reason it did not, and the intonation of the sentence he had begun required an ending, he inserted a ". . . don't you?"

"Yeah, sure do. Thanks very much, Mikael."

"Thank you, Chief of Police," Bellman said, fumbling for a moment with the mouse before he managed to disconnect the link, leaned back in his chair and whispered: "*Outgoing* Chief of Police."

Prim looked at Fredric Steiner sitting on the bed. His eyes were childlike in their clarity, but his stare was vacant, as though a curtain were drawn within.

"Uncle," Prim said, "can you hear me?"

No response.

He could say anything to him, it wouldn't go in. Ergo nothing would come out either. Not in a way anyone would believe, at any rate.

Prim closed the door to the corridor and sat down by the bed again. "You're going to die very soon," he said, relishing the sound of the words. His uncle's expression didn't change, he was gazing at something only he could see that seemed a long way off.

"You're going to die, and I suppose in a sense I should be sad. I mean, after all, I am your"—he glanced at the door just in case—"biological son."

The only sound to be heard was the low whistle of the wind in one of the gutters of the nursing home.

"But I'm not sad. Because I hate you. Not in the way I hate him. The man who took over your problems, who took over Mom and me. I hate you because you knew what my stepfather was up to, what he was doing to me. I know you confronted him about it, I heard you that night. Heard you threaten to expose him. And how he threatened to then expose you. The two of you left it at that. You sacrificed me to save yourself. Save yourself, Mom and the family name. What was left of it—you didn't even use it yourself any longer, after all."

Prim reached into the bag, took out a cookie and let it crunch between his teeth.

"And now you're going to die, nameless and alone. You'll be forgotten and disappear. While I, the spawn of your loins, the sinful fruit of your lust, will see my name shine in the heavens. You hear me, Uncle Fredric? Doesn't it sound poetic? I've written all that down in my diary, it's important to give the biographers some material to work with, isn't it?"

He stood up.

"I doubt I'll be back. So this is farewell, Uncle." He walked to the door, turned. "I don't mean *fare well*, of course. I hope your journey to hell is anything but."

Prim shut the door behind him, smiled at a nurse walking towards him and left the nursing home.

*

341

The nurse entered the old professor's room. He was sitting on the edge of the bed with a blank expression, but tears were running down his cheeks. That was how it was with the elderly, they lost control of their emotions. Especially the senile. She sniffed. Had he soiled himself? No, it was just that the air in here was stale and smelled of bodily odors and . . . musk?

She opened a window to air the room.

It was eight in the evening. Terry Våge listened to the metallic whining from the inner courtyard, where the rising wind was making the communal rotary clothes line turn. He had resumed the crime blog. There was so much to write about. Even so, he had been sat staring at the empty white page on the PC screen.

The phone rang.

Maybe it was Dagnija, they'd had a fight last night, and she said she wasn't coming for the weekend. Now she probably regretted it, as usual. He could feel how he hoped it was her.

He looked at the cell phone. Unknown number. If it was that phoney from yesterday, he shouldn't take it, nutcases you had responded to once or twice could be impossible to get rid of. Once—after he had written the truth about The War on Drugs being the most boring band in the world both live and on record—he had been stupid enough to answer a pissed-off fan one time—and had ended up with a pest who phoned, emailed and even collared him at gigs, and who it took two years of ignoring to shake off.

It continued ringing.

Terry Våge cast another glance at the empty screen. Then he answered the phone.

"Yeah?"

"Thanks for coming alone yesterday and waiting on the roof until twenty to ten."

"You . . . were there?"

"I was watching. I hope you understand that I had to be sure you wouldn't try and trick me."

Våge hesitated. "Yeah, yeah, OK. But I don't have time for any more hide-and-seek."

"Oh yes you do." He heard a small chuckle. "But we'll drop it, Våge. In fact, you're going to drop everything . . . right now."

"What do you mean?"

"You're going to go to the end of a road called Toppåsveien in Kolsås as quickly as possible. I'll call again, I'm not telling you when, it could be in two minutes. If I get a busy signal, this will be the last time you and I have contact. Understood?"

Våge swallowed. "Yes," he answered. Because he understood. Understood it was to prevent him from contacting someone, like the police. Understood that this wasn't a mindless nutjob. Crazy, yes, but not a nutjob.

"Bring a flashlight and a camera, Våge. And a weapon if it makes you feel safe. You're going to find tangible, irrefutable evidence that you've been talking to the killer, and you're free to write about it afterwards. That includes this conversation. Because we want people to believe you this time, don't we?"

"What will—"

But the man had hung up.

Harry was lying in Alexandra's bed, his bare feet sticking out just over the end.

Alexandra was also naked, lying crosswise, with her head on his stomach.

They had made love the night they had been at the Jealousy Bar, and now they had made love again. Now had been better.

He was thinking about Markus Røed. About the fear and hatred in his eyes while he fought for air. The fear had been greater. But had it remained so after he was able to breathe again? In that case—if Røed hadn't reversed the money transfer—they must have released Lucille by now. As he had been instructed not to try to find her or contact her before the debt was paid, he had decided to wait a couple of days before calling her number.

343

She didn't have his number or details, so it wasn't strange he hadn't heard anything. He had looked up Lucille Owens online and the only hits had been old articles in the *Los Angeles Times* about the *Romeo and Juliet* film. Nothing about her being missing or kidnapped. And he had realized what it was they shared, what connected them. It wasn't the outward danger after what happened in the parking lot. Nor was it that he saw his own mother in Lucille, that she was the woman in the doorway of the classroom or the woman in the hospital bed whom he had a fresh opportunity to save. It was the loneliness. That they were two people who could vanish from the face of the earth without anyone noticing.

Alexandra passed him the cigarette they were sharing, and Harry inhaled and looked at the smoke curling up towards the ceiling while "Hey, That's No Way to Say Goodbye" came from a little Geneva speaker on the bedside table.

"Sounds like that's about us," she said.

"Mm. Lovers who break up?"

"Yeah. And what Cohen says about not talking of love or chains."

Harry didn't respond. Held the cigarette and gazed at the smoke, but was aware of her still lying with her face turned to him.

"It's in the wrong order," he said.

"Wrong because Rakel was already in your life when we met?"

"I was just thinking of something a woman said to me. How we're fooled when the writer changes the order of the sentences around." He took a fresh drag of the cigarette. "But, yeah, probably that about Rakel too."

After a while he felt the warmth of her tears on his stomach. He wanted to cry himself.

The window creaked, as though what was out there wanted to get in to them.

37

WEDNESDAY

Reflex

TOPPÅSVEIEN DIDN'T QUITE LIVE UP to the name. The road wound its way between villas a fair way up to higher ground, but the top of Kolsås was still a good distance away when the road ended. Terry Våge parked by the side of the road. There was forest above him. In the darkness he could make out something lighter farther up, which he knew were rock faces popular with climbers and other boneheads.

He fiddled with the sheath of the knife he had taken with him, looked over at the flashlight and the Nikon camera on the passenger seat. The seconds passed. The minutes passed. He peered down towards the lights in the darkness below. Rosenvilde High School was down there some-where. He knew that because Genie had been a pupil there when he had discovered her. Because it was he, Terry Våge, who had done it, who had used his influence as a music critic to lift her and that talentless band of hers up from the underground into the light, into the mainstream, the marketplace. She had been eighteen, attending school there, and he had

345

driven over a couple of times because he was curious to see her in a school setting. Was there something wrong with that? He had just hung around outside the schoolyard to catch a glimpse of the star he had created, hadn't even taken any pictures, which he easily could have. The telephoto lens he had taken with him would have rendered razor-sharp pictures of a different Genie from the performer playing a role as a dangerous seductress. It would have shown the innocence, the little girl. But hanging around a schoolyard like that could easily have been misunderstood if he'd been discovered, so he had left it at those two times and sought her out at the concerts instead.

He was about to check the time when the phone rang.

"Yes?"

"You're in position, I see."

Våge looked around. His car was the only one parked on the road, and he would have seen anyone in the street light. Was the guy watching him from somewhere in the woods? Våge's hand squeezed the handle of the knife.

"Take your flashlight and camera, walk along the forest trail past the barrier, keep an eye on the left-hand side. After about one hundred yards you'll see reflective paint on a tree trunk. Leave the trail and follow the reflective paint. Got it?"

"Got it," Våge said.

"You'll know when you've reached the spot. Once you do, you have two minutes to take pictures. Then you walk back, get into your car and drive straight home. If you haven't left after those one hundred and twenty seconds, I will come for you. Do you understand?"

"Yes."

"Then it's time to reap your reward, Våge. Hurry up."

The connection was broken. Terry Våge drew a deep breath, and a thought struck him. He could still turn the key in the ignition and get the hell out of there. He could go and have a beer at Stopp Pressen! Tell anyone who would listen that he had spoken to the serial killer on the phone and they had arranged a rendezvous, but that Terry had chickened out at the last minute.

Våge heard his own barking laughter, grabbed the camera and the flashlight and stepped out of the car.

Perhaps this was the lee side of the hill, because strangely enough the wind wasn't as strong up here as it had been lower down or in the city center. He spotted the forest trail a few yards in from the road. He walked past the barrier, turning towards the street light one last time before switching on the flashlight and continuing into the darkness. The wind soughed in the treetops and the gravel crunched beneath his shoes as he counted the steps and alternated between shining the light on the ground and at the tree trunks on the left side. He had made it to one hundred and five when he caught sight of the first patch of reflective paint shining in the beam. He saw the second patch farther into the forest.

He touched the sheath of the knife in his jacket pocket again before swinging the strap of the camera over his shoulder, hopping over the ditch and making his way in among the trees. It was pine forest, and the space between the trees meant he could move through without great effort and be afforded some visibility. The paint had been applied at eye level at ten- to fifteen-yard intervals on selected tree trunks. The terrain grew gradually steeper. At one spot he paused to catch his breath and ran a finger over the blotch on the tree. Looked at his finger. Fresh paint. He was standing on a carpet of pine needles in a cluster of mighty pines. The rustle from the treetops was distant, but that only served to make the cracking and creaking from the almost imperceptible swaying of the trunks all the more present. The sounds were coming from all around, as though a conversation were taking place, as though they were discussing among themselves what to do with their nocturnal guest.

Våge continued.

The forest grew more dense, visibility poorer and the distance between the smudges of paint less, and now the ground was so rugged and steep that there was no point in counting steps any longer.

Then—suddenly—he made it to a plateau and the forest opened up. The beam from his flashlight shone into a small clearing and had to search before it found more paint. This time it wasn't just a patch, it was a T-shape. He went closer. No, it was a cross. In the center of the clearing he raised the flashlight. He couldn't see any more reflective patches beyond the cross. He was at the end of the journey. He held his breath. A sound could be heard, like when you hit two wooden sticks against one another, but he couldn't see anything.

Then, as if to help him, the moon appeared between the scudding clouds, bathing the clearing in a soft, yellow light. And he saw them.

He shuddered. The first thing he thought of was an old number Billie Holiday sang, "Strange Fruit." Because that was what they looked like, the two human heads hanging from the branch of the birch tree. The long hair on both heads swaying in the wind, and when they knocked against each other, they made a hollow sound.

It struck him at once that it must be Bertine Bertilsen and Helene Røed. Not because he recognized the stiff mask-like faces, but because one was dark and the other blonde.

His pulse was racing as he swung the camera off his back and began to count again. Not steps this time but seconds. He pressed the shutter release again and again, the flash went off and continued going off as the moon disappeared back behind the clouds. He had counted to fifty, moved closer, refocused and continued taking pictures. More excited than terror-struck, he no longer thought of the two heads as people who had been alive not too long ago, but as proof. Proof that Markus Røed was innocent. Proof that he—Terry Våge—wasn't a fraud, but had spoken to the killer. Proof that he was Norway's best crime journalist, a person demanding of everyone's respect, his family's, Solstad's, Genie's and that crappy band of hers. And—most important of all—the respect and admiration of Mona Daa. He had pushed the thought from his mind after being fired, how he must have fallen in her esteem. But now that would be turned on its head, everybody loves a comeback kid. He couldn't wait for them to meet again. No, he literally couldn't wait, so he would have to *ensure* that they did meet, and he promised himself it would happen as soon as Dagnija left for Latvia.

Ninety. He had thirty seconds left.

Then I'll come for you.

Like a troll in a folk tale.

Våge lowered the camera and filmed with his phone. Turned the camera towards himself so he had proof he was the one who had been there and taken pictures.

Time to reap your reward, the guy had said. Was that why Våge had picked up on the association with the Billie Holiday song when he saw the heads in the trees? That was about the lynching of black Americans in the South, not about . . . this. By reap, had he meant he could take the heads with him? Våge took a step closer to the birch tree. Stopped. Had he lost his mind? These were the killer's trophies. And time was up. Våge slung the camera behind his back and held his hands up in the air to show any watching eyes in the forest that he had finished and was leaving.

The return journey was more difficult, given that he didn't have any reflective paint to navigate by, and even though he hurried, it took nearly twenty minutes before he found the forest trail again. When he was back in the car and had started the engine, a thought occurred to him.

Even though he hadn't taken the heads, he should have taken something. A strand of hair. As it was, he had photos of two heads that even he—who had seen countless pictures of Bertine Bertilsen and also some of Helene Røed—couldn't say for certain was them. Or if they were real human heads. Fuck! If it hadn't been for him having to engage in a little artifice after Truls Berntsen had let him down and he had been found out, they would have believed in solid pictorial proof like this without question. Now he risked it being viewed as fresh deception and then he really was finished. Should he call the police right away? Would they get here before the murderer made off?

He was steering the car down Toppåsveien when he remembered what the guy had said. *Get into your car and drive straight home.*

The guy had been worried about Våge waiting for him. Why? Maybe this was the only road down from the forest.

He slowed down and tapped his phone. Kept an eye on the road while he brought up the window with the map he had used on the way there.

After consulting it, he concluded that if the guy had come by car there were only two roads he could have parked on. Våge drove all the way down Toppåsveien and up the alternative road that ended where the forest trail began. No cars parked on either road. OK, then maybe he had walked all the way up from the main road. Walked beneath the street lamps through a quiet neighborhood with the residents' eyes on him as he carried a couple of heads and a can of paint in his backpack. Maybe. Maybe not.

Våge studied the map a little more. Getting to the top of the mountain and to the main road around the back looked like a steep and arduous hike, and he couldn't see any trails shown on the map. But the climbing wall was shown, with a path along the base. And there, towards the west, a path led to a residential area and a football pitch. From there, you could drive down past Kolsås Shopping Center to the main road without going close to Toppåsveien.

Våge thought for a moment.

If the guy was up in the forest, and if he were in his shoes, Våge had no doubt which retreat route he would have chosen.

Harry woke with a start. He hadn't meant to fall asleep. Was it a sound that woke him? Something blown over by a gust of wind in the courtyard perhaps? Or a dream, a nightmare he had struggled his way out of? He turned, and in the semi-darkness he made out the head lying turned away from him, the black hair cascading over the white pillow. Rakel. She stirred. Maybe the same sound had woken her, maybe she sensed he had woken, she usually did.

"Harry," she mumbled drowsily.

"Mm."

She turned to him.

He stroked her hair.

She reached towards the bedside light.

"Leave it," he whispered.

"OK. Shall I—"

"Shush. Just . . . shush for a moment. A few seconds."

They lay silent in the darkness, and he ran a hand over her neck, shoulder and hair.

"You're pretending I'm Rakel," she said.

He didn't answer.

"You know what?" she said, caressing his cheek. "It's fine."

He smiled. Kissed her on the forehead. "Thank you. Thanks, Alexandra. But I'm done with all that. Cigarette?"

She reached across to the bedside table. She usually smoked another brand but had bought a pack of Camel today because they were what he used to smoke and she didn't have any strong preference. Something lit up on the bedside table. She handed him the phone and he looked at the display.

"Sorry. I need to take this."

She smiled wearily and flicked the lighter into a flame. "You never get calls you don't need to take, Harry. You should try it now and then, it's pretty nice."

"Krohn?"

"Um . . . good evening, Harry. It's about Røed. He wants to revise his statement."

"OK?"

"He now claims to have met Susanne Andersen in secret earlier in the day at his other apartment, the one in Thomas Heftyes gate. And that they had sex and he kissed her breast. He says he didn't want to say anything before, first and foremost because he was afraid it would tie him to the murder, but also so as to keep it hidden from his wife. He says that seeing how he had given a false statement and been found out, he was worried it would only seem even more suspicious were he to change it. Furthermore, he had neither witnesses nor other supportive evidence to confirm he had a visit from Susanne. He foolishly maintained, therefore, that he had not met her in anticipation of you or the police finding the guilty party or other evidence which would clear his name. He says."

"Mm. Was it stewing in the slammer that softened him up?"

"If you ask me I'd say it was you. I think being grabbed by the throat was a wake-up call. He realizes there's such a thing as punishment. And he can see there's no headway being made on the case and that he can't endure four weeks in custody."

"Four weeks without cocaine, you mean?"

Krohn didn't answer.

"What's he say about Villa Dante?"

"He's still denying that."

"OK," Harry said. "The police aren't going to let him go. He has no witnesses, and he's right about changing his story only making him look like a worm trying to wriggle off the hook."

"I agree," Krohn said. "I just wanted to keep you informed."

"Do you believe him?"

"Is that important?"

"Me neither. But he's a pretty good liar. Thanks for keeping me up to speed."

They hung up. Harry lay with the phone in his hand, staring into the darkness, trying to make the pieces fit. Because they fit, they always did. So the problem was with him, not the pieces.

"What are you doing?" Alexandra asked, taking a drag of the cigarette.

"I'm trying to see but it's so bloody dark."

"You can't see anything?"

"Yeah, something, but I can't make out what it is."

"The trick in darkness is not to look directly at an object but a little to the side. Then you actually see the object more clearly."

"Yes, and that's what I'm doing. But it's as though that's where the object is situated."

"To the side?"

"Yeah. It's like the person we're looking for is in our field of vision. Like we've seen him, but without knowing he's the one we've seen."

"How do you explain it?"

"That"—he sighed—"is something I have no insight into and will not attempt to explain."

"Some things we just know?"

"There's no mystery to it, there is just some stuff the brain figures out by putting together the information available, but neglects to tell us the details, merely offers us the conclusion."

"Yeah," she said softly, taking another drag of the cigarette and passing it to him. "Like me knowing that Bjørn Holm murdered Rakel."

Harry dropped the cigarette on the duvet. He got hold of it again and put it between his lips.

"You know?" he asked, inhaling.

"Yes. And no. It's like you said. Information the brain adds up without you consciously trying or even wanting it to. And then you have the answer, but not the calculation, and you have to do the math backwards to see what your brain was thinking while you were thinking of something else."

"And what was your brain thinking?"

"That when Bjørn discovered you were the father of the child he believed was his, he needed to seek revenge. He murdered Rakel and let the evidence point to you. You told me it was you who killed Rakel. Because you feel it's your fault."

"It was my fault. It *is* my fault."

"Bjørn Holm wanted you to feel the same pain as him, didn't he? Lose the person you love the most. And feel guilt. I sometimes think about how lonely you both must have been. Two friends without any friends. Separated by . . . things that happen. And now neither of you has the woman you loved."

"Mm."

"How much did it hurt?"

"It hurt." Harry sucked desperately at the cigarette. "I was going to do the same as him."

"Take your own life?"

"I'd sooner call it ending my own life. There wasn't much life left to take."

Alexandra accepted the cigarette. It was almost down to the filter and she put it out in the ashtray and snuggled up to him. "I can be Rakel for a little longer if you like."

Terry Våge tried to block out the annoying sound of the halyard continuously slapping against the flagpole in the wind. He had parked in the parking lot in front of the unassuming Kolsås Shopping Center. The stores were closed so there were not many cars there, but a sufficient number for his own vehicle not to be noticed by the few cars coming down the road from the residential area. He had been sitting there for half an hour now, and had only counted forty passing cars. Without using the flash, he took a photo of each car as they drove into the light from the street lamp just forty or fifty yards from where he was sitting. The pictures were more than sharp enough for him to read the license plates.

It had now been nearly ten minutes without a single vehicle. It was late, and people were probably staying home in this weather if they could. Våge listened to the sound of the halyard and decided he had waited long enough. Besides, he needed to publish the pictures.

He'd had a little time to think about how to do that. Using his own platform and blog would of course breathe life back into it. But if he wanted to get the blog up and running and not just back on its feet, then he needed the help of a bigger medium.

He smiled at the thought of Solstad choking on his morning coffee.

Then he turned the key in the ignition, opened the glove compartment and pulled out an old, scratched CD he hadn't played in a long, long time and pushed it into the aged player. Turned up the sound of Genie's lovely, nasal voice and put his foot on the accelerator.

Mona Daa did not believe her ears. Not the story nor the man who told it to her. But she did believe her eyes. Which was why she was now reconsidering her opinion about Terry Våge's story. When he had called she had almost inadvertently answered the phone to spare herself yet another of Isabel May's pretentious monologues in the TV series 1883, left Anders on the sofa and gone into the bedroom. Her irritation at May's words of wisdom was not lessened by her suspicions that Anders had a crush on the actress.

But she had forgotten about all that now.

She stared at the pictures Våge had sent to back up his story and his suggestion. He had used a flash, so even though it had been dark and the heads were moving in the wind, the photos were pin-sharp.

"I sent the video as well, so you can see I was the one there," Våge said.

She opened the video and was no longer in any doubt. Even Terry Våge wasn't crazy enough to stage such an outrageous lie.

"You need to call the police," she said.

"I have," Våge said. "They're on their way, and they'll find the reflective markings, I doubt he's had time to remove them. For all I know he's left the heads hanging there too. Whatever they do find, they'll make public, which means you and the paper don't have much time to decide if you want this."

"And the price?"

"I'll take that up with your editor. Like I said, you can only use the one photo I've tagged that's a little out of focus, and the reference to my blog has to be in the opening sentence after the lead-in. It also has to clearly state that there are more pictures and a video on the blog. Does that sound all right? Oh yeah, one more thing. The byline is yours and yours alone, Mona. I'm an outsider here."

She looked at the pictures again and shuddered. Not because of what she saw but because of the way he had articulated her first name. Half of her felt like yelling no and hanging up. But that was the half which wasn't at work. She couldn't *not* do something. And ultimately, she wasn't the one who had to make the decision, that fell under editorial responsibility, thank God.

"All right."

"Good. Ask the editor to ring me within the next five minutes, OK?"

Mona ended the call and brought up Julia's name. While waiting for Julia to answer the phone she felt her heart beating. And heard eight words echoing in her head. *The byline is yours and yours alone, Mona.*

38

THURSDAY

ALEXANDRA MOVED THE MAGNIFYING GLASS millimeter by millimeter over Helene Røed's entire head. She had been at it since arriving this morning, and soon it would be lunchtime.

"Can you come here for a sec, Alex?"

Alexandra took a break in the hunt for clues and walked to the far end of the bench where Helge was busy with Bertine Bertilsen's head. She didn't allow anyone other than him to shorten her name to an androgynous one, perhaps because coming from his mouth it sounded so natural, almost affectionate, like she was his sister.

"What is it?"

"This," Helge said, pushing down the decomposing lower lip on Bertine's head and holding the magnifying glass up in front of the teeth in the lower jaw. "There. It looks like skin."

Alexandra leaned closer. It was barely visible to the naked eye but under the magnifying glass there was no doubt. A white, dried-up flake protruding between two teeth.

"Jesus, Helge," she said. "It *is* skin."

It was a minute to twelve. Katrine looked out over the audience in the Parole Hall and concluded that, like the last time, the press had turned out in strength. She saw Terry Våge seated next to Mona Daa. Not so strange considering the story he had served up on a plate to *VG*. Still, she thought Daa looked slightly uneasy. She let her eyes wander towards the back, noticed a man she hadn't seen before and assumed must be from a church magazine or Christian newspaper as he was wearing a clerical collar. He was sitting very straight-backed, looking right at her, like an expectant, attentive schoolboy. With a constant smile and unblinking eyes, putting her in mind of a ventriloquist's dummy. At the very back of the room, leaning against the wall with arms folded, she saw Harry. Then the press conference began.

Kedzierski outlined what had happened, that the police, acting on information from journalist Terry Våge, had arrived at Kolsåstoppen, where the heads of Bertine Bertilsen and Helene Røed had been found. That Våge had given a statement and how at present the police had no plans to bring any charges against the journalist for his conduct in the case. That they could of course not rule out the possibility of two or more people cooperating to carry out the murders, but as things stood, Markus Røed would be released.

Afterwards—like an echo of the previous night—a storm of questions followed.

Bodil Melling was seated on the podium to handle questions of a more general character. And—she had informed Katrine—to answer any questions about Harry Hole.

"I think it would be best if you didn't mention Hole at all in your answers," the Chief Superintendent had said. Nor should Røed's new alibi be touched upon—that he had been at a club for men at the time of two of the murders—since the manner in which this information had been obtained was highly dubious. The first questions concerned the discovery of the heads, and Katrine responded with the standard phrases about not being in a position to answer or being unable to comment.

"Does that also mean you haven't found forensic evidence at the crime scene?"

"I said we couldn't comment on that," Katrine said. "But I think we can safely say that Kolsås is not considered a primary crime scene."

Some of the more seasoned reporters chuckled.

After several questions of a technical character the first awkward one was asked.

"Is it embarrassing for the police to have to release Markus Røed four days after placing him in custody?"

Katrine glanced at Bodil Melling, who nodded to signal her intent to take it.

"As with every other case, the police are investigating this one with the tools we have at our disposal," Melling said. "One of these tools is the detention of individuals who suspicions fall upon due to technical or tactical circumstantial evidence, and this is utilized to mimimize the risk of flight or tampering with evidence. This is not the same as the police being convinced they have found the guilty party, or that mistakes have been made should further investigation lead to detention no longer being deemed necessary. Given the information we had on Sunday we would do the same thing again. So no, it's not embarrassing."

"But it wasn't the investigation that saw to it, it was Terry Våge."

"Having open lines so that people can call in with information is an element of the investigation. Part of the job is sifting through this information, and the fact that we took Våge's call seriously is an example of correct judgment on our part."

"Are you saying it was difficult to judge whether or not Våge should be taken seriously?"

"No comment," Melling said curtly, but Katrine saw the trace of a smile.

The questions were coming from all directions now, but Melling answered calmly and confidently. Katrine wondered if she had been wrong about the woman, perhaps she was more than a gray careerist after all.

Katrine had time to study the people in the audience, and saw Harry take out his phone, look at it and stride out of the hall.

As Melling finished responding to one question and the next journalist in Kedzierski's line was allowed to direct one to the people on the podium, Katrine felt her phone vibrate in her jacket pocket. The next question was also addressed to Melling. Katrine saw Harry re-enter the hall, catch her eye and point to his own phone. She understood and slipped her phone out from under the table. The text was from Harry.

Forensic Med Inst have DNA and 80% match.

Katrine read it again. Eighty per cent didn't mean that the DNA profile matched eighty per cent—then you would have to include all mankind and every animal down to snails. Eighty per cent match in this context meant there was an eighty per cent chance they had the right person. She felt her heart rate soar. The journalist had been right about them not finding any evidence around the tree on Kolsåstoppen, so this was simply fantastic. Eighty per cent wasn't one hundred per cent but it was . . . eighty per cent. And seeing as it was only midday they wouldn't have had time to get a full DNA profile yet, so that figure could increase during the course of the day. But might it also decline? In fairness, she hadn't taken in everything those times Alexandra had explained the finer points of DNA analysis. No matter, she just wanted to get up and rush out, not sit here feeding the vultures, not now that they finally had a lead, a name! Someone they had in the database, probably with a previous conviction, or someone they had arrested at least. Someone . . .

A thought had crossed her mind.

Not Røed! Oh God, don't let it be Røed again, she couldn't face that rigmarole one more time. She had closed her eyes and realized it had gone quiet.

"Bratt?" It was Kedzierski's voice.

Katrine opened her eyes, apologized and asked if the journalist could repeat the question.

"The press conference has finished," Johan Krohn said. "Here's what *VG* wrote."

He handed Markus Røed the phone.

They were sitting in the back of an SUV on the way from the custody block to the apartment in Oslobukta. They had been allowed to leave via the subterranean tunnel to Police HQ to avoid the posse of journalists at the exit. Krohn had hired a car and people from a security company Røed had used before, Guardian. It had been done on the advice of Harry Hole and his rationale had been simple. Six people had at one point been in the same room with a few lines of green cocaine. Of these, three had been murdered by what increasingly seemed to be an insane serial killer. The likelihood of one of the three remaining people being next in line was not sky-high, but high enough for it to make good sense to hole up in a breach-proof apartment with bodyguards for a while. Røed had, after some deliberation, agreed. Krohn suspected the two bull-necked men in the front seats were inspired by the Secret Service in choice of suits, sunglasses and workout regimens. He was unsure if the reason the black off-the-peg suits appeared so tight was due to muscle mass or bulletproof vests. But he was sure that Røed was in good hands.

"Ha!" Røed exclaimed. "Listen . . ."

Krohn had of course read Daa's column but could bear to hear it again.

"*Melling claims the release of Markus Røed isn't embarrassing, and she's right. It's his being remanded in custody that's embarrassing. Just as the Fraud Squad tarnished their reputation a few years ago by engaging in a desperate hunt of high-profile business leaders and captains of industry to acquire a feather for their hat, Melling's department has fallen into the same trap. You can like Markus Røed or not, and you can swear to equality before the law, but there isn't more justice in going harder out against Ebenezer Scrooge than Bob Cratchit. The time the police have wasted in the hunt for a big bear would have been better spent hunting down what this has all the earmarks of: a mentally disturbed serial killer.*"

Røed turned to the lawyer.

"Do you think that part about the bear is a pun on . . . ?"

"No." Johan Krohn smiled. "What are you going to do now?"

"Good question, what am I going to do?" Røed asked, handing Krohn back his phone. "What do released prisoners usually do? Party, of course."

"I would advise against that," Krohn said. "The eyes of the whole country are on you, and Helene . . ." His voice trailed off.

"Her body isn't cold yet, you mean?"

"Something like that. Besides, I'd like as little traffic as possible."

"Meaning?"

"Meaning that you stay put in the apartment, just you and your two new friends. At least for the time being. You can work from there."

"Fine," Røed said, "But I'll need a little something . . . to keep my spirits up. If you know what I mean."

"I think I do," Krohn sighed. "But can't that wait?"

Røed laughed and laid a hand on Krohn's shoulder. "Poor old Johan. You don't have many vices but you probably haven't had too much fun either. I promise not to take any chances. I do actually want to keep this beautiful, unique . . ." He drew a circle over his head.

"Good," Johan said, and looked out the window, at the strict yet playful design of the Barcode buildings that had brought Oslo into this century. He dismissed the thought that had been in his mind for a fraction of a second. That he would not have mourned very long if Markus Røed were to be decapitated.

"Shut the door behind you, please," Bodil Melling said as she stepped out from behind her desk.

Katrine closed the door behind her and Harry, and sat down at the table where Sung-min was already in place.

"What do we have?" Melling said, sitting at the end.

She was looking directly at Katrine, but Katrine nodded towards Harry, who was still getting settled in his chair.

"Well," Harry said, pausing until he had found his preferred, half-lying position. Katrine saw the impatience on the Chief Superintendent's face. "The Forensic Medical Institute called me and—"

"Why you? If they have something to report then they ought to ring the detective leading the investigation."

"Maybe so," Harry said. "Anyway, they said—"

"No, I want this cleared up first. Why didn't they contact the lead detective?"

Harry grimaced, stifled a yawn and looked out the window as though the question were immaterial.

"It was perhaps not formally correct," Katrine said. "But they called the individual who in effect has been leading this investigation, in the sense of being at the forefront. Can we move on?"

The two women's eyes met.

Katrine was aware that what she had said—and the way she had said it—could be perceived as provocative. And maybe it was. So what? This wasn't the time for office politics and pissing contests. And perhaps Melling realized that too. In any case, she gave Katrine a curt nod.

"Ok, Bratt. Go on, Hole."

Harry nodded in the direction of the window as though he'd had a silent conversation with someone outside and turned to the others again.

"Mm. Pathology found a skin fragment between Bertine Bertilsen's teeth. According to the post-mortem technicians, it was so loose that it would have disappeared had she rinsed her mouth or brushed her teeth, so it's reasonable to assume it ended up there just prior to death. For example, by her biting her killer. There is a preliminary profile with a very likely match in the database."

"Criminal?"

"Not convicted, but yes."

"How high is the probability?"

"High enough to merit arrest," Harry said.

"In your opinion. We can't afford to make yet another arrest where the press—"

"This is our man." Harry said it in a low voice, but the words seemed to resound in the room.

Melling shifted her gaze to Katrine, who nodded.

"And you, Larsen?"

"The latest information from Pathology is a probability of ninety-two per cent," Sung-min said. "This is our man."

"Good," Melling said and clapped her hands together. "Get to it."

They stood up.

On the way out Melling held Katrine back.

"Do you like this office, Bratt?"

Katrine looked at Melling, uncertain. "Yes, the place looks nice."

Melling ran a hand over the back of one of the meeting chairs. "I only ask because I haven't got the green light yet, but I might be moving to another one, which means this will be vacant." Melling smiled with a warmth Katrine didn't know she possessed. "But don't let me keep you, Bratt."

39

THURSDAY

Ornamental kale

HARRY ENTERED THE CEMETERY. The florist in Grønlandsleiret had suggested he place ornamental kale on the grave. Not only because it resembled a beautiful flower, but because the colors would only turn prettier as the temperature dropped over the fall.

He picked up a branch that must have broken off in the previous night's storm and now lay partly across the headstone, placed it by the trunk of the tree, walked back, squatted down and used his hands to work the pot of flowering kale down into the soil.

"We've found him," Harry said. "I thought you'd like to know, because I expect you're keeping tabs."

He peered up at the crisp blue sky. "I was right about it being someone on the periphery of the case, a person we had seen but not seen. As regards everything else, I was wrong. I'm always looking for motive, you know that, believe that's what will lead us in the right direction. And of course, there's always a motive. But it's not always shining so brightly that we can use it as a lodestar, is it? Not when the motive is so locked away in the darkness of insanity as here, at any rate. Then I give up on the *why* and concentrate on the *how*. It's better to just let Ståle and his people take care of the sick *why* afterwards." Harry cleared his throat. "Stop beating around the bush and get to the *how*? OK, then."

It was three o'clock when Øystein Eikeland entered Jernbanetorget, where he had met Harry a week and a half earlier. It seemed like an eternity ago. Passing the tiger statue, he saw Al bent double with one hand resting on the wall of the old Central Station building.

"How's it going, Al?" Øystein said.

"Took some bad shit," he said, retching one more time before straightening up. Wiping his mouth with the sleeve of his parka. "Otherwise good. What about you? Long time . . ."

"Yeah, I've been busy with some other stuff," Øystein said, looking down at the pool of vomit. "Remember I asked you about that party at Markus Røed's. Told you it was because I was wondering who the other dude selling beak was."

"He was handing it out for free, but yeah, what about him?"

"I probably should have told you that I was asking because I'm working for a private investigator."

"Oh?" Al fastened his blue eyes on Øystein. "The cop who was here, Harry Hole?"

"You know who he is?"

"I do read the newspapers!"

"Really? Wouldn't have thought that."

"Not that often, but after you told me about those two girls at the party I've been following that particular case."

"Have you now?" Øystein looked around. The square looked the same as always. The same clientele. Tourists looking like tourists, students like students, buyers like buyers. He should stop now. Was supposed to stop now. Or rather, was supposed to leave now. Why did he always have to overdo things, why couldn't he abide by Keef's commandment about moderation? All he was meant to do was point out Al in the crowd and distract him slightly. But no, he had to . . .

"Or have you been doing a little more than just following the case, Al?"

"What?" Al's eyes appeared to grow bigger. The whites were now visible all the way around.

"He met the girls at the party, or maybe he provided them with cocaine before," Harry said to the headstone. "I suppose he liked them. Or hated them, who knows. Maybe the three girls liked him too, he is a good-looking kid and has a charisma about him. The charisma of loneliness, Øystein calls it. So, yeah, perhaps that was how he lured them in. Or he lured them with cocaine. He wasn't at home during the raid on his apartment this morning—according to Øystein he keeps regular working hours at Jernbanetorget. Single, apparently, but the bed was neatly made up. They found a lot of interesting stuff. All kinds of knives. Hard porn. A car Forensics are going over as we speak. A poster of Charles Manson above the bed. And a gold snuff bullet with the initials B.B. on it, which I'm guessing someone who knew Bertine Bertilsen will identify as hers. It contained green cocaine. You liked that, huh? But listen to this. There were eight bricks of white cocaine underneath the bed which they said seemed pretty pure. Eight bricks, mind. Cut it a little and you're talking a street value of over ten million kroner. He doesn't have any convictions but has been arrested twice. One was a gang-rape case. Seems he wasn't even there, but that was how his DNA ended up in the database. We haven't had time to dig around in his past yet, or his childhood, but you wouldn't get high odds betting on it being of the shitty kind. So there you have it." Harry checked the time. "They're taking him into custody around now, I imagine. He's known to be vigilant bordering on paranoid, and the combo of the collection of knives together with how crowded with people it gets down there means they're using Øystein as a distraction. Bad idea involving amateurs, if you ask me, but they were the orders from above apparently."

*

"What the fuck do you mean?" Al said.

"Nothing," Øystein said, keeping an eye on Al's hands, buried deep in the pockets of his parka.

It occurred to him that he was possibly in danger now. So why was he standing here dragging this out? He looked at Al's hands. What did he have in those pockets? At that moment he realized what it was he liked. That finally for once he was the center of attention, that at this very moment radio communications were probably squawking: "Why is he still standing there?", "He's got some balls," "Fuck me, talk about cool!"

Øystein saw two dancing red dots of light appear on the chest of Al's parka.

His moment in the limelight was over.

"Have an all right day, Al."

Øystein turned and walked towards the road and the bus stops.

A red bus passed right in front of him, and in the reflection flickering across the windows he saw three people in the square start to move simultaneously as they each slipped a hand inside their clothing.

He heard Al's screams and just had time to catch sight of them wrestling him to the ground, two of them with pistols pointed at Al's back, the third with handcuffs which he clamped around Al's wrists. Then the bus drove past, and he looked up Karl Johans gate towards the Palace, watched the people streaming towards him and away from him, and he thought for a second about all the people he had met and left behind in his life.

Harry rose on stiff knees and looked down at the pink-tinged flower. Which was cabbage. Raised his gaze to the name on the headstone. Bjørn Holm.

"So now you know, Bjørn. And I know where you lie. Maybe I'll be back some day. They miss you at the Jealousy Bar as well, by the way."

Harry turned and walked in the direction of the gate he had entered by.

Took out his phone and called Lucille's number again.

No answer this time either.

*

Mikael Bellman was standing by the window as Vivian handed him a short report on the successful arrest at Jernbanetorget.

"Thanks," he said, his gaze as usual seeking out the center of things. "I'd actually like to issue a statement. A press release praising the tireless work of the police, their work ethic and professionalism in dealing with difficult cases. Could you work up a draft?"

"Of course," she said, and he heard the enthusiasm in her voice. It was the first time she had been entrusted with writing anything from scratch. Still, he sensed trepidation.

"What is it, Vivian?"

"You're not concerned that it might be perceived as presumption of guilt?"

"No."

"No?"

Bellman turned to face her. She was so pretty. So smart. But so young. Was he beginning to prefer them a little older? Wise rather than bright?

"Write it as a general tribute to the police all across the country," he said. "A Minister for Justice doesn't comment on individual cases. Then those who want to link it to the solving of this specific case can do so if they wish."

"But this case is what everyone is talking about so most people will make that connection?"

"I hope so." Bellman smiled.

"And that will be perceived as . . . ?" She looked at him, uncertain.

"Do you know why prime ministers send telegrams of congratulation when someone wins a gold medal at the Winter Olympics? Because those telegrams end up in the newspapers so that the Prime Minister can bask a little in the reflected glory and remind the people who created the conditions to facilitate such a small country being able to take so many gold medals. Our press release will be correct, but also show that I'm on the same wavelength as the people. We've put a drug-pushing serial killer behind bars, and that's even better than a rich guy. We won the gold medal. You understand?"

She nodded. "I think so."

40

THURSDAY

Absence of fear

TERRY VÅGE LIFTED THE CHAIR—just to hip height, he couldn't raise it higher—and flung it at the wall.

"Fuck, fuck, fuck!"

Locating the owners of the vehicles that had passed Kolsås Shopping Center had been easy. All you had to do was go into REGNR online and type in the license plate, then—for a certain fee—you were given a name and address. It had cost him over two thousand kroner and taken a couple of hours, but finally he had a complete list with fifty-two names and addresses and was about to start calling them. But now on *VG* 's website he just read the guy had been caught, arrested at Jernbanetorget!

The chair didn't even tip over, just came rolling back towards him on the sloping floor, as though bidding him to sit down and calmly evaluate things.

He put his head in his hands and tried to do as the chair suggested.

The plan had been to land the scoop of all time, one that would even

369

top the photographs he had taken of the heads in Kolsås. He was going to find the killer on his own and—here was the genius of it—demand an exclusive, in-depth interview about the murders and the man behind them in exchange for complete source protection. Våge would explain that source confidentiality would be cemented by going public, safeguarding them both against prosecution by the police or other authorities. He would, however, fail to mention that this protection of sources—just like the privileged information and duties of confidentiality of certain professions—only stretched so far, and certainly not past the point where life was in danger. Våge would, therefore—as soon as the interview was published—tell the police where they could find the murderer. He was a journalist, and nobody could hold the fact he was doing his job against him, especially when it was he, Terry Våge, who had found the killer!

But now someone had beaten him to it.

Fuck!

He scrolled through the other newspapers' sites. No pictures of the guy, and no name. Common practice when the person concerned wasn't a high-profile figure, like Markus Røed, for example. It was just typical bloody Scandinavian mollycoddling, protecting the bastards, it made you want to emigrate to the USA and other places where journalism got a bit of elbow room. Oh well. Anyway, so what if he did find the name? All he could do was berate himself for not having found it sooner and calling the guy.

Våge sighed heavily. He was going to be in a bad mood the rest of the weekend. And that would impact Dagnija. But she would just have to put up with it, he had paid half the cost of her tickets, after all.

At six o'clock, everyone in the Aune group was in room 618.

Øystein had brought a bottle of champagne and plastic cups.

"I got it at Police HQ," he said. "As a thank-you, like. Think they must've had a few bottles themselves. Never seen so many jolly cops."

Øystein popped the cork and poured into the cups, which Truls distributed to everyone, a smiling Jibran Sethi included. They toasted.

"Can't we just continue having these meetings?" Øystein said. "We don't need to be solving cases either. We can argue about . . . who the most underrated drummer in the world is, for instance. The correct answer is Ringo Starr, by the way. The most overrated is Keith Moon from the Who, and the best is of course John Bonham from Led Zeppelin."

"Would make for pretty short meetings by the sound of it," Truls said, and everyone laughed, not least Truls himself upon realizing he had actually been funny.

"Well, well," Aune said from the bed when the laughter had subsided. "I guess it's time for a summary."

"Yep," Øystein said, tilting back on his chair.

Truls merely nodded.

All three looked at Harry expectantly.

"Mm," he said, fidgeting with the plastic cup, which he had yet to drink from. "We don't have all the details yet, and some questions remain. But let's draw some lines between the dots we have and see if we get a clear picture. OK?"

"Hear, hear," Øystein said, and stamped approvingly on the floor.

"We have a killer with a motive unknown to us or that we can't understand," Harry said. "Hopefully the interviews will tell us something more. Otherwise, it seems clear to me that the whole thing started at the party at Røed's place. As you'll recall, I thought we should track down the cocaine dealer, but I have to admit my focus was on the wrong dealer. After all, it's easy to believe that the guy wearing a face mask, sunglasses and a baseball cap is the bad guy. Let's go through what we know about him before we look at the murderer. What we know is that this guy was an amateur with samples of green cocaine originating from a recent seizure. Let's call him the Greenhorn. My guess is the Greenhorn is someone who happens to be at one of the stops along the way before the drugs are sent for analysis, so one of the customs officers or someone working at police storage. He realizes the quality of this stuff is off the charts and spots his chance to hit the jackpot. What he needs to do after stealing so much from the seizure is sell the whole lot in one go to one individual who appreciates quality product and can pay for a batch that size."

"Markus Røed," Øystein said.

"Exactly. And that's the reason the Greenhorn is so insistent on Røed having a taste. He was the target."

"And I was the one who got the blame," Truls said.

"But let's forget the Greenhorn for now," Harry said. "After Markus sneezes on the table and ruins everything for the poor guy, it's Al who provides Markus with cocaine. And probably the girls too, even though they got some of the green type first. The girls like Al. He likes them. And he lures them into taking a walk in the forest. And that's where we get to what for me is a mystery. How did he manage that? How does he get Susanne to willingly travel all the way across the city and meet him at a secluded spot? By dangling some mediocre cocaine under her nose? Hardly. How does he get Bertine to readily agree to meet him in the forest after another girl, who she knows about, has just disappeared. And after these two murders, how on earth does he persuade Helene Røed to willingly leave with him in the intermission at *Romeo and Juliet*?"

"Do we know that?" Aune asked.

"Yeah," Truls said. "The police checked with the ticket office and found out which seat numbers they'd sent to Røed and who'd been sitting next to her as well. And they said the woman sitting beside them hadn't returned after the intermission. The cloakroom attendant also remembered a lady picking up her coat, and a man standing waiting a little way off with his back turned. She remembered because they were the only people she had seen leave that particular play during the break."

"I spoke to Helene Røed," Harry said. "She was a smart woman and capable of taking care of herself. It just doesn't make sense to me that she would willingly leave a play with a drug dealer she doesn't know. Not after everything that's happened."

"You keep bringing up *willingly*," Aune said.

"Yes," Harry said. "They ought to be . . . scared."

"Go on."

"Yes. Terrified." Harry was no longer sitting in his usual slumped position, but on the edge of the chair, leaning forward. "It reminds me of this mouse I saw one morning when I woke up in Los Angeles. It just walked right over to the house cat. Who of course killed it. And a few days ago I saw the same thing happen in a backyard here in Oslo. I don't know what's wrong with these mice, maybe they were drugged or had lost their natural instinct of fear."

"Fear is good," Øystein said. "A little bit at least. Fear of strangers, for instance. Xenophobia is a pretty negatively charged word, and yeah, it's to blame for a lot of seriously evil shit. But the world we live in is eat or be eaten, and if you're not suitably scared of what's unfamiliar to you, then sooner or later you're fucked. Don't you think, Ståle?"

"Certainly," Aune said. "When our senses perceive something they recognize as a danger, the amygdala excretes neurotransmitters like glutamate, so we become fearful. It's a smoke alarm from evolution, and without it . . ."

"We burn up," Harry said. "So what's wrong with these murder victims? And the mice?"

The four of them looked at one another in silence.

"Toxoplasmosis."

They turned to the fifth person.

"The mice have toxoplasmosis," Jibran Sethi said.

"What's that?" Harry asked.

"It's a parasite that's infected the mouse, blocking the fear response, and replacing it with sexual attraction instead. The mouse approaches the cat because it's sexually attracted."

"You've got to be kidding," Øystein said.

Jibran smiled. "No, the parasite is called *Toxoplasma gondii* and is actually one of the most common in the world."

"Wait," Harry said. "Is it only found in mice?"

"No, it can live in almost any warm-blooded animal. But its life cycle goes through animals which are prey for cats because the parasite needs to get back into the intestines of the main host to reproduce, and that has to be a feline."

"So the parasite can in principle be present in people?"

"Not just in principle. In certain areas of the world it's quite common for humans to be infected with the gondii parasite."

"And they are then sexually attracted to . . . eh, cats?"

Jibran laughed. "Not that I've heard of. Perhaps our psychologist knows something about that?"

"I'm familiar with the parasite, so I should have made the connection," Aune said. "The parasite attacks the brain and the eyes, and there's research to show that people with no history of mental problems begin to display abnormal behavior. Not that they start carrying on with cats, but they do exhibit violence, directed primarily at themselves. There are numerous instances of suicide where it's believed the parasite is to blame. I read in a research paper that the reaction times of people with the gondii parasite are diminished, and that the probability of them being involved in road accidents is three to four times greater. And there's an interesting study showing that students with toxoplasmosis are more likely to become businessmen. They reasoned that this was due to an absence of fear of failure."

"Absence of fear?" Harry said.

"Yes."

"But not sexual attraction?"

"What are you thinking?"

"I'm thinking that the women didn't just leave willingly, they went all the way across town or left a theater production they liked to be with their killer. No signs of rape were found, and the footprints in the forest may indicate that they had their arms linked as they walked, like lovers."

"It's the scent of the cat and cat's urine that attracts infected mice," Jibran said. "Imagine, the parasite eats away at the mouse's brain and eyes, while at the same time it knows it needs to return to the cat because it's only within the bowels of the cat that the environment is conducive to reproduction. So it alters and manipulates the mouse's brain to be attracted sexually by the smell of the cat. So that the mouse voluntarily helps the parasite return to the cat's intestines."

"Holy shit," Truls said.

"Yes, it's gruesome," Jibran conceded. "But that's how parasites function."

"Mm. Is it conceivable that the killer has taken on the role of the cat, as it were, after he's infected them with the parasite?"

Jibran shrugged. "It's perfectly conceivable that it's a mutated parasite or that someone could breed a gondii parasite that requires human intestines as a primary host. I mean, in this day and age even a biology student can engage in gene manipulation on a cellular level. But you'd have to ask a parasitologist or a microbiologist about that."

"Thanks, but first we'll hear what Al has to say." Harry checked the time. "Katrine said they were going to question him as soon as he's had a chance to talk to the lawyer appointed to him."

It was rare anyone at the Custody Unit dared to ask Duty Officer Groth the reason behind his chronically bad humor and ill temper. Those who had were now gone. His hemorrhoids, however, were not. They had been at the Custody Unit as long as Groth—for twenty-three years. He had been interrupted in the middle of a promising game of solitaire on the PC, and now winced in pain on the chair as he looked at the ID card the man in front of him had placed on the counter. The man had introduced himself as the lawyer for the prisoner arrested at Jernbanetorget earlier that day. Groth didn't care much for lawyers in expensive suits, even less for ones like this, slumming it in a bomber jacket and wearing a flat cap like some dock worker.

"Would you like an officer present in the room, Beckstrøm?" Groth asked.

"No thank you," the lawyer said. "And no one listening at the door either."

"He's killed three—"

"Suspected of having killed."

Groth shrugged and pressed the button that opened the full-height turnstile. "The guard on the inside will search you and open the cell door."

"Thanks," the lawyer said, picking up his ID card and going through.

"Idiot," Groth said, not bothering to look up from the PC screen to see if the lawyer had heard.

Four minutes later it was clear the game of solitaire wasn't working out after all.

Groth swore, and just then heard someone clear their throat and saw a man wearing a face mask standing behind the full-height turnstile. Groth was momentarily taken aback before he recognized the flat cap and the bomber jacket.

"That was a short conversation," Groth said.

"He's in pain, just bawling and wailing," the lawyer said. "You need to get him medical help, and then I'll come back later."

"Oh, the doctor was just in there, but he couldn't find anything the matter with him. The guy got painkillers, so I'm sure he'll stop his wailing soon."

"He's screaming like he's about to die," the lawyer said, walking towards the exit. Groth watched him leave. Something wasn't right but he couldn't put his finger on it. He pressed the call button.

"Svein, how are things in number 14? Is he still screaming?"

"He was when I unlocked to let the lawyer in, but when I went to let the lawyer out he'd stopped."

"Did you take a peek inside?"

"No. Should I?"

Groth hesitated. The line he took—and it was built on experience—was to let the prisoners scream, cry and yell without giving it too much attention. They'd been stripped of anything they could use to harm themselves and if you came running every time they started whining, they soon learned it got them attention, just like wailing infants. In the box that was still in front of him lay the possessions the prisoner in number 14 had had on him when they brought him in, and Groth automatically took a look for something that could give an answer. Evidence and Seizure had already been to collect the bags of cocaine and money, and all he saw were house keys, car keys and a crumpled theater ticket that said "Romeo and Juliet" on it. No meds, prescriptions or anything to give an indication. He twisted in the chair, felt a jolt of pain as one of the hemorrhoids became pinched and swore under his breath.

376

"Well?" Svein said.

"Yeah," Groth said gruffly. "Yeah, check on the prick."

Aune and Øystein were sitting at one of the tables in the Radium Hospital's almost deserted cafeteria. Truls had gone to the restroom, and Harry was standing on the terrace outside the cafeteria with the phone to his ear and a cigarette in the corner of his mouth.

"You're the doctor in these sorts of things," Øystein said and nodded out in the direction of Harry. "What's bugging him?"

"Bugging?"

"Driving him on. He never stops working, even now the guy's been caught and he's not getting paid any more."

"Oh, that," Aune said. "I suppose he's seeking order. An answer. The need for that is often more keenly felt when everything else in your life is chaotic and seems to lack meaning."

"OK."

"OK? You don't sound convinced. What do you think the reason is?"

"Me? Well. Same as Bob Dylan answered when he was asked why he keeps on touring long after he'd become a millionaire and his voice had gone to shit. " 'It's what I do.' "

Harry leaned against the railing with the phone in his left hand while he sucked on the single cigarette he had allowed himself to take from Alexandra's Camel pack. Perhaps the principle of moderation could be applied to smoking. While waiting for an answer on the other end, he caught sight of a person standing down below in the sparsely lit parking lot. A man with his face tipped up towards Harry. It was hard to make out at this distance, but he had something white on his neck. A freshly laundered shirt collar, a neck brace. Or a clerical collar. Harry tried to put the thought of the man in the Camaro out of his mind. He had gotten his money, why would he be coming for Harry now? Another thought occurred to him. What he had said to Alexandra when she asked if he thought he had killed the man with that blow to the throat. *If he had died,*

I don't think his friends would have let me live afterwards. Afterwards. *After* he had made sure they got their money.

"Helge."

Harry was jarred out of his thoughts. "Hi, Helge, Harry Hole here. I got your number from Alexandra, she was saying you might be at the Forensic Medical Institute working on your doctorate."

"She's not wrong," Helge said. "Congrats on the arrest, by the way."

"Mm. I was going to ask you for a favor."

"Shoot."

"There's a parasite by the name of *Toxoplasma gondii*."

"Yeah."

"You're familiar with it?"

"It's very common, and I am a bioengineer."

"OK. What I was wondering was if you could check to see if the victims might have had the parasite. Or a mutated version of it."

"I understand. I wish I could, but the parasite is concentrated in the brain, and we don't have theirs."

"Yes, but the parasite can also be present in the eyes, I'm told, and the killer left one eye on the corpse of Susanne Andersen."

"True, they are also concentrated in the eyes, but it's too late. Susanne's remains were sent for the funeral, and that was to take place earlier today."

"I know, but I checked. The funeral did go ahead today, but the body is still lying in the crematorium. There's a line so she won't be cremated until tomorrow. I got an oral court order over the phone, so I can go up there now, get the eye and then come over to you. That OK?"

Helge let out a laugh of disbelief. "All right, but how were you planning to remove the eye?"

"You've got a point. Any suggestions?"

Harry waited. Until he heard Helge sigh.

"It would, strictly speaking, be regarded as part of the post-mortem, so I'd better get down there and do it."

"The country owes you a debt of thanks," Harry said. "See you there in thirty minutes."

Katrine walked as quickly as she could across the floor of the Custody Unit. Sung-min was right behind her.

"Open up, Groth!" she called out, and the duty officer did as he was told without a murmur. For once Groth looked more shocked than grumpy. But that was small comfort.

Katrine and Sung-min squeezed through the rotating bars of the turnstile. A guard held open the door leading into the corridors between the detention cells.

The door of cell 14 was open. Even in the corridor she could smell the stench of vomit.

She stopped in the doorway. Over the shoulders of the two medics, she saw the face of the person lying on the floor. Or rather, what should have been a face but was now only a bloody mass, the front of a head where fragments of nasal bone were the only white in a red pulp of flesh. Like a . . . Katrine didn't know where the words came from . . . blood moon.

Her eyes moved to the spot on the brick wall the man had obviously dashed his head against. He must have done it recently, because half-coagulated blood was still making its way down the wall.

"Inspector Bratt," she said. "We just got the message. Is he . . . ?"

The doctor looked up. "Yes. He's dead."

She shut her eyes and cursed to herself. "Is it possible to say anything about the cause of death?"

The doctor grinned grimly and shook his head wearily, as though it were an idiotic question. Katrine felt anger bubbling up. She saw the Médecins Sans Frontières logo on his jacket, he was probably one of those doctors who had spent a few weeks in some war zone and played the role of hardcore cynic the rest of his life.

"I asked—"

"Miss," he interrupted, his voice sharp, "as you can see, it's not even possible to tell who he is."

"Shut up and let me finish my question," she said. "*Then* you can open your mouth. Now, how—"

The doctor without borders laughed, but she could see the vein in his neck become more pronounced and more color come into his face. "You may be an inspector, but I'm a doctor and—"

"And have just declared our prisoner dead, so your job here is done, pathology will take care of the rest. You can either answer here or be locked up in one of the neighboring cells. OK?"

Katrine heard Sung-min clear his throat softly beside her. She ignored the discreet admonition about having gone too far. Fuck it, their party was ruined, she could already see the newspaper headlines—*Murder Suspect Dies in Police Custody.* The biggest murder case she had ever had would probably never be completely resolved now that the central figure couldn't talk. The families would never know what had really happened. And here was this puffed-up doctor guy trying to play cool?

She breathed in. Out. Then in again. Sung-min was of course right. That was the old Katrine Bratt who had surfaced, the one *this* Katrine had hoped was buried for good.

"Sorry." The doctor sighed and looked up at her. "I'm being childish. It's just that it looks like he was suffering for a long time without anything being done, and then . . . then I react emotionally and blame you guys. Sorry."

"It's fine," Katrine said. "My own apology was close on the heels of yours. *Can* you say anything about the cause of death?"

He shook his head. "It could have been that." He nodded at the blood on the whitewashed wall. "But I've yet to see someone manage to take their own life by banging their head against a wall. So maybe the pathologist should check that out as well." He pointed to the yellowish-green pool of vomit on the floor. "I heard he'd been in pain."

Katrine nodded. "Any other possibilities?"

"Well," the doctor said, getting to his feet, "possibly someone killed him."

41

THURSDAY

Reaction speed

IT WAS SEVEN O'CLOCK, AND at the Forensic Medical Institute the only lights on were those in the laboratory. Harry stared first at the scalpel in Helge's hand and then at the eyeball lying on one of the glass plates.

"Do you really . . . ?" he asked.

"Yeah, I have to get to the inside," Helge said and cut.

"Yeah, well," Harry said. "The funeral is over, I suppose, no one in the family is going to see her again."

"Well, actually they're going there tomorrow," Helge said, placing the piece he had cut away under the microscope. "But the guy from the undertakers had already put in a glass eye and will just put in one more. Look at this."

"You see something?"

"Yeah. Gondii parasites. Or at least something similar. Look . . ."

Harry leaned forward and peered into the microscope. Was he imagining things, or did he detect an almost imperceptible odor of musk?

He asked Helge.

"It *could* be from the eye," he said. "In which case you have an exceptional sense of smell."

"Mm. I have parosmia, I can't smell corpses. But maybe it means I smell other things all the better. Like with blindness and hearing, you know?"

"You believe that?"

"No. I do, however, believe that the killer might have used the parasite to render Susanne fearless, and that she felt sexually attracted to him."

"No way. That he's made himself the primary host, you mean?"

"Yeah. Why no way?"

"Just that it's not that far off from the field I'm toiling in to obtain a doctorate. Theoretically, it is possible but if he's managed to do it, we're talking the Odile Bain Prize. Eh . . . that's like the Nobel Prize in parasitology."

"Mm. I'm thinking he'll get life instead."

"Yeah, of course. Sorry."

"Another thing," Harry said. "The mice are attracted by the smell of cat, any cat I mean. So why are these women attracted to just one man in particular?"

"You tell me," Helge said. "The key is the smell the parasites can direct an infected person towards. Perhaps he carried something the women caught the scent of. Or he might have smeared it directly on his body."

"What kind of smell?"

"Well, the most direct way is a smell from the intestinal tract where the parasites know they can reproduce."

"Excrement, you mean?"

"No, he'd use excrement to spread the parasite. But to attract an infected person he might use the intestinal juices and enzymes in the small intestine. Or the digestive secretions from the pancreas and gall bladder."

"You're saying he's spreading the parasite with his own feces?"

"If he has created his own parasite, then he's probably the only possible compatible host, so he alone must ensure the life cycle continues running its course so the parasites don't die out."

"And how does he do that?"

"Same as the cat. He could see to it, for example, that the water the victims drink is infected with his feces."

"Or the cocaine they snort."

"Yes, or the food they eat. It will take a while before the parasite reaches the victim's brain and can manipulate it."

"How long?"

"Well . . . if I had to guess how long it took with a mouse, I'd say two days. Maybe three or four. The point is that in humans the immune system would generally eradicate the parasite, and that would occur after a couple of weeks or a month, so he doesn't have all the time in the world if he's trying to keep the life cycle going."

"So, he'd need to wait a couple of days, but not too long, before killing them."

"Yes. And then he'd have to eat the victim."

"All of the victim?"

"No, the parts where parasites ready to reproduce are most concentrated should do it. So, the brain . . ." Helge stopped abruptly and stared at Harry as though it just dawned on him. He swallowed. ". . . or the eyes."

"Last question," Harry said hoarsely.

Helge just nodded.

"Why don't the parasites take over the brain of the primary host as well?"

"Oh, but they do."

"Really? And what do they do to him?"

Helge shrugged. "Pretty much the same thing. He becomes fearless. And seeing as how he is receiving a continuous top-up as is the case here, the immune system won't be able to get rid of the parasite, and he risks a dulling or a slowing down of reaction times, for instance. And schizophrenia."

"Schizophrenia."

"Yes, recent research indicates it. Unless he keeps the number of parasites in his own body in check."

"How?"

"Well. That I don't know."

"What about parasiticides? Like Hillman Pets, for example?"

Helge gazed into the air thoughtfully. "I'm not familiar with that brand, but theoretically the right dosage of a parasiticide could create a balance of sorts, yes."

"Mm. So the quantity of parasites you have in you is important?"

"Oh yeah. Were you to give someone a large dose with a high concentration of gondii the parasites would block the brain, paralyzing the person in the space of a few minutes. They'd be dead within an hour."

"But you wouldn't die from snorting a line of infected cocaine?"

"Maybe not within an hour, but if the concentration is high enough, it could easily kill you within a day or two. Excuse me . . ." Helge picked up a ringing phone. "Yes? All right." He hung up. "Sorry, I'm going to be busy now, they're on their way up with a body from the Custody Unit I have to carry out a preliminary post-mortem on."

"OK," Harry said, buttoning up his suit jacket. "Thanks for your help, I'll find my own way out. Sweet dreams."

Helge gave him a faint smile.

Harry had just walked out the door of the lab when he turned and went back in.

"Whose body are they bringing over, did you say?"

"I don't know his name—the guy arrested at Jernbanetorget today."

"Fuck," Harry said in a low tone, gently striking the doorjamb with his fist.

"Something wrong?"

"That's him."

"Who?"

"The primary host."

Sung-min Larsen was standing behind the counter at the Custody Unit peering down into the box containing the property of the deceased. There was no great hurry on the house keys, since they had already broken in and searched his place, but a forensics officer was on the way to collect the keys to the car, which had been found in the multi-story parking lot closest to Jernbanetorget. Sung-min turned the theater ticket. Had he been to the same performance as Helene? No, there was an earlier date on the ticket. But maybe he had gone to the National Theater to reconnoitre, to plan the abduction and murder of Helene Røed.

His phone rang.

"Larsen."

"We're at Beckstrøm's now but only the wife is home. She says she thought he was at work."

Sung-min was puzzled. No one at Beckstrøm's office knew where the defense lawyer was either. Beckstrøm was a key witness given that he was the last person who had seen the detainee alive. This was urgent. True, the media hadn't linked the arrest on Jernbanetorget to anything in particular so far; after all it wasn't unusual for the police to apprehend dealers there. But it might only be a matter of minutes or hours before a journalist got wind of a death in the Custody Unit, and then they'd all be on the warpath.

"Groth," Sung-min called out to the shift commander, leaning on the other side of the counter, "how did Beckstrøm seem when he came out?"

"Different," Groth said sourly.

"Different how?"

Groth shrugged. "He'd put on a face mask, maybe that was it. Or he was distressed by seeing the prisoner so sick. Wild-eyed, anyway, completely different from when he arrived. Maybe he's the sensitive type, what do I know?"

"Maybe," Larsen said, his gaze lingering on the theater ticket while he ransacked his brain for the reason why this alarm clock was going off in his head.

It was almost nine o'clock in the evening when Johan Krohn tapped in the number of the apartment and looked up at the video camera above the entrance. After a few moments he heard a deep voice not belonging to Markus Røed. "Who are you?"

"Johan Krohn. The lawyer who was in the car earlier today."

"Right. Come in."

Krohn took the elevator up and was let into the apartment by one of the bull-necked security men. Røed seemed irritable and was restlessly pacing the living room, back and forth, like one of the mangy old lions Krohn had seen as a little boy in Copenhagen Zoo. His white shirt was open and was ringed with sweat under the arms.

"I come bearing good news," Krohn said. And added drily when he saw his client's face light up: "News, not coke."

As Krohn saw the anger flare up in the other man's face he hurried to extinguish it: "The suspected killer has been caught."

"Really?" Røed blinked in disbelief. Then he laughed. "Who is it?"

"His name is Kevin Selmer." Krohn saw the name didn't ring a bell with Røed. "Harry says he's one of your cocaine suppliers."

Krohn was half expecting Røed to dispute the allegation he had anyone who supplied him with cocaine, but instead it looked as though he was trying to recall the name.

"He's the guy who was here at the party," Krohn said.

"Ah! I didn't know his name, he never told me. Said I should just call him K. I just figured he couldn't spell and thought it stood for . . . well, you can probably guess."

"That I can."

"So K killed them? That's baffling. He must be nuts."

"I think that's a safe assumption, yes."

Røed stared out at the roof terrace. A neighbor was leaning with his back against the wall beside the fire escape smoking a cigarette. "I should buy his apartment, and the other two as well," Røed said. "I can't bear them standing out there looking like they own . . ." He didn't finish the sentence. "Well, I can get out of this prison, at least."

"Yes."

"Good, then I know where I'm going." Røed strode towards the bedroom. Krohn followed.

"Not out to party, Markus."

"Why not?" Røed walked past the big double bed and opened one of the built-in closets.

"Because it's only been a few days since your wife was killed. Think how people will react."

"You're wrong," Røed said as he browsed the suits. "They'll understand that I'm celebrating the fact her killer has been caught. Hello, long time since I've worn this," He took out a navy-blue, double-breasted blazer with gold buttons and put it on. Felt in the pockets and pulled something out that he tossed on the bed. "Whoa, has it been *that* long?"

Krohn saw it was a black masquerade mask shaped like a butterfly.

Røed did up the blazer while he looked in a gold-framed mirror.

"Sure you don't want to come on a bender, Johan?"

"Quite sure."

"Maybe I can take my bodyguards instead. How long have we paid them for?"

"They're not allowed to drink on the job."

"Right, that would make for boring company." Røed went out to the living room and, with laughter in his voice, shouted: "Have you heard, boys? You're discharged!"

Krohn and Røed took the elevator down together.

"Ring Hole," Røed said. "He likes to drink. Tell him I'm going on a bar crawl on Dronning Eufemias gate, from east to west. And the drinks are on me. Then I can congratulate him right away."

Krohn nodded as he posed himself that perennial question: if he'd known that as a lawyer he would have to spend such a large portion of his life with people he disliked so much, would he still have chosen the same career?

"Creatures."

"Hi. Is that Ben?"

"Yeah, who's this?"

"Harry. The tall, blond—"

"Hi, Harry, long time. What's up?"

Harry looked down from Ekeberg, out over the city that lay like an inverse starry sky below him.

"It's about Lucille. I'm in Norway and I can't get hold of her on the phone. Have you seen her?"

"Not for . . . about a month?"

"Mm. She lives on her own, as you know, and I was worried something might have happened to her."

"OK?"

"If I give you an address on Doheny Drive, could you check on her for me? If she's not there, you should probably contact the police."

There was a pause.

"OK, Harry, I'm jotting it down."

After the call, Harry walked to the Mercedes parked behind the old German bunkers. Sat on the hood next to Øystein again, lit up a cigarette and continued from where they had left off while the music streamed out of the two open car windows. About all the others and what had become of them, about the girls they never got, about the dreams that didn't shatter but faded away like a half-baked song or a long joke without a punchline. About the life they chose or the life that chose them, which was one and the same, since you—as Øystein said—can only play the hand you're dealt.

"It's warm," Øystein said, after they had sat in silence for a while.

"Old engines give the best heat," Harry said, patting the hood.

"No, I meant the weather. I thought it was over but the warm weather's back. And tomorrow that there will be eclipsed by blood." He pointed up at a pale full moon.

Harry's phone rang. "Talk to me."

"So it's true," Sung-min said. "You really do answer the phone like that."

"I saw it was you and was just trying to live up to the myth," Harry said. "What's going on?"

"I'm at the Forensic Medical Institute. And to be completely honest, I don't quite know what's going on."

"Oh yeah? Are the press onto you about the death of the suspect?"

"Not yet, we're holding off a little before making it public. Until he's identified."

"If he's really named Kevin Selmer, you mean? Øystein here called him Al."

"No, if the man we found dead in cell 14 is the same man we brought in."

Harry pressed the phone harder against his ear. "What do you mean, Larsen?"

"His legal counsel has disappeared. He was alone in the cell with Kevin Selmer. Five minutes after he arrived, he left again. If it was him. The man who left was wearing a face mask and the lawyer's clothes, but the shift commander of the Custody Unit thought the person seemed different."

"You think that Selmer . . ."

"I don't know what I think," Sung-min said. "But yeah, it's possible Selmer might have escaped. That he killed Beckstrøm, smashed his face in, switched clothes and just walked out of there. That the corpse we're sitting with is Beckstrøm, not Al. Or Selmer, that is. The face is totally beyond recognition, we can't find any friends or relatives of Kevin Selmer who know him well enough to identify him. And on top of that, Beckstrøm is nowhere to be found."

"Mm. Sounds a bit far-fetched, Larsen. I know Dag Beckstrøm, he's probably gone off the deep end. You have heard about Judgment Dag?"

"Eh, no."

"Beckstrøm has a reputation for having a rather sensitive nature. If a case has upset him he goes out and drinks, and then he turns into Judgment Dag and pronounces verdicts on all and sundry. Sometimes for days. That's probably what happened here."

"Well, let's hope so. We'll find out soon enough, Beckstrøm's wife is on her way over here. I just wanted to give you a heads-up."

"OK. Thanks."

Harry hung up. They sat in silence listening to Rufus Wainwright singing "Hallelujah."

"I think I might have underrated Leonard Cohen," Øystein said. "And overrated Bob Dylan."

"Easily done. Put out the cigarette, we need to go."

"What's happening?" Øystein asked, hopping off the hood.

"If Sung-min is right, Markus Røed could be in danger." Harry swung into the passenger seat. "Krohn called while you were in the bushes taking a piss. Røed's gone on a bar crawl and wants my company. I said no but maybe we need to find him all the same. Dronning Eufemias gate."

Øystein turned the key in the ignition. "Can you say step on it, Harry?" He revved the engine. "Please?"

"Step on it," Harry said.

Markus Røed lurched to the side, took a step to steady himself, and stared down at the glass on the table in front of him.

It had spirits in it, he was sure of that. He wasn't so sure what the rest of the stuff in there was but the colors were nice. Both in the glass and in the bar. Which he didn't know the name of. The other guests were younger and looked over at him with stolen—and not so stolen—glances. They knew who he was. No, they knew what his *name* was. Had seen his picture in the papers, especially lately. And would have formed an opinion on him. Choosing this particular street for a pub crawl had been a mistake; you only had to look at the pretentious name of Oslo's newest attempt at an avenue: Dronning Eufemias gate. Ouch! Femi. There you have it, a bloody gay street. He should have gone to some of the old spots. Places where people accepted the offer and flocked to the bar when a capitalist got to his feet and announced the next round was on him. In the last two bars he had been in they had just gawped at him as if he had spread his cheeks and shown them his balloon knot. In one place the barman had even asked him to sit down. As if they didn't need the revenue. Those places would be out of business within a year, just wait. It was the old hands who survived, those who knew the game. And he—Markus Røed—knew the game.

His upper body began tipping forward, his dark hair flopping down towards the glass. He managed to straighten up at the last moment. A full head of hair. Real hair that didn't need dyeing every fucking week. Put that in your pipe.

He gripped the glass, something to hold on to. Drained it. Maybe he should drink a little slower. On the way between the two first bars he had been crossing the street—sorry, avenue—when he heard the piercing clatter of a tram bell. He had reacted so sluggishly, as though wading through mud. But that drink he'd had in the first bar must have been strong, because not only were his reflexes poor, it was as if he had lost all sense of fear too. When the tram passed, so closely that he could feel the air pressure on his back, his pulse had hardly increased. Now that he wanted to live again as well! It was like a distant memory that he had asked to borrow Krohn's tie when he was in custody. Not to improve his appearance but to hang himself. Krohn had said he wasn't allowed to hand anything over. Idiot.

Røed looked around the room.

They were all idiots. His father had taught him that, beaten it into him. That everyone—except those with Røed as a surname—was an idiot. That it was an open goal, all you had to do was tap the ball in every time. But you had to do it. Don't feel sorry for them, don't feel you had enough, you had to keep going. Increase the wealth, get further ahead, take what came your way and then some. Damn it, he might not have been the most academically gifted in the family but unlike the others he had always done what his father said. And didn't that give him the right to live it up once in a while? Snort a few lines. Slap a few boys on their tight asses. If they were under that idiotic age of consent, so what? In other countries and cultures they saw the big picture; knew that it did the boys no harm, that they grew up and moved on, became solid, decent citizens. Not drama queens and queers; it wasn't contagious or dangerous getting a grown man's cock in you when you were young, you could still be saved. He had often seen his father strike out but only once seen him lose his temper. It was when Markus was in the fourth grade and his father had walked into his bedroom to find Markus and the boy next door playing mommies and daddies in bed. Jesus, how he had hated that man. How frightened he had been of him. And how much he had loved him. One single word of approval from Otto Røed and Markus felt like the master of the world, invincible.

"So this is where you are, Røed."

Markus looked up. The man standing in front of his table was wearing a face mask and a flat cap. There was something familiar about him. About the voice too, but Markus was too drunk, everything was blurry.

"Got any coke for me?" Markus asked automatically, and wondered in the same moment where that had come from. Probably just the craving.

"You're not getting any coke," the man said, sitting down at the table. "You shouldn't be out drinking at a bar either."

"I shouldn't?"

"No. You should be at home crying over that lovely wife of yours. And over Susanne and Bertine. And now another person is dead. But here you sit, looking to party. You worthless, fucking pig."

Røed winced. Not because of what he said about the women. It was the word "worthless" that had struck home. An echo from childhood and the man who had stood over him frothing at the mouth.

"Who are you?" Røed slurred.

"Can't you see? I've come from the Custody Unit. Jernbanetorget. Kevin Selmer. Ring any bells?"

"Should it?"

"Yes," the man said, removing his face mask. "You recognize me now?"

"You look like my fuck," Markus slurred. "My *father*." He had the vague feeling he ought to be scared. But he wasn't.

"Death," the man said.

Maybe it was the sluggishness and the absence of fear that caused Markus not to raise a hand in defense when he saw the man lift his. Or maybe it was just automatic, the conditioned response of the boy who has learned that his father has the right to hit him. The man was holding something in his hand. Was it a . . . hammer?

*

Harry entered the bar, which—if the red neon letters over the door spelled the name—was simply called Bar. This was the third place he had tried, and it was indistinguishable from the other two: glossy, probably stylish and no doubt pricey. He scanned the room and spotted Røed seated at a table. In front of him, with his back to Harry, a man was sitting in a flat cap with his hand raised. He was holding something. Harry saw what it was and knew in the same instant what was going to happen. And that he was too late to prevent it.

Sung-min and Helge were standing next to the woman gazing down at the body.

She was somewhere in her sixties and had the hair, clothes and makeup of a hippy; Sung-min expected she was one of those women who turned up at music festivals featuring old acoustic heroes from the seventies. She had already been crying when they opened the door of the Forensic Medical Institute to her, and Helge had given her some paper towels which she was now using to wipe away tears and running mascara with.

Now that Helge had washed away all the coagulated blood, Sung-min could see that the face of the dead man was more intact than he had previously thought.

"Take your time, fru Beckstrøm," Helge said. "We can leave you alone if you wish?"

"No need," she sniffed. "There's no doubt."

The buzz of voices in Bar fell silent instantly and the customers turned in the direction of the sound. A bang as loud as a pistol shot. Half in shock, they stared at the man in the flat cap who had risen to his feet; some had picked up on the fact that the other person at the table was the real estate magnate, the husband of the woman found dead on Snarøya. In the silence they heard the man's voice clear as a bell and saw him raise the hand with the blunt weapon.

"I said death! I sentence you to death, Markus Røed!"

There was another loud bang.

They saw a tall man in a suit walking quickly towards the table. And as the man in the cap lifted his hand a third time, the tall man snatched the object from his grip.

"It's not him," fru Beckstrøm sobbed. "It's not Dag, thank God. But I don't know where he is. I'm beside myself with worry every time he disappears like this."

"There, there," Sung-min said, and wondered if he should place a hand on her shoulder. "I'm sure we'll find him. And we're also relieved it's not your husband. I'm sorry you had to go through this, fru Beckstrøm, but we just had to be certain."

She nodded mutely.

"That's enough now, Judgment Dag."

Harry pushed Beckstrøm back down into his chair and put the gavel in his own pocket. The two drunk men, Røed and Beckstrøm, gawped stupidly at each other, as if they had both just woken up and were wondering what had happened. The glass-topped table had a large crack in it.

Harry sat down. "I know you've had a long day, Beckstrøm, but you should contact your wife. She went to the Forensic Medical Institute to see if the body of Kevin Selmer was you."

The defense lawyer stared at Harry. "You didn't see him," he whispered. "He couldn't handle the pain. He'd told them his stomach and head were hurting, but the doctor had just given him some mild painkillers, and when they didn't work and no one came to help he bashed his head against the wall to knock himself unconscious. *That's* how much pain he was in."

"We don't know that," Harry said.

"Yes," Beckstrøm said, his eyes now wet with tears, "we do, because we've seen this type of thing before. While his sort"—he pointed a trembling finger at Røed, who was sitting with his chin on his chest—"don't give a fuck about anyone or anything, they just want to be rich, and along the way they trample on and exploit anybody weaker in society, all those who never had the silver spoon they suck on. But the day will come when the sun will be turned into darkness, the great and terrible—"

"Judgment Day, Judgment Dag?"

Beckstrøm glowered at Harry while looking like he was making a great effort to keep his head straight.

"Sorry," Harry said, placing a hand on his shoulder. "Let's do this another time. Right now, I think you need to call your wife, Beckstrøm."

Dag Beckstrøm opened his mouth to say something but shut it again. Nodded, took out his phone, got to his feet and left.

"You handled that well, Harry," Røed said clearly sloshed, almost missing the table as he put his elbows on it. "Can I buy you a drink?"

"No thanks."

"No? Now that you've solved the case and everything? Or almost everything . . ." Røed motioned to a waiter for another drink but he ignored him.

"What do you mean by almost?"

"What do I mean?" Røed said. "Well, you tell me."

"Out with it."

"Or what?" The tip of Røed's tongue emerged, he smiled, and his voice became a hoarse whisper. "Or else you'll put me in a chokehold?"

"No," Harry said.

"No?"

"I can put you in a chokehold *if* you tell me."

Røed laughed. "Finally, a man that understands me. It's just that I have a little confession to make now that the case is solved. I lied when I said Susanne and I had sex on the same day as she was killed. I didn't meet her at all."

"No?"

"No. I only said it to give the police a plausible explanation as to why my saliva was found on her body. It was what they wanted to hear, and it was also going to save me a lot of trouble. The path of least resistance, you might say."

"Mm."

"Can we keep that between ourselves?"

"Why? The case has been cleared up. And you hardly want it known you were screwing another woman behind your wife's back?"

"Ah," Røed said, and smiled. "I'm not worried about that. There are . . . other rumors to consider."

"Are there?"

Røed twirled the empty glass in his hand. "You know, Harry, when my father died, I was both devastated and relieved. Can you understand that? What a release it was to be rid of a man you didn't want to disappoint for anything in the world. Because you know that sooner or later the day will come when you have to disappoint him, when he has to find out who you *really* are. And so you hope to be saved by the bell. And I was."

"Were you afraid of him?"

"Yes," Røed said. "I was afraid. And I suppose I loved him too. But above all"—he put the empty glass to his forehead—"I wanted him to love me. You know, I would happily have let him kill me if I just knew that he loved me."

42

FRIDAY

TERRY VÅGE BLINKED. HE HAD slept poorly. And was in a bad mood. Anyway, no one liked press conferences that started at nine in the morning. Or perhaps he was mistaken, the other journalists in the Parole Hall looked annoyingly perky. Even Mona Daa—the seats next to her already occupied when he arrived—appeared wide awake and animated. He had tried to make eye contact but to no avail. None of the other journalists had paid any attention to him when he entered either. Not that he was expecting a standing ovation, but you would think that going into the woods in the middle of the night and running the risk of encountering a serial killer might garner you a modicum of respect. Especially when you came back alive with pictures that had been sold to media outlets and appeared all around the world. Happiness is short-lived, as they say. A real win would have meant his getting that exclusive interview, but that scoop had been snatched away at the last minute. So yes, he had more reason than the rest to be in bad form today. Moreover, Dagnija had called last night to say she couldn't come that weekend after all. When she told him she couldn't make it—although he wasn't convinced that she *couldn't*—he had naturally attempted to persuade her, which had ended in an argument.

"Kevin Selmer," Katrine Bratt said from the podium. "We've chosen to go public with the name because the suspect is deceased, because of the seriousness of the crime, and in order to spare others who have been under police scrutiny from public suspicion."

Terry Våge watched the other journalists take notes. Kevin Selmer. He searched his brain. He had the list of car owners on the PC at home but couldn't remember anyone with that name offhand. But his memory wasn't what it once was, not like when he was able to reel off the name of every notable band, their members, records and release dates from 1960 to . . . well, 2000?

"I'll now hand over to Helge Forfang from the Forensic Medical Institute," Head of Information Kedzierski said.

Terry Våge was slightly puzzled. Wasn't it uncommon for forensic scientists to be present at press conferences? Didn't they usually just have their reports quoted? And he was puzzled by what Forfang presented. That at least one of the victims had been infected with a mutated or manipulated parasite and the evidence suggested the killer had been responsible. And that the killer had also been infected.

"The post-mortem carried out on Kevin Selmer last night revealed a high concentration of the *Toxoplasma gondii* parasite. High enough for us to say with a large degree of certainty that the parasite was the cause of death, not the self-inflicted injuries to the head and face. Although speculative, it might appear as if Kevin Selmer acted as a primary host for the parasite and was able for a time to control the population, perhaps by use of antiparasitic agents, but, again, we don't know that for sure."

Terry Våge stood up and left when they opened for questions from the floor. He had found out what he needed to know. He was no longer puzzled. He just needed to get home and confirm it.

Sung-min walked through the cafeteria and out onto the terrace. He had always envied the employees of Police HQ this view from the top of the glass palace. At least on a day like this, when Oslo lay bathed in sunshine and the temperature had spiked unexpectedly. He made his way over to Katrine and Harry, both standing by the railing, each smoking a cigarette.

"Didn't know you smoked," Sung-min said, smiling at Katrine.

"I don't really," she said, smiling back. "I just bummed one off Harry to celebrate."

"You're a bad influence, Harry."

"Yep," Harry said, holding out a pack of Camels.

"Sung-min hesitated. "Why not?" he said, taking a cigarette that Harry lit up for him.

"How are you going to celebrate?" Katrine asked.

"Let me see," Sung-min said. "I have a dinner date. What about you?"

"Me too. Arne told me to meet him up at Frognerseteren Restaurant. It's going to be a surprise."

"A restaurant on the edge of the forest with a view from the mountain. Sounds romantic."

"Sure," Katrine said, looking with momentary fascination at the smoke she was blowing out through her nose. "I'm just not that big into surprises. You going to mark the occasion, Harry?"

"I was. Alexandra invited me up onto the roof of the Forensic Medical Institute. She and Helge are going to share a bottle of wine and watch the lunar eclipse."

"Ah, the blood moon," Sung-min said. "And it looks like it's going to be a nice night."

"But?" Katrine said.

"We'll see," Harry said. "Been some bad news. Ståle's wife called. He's taken a turn and wants me to come visit. I'll probably stay as long as he has the energy."

"Shit."

"Yeah." Harry took a long drag of his cigarette.

They stood in silence for a while.

"You see the tribute we received today, from the Minister of Justice no less?"

Katrine sounded sarcastic.

The other two nodded.

"Just one thing before I go," Harry said. "Røed told me last night that he wasn't with Susanne the day she was killed. And I believe him."

"Me too," said Sung-min, who, with the cigarette in his hand, angled his wrist in a way he otherwise managed to avoid.

"Why?" Katrine asked.

"Because it's obvious he prefers men to women," Sung-min said. "I reckon his sex life with Helene was a compulsory exercise."

"Mm. So we're inclined to believe him. Then how did Røed's saliva wind up on Susanne's breast?"

"Indeed," Katrine said. "I was slightly confused myself when Røed came up with that story about sex earlier in the day, that the spit was from then."

"Oh?"

"What do you think I'll do before I meet Arne tonight? And this goes for all my dates, no matter what, even the ones where sex isn't in the cards."

"You'll take a shower," Sung-min said.

"Correct. I thought it strange that Susanne wouldn't shower before she took the metro to Skullerud. Especially if she'd had sex."

"So, I repeat the question," Harry said. "Where did the saliva come from?"

"Eh . . . after she was killed?" Sung-min said.

"Theoretically possible," Harry said, "But highly unlikely. Think about how meticulously planned these three murders have been. I think the killer planted Røed's saliva on Susanne with the intention of misleading the police."

"Perhaps," Sung-min said.

"I could buy that," Katrine said.

"Of course we'll never get an answer," Harry said.

"No, we never get all the answers," Katrine said.

They stood for a while, closed their eyes to the sun as if they already knew that this would be the last warm day of the year.

It was just before closing time when Jonathan asked. He was standing by the rabbit hutches, and the question, whether Thanh had any plans for the evening, was meant to come across as casual.

If Thanh had suspected anything, naturally she would have answered yes. But she hadn't, so she replied truthfully, that she did not.

"Good," he said. "Then I'd like you to accompany me someplace."

"Someplace?"

"Someplace where I'm going to show you something. But it's secret so you mustn't tell a soul. OK?"

"Eh . . ."

"I'll pick you up at home."

Thanh felt panic mount. She didn't want to go anywhere. And certainly not with Jonathan. True, he no longer seemed angry she had taken a walk with the policeman and his dog. Yesterday he had even brought her a large coffee, something he had never done before. But she was still a little afraid of him. He was so difficult to read, and she considered herself pretty good at reading people.

But now she had painted herself into a corner. She could of course say that she had another appointment that had slipped her mind, but he wouldn't believe her, she was also a terrible liar. And he was her boss after all, and she needed this job. Not at all costs, of course, but at a certain cost. She swallowed.

"What is it you want to show me?"

"Something you'll like," he said. Did he sound grumpy because she didn't say yes straight away?

"What?"

"It's a surprise. Nine o'clock all right?"

She needed to decide. She looked at him. Looked at the odd, closed-off man whom she feared. Tried to make eye contact as though that might give an answer. And then she caught a glimpse of something she hadn't seen before. It wasn't big, just an attempt at a smile that seemed to slip, as it were, as though behind the hard exterior he was nervous. Was he afraid she would say no? Perhaps that was the reason she suddenly felt she wasn't so scared of him after all.

"OK," she said. "Nine o'clock."

And then it was as though he regained self-control. But he smiled. Yes, he smiled, she didn't know if she had seen him smile like that before. It was a nice smile.

But on the metro on the way home she began having doubts again. She wasn't too sure it had been wise to say yes. And then there was one thing she had thought was a little strange, although perhaps it wasn't. He'd said he would pick her up but had not asked where she lived, and she couldn't remember ever having told him.

43

FRIDAY

The alibi

SUNG-MIN WAS COMING FROM THE shower when he saw the phone that lay charging beside the bed was ringing.

"Yes?"

"Good afternoon, Larsen. This is Mona Daa from *VG*."

"Good evening, Daa."

"Oh, it's late you mean? Sorry if your working day is done, I just wanted a couple of quotes from the people involved in the investigation. About how it's been and how it feels to have finally solved the case. I mean, it must be a great relief and a triumph for you and Kripos, who were involved from the start, when Susanne Andersen went missing on the thirtieth of August."

"I think you're a good crime reporter, Daa, so I'm going to give you some short answers to your questions."

"Thanks so much! My first question concerns—"

"I meant the ones you've already asked. Yes, it is evening and my workday is done. No, I have no comments to make, you'll need to call Katrine Bratt who was in charge of the investigation or my boss Ole Winter. And no, Kripos was not involved from the start, when Susanne Andersen was reported missing on the . . . eh . . ."

"Thirtieth of August," Mona Daa repeated.

"Thanks. We hadn't been brought in at that stage. That didn't happen until two people went missing and it became clear that it was a murder case."

"Sorry, again, Larsen. I'm aware I'm being pushy now, but it is my job. Could I get a quote, whatever, just something general, and use a picture of you?"

Sung-min sighed. He had an idea of what she was after. Diversity. A picture of a police officer who was not a fifty-year-old, ethnically Norwegian, heterosexual man. He ticked those boxes anyway. Not that he had anything against diversity in the media, but he knew that once he opened that door it wouldn't take long before he was sitting on a sofa in a TV studio answering questions from a certain TV anchor about what it was like to be gay in the police. Not that he had anything against it, someone should do it. Just not him.

He declined, and Mona Daa said she understood and apologized again. Good woman.

After they had broken the connection, he stood staring into space. He froze. He was naked but that was not why. It was the alarm clock in his head, the same one that had rung when he was at the Custody Unit. It had begun to ring again. It wasn't what Groth had said about Beckstrøm seeming different when he left that had made the alarm go off. It was something else. Something altogether—and distinctly—different.

Terry Våge stared at the PC screen. Checked the names again.

It *might* of course be a coincidence—Oslo was a small town, when it came down to it. He had spent the last few hours deciding what to do. Go to the police or carry out the original plan. He had even considered calling Mona Daa to bring her in on his scheme and—if it was whom he

404

suspected and they hit the jackpot—get the story published in the country's leading newspaper. The two of them on an adventure together, wouldn't that be something? But no, she was too proper, she would insist on notifying the police, he was sure of it. He stared at the phone, on which he had already tapped in the number, all he had to do was press Call. He was done debating with himself now, and the winning argument had been this: it *might* be a coincidence. He had no absolute proof to present to the police, so surely that meant it had to be all right to continue digging on his own. So what was he waiting for? Was he scared? Terry Våge chuckled. Bloody right he was scared. He pressed his forefinger firmly on the Call icon.

He could hear his own ragged breathing against the phone while it rang. For a brief moment he hoped no one would take it. Or if they did, that it wasn't him.

"Yes?"

Disappointment and relief. But mostly disappointment. It wasn't him; this wasn't the voice he had heard on the phone the other two times. Terry Våge took a deep breath. He had decided beforehand that he would go through with the whole plan no matter what so as not to be left in any doubt afterwards.

"It's Terry Våge," he said, managing to control the quaver in his voice. "We have spoken previously. But before you hang up, you should know I haven't contacted the police. Not yet. And I won't either, not if you talk to me."

There was silence on the line. What did that mean? Was the person on the other end trying to decide whether it was a crazy person or a pal playing a prank? Then, quietly and slowly, a different voice sounded.

"How did you find out, Våge?"

It *was* him. It was that deep, rasping voice he had used when he had called Våge from the hidden number, probably on an unregistered phone.

Våge shuddered, without knowing how much it was out of delight and how much it was out of pure dread. He swallowed.

"I saw you driving past Kolsås Shopping Center two nights ago. You went by twenty-six minutes after I'd left the place where you'd hung up the heads. I have all the timestamps on the photos I took."

There was a long pause.

"What do you want, Våge?"

Terry Våge took a deep breath. "I want your story. The whole story, not just about these killings. A true picture of the person behind them. So many people have been affected by what's happened, not only those who knew the victims. And they need to understand, the entire country needs to understand. I hope you realize I have no interest in portraying you as a monster."

"Why not?"

"Because monsters don't exist."

"Don't they?"

Våge swallowed again. "You have of course my word that you will remain anonymous."

A brief snort of laughter. "Why would I take your word for it?"

"Because," Våge said, stopped to get his voice under control. "Because I'm an outcast in journalism. Because I'm stuck on a desert island and you're my only salvation. Because I have nothing to lose."

Another pause.

"And if I don't grant you an interview?"

"Then my next call is to the police."

Våge waited.

"All right. Let's meet at Weiss behind the Munch Museum."

"I know where it is."

"Six o'clock sharp."

"Today?" Våge checked the time. "That's in three-quarters of an hour."

"If you come too early or too late, I'm leaving."

"Fine, fine. See you at six."

Våge put the phone down. Took three shaky breaths. Then laughter took hold, and he lay his head on the keyboard as he slammed his palm on the desk. Fuck you! Fuck all of you!

*

Harry and Øystein were sitting on either side of the bed when the door opened gently and Truls stole into the room.

"How's he doing?" Truls whispered, found a seat and looked at Ståle Aune lying there pale with eyes shut.

"You can ask me," Aune said sharply, opening his eyes. "I'm fair to middling. I asked Harry to come but don't the two of you have something better to do on a Friday night?"

Truls and Øystein looked at each other.

"Nope," Øystein said.

Aune shook his head. "Where were you, Eikeland?"

"Yeah," Øystein said. "So, I had a fare from Oslo to Trondheim, three hundred miles, and this guy was playing a cassette with a panpipe version of 'Careless Whisper,' and in the middle of the Dovrefjell mountain range I snapped, ejected the tape, rolled down the window . . ."

Harry's phone rang. He presumed it was Alexandra wondering if he was going to make it over for the lunar eclipse at 10:35 p.m., but he saw it was Sung-min. He hurriedly stepped out into the corridor.

"Yeah, Sung-min?"

"No. Say *talk to me*."

"Talk to me."

"I will. Because it doesn't add up."

"What doesn't add up?"

"Kevin Selmer. He had an alibi."

"Oh?"

"I was at the Custody Unit and it was right in front of me. Selmer's ticket to *Romeo and Juliet*. If my brain was a little more efficient I'd have realized it there and then. That is to say, my brain tried to tell me, but I didn't listen. Not until Mona Daa spelled it out for me on the phone."

Sung-min paused.

"On the date Susanne Andersen was reported missing, Kevin Selmer was at *Romeo and Juliet* at the National Theater. I've traced the ticket, it was one of several sponsor tickets that were sent to Markus Røed, the same type as Helene used."

"Yeah. She told me she handed out a few of them at the party. Probably where Selmer got his. And I assumed that was where he found out when Helene would be going to the theater too—her ticket was stuck to the fridge door."

"But it wasn't him. Not if it was the same man who killed Susanne Andersen. Because the ticket office at the theater contacted the people next to Selmer that night and they confirmed the man in the seat beside them fit his description, they remembered because he sat there in his parka. And he *didn't* disappear at the intermission."

Harry was surprised. Mostly by the fact he wasn't *more* surprised.

"We're back where we started," Harry said. "It's the other guy, the Greenhorn."

"Sorry?"

"The killer, it's the amateur with the green coke. It's him after all. Fuck, fuck!"

"You sound . . . eh, sure."

"I am sure, but if I were you, I wouldn't trust someone who's been wrong as many times as me. I need to call Katrine. And Krohn."

They hung up.

Katrine was in the process of putting Gert to bed when she took the call, so Harry quickly informed her of the development in the case. After that he called Krohn and explained the indications were that the case wasn't solved after all. "Put Røed back under house arrest. I don't know what this guy's planning, but he's had us fooled the whole way, so we'll take every precaution."

"I'll call the Guardian company," Krohn said. "Thanks."

44

FRIDAY

Interview

PRIM CHECKED THE TIME.

One minute to six.

He had taken a seat at one of the window tables at Weiss. From where he was sitting, he had a view of the two freshly pulled beers in front of him, the Munch Museum in the light of the low sun outside, and the building where he had gatecrashed the terrace party.

A half-minute to six.

He let his eyes drift around. The customers looked so happy. They were standing in groups, smiling, chatting, laughing and patting each other on the shoulders. Friends. It looked nice. It was nice to have some-one. To have Her. Then they would drink beer, and Her friends would be his.

A man wearing a porkpie hat came in. Terry Våge. He stopped and scanned the room as the door slid closed behind him. At first he didn't notice Prim discreetly waving his hand, his eyes no doubt needing to adjust to the dimly lit premises. But then he gave a brief nod and steered towards Prim's table. The reporter looked pale and out of breath.

"You're . . ."

"Yes. Sit down, Våge."

"Thanks." Våge took his hat off. His forehead glistened with sweat. He nodded at the beer on his side of the table.

"Is that for me?"

"I was going to leave as soon as the head was beneath the rim of the glass."

Våge smirked in response and lifted the glass. They drank. Put down the beers and wiped the foam from their lips with the back of their hands in an almost synchronized motion.

"So here we are at long last," Våge said. "Sitting drinking like two old friends."

Prim understood what Våge was trying to do. Break the ice. Gain trust. Get under his skin as quickly as possible.

"Like them?" Prim nodded towards the boisterous people at the bar.

"Oh, they're paper-pushers. The Friday drinks they're having now are the highlight of their week, before they head home to their dull family lives. You know: eat tacos with the kids, put them to bed and watch TV with the same woman until they're both bored enough to fall asleep. Then it's up in the morning to more nagging from the kids and a trip to playland. I imagine that's not the sort of life you live?"

No, Prim thought. *But it might not be far off the kind of life I could see myself living. With Her.*

Våge knew there wouldn't be much opportunity to drink once he had taken out his notebook, so he took a big mouthful of the beer. Jesus, he needed that.

"What do you know about the kind of life I live, Våge?"

Våge looked at the other man, tried to read him. Was this resistance? Had being so direct so early been a mistake? Profile interviews were often a delicate dance. After all, he wanted the interviewees to feel safe, regard him as a friend who understood them, open up and tell him things they wouldn't otherwise. Or to be more precise: say things they'd regret. But sometimes he could be a bit pushy, too overt in his intentions.

"I know a little," Våge said. "It's unbelievable what you can find online when you know where to look."

He noticed the other man's voice was different than on the phone. And that he smelled of something. An odor that conjured up memories of a childhood holiday, his uncle's barn, the smell of the horses' sweaty harnesses. Våge felt a slight sting of pain in his stomach. Probably the old ulcer saying hello, as was its wont following periods of stress and indulgence in bad habits. Or when he drank too quickly, like now. He pushed the glass away and placed the notebook on the table.

"Tell me, how did it start?"

Prim didn't know how long he had been talking when he mentioned that his uncle was also his biological father, but that he only found that out after his mother had died in the fire.

"Initial inbreeding isn't necessarily so unfortunate, it can, on the contrary, yield excellent results. It is through persistent inbreeding that family defects arise. I had noticed there were some distinguishing features that I and Uncle Fredric shared. Small things, like the way we both put our middle finger to the corner of our mouth when thinking. And larger things, like us both having an exceptionally high IQ. But it was only when I began to immerse myself in animals and breeding that I suspected there was a connection and sent in both our DNA for testing. I'd harbored thoughts of revenge long before that. I was going to humiliate my stepfather the way he'd humiliated me. And he was indirectly responsible for the death of my mother. But now I realized the two of them were to blame, Uncle Fredric had also left my mother and me in the lurch. So, I gave him a box of chocolates for Christmas. Uncle Fredric loves chocolates. I'd injected a subspecies of *Angiostrongylus cantonensis* into them, a rat lungworm that is especially fond of human brains and

411

which is only to be found in the slime of the Mount Kaputar slug. The result is a slow, agonizing death with increasing dementia. But I can see I'm boring you. So let's cut to the chase. I spent years developing my own subspecies of *Toxoplasma gondii*, and once it was ready the plan also began to form. The first and biggest problem proved to be getting close enough to Markus Røed to plant the parasite in him. Wealthy people are so less accessible, so much harder to get close to, as a journalist you'd know all about that, when you're trying to get a few words out of rock stars, right? The solution cropped up more or less by accident. I'm not the kind of person who goes out on the town much, but I'd gotten wind of a party being held on the rooftop where Røed lives. Up there . . ." Prim pointed out the window. "And at the same time, through my job, I happened to come across a batch of green cocaine that I realized I could skim. You're familiar with the expression? Yes, so I mixed it with my gondii friends. Not much, just enough to be sure it would have the desired effect once Røed consumed it. The plan was to wait for a couple of days after the party and then visit him again. That would be enough for him to get a scent of me, of the primary host, and be unable to reject me. On the contrary, he'd have done exactly what I asked of him, because from then on, he'd only have had one thought on his mind. Having me. I may no longer have had that little boy's ass he wanted, but no one with gondii in their brain can resist the primary host."

The Aune group was once more gathered around the bed in room 618.

Harry had explained to them how the case now appeared in a fresh light.

"But that can't be bloody right," Øystein exclaimed. "Bertine had a bit of Selmer's skin between her teeth. So where did that come from? Maybe she screwed him earlier on the day she went missing?"

Harry shook his head. "The Greenhorn planted it. Just like he planted Røed's saliva on Susanne's breast."

"How?" Truls asked.

"I don't know. But he must have. He did it to mislead us. And it worked."

"Fine in theory," Øystein said. "But running around planting DNA. Who the fuck does that?"

"Mm." Harry looked thoughtfully at Øystein.

"Unfortunately, things didn't go according to plan at the party." Prim sighed. "While I was arranging the lines on the coffee table, the other dealer, the guy I would later read in the newspaper was called Kevin Selmer, was talking about how he'd never tried green cocaine before, only heard about it. His eyes were shining and when the lines lay ready, he dived in to snort the first one. I grabbed his arm and pulled him away—after all, I had to be sure there was enough for Røed. I clawed at him . . ." Prim looked down at his hand. "Got blood and skin under my nails. Later, when I got home, I picked it out and preserved it. You never know when you might have use for that sort of thing. Anyway, the problems at the party just continued. Røed insisted that his two female friends each snort a line before him. I didn't want to risk raising any objections, but at least the girls were well mannered enough to do the two thinner lines of the three I had arranged. When it was Røed's turn, his wife, Helene, walked in and started telling him off, and maybe that was what stressed him out and caused him to sneeze and blow away the cocaine. That was bad, I didn't have any more with me. So I ran to the kitchen counter, found a dishcloth and cleaned the cocaine up off the table and the floor. Showed the dishcloth to Røed and told him there was enough there for a line. But he wouldn't hear of it, said it was full of fucking snot and spit, and that he'd get some off K, Kevin that is, instead. Kevin was mad at me, so I told him maybe he could get a taste another time. He said he'd like that, that he didn't do drugs, but that everyone had to test things once. He wouldn't tell me his name or where he lived, but that I could find him at Jernbanetorget during normal working hours if I wanted to trade a little of my cocaine for his. I said yeah, sure, figured I'd never see him again. In any event, the party had been a fiasco, and I went back to the kitchen counter to rinse the cloth and leave it when I noticed something on the door of the fridge. A theater ticket to *Romeo and Juliet*. Like the ones Røed's wife had handed out to some of us on the rooftop terrace. I'd stuffed the one I'd been given into my pocket without any intention of using it, and I'd seen Kevin getting one too. Anyway, while I was standing there, my mind began hatching a plan B. And my mind works quickly, Våge. It's incredible how many moves ahead a brain can think when under pressure. And mine was—like I've said—both fast and under pressure. I don't know how long I stood there, scarcely more than a minute, perhaps two. Then I stuffed the cloth in my pocket and approached the girls. First one, then the other. They were favorably disposed towards me after the cocaine I'd given them, and I pumped them for as much information as possible. Not personal stuff, but the kind of things that could tell me where I might find them. Susanne wondered why I still wore a face mask. Bertine wanted more cocaine. But in both cases other men moved in and it was obvious that they were more interested in them than in someone like me. I went home happy, however; after all, I knew it would only be a matter of days until the parasites reached their brains, until they'd be screaming within like little girls in front of a boy band when they caught my scent." Prim laughed and raised his glass to Våge.

"So the question is," Harry said, "where do we start looking for the Greenhorn?"

Truls grunted.

"Yes, Truls?"

Truls made a few more sounds before he managed to speak. "If he's managed to get ahold of green cocaine, we need to check the people who were near the seizure before it was sent for analysis. By that I mean people at the airport and at evidence storage. And, yes, me and the ones who drove it from Gardermoen to Police HQ. But also the guys who transported it from the evidence storage to Krimteknisk."

"Whoa," Øystein said. "We don't know for sure that that seizure was the only batch of green cocaine to have come into the country."

"Truls is right," Harry said. "First we search in the light."

*

414

"As I suspected, I didn't get another chance to get close to Røed," Prim said with a sigh. "I'd mixed all the parasites I had into the cocaine and those in my own body had been killed off by my immune system and a slight overdose of insecticide. So, in order to infect Røed I needed the parasites in the girls before their immune systems destroyed them. In other words, I had to eat some of the girls' brains and eyes. I opted for Susanne, because I knew the gym where she worked out. Given that the human sense of smell is about as strong as that of a mouse, I had to enhance my appeal a tad. So I smeared myself with intestinal juices distilled from my own excrement."

Prim smiled broadly and looked up. Våge didn't return the smile, just stared at him with what looked like disbelief.

"I waited for her outside the gym, and I was excited. I'd tested the parasite on animals that usually shy away from humans, like foxes and deer, and they had been attracted to me, especially the fox. But I couldn't know for sure if it would work on people. She came out and I could tell straight away she was attracted. I arranged to meet her at the parking lot by the forest trails in Skullerud. When she didn't turn up on time I wondered if I'd made a mistake, if she'd gotten her wits back about her when she no longer had the smell of my intestines in her nostrils. But then she appeared, and I was exultant, believe you me."

Prim took a gulp of his beer, as though getting ready to dive in.

"We walked into the forest, arm in arm, and when we were a little distance from the road, we left the trail and had sex. Then I slit her neck." Prim felt tears coming and had to clear his throat. "I am aware that you might like more details at this point, but I think I must have suppressed some parts. Anyway, I'd also brought along a vial of saliva from Røed that I smeared on her breast. I dressed her upper body so that the saliva wouldn't be washed away in the rain before the police found her. The spit seemed like a good idea at the time, but it only served to complicate matters." He took a sip of beer. "With regards to Bertine, it was quite similar. I met her at a bar she told me she frequented and arranged to meet her in Grefsenkollen. She came by car and when I asked her to leave her phone and accompany me on an adventure in my car she had no qualms, only pure lust. She brought something she called a snuff bullet, a sort of mini-peppermill you inhale cocaine from. She persuaded me to take a sniff. I said I wanted to take her from behind and put a leather strap around her neck. No doubt assuming it was a sex game, she let me do it. It took a little longer to strangle her than I thought. Nevertheless, she stopped breathing in the end."

Prim sighed heavily and shook his head. Wiped a tear away.

"I must point out that I was very careful to remove any traces of myself the police might find, so I took her snuff bullet, seeing as DNA from my nose could have made its way inside. At the time I didn't know that I would have use for it later. I had learned, incidentally, that if you're going to kill someone and procure their brain and eyes, it's a lot smarter to take their entire head home."

Prim flexed his feet under the table, they felt like they were going to sleep.

"Over the following weeks I ate little bits of brain and eyes. I needed to keep the reproduction of the annoyingly short-lived parasites going while I waited to get within striking distance of Røed. I sat a number of times at this very table wondering if I should drop by and ask if we could speak. But he was never home, I only saw Helene coming and going. Perhaps he was living someplace else, but I never managed to find out where. In the meantime, I'd eaten up the brains, the parasites were dead, so I needed a new mouse. Helene Røed. I figured it would cause Markus Røed pain—at least a certain amount—if I took her from him. And I knew of two locations I could get close to her. At the National Theater on the date of the ticket on the fridge door. And at a place called Danielle's. When I asked Susanne, she told me that was where she first met Markus Røed. And she couldn't understand why Helene Røed still went to those Monday lunches—after all, she'd already reeled in her big fish. So I went along on a Monday, and sure enough, Helene Røed showed up. I ordered the same drink I'd seen her have at the party, a dirty martini, and poured an appropriate dose of gondii juice into it. Then I summoned the waiter, gave him a 200-krone note and had him take the drink to her table. I told him to point out another sender, that it was a joke between friends. I waited until I saw her drink and then left. I found out what time the intermission for *Romeo and Juliet* was and that you only needed a ticket to get into the auditorium, that anybody could walk in when there was an intermission and mingle with the audience. So I did what I already felt fairly experienced at, I went in and picked her up and . . ." Prim grimaced and kicked out with one foot. Didn't know whether it was the leg of the table or Våge's leg he hit. "The next day she was found and Røed was taken into custody. And that was when I realized I'd shot myself in the foot. I had ensured he would wind up there because I wanted him to suffer, but then they said he'd probably be sitting there for months. So, I had to solve that problem. Fortunately, I have this . . ."

Prim tapped a finger against his forehead.

"I used it and found another innocent person who could take Røed's place. Kevin the cocaine dealer. After all, he'd been so excited to try green cocaine. He was perfect."

45

FRIDAY

Collection

PRIM GLANCED TOWARDS THE OFFICE gang celebrating Friday while slowly turning his own glass.

"I also had a small shred of skin preserved. Skin from Kevin Selmer's forearm. He wasn't the only person I had a tissue sample of; they were something I collected and sometimes had use for in my project to cultivate the perfect parasite. With a toothpick, I lodged a flake of skin between two of the teeth in Bertine's skull. And then you ensured the evidence landed in the hands of the police. But I expected that sooner or later it would be discovered that the bodies had a variant of the gondii parasite. And if someone understood the connection, they would begin to hunt for the primary host. Could I make Kevin appear to be both the killer and the primary host? Apologies if I sound a little smug, but the solution was as ingenious as it was simple. I prepared a mixture of green cocaine and gondii, a dose guaranteed to be lethal, put it into Bertine's snuff bullet and went down to Kevin at Jernbanetorget to make the trade I had agreed to at the party. He was thrilled, especially when I threw the snuff bullet into the bargain. I can only imagine the pains he must have had in his stomach before he died, I don't doubt I would have butted my head against a wall to render myself unconscious as well."

Prim drained the rest of his beer glass.

"That was a long monologue, so enough about me, Terry. How are you doing?" Prim leaned across the table. "Like, really.. Are you feeling . . . paralyzed? Because it happens very quickly when you drink a beer containing such a strong concentration of gondii. Even stronger than Kevin got. After a few minutes you're simply unable to lift a finger. Not make a sound either. But I can see you're still breathing. Heart and respiratory failure are actually the last things to occur. Well, the brain ceases to function too, of course. So I know you can hear this. I'm going to take your house keys and collect your PC. Throw it and your phone in the fjord."

Prim looked outside. The daylight was beginning to dwindle.

"Look, there's a light on in my stepfather's apartment. He'll be on his own now. Do you think he'd like a visitor?"

The time was a little past six thirty when Markus Røed heard the doorbell ring.

"You expecting anyone?" asked the older of the two bodyguards.

Røed shook his head. The bodyguard walked from the living room towards the hallway and the intercom.

Once he had left the room, Røed made use of the opportunity.

"And what do you want to do after you finish working as a bodyguard?"

The young man looked at him. He had long eyelashes and soft brown eyes. The unnecessarily large muscles were compensated by the naive, childish mien. If you added some goodwill and imagination, he could pass for five or six years younger than he was.

"Dunno," he said, letting his gaze sweep around the living room. Probably something they were taught in training: no unnecessary conversation with the client and constantly check the surroundings, even when sitting behind locked doors in the cosy cocoon of a home.

"You could come and work for me, you know?"

The young man eyed Røed briefly, and Røed saw something resembling contempt, disgust. Then, without responding, the young man began to scan the room again. Røed cursed to himself. Fucking pup, didn't he understand what he was being offered?

"It's a guy who says he knows you," the guard called from the hallway.

"Krohn?" Røed called back.

"No."

Røed frowned. He couldn't think of anyone who would just call at his place unannounced.

He went out to the hall, where the bodyguard had assumed a wide stance and was pointing at the video screen. There was a young man staring up at the camera above the entrance door down on the street. Røed shook his head.

"I'll ask him to leave," the bodyguard said.

Røed peered at the screen. Hadn't he seen the guy before, just a while back? And hadn't he recognized something then as well, from long ago, but dismissed it as just another face that brought back memories? But now when he was standing out there, might it . . .

"Wait," Røed said and held out his hand.

The bodyguard gave him the handset.

"Go back inside," Røed said.

The bodyguard hesitated for a moment before doing as he was instructed.

"Who are you and what do you want?" Røed said into the intercom. It sounded more negative than he'd intended.

"Hi, Dad. It's your stepson. And I just wanted to talk to you."

Røed gasped for breath. There was no doubt. The boy from so many dreams, the fear from so many nightmares about being found out. No, it wasn't the boy, but it was him. After all these years. Talk? That didn't bode well.

"I'm a bit busy," Røed said. "You should have called ahead."

"I know," the man said into the camera. "I wasn't planning on getting in touch, I just decided today. You see, I'm going away tomorrow on an extended trip, and I don't know when I'll be back. I didn't want to leave with matters unresolved, Dad. It's time for forgiveness. I had to see you one last time, face-to-face, to get it off my chest. I think it'll be good for both of us. It doesn't need to take more than a few minutes, and we'll both regret it if we don't, I'm sure of that."

Røed listened. He hadn't heard that deep voice before, not back then or recently. From what he could remember of those last days in the house in Gaustad, the boy's voice had just begun to break. Of course, the thought had crossed his mind that he may show up one day and cause trouble for him. It would be one person's word against another's and the only person who could confirm that any so-called sexual abuse had occurred had perished in a fire. But even an allegation would damage his reputation if it came out. Stain the facade, as the people in this country so contemptuously put it. Because Norway was a country where concepts like family honor had been eroded by social bloody democracy, because the state was the family for most people now, and the small individuals had nobody to answer to but their equals, social democracy's gray mass, so lacking in tradition. It was different if your name was Røed, but that was something the average citizen would never understand. Understand the expectation to sooner take your own life than drag the family name through the mud. So, what should he do? He had to decide. His stepson had resurfaced. Røed wiped his forehead with his free hand. And was astonished to find he was not afraid. It was like when the tram nearly ran him over. Now that what he had been so terrified of was finally happening, why didn't it scare him more? What if they did talk together? If his stepson had bad intentions, then talking wasn't going to make the situation any worse. And at best it was just a matter of forgiveness. All forgotten, thank you and goodbye, maybe he would even sleep better at night. The only thing he had to be careful about was not to say anything, confess directly or indirectly to something that could be used against him.

"I can give you ten minutes," Røed said, and pressed the button that opened the street door. "Take the elevator to the top floor."

He replaced the handset. Could the boy be planning on making a recording? He returned to the living room. "Do you frisk visitors?" he asked the bodyguards.

"Always," the older one said.

"Good. Check if he has any microphones taped to him and keep his phone until he leaves."

Prim was sitting in a soft armchair in the TV room looking at Markus Røed. The bodyguards were standing just outside with the door ajar.

It had come as a surprise to find he had bodyguards, but it didn't really matter much. The important thing was that he had him on his own.

The whole thing could of course have been made easier. Had he wanted to kill Markus Røed or cause him physical harm, it would not have been very difficult; after all, only now did he have bodyguards, and in a city like Oslo the inhabitants are so naively trusting that no one thinks the guy they meet on the street might have a weapon under his jacket. It just doesn't happen. And that wasn't what was going to happen to Markus Røed either. That wouldn't be enough. Yes, it would be easier to shoot him, but if the vengeance he had planned for his stepfather gave him just a fraction of the delight it had given him in his imagination, it would be worth all the work. Because the revenge Prim had composed was akin to a symphony, and the climactic crescendo was building.

"I'm sorry about what happened to your mother," Markus said. Loud enough for Prim to hear him clearly, low enough for the bodyguards in the hallway not to catch it.

Prim could see the big man was uncomfortable sitting there in the chair. His fingers picking at the material on the armrests, his nostrils flaring. A sure sign he had caught the odor of the intestinal juices. The dilated pupils told Prim that the scent signals had already reached the brain, where the parasites, eager to breed, had been in place for several days. The result of a little work of art, if he might say so himself. When the original plan to infect his stepfather at the party had gone awry, Prim had been forced to improvise and come up with a fresh plan. And he had carried it out, he had infected Markus Røed right in front of all of them, the lawyers, the police, even Harry Hole.

Markus Røed looked at his watch and sneezed. "Not to rush you, but as I said I'm pressed for time, so we need to be brief. What country is it you're trav—"

"I want you," Prim said.

His stepfather gave such a start in the chair that his jowls quivered.

"I'm sorry, what?"

"I've fantasized about you all these years. There's no doubt it was abuse, but I . . . well, I guess I learned to like it. And want to try it again."

Prim looked straight into Markus Røed's eyes. Saw the parasite-infested brain working behind them and drawing the wrong conclusions: *I knew it! The boy liked it, he was only pretending to cry. I didn't do anything wrong—on the contrary, I merely taught someone to like what I like!*

"And I think we should make it as similar as possible to how it was before."

"Similar?" Markus Røed said. His throat was already tight with excitement. That was the paradox of toxoplasmosis, how the sexual drive—which is essentially the desire to reproduce—suffocates the fear of death, ignores dangers, giving the infected being that delightful, hopeless tunnel vision, a tunnel leading right into the cat's maw.

"The house," Prim said. "It's still there. But you have to come alone, you have to give your bodyguards the slip."

"You mean"—Markus swallowed—"*now?*"

"Of course. I can see you"—Prim leaned forward and placed a hand on the other man's crotch—"want to?"

Røed's jaw was moving up and down uncontrollably.

Prim got to his feet. "You remember where it is?"

Markus Røed just nodded.

"And you'll come alone?"

Another nod.

Prim knew he didn't need to tell Markus Røed not to let anyone know where he was going or who he was planning to meet. Toxoplasmosis renders the infected person horny and fearless, but not stupid. That is to say, not stupid in the sense that they would do something that might potentially prevent them from getting the only thing on their minds.

"I'll give you thirty minutes," Prim said.

The older bodyguard, Benny, had been in the business for fifteen years.

When he opened the door, he saw the visitor had put on a face mask. Benny watched as the younger bodyguard patted him down. Apart from a set of keys, the visitor had nothing on him that could be used as a weapon. Neither did he have a wallet nor any form of ID. He gave his name as Karl Arnesen, and even though it sounded like something he had made up on the spot, Røed had confirmed it with a curt nod. The visitor was relieved of his cell phone as Røed had requested, and Benny insisted on the door to the TV room remaining slightly open.

It took just five minutes—at least that was the length of time Benny would give in his statement to the police later—for this young "Arnesen" to emerge from the TV room, get his phone and leave the apartment. Røed called out from the TV room that he wanted to be alone and closed the door. It took another five minutes before Benny knocked to say that Johan Krohn wanted to speak to him. But Benny got no answer, and when he opened the door, the room was empty and the window out to the terrace was open. His eyes fell on the door of the fire escape leading down to the street. It was hardly any great mystery; the client had hinted three times within the last hour that he would pay exceptionally well if Benny or his colleague would head over to Torggata or Jernbanetorget and procure some cocaine.

46

FRIDAY

Blood moon

MARKUS GOT OUT OF THE taxi by the gate at the end of the drive.

The first thing the taxi driver had asked him when he got into the car at Oslobukta had been if he had any money. A reasonable question given that Markus wasn't wearing his jacket over his shirt and had slippers on. But he had his credit card with him, as always—no matter what, he felt naked without it.

The hinges screeched as he opened the gate. He walked up the gravel drive, reached the top and was a little shocked when he saw the half burnt-out house standing there in the dusk. He hadn't been here since leaving Molle and the boy with that idiotic nickname, Prim. He had read about her death in the paper, had gone to the funeral, but hadn't known the house was so badly damaged. He only hoped enough of the backdrop was preserved for them to act out the scene in a credible manner, so to speak. Reconstruct what they had done and what they had been to one another back then. Although, what he had been to the boy God only knew.

As Røed began walking down towards the house he saw a figure step out of the front door. It was him. The desire Røed had felt sitting in the TV room across from the boy had been overwhelming, almost making him lose control and lunge. But he had done that sort of thing one too many times in his life and had only barely gotten away with it. Now his desire was under control, enough to enable rational thought, he felt. Still the craving, after so many years of stored-up memories about Prim, was so strong that nothing could have stopped him now.

He walked down to the young man, who extended his hand in welcome and smiled. It hadn't crossed Røed's mind until now but the two big, rodent-like front teeth were gone, and the boy had a line of nice, even teeth. For the sake of illusion, he would have preferred the childhood teeth but forgot about that as soon as he drew close and was led into the house.

Another small shock. The hallway, living room, everything black and burnt-out. The partition walls were gone rendering everything more open. The man—the boy—led him straight to the floor space that had been his room on the ground floor. With a shudder of delight, Røed realized he didn't need any light, he had walked these steps from the bottom of the staircase to the boy's room in the darkness of night so many times that he could do it with his eyes closed.

"Undress yourself and lie down there," the boy said, shining his phone's flashlight.

Røed stared at the filthy mattress and the burnt-out skeleton of an iron bed.

And did as he was told, laying his clothes over the headboard.

"Everything," the boy said.

Røed took off his underpants. His erection had grown ever since the boy had taken his hand. Røed liked to dominate, not be dominated. Not up until this point anyway. But now he was enjoying the sound of the commanding voice, the cold giving him goose pimples, the humiliation in being naked while the boy was fully dressed. The mattress stank of urine and was wet and cold against his back.

426

"Let's get these on." Røed felt his arms being pulled upwards and something being tightened around his wrists. Looked up. In the light from the boy's phone, he saw his hands being tied to the headboard with leather straps. Then the same with his feet. He was at the mercy of the boy. The same way the boy had been at the mercy of him.

"Come," Røed whispered.

"We need more light," the boy said. He had taken Røed's cell phone from the jacket on the headboard. "What's the code?"

"Eye recog—" Røed began before the screen appeared in front of his face.

"Thanks."

Røed was blinded by the two light sources and couldn't see what the boy was doing before discerning his figure between the two phones. He realized they must have been mounted on two stands at head height. The boy was older. Had become a man. But was still young enough for Røed to want him. Clearly. His erection was beyond reproach and the tremor in his voice owed as much to excitement as the cold when he whispered: "Come! Come to me, boy!"

"First, tell me what you want me to do to you."

Markus Røed moistened his dry lips. And told him.

"Say it again," the boy said, pulling down his pants and placing his hand around his own still flaccid penis. "This time without using my name."

Røed was nonplussed. But fair enough, more than a couple of the ones at Tuesdays got off on the whole impersonal thing, preferring a stiff cock in a glory hole instead of seeing the entire person. Fortunately. He repeated his wish list without mentioning any names.

"Tell me what you did to me when I was a little boy," the man between the lights said, now masturbating.

"Just come here and let me whisper it in your ear—"

"Tell me!"

Røed swallowed. So that was how he wanted it. Direct, crude, a harsh tone and in glaring light. Fine. Røed just needed to tune in his own receiver and transmit on the same frequency. Jesus, he'd do anything to have him. Røed began hesitantly, skirting around at first, but got going after a while. Told him. Directly. In detail. And found the frequency. Was aroused by his own words, of the memories they conjured up. Told it how it was. Used words like "rape," both because that was what it had been and because it further increased the excitement, both his and the boy's, he was groaning in any case, although no longer visible, he had taken a few steps back, into the darkness behind the light. Røed had told him everything, up to how he wiped his penis on the boy's duvet before tiptoeing back to the first floor.

"Thanks!" the boy said, his voice sharp. One light was switched off and he stepped into the light of the other. He had pulled his pants up, was fully dressed. He was holding Røed's phone and tapping something into it.

"Wh-what are you doing?" Røed moaned.

"I'm sharing the last video recording with all your contacts," the boy said.

"You . . . recorded it?"

"On your phone. Want to see?" The boy held the phone up in front of Røed. On the screen he saw himself, a portly man well into his sixties, pale, almost white in the harsh light, lying on a dirty mattress with an erection, going slightly to the right. No mask this time, nothing to hide his identity. And the voice, slightly thick with excitement but clear as a bell at the same time, eager for the other man to hear the words. He noticed that the clip was framed so that a viewer couldn't see his hands and feet were bound to the bedposts.

"I'm sending it together with a short text message I prepared," the boy said. "Listen. *Hello, world. I've been doing a lot of thinking lately, and I've decided that I can no longer live with what I've done. So, I'm going to burn myself to death in the same house where Molle did. Goodbye.* What do you think? Not exactly poetry, but loud and clear, right? I'll send it to your list of contacts with a time delay so they get it just after midnight."

Røed opened his mouth to say something but didn't manage to get a word out before something was forced between his lips.

"Soon everyone you know will discover what a perverted pig you are," Prim said, fixing a piece of tape over Røed's mouth, into which he had stuffed one of the Bulgarian's left-behind wool socks. "And after a day or so the rest of the world will know as well. What do you think of that?"

No answer. Just a pair of wide-open eyes and tears rolling down round cheeks.

"There, there," Prim said. "Let me offer you a little comfort, Father. I'm not going to carry out my original plan, which was to out you, then take my own life, and let you live with the public humiliation. Because I want to live after all. You see, I've found a woman I love. And tonight, I'm going to propose. Look what I bought for her today."

Prim took the burgundy velvet-covered box from his trouser pocket and opened it. The small diamond on the ring glittered in the light from the phone on the stand.

"So I've decided to live a long and happy life instead, but of course that entails my identity not being revealed. And that means those who do know need to die in place of me. *You* must die, Father. I realize that's hard enough in itself, never mind doing so in the knowledge that your family name is ruined. Mom told me how important that sort of thing was to you. But at least you don't have to live with the humiliation. And that's nice, isn't it?"

Prim wiped away one of Røed's tears with his forefinger and licked at it. They wrote about bitter tears in literature, but didn't all tears actually taste the same?

"The bad news is I was planning to kill you slowly to compensate for you avoiding the humiliation. The good news is I'm not going to kill you *very* slowly, given that I have a date with my beloved in not too long." Prim checked the time. "Oops, I need to get home to shower and change, so we'd best get started here."

Prim took hold of the mattress with both hands. After two or three hard yanks he managed to pull it from under Røed, the iron bedsprings issuing a screech as the weight of his body landed on them. Prim walked over to the blackened brick wall and fetched the camping stove beside the jerrycan. He placed the camping stove on the floor beneath the bed directly below his stepfather's head, turned on the gas and lit it.

"I don't know if you remember, but this is the best torture method in that book about Comanches you gave me as a Christmas present. The skull is the pot and in a while your brain will begin to bubble and boil. The consolation is the parasites will die before you."

Markus Røed writhed and thrashed about. Some of the iron springs pierced his skin and drops of blood fell on the ash-covered floor. And then sweat also began to drip from his back. Prim watched as veins protruded on Markus Røed's neck and forehead as he tried to scream behind the wool sock.

Prim watched him. Waited. Swallowed. Because nothing was happening inside him. That is to say, something was happening, but not what was supposed to happen. Yes, he had been prepared for vengeance not tasting as sweet as it had in his imagination, but not this. Not that it would taste like his stepfather's bitter tears. It came as more of a shock than a disappointment to feel this way. He felt sorry for the man lying there. The man who had destroyed his childhood and was to blame for his mother killing herself. He didn't want to feel this way! Was it Her fault, was it because She had brought love into his life? In the Bible it said that Love was the greatest. Was that true, was it greater than revenge?

Prim began to cry, could not stop. He walked over to the charred staircase, found the heavy old spade lying half buried in ash. Took hold of it and went back over to the iron bed. This wasn't the plan, long drawn-out suffering had been the intention, not compassion! But he raised the spade above his head. Saw the desperation in Markus Røed's eyes as he jerked his head this way and that to avoid the flat blade, as though he would rather live a few more torturous minutes than die quickly.

Prim aimed. Then brought the spade down. Once, twice. Three times.

Wiping away the spray of blood that had hit his eye, he bent down and listened for breathing. Straightened up and lifted the spade above his head again.

Afterwards, he exhaled. Checked the time again. All that remained was to remove every trace. Hopefully the impact of the spade hadn't left any marks on the cranium to cast doubt on it being suicide. The flames would soon remove all else. He undid the straps and stuck them in his pocket. He cut the start and the end of the film on Røed's phone so no one would suspect another person had been present but it would seem as though Røed himself had edited the recording before he sent it out. Then he marked every contact on Røed's list, set the time to 00.30 and pressed Send. Thought about all the horrified, disbelieving faces lit up by screens. Then he wiped his fingerprints off the phone before slipping it into Røed's suit jacket, noticed he had eight missed calls, three of them from Johan Krohn.

He poured gasoline on the body. Let it soak in and repeated the process three times until he was certain the body was properly marinated. Doused the remaining beams and the walls still standing which were flammable. He walked around igniting it. Remembered to place the lighter by the bed so it appeared as though the last thing his stepfather had done was to set himself alight. Walked out of the shell of his childhood home, stood on the gravel drive and turned his face to the sky.

The ugliness was over. The moon had risen. It was beautiful and would soon be even more beautiful. Darkened, covered by blood. A celestial rose for his beloved. He would tell her that, use exactly those words.

47

FRIDAY

Blueman

"*BLUEMAN, BLUEMAN, MY BUCK, THINK of your small boy.*"

Katrine sang the last note almost soundlessly as she tried to gauge from Gert's breathing if he had fallen asleep. Yes, it was deep and even. She pulled the duvet a little higher up and got ready to leave.

"Whew is Uncle Hawny?"

She looked down into his blue, wide-open eyes. How had Bjørn not seen that they were Harry's? Or had he, had he known right from day one in the delivery room?

"Uncle Harry is at the hospital with a friend who's sick. But Granny is here."

"Whew aw you going?"

"To a place called Frognerseteren. It's almost in the forest, high up in the hills. Maybe you and I can take a trip up there one day."

"And Uncle Hawny."

She smiled at the same time as she felt a prick in her heart. "And maybe Uncle Harry," she said, and hoped she wasn't lying.

"Is de beaws deh?"

She shook her head. "No bears."

Gert closed his eyes and moments later was asleep.

Katrine looked at him, could hardly tear herself away. Looked at the clock. Eight thirty. She had to get going. She kissed Gert on the forehead and left the room. Heard the faint clink of her mother-in-law's knitting needles from the living room and stuck her head in.

"He's asleep," she whispered. "I'm off."

Her mother-in-law nodded and smiled. "Katrine."

Katrine stopped. "Yeah?"

"Can you promise me something?"

"What?"

"That you'll have a nice time."

Katrine met the older woman's gaze. And understood what she was saying. That her son was long dead and buried, that life had to go on. That she, Katrine, had to go on. Katrine felt a lump in her throat.

"Thanks, Gran," she whispered. It was the first time she had called her Gran, and she could see the other woman's eyes filling with tears.

Katrine walked quickly towards the metro station by the National Theater. She hadn't dressed up too much. A warm jacket and practical shoes, as per Arne's recommendation. Did that mean they would be dining in the outdoor part of the restaurant, under patio heaters and with the view all around? With only the sky above? She glanced up at the moon.

Her phone rang. It was Harry again.

"Johan Krohn called," he said. "Just so you know, Markus Røed has given his bodyguards the slip."

"Not exactly a shock," she said. "He's a drug addict."

"The security company sent people to Jernbanetorget. No sign of him there. He hasn't come back, nor is he answering his phone. Of course he might headed somewhere else to score and then gone on to celebrate his release. I just thought you should know."

"Thanks. I was planning on having a night where I don't give Markus Røed a thought but concentrate on the people I like. How's Ståle?"

"Astonishingly well for a man so close to death."

"Really?"

"He thinks it's the Grim Reaper's way of welcoming him. Have him step voluntarily over the threshold of the underworld."

Katrine couldn't help smiling. "Sounds like Ståle. How are his wife and daughter doing?"

"They're bearing up well. Coping."

"OK. Give him my love."

"Will do. Is Gert asleep?"

"Yeah. He mentions you a little too often, I feel."

"Mm. A new uncle you never knew about is always exciting. Enjoy your restaurant date. Bit late to be eating now, isn't it."

"Was inevitable, they're having trouble getting through the workload at Krimteknisk. Sung-min was supposed to be going out to dinner with his partner. Does he know—"

"Yeah, I called about Røed."

"Thanks."

They hung up as Katrine made her way down into the metro.

Harry looked down at his phone. He had received one missed call while talking to Katrine. Ben's number. He called back.

"Good morning, Harry. Me and a friend went down to Doheny. No Lucille there, I'm afraid. I called the police. They may wanna talk to you."

"I see. Give them my number."

"I did."

"OK. Thank you."

They broke the connection. Harry shut his eyes and swore silently. Should he call the police himself? No, if the scorpion guys still had Lucille he'd be running the risk of them killing her. He couldn't do anything but

434

wait. So he had to put Lucille out of his mind for the moment, because he was encumbered with the brain of a man and could only concentrate on one thing at a time, and sometimes not even that, and right now he required it to stop a killer.

When Harry returned to room 618, Jibran had gotten out of bed and was sitting with Øystein and Truls by Aune's bed. A phone was lying on the middle of the duvet.

"Hole just came in," Aune said to the phone before turning to Harry. "Jibran thinks that if the killer has bred a new parasite, then he must have done some sort of research in microbiology."

"Helge at the Forensic Medical Institute thought the same," Harry said.

"And there aren't too many with a background in that," Aune said. "We've got Professor Løken on the line, he's the head of research at the Department of Microbiology at Oslo University Hospital. He says he only knows of one person who has been involved in researching mutated *Toxoplasma gondii* parasites. Professor Løken, what did you say his name was?"

"Steiner," a voice from the duvet crackled. "Fredric Steiner, parasitologist. He came a long way in developing a variant that could use humans as a primary host. Although there was a relative of his who tried to continue the research, but he lost financial support and a research place here."

"Can you say why?" Aune asked.

"As far as I can recall there was mention of unethical research methods."

"Meaning?"

"I don't know, but in this case I believe it concerned experimentation on living subjects."

"Harry Hole here, Professor. Do you mean he infected people?"

"Nothing was ever proved but there were rumors, yes."

"What was the name of this person?"

"I don't remember, it was a long time ago, and the project was simply stopped. That's not an uncommon occurrence, nothing needs to have gone wrong necessarily, sometimes projects don't demonstrate sufficient progress. While we've been talking I've done a search for Steiner in the historical overview of research personnel, not just at our hospital but for the whole of Scandinavia. Unfortunately, I can only find Fredric. If it's important, I can speak to someone who worked with parasitology at the time."

"We'd really appreciate that," Harry said. "How far did this relative get in their research?"

"Not far, I would have heard about it otherwise."

"Do you have the time for a question from an idiot?" Øystein asked.

"They're generally the best kind of questions," Løken said. "Go ahead."

"Why on earth would you finance research on breeding or retraining parasites so that they can use people as hosts? Isn't that just destructive?"

"What did I say about the best questions?" Løken chuckled. "People often recoil when they hear the word parasite. And that's understandable, since many parasites are dangerous and detrimental to the hosts. But many parasites also serve a medically valuable function for the host as it's in their interest to keep the host alive and as healthy as possible. Seeing as they serve this function for animals, it's not inconceivable they can also do so for people. Although Steiner was one of the few in Scandinavia engaged in the research of breeding beneficial parasites, internationally it's been a large field for years. It's only a question of time before someone in the field wins a Nobel Prize."

"Or provides us with the ultimate biological weapon?" Øystein asked.

"I thought you said you were an idiot," Løken replied. "Yes, that's correct."

"We'll have to save the world another day," Harry said. "Right now we're interested in saving the next person on the list of a murderer. We're aware that it's Friday evening but you did ask if it was important . . ."

"Which I now understand it is. I've read about you in the newspapers, Hole. I'll make a few calls straight away, then I'll get back to you."

They hung up.

Looked at one another.

"Anyone hungry?" Aune asked.

The four others shook their heads.

"None of you have eaten in a while," he said. "Is it the smell causing people to lose their appetite?"

"What smell?" Øystein asked.

"The smell from my intestines. I can't do anything about it."

"Dr. Ståle," Øystein said, patting Aune's hand on the duvet, "if there's any smell then it's coming from me."

Aune smiled. Whether his tears were of pain or he was touched was impossible to say. Harry looked at his friend while the thoughts raced through his mind. Or rather: as though he was racing through his mind searching for a thought. He knew he was missing something and needed to ferret out. And all he knew and was aware of was that it was urgent.

"Jibran," he said slowly.

Perhaps hearing something in his tone, the others turned to him as though he was going to say something important.

"What do intestinal juices smell like?"

"Intestinal juices? I don't know. Judging by the breath of people with acid reflux, it would perhaps smell rather like rotten eggs."

"Mm. So not like musk, then?"

Jibran shook his head. "Not in humans, I know that."

"What do you mean, not in humans?"

"I've opened the stomachs of cats with a distinct odor of musk. It comes from the anal glands. Various animals use musk to mark their territory or to attract partners in the mating season. In ancient Islamic tradition they said that the smell of musk was the smell of paradise. Or of death, depending on how you look at it."

Harry stared at him. But it was Lucille's voice he heard in his head. *We think the author is thinking in the same sequence as he writes. Little wonder really; after all, people are inclined to believe that what is happening is a result of what's gone before, and not the other way around.*

The skimming, suspicion and disclosure about the shipment being diluted. That was the sequence of events they had automatically accepted. But someone, the author, had changed the order around. Harry understood that now, that they had been fooled, and that perhaps he had—literally—sniffed out the author.

"Truls, can we have a word outside?"

The other three watched Harry and Truls as they stepped out into the corridor.

Harry turned to him.

"Truls, I know you've told me it wasn't you who skimmed the cocaine. I also know you have every reason in the world to lie about it. I don't give a shit what you've done, and I think you trust me. So that's why I'm going to ask you one more time. Was it you or someone you know of? Take five seconds to think about it before you answer."

Truls had lowered his forehead like a surly bull. But nodded. Said nothing. Drew five deep breaths. Opened his mouth. Closed it again as if he had thought of something. Then he spoke.

"You know why Bellman didn't shut down our group?"

Harry shook his head.

"Because I went to his house and told him that if he did, I'd make it known he killed a drug dealer from a motorcycle club in Alnabru, whose body I hid by pouring cement on it in the terrace of that new house of his in Høyenhall. All you've got to do is dig it up if you don't believe me."

Harry looked at Truls for a long time. "Why are you telling me this?"

Truls snorted, his forehead still reddish. "Because it should prove that I trust you, shouldn't it? I've just given you enough ammo to put me away for years. Why would I admit to that and not admit to skimming some cocaine that would put me behind bars for a couple of years at most?"

Harry nodded. "I understand."

"Good."

Harry rubbed the back of his neck. "What about the two others with you when the dope was collected?"

"Impossible," Truls said. "I was the one who carried the dope all the way to the car from Customs at the airport, and from the car into Seizures."

"Good," Harry said. "I already said I think it was one of the customs officers or someone in Seizures who skimmed. What do you think?"

"I don't know."

"No, but what do you *think*?"

Truls shrugged. "I know the people who handled it in Seizures and none of them are dirty. I think they just got the weight wrong."

"And I think you're right. Because there's a third possibility that I—idiot that I am—haven't considered. Go on back inside, I'll join you in a second."

Harry tried to call Katrine but got no answer.

"Well?" Øystein said when Harry came back in and sat down by the bed again. "Something the three of us couldn't hear after all we've been through together?"

Jibran smiled.

"We've been fooled by the sequence," Harry said.

"What do you mean?"

"When the cocaine seizure arrived at Krimteknisk, no one had skimmed it. It's like Truls said, they were just a little inaccurate when they weighed it, so that was a small anomaly. The skimming took place *afterwards*. By the person at Krimteknisk who analyzed the cocaine."

The others stared at him in disbelief.

"Think about it," Harry said. "You work at Krimteknisk and are sent a batch of almost pure cocaine because Seizures suspect someone may have cut it with something and stolen the difference in weight. You see that no, it's completely pure, no one has tampered with the batch. But seeing as Seizures already suspect someone else, you spot your chance. You take a little of the pure cocaine, add some levamisole and send the batch back with a conclusion confirming that, yes, someone diluted the dope before it arrived at Krimteknisk."

"Beautiful!" Øystein sang in a fast vibrato. "If you're right, then the guy has, like, serious bloody guile."

"Or she," Aune said.

"He," Harry said.

"How do you know?" Øystein said. "Aren't there women working at Krimteknisk?"

"Yes, but remember that guy who came over to us at the Jealousy Bar

439

and told us he'd applied to Police College, but skipped it because he wanted to study something else?"

"Bratt's boyfriend?"

"Yeah. I didn't give it much thought at the time, but he said his chosen field meant he could maybe do investigative work after all. And earlier this evening Katrine let it slip that they were going to eat at a restaurant at Frognerseteren so late because there was so much to do at Krimteknisk. She's not the one who has a lot to do, he is. Have you heard of someone called Arne at Forensics, Truls?"

"There're a lot of new people there now, and it's not like I go around . . ." He wobbled his head as if searching for the word.

". . . making new friends?" Øystein suggested.

Truls shot him a warning glare but nodded.

"I can see how it could be someone at Forensics," Aune said. "But what makes you so sure, and why this boyfriend of Katrine's? Is it Kemper you're thinking of?"

"That too."

"Hello," Øystein interjected. "What are the two of you on about now?"

"Edmund Kemper," Aune said. "A serial killer in the 1970s who liked to fraternize with police officers. Typical of several serial killers. They seek out cops they anticipate will investigate them, before and after the murders. Kemper had also applied to Police College."

"Those are the parallels," Harry said. "But most of all it's that pungent odor. Musk. Like wet or warm leather. Helene Røed said she had smelled it at the party. I smelled it in the morgue when Helene Røed was lying there. I smelled it when we cut open Susanne Andersen's eye. And I smelled it at the Jealousy Bar the night we met this Arne guy."

"I didn't smell anything," Øystein said.

"It was there," Harry said.

Aune raised an eyebrow. "You noticed this smell among a hundred other sweating men?"

"It's a specific fucking odor," Harry said.

"Maybe you've got toxoplasmosis," Øystein said with feigned concern. "Were you horny?"

Truls grunted a laugh.

Harry experienced a sudden painful déjà vu. Bjørn Holm tidying so meticulously after the murder of Rakel. "That would also explain why we found no evidence at the crime scenes or on the bodies," he said. "It was a pro who'd cleaned up after himself."

"Of course!" Truls said. "If we'd found any of his DNA . . ."

"Everyone who works murder scenes and with corpses has their DNA profile on the database," Harry added. "So we can see if a hair that's been found only comes from a forensics officer who hasn't been careful enough."

"If it is this Arne," Aune said, "then he's out with Katrine tonight. At Frognerseteren."

"Which is practically in the forest," Øystein said.

"I know, and I've tried calling her," Harry said. "She's not picking up. How worried should we be, Ståle?"

Aune shrugged. "As I understand it, he and Katrine have been dating for a while. If he intended to kill her, then he probably would have already done so. He must have changed his mind for some reason."

"Such as?"

"The real danger would be if she did something that left him feeling humiliated. Rejecting him, for instance."

48

FRIDAY

The forest

IN AN APARTMENT BUILDING IN Hovseter, Thanh was standing by a window on the third floor staring down below. She was holding her phone in her hand. It was one minute to nine. She was looking down at the car parked right outside the front door. It had been there for almost five minutes. It was Jonathan's car. She gave a start as the phone began to ring. The digits on the screen showed that the time was nine o'clock. Exactly.

She thought about all the excuses she had come up with over the last hour only to dismiss them. She pressed Accept.

"Yes?"

"I'm outside."

"OK, coming," she said and dropped the phone into her handbag.

"I'm off!" she called out from the hall.

"*Tam biêt*," her mother answered from the living room.

Thanh closed the door behind her and took the elevator down. Not because she couldn't face the stairs, she usually took them, but because there was a theoretical possibility the elevator might break down, get stuck, necessitating a call to the fire department and the cancellation of all other plans.

But the elevator didn't break down. She walked out into the street. The night was oddly warm for one so late in September, especially as the sky was cloudless.

Jonathan leaned across the passenger seat and pushed open the door for her. She got in. "Hi."

"Hi, Thanh."

The car pulled out. It struck her that he had used her name, which he never did when they were in the store.

When they came to the main road, he headed west.

"What was it you wanted to show me?" she asked.

"Something beautiful. Something just for you."

"For me?"

He smiled. "And for me too."

"Can't you tell me what it is?"

He shook his head. She sat looking at him out of the corner of her eye. He was so different. For one thing he used her name, but she had never heard him use a word like "beautiful" or say something was for her. She had been fretting, yes, frightened almost, before getting into the car but something—perhaps the way he spoke—calmed her.

And now he smiled as though he was aware of her peeking over at him. Maybe this is how he is when he's not at work, she thought. But then she remembered that she was an employee, and he was the boss, so this was work, in a way. Or maybe it wasn't?

Hovseter was on the west side of the city, and after a few minutes they had passed Røa, the golf course at Bogstad, and were deep into Sørkedalen with extensive, dense spruce forest on both sides.

"Did you know bears have been sighted around here?" he asked.

"Bears?" she said in alarm.

He didn't laugh at her, merely smiled. He had a nice smile, Jonathan, she hadn't noticed before. Or maybe she had, just not let the thought fix in her mind. After all, it was so seldom he smiled in the store you could easily forget how it looked in the intervening time. As though he were afraid of exposing something he didn't want to show her if he smiled. But now he did want to show her something. Something "beautiful."

Her phone rang, giving her a start once again.

She looked at the display, declined the call and put the phone back in her bag.

"Feel free to answer it if you want," he said.

"I don't answer if I don't know who's calling," Thanh said. That was a lie, she had recognized the number of the policeman, Sung-min. But, of course, she couldn't take it and risk Jonathan becoming angry again.

He indicated and slowed down. Thanh couldn't see any turn-off but suddenly it was there. Her heart beat faster as the wheels crunched along a narrow gravelly road. The headlights were the only light on a wall of black forest.

"Where . . ." she began but stopped for fear he would hear the tremor in her voice.

"Don't be scared, Thanh. I just want to make you happy."

She had been found out. Just make you happy? She wasn't so sure she liked him saying strange things like that to her any more.

He stopped the car, switched off the engine and the lights, and suddenly they were sitting in total darkness.

"Right," he said. "We're getting out here."

She drew a deep breath. It must be that calm in his voice, it was almost hypnotic, because now she wasn't frightened any longer, just excited. *Show her alone. Something beautiful.* She didn't know why, but it suddenly occurred to her that this really wasn't so strange. That it was something she had been waiting for, yes, hoping for. That the intense anxiety she had felt all day must be like how a bride feels on her wedding day. She stepped out of her side of the car and inhaled the fresh evening air and the smell of spruce. Then the panic returned. Since he had been so emphatic about her not telling a soul, she had—being the idiot she was—not told anyone. Absolutely no one knew she was there. She swallowed. At what point would she say stop, that she wanted to go home? If she did it now, wouldn't that just make him very angry and maybe . . . maybe what?

"You can leave the bag," he said, opening the rear door on his side.

"I'd like to bring my phone," she said.

"Suit yourself, but you should put it in the pocket of this, it could be cold." He handed her a padded jacket. She put it on. It smelled. Of Jonathan, probably. And of campfire. At least of recently being near to an open fire.

Jonathan had put on a headlamp and turned away before switching it on so as not to blind her. "Follow me."

He stepped over a shallow roadside ditch right into the woods, and Thanh had no choice but to jump over after him. They made their way into the forest. If there was a trail, she couldn't see it. The terrain rose and he stopped here and there to hold branches aside so she could make her way through more easily.

They emerged onto open moorland bathed in moonlight and she took the opportunity to take her phone out and check it. Her heart sank. The coverage wasn't just poor, there was *no* coverage.

When she looked up again, she realized the light from the phone had ruined her ability to see in the dark, and all she saw was a black wall. She stood blinking.

"Over here."

She moved in the direction of the voice. Made out Jonathan standing at the edge of the forest holding his hand out to her. She took it without thinking. It was warm and dry. He led her farther in. Should she peel off and run? Where? She no longer had any idea in which direction the road or the city were, and here in the forest he would catch up with her anyway. If she were to resist, it would probably only accelerate the plans he had for her. She felt a welling in her throat, but defiance at the same time. She wasn't some helpless, naive little girl, there had to be some part of her brain telling her this was OK, so why feed her fear with paranoid thoughts? Soon she would understand what it was he wanted, and it would be like those nightmares you wake from and realize that you've been lying safely in bed the entire time. He was going to show her something beautiful and that was that. And instead of letting go, she held a little tighter around his hand, which in spite of everything felt strangely safe.

She was startled when he stopped.

"We've arrived," he whispered. "Lie down here."

She looked at the place his headlamp illuminated, it was a sort of lair, a bed of pine-needle branches. As if sensing her hesitation and wanting to show it was safe, he lay down himself and motioned for her to lie down next to him. She drew a deep breath. Wondered how to formulate her refusal. Moistened her lips. Saw that he had placed his forefinger over his own lips and was looking at her with a happy, boyish expression. It reminded her of her little brother when the two of them did something they weren't allowed, that bond of conspiratorial delight. Whether it was that or something else she didn't know, but she suddenly found she had lain down beside him. She could see the remains of a small fire next to them, as though someone had been here a few times before, even though it was in the middle of the forest and hardly a logical place to make camp. From where they were lying, she could see the sky and the moon between the treetops. What was there here for him to show her?

She felt his breath close to her ear. "You must be completely quiet, Thanh. Can you turn over onto your stomach?" His voice, his smell, yes, it was as if the person she had always known had been inside Jonathan had finally stepped out into the light. Or rather, into the dark.

She did as he said. She wasn't afraid. And when she saw his hand right in front of her face, her only thought was this is it, now it's going to happen.

Sung-min raised his glass to Chris. After Harry had called, Sung-min had put an end to the working week by calling Thanh's number to book a dog walker and hear if she wanted to take the opportunity to tell him anything about her boss. She hadn't answered. It didn't matter much; he had checked out this Jonathan very thoroughly without finding a trace of anything criminal, either past or present. He had made up his mind there and then to put suspicion aside. After all, that was the method he had always sworn by: follow rigorous and proven principles of investigation. He should have learned by now that listening too much to that so-called gut feeling was only tempting due to it being so easy. He had also learned that if you wanted to survive as a homicide detective, you had to put the case aside in your free time. And in order to do that, you had to focus on something else. So now he was focusing on Chris. On them. On this meal and the evening they were going to spend together. Things had been slightly strained when he had arrived, the echo of their argument still lingering. But the atmosphere had already improved. It was going to be a nice dinner, and afterwards there was going to be good make-up sex.

So when he felt the phone vibrate, saw it was Harry again and Chris looked at him with one eyebrow raised as if to let him know that make-up sex was at stake, Sung-min decided not to take the call. Surely it was something that could wait. Couldn't it? Sung-min had instructed his right forefinger to press Decline but it didn't obey. He sighed heavily and made an apologetic face.

"If I don't answer they're just going to keep on calling all night. I promise, this will only take twenty seconds." Without waiting for a reply, he pushed his chair back and ran out to the kitchen to show Chris that he meant it literally when he said twenty seconds.

"You need to make this quick, Harry."

"OK. Is there anyone working at Krimteknisk by the name of Arne?"

"Arne. Not that I can think of. What's his second name?"

"I don't know. Could you find out who at Krimteknisk analyzed the seizure of green cocaine?"

"Sure, I'll get on it tomorrow."

"I was thinking now."

"Now tonight?"

"Now within the next fifteen minutes."

Sung-min paused to allow Harry time to realize how unreasonable such a request was on a Friday night, and to someone who was technically his superior to boot. When it was apparent neither an emendation nor an apology was forthcoming, Sung-min cleared his throat.

"Harry, I'd like to help, but right now I have some private matters I need to prioritize, and the truth isn't going to disappear in the space of twelve hours. My lecturer at Police College maintained he was quoting you when he said that the investigation of a serial killer wasn't a sprint but a marathon. That you need to pace yourself. But now my twenty seconds are up, Harry. I'll call you first thing tomorrow."

"Mm."

Sung-min wanted to take the phone from his ear, but again his hand refused to obey.

"Katrine is together with this Arne guy at the moment," Harry said.

Chris had counted the seconds. It annoyed him that over thirty of them had passed when Sung-min sat down across from him again. And it annoyed him even more that his boyfriend did not look him in the eye. At least not until he had taken a mouthful of the red wine Chris had already forgotten the name of. He could sense Sing-min's restlessness, which always made him feel like—at best—number two.

"You're going to work, aren't you?"

"No, no, relax. Tonight, you and I are going to enjoy ourselves, Chris. Why don't you take that glass of wine to the sofa and I'll put on that recording of Brahms's third symphony I brought with me?"

Chris looked at Sung-min suspiciously, but they went into the living room. It was Sung-min who had persuaded him to buy a turntable and while Sung-min put the record on he sat back on the sofa.

"Close your eyes!" Sung-min ordered.

Chris did as he was told and a moment later the music streamed out into the room. He waited to feel the sofa yield to the weight of Sung-min where he had left space but it didn't happen. He opened his eyes.

"Hey! Sung! Where are you?"

The reply came from the kitchen. "Just making a few quick calls. Listen in particular to the cellos."

49

FRIDAY

The ring

FROGNERSETEREN RESTAURANT WAS SITUATED HIGH above Oslo, between the villas of its more bourgeois inhabitants and the hiking terrain of those same inhabitants. The people on their way to the restaurant were wearing suits and dresses; those going to the cafe adjacent were dressed in trekking attire. It was a six-minute walk from the terminus of the metro, and when Katrine arrived, she had no trouble spotting Arne, he was sitting alone outside at one of the large, solid wooden tables. He had stood up and spread his arms wide, smiling with those nice, sad eyes from under his flat cap, and she had stepped slightly reluctantly into his imperious embrace.

"Won't it get a little cold?" she asked when they had sat down. "They haven't put out any patio heaters. It looks like they have tables inside."

"Yes, but if we're in there we won't get to see the blood moon."

"I see," she said, shivering. It was unseasonably warm in the city below, but up here the temperature was considerably lower. She looked up at the white moon. It was full but looked normal otherwise. "When's the blood coming out?"

"It's not blood," he said with a chuckle.

For a while she had found it irritating that he took everything she said so literally, as if he thought she were a child. But tonight she found it perhaps a little extra irritating when so many stressful thoughts were swirling in her head, and she had a nagging feeling that she should be at work, because *time* was at work—and not in their favor.

"The eclipse occurs because the earth is between the sun and the moon. So for a short time the moon is in the earth's shadow," he said. "Ergo the moon should be black. But the direction of light changes when it strikes something with a different density. Don't you remember this from your school physics, Katrine?"

"I took languages."

"Oh, well, when the sunlight strikes the earth, the atmosphere bends the red portion of the light inwards, around the earth, and it hits the surface of the moon."

"Aha!" Katrine said with ironic exaggeration. "So it's light and not blood."

Arne smiled and nodded. "Man has been staring at the sky in wonder since time immemorial. But we continue to do so even now when we have so many answers. And I think it's because there's a comfort of sorts in the vastness of space. It makes us and our short lives seem so small and insignificant. Ergo our problems also seem small. We're here one moment and gone the next, so why spend what little time we have worrying? We need to use it as best we can. That's why I'm now going to ask you to switch off your mind, switch off your phone, switch off this world. Because just for tonight you and I are only going to relate to the two greatest things. The universe . . ." He placed his hand on hers. "And love."

The words touched Katrine's heart. Of course they did, she was a simple soul. At the same time, she knew they would have probably touched her more deeply if someone else had said them. She also didn't know if she was comfortable about turning off her phone; she had a babysitter at home and responsibility for a murder investigation that might not turn out to be as cut and dried as they had believed only hours before.

But she had done as he said, switched off her phone. That was an hour ago. Since then they had eaten and drunk and there had only been one thing on her mind: sneaking off to the bathroom and turning on her phone to check for missed calls or texts. She could of course have said it straight out, that just like Arne's planets didn't stop rotating, reality in Oslo didn't stop to take a break. As though to emphasize the thought she heard the low sing of the distant siren of a fire engine far below in the urban cauldron. But she didn't want to ruin this night for Arne. After all, he didn't know it would be his last one with her. Yes, all those things he said were sweet, but it was too much. Too Paulo Coelho, as Harry would have said.

"Shall we go?" Arne asked after he had paid.

"Go?"

"I know a place up here where there's less light and we'll get an even better view of the blood moon."

"Up where?"

"By Tryvann. It's only a few minutes' walk. Come on, the eclipse is starting in . . ." He checked his watch. "Eighteen minutes."

"Well, let's walk then," she said, getting to her feet.

Arne pulled on a small knapsack. He just gave her a sly wink and offered her his arm when she asked what he had in it. They set off towards Tryvann. On the mountaintop right over the lake they could see the radio and TV tower stretching over a hundred yards into the sky. It had ceased transmitting signals years ago and now just stood there like a disarmed guard at the gate of Oslo. The occasional car and jogger passed them, but when they turned onto the path along the lake there wasn't a soul to be seen.

"That's a good spot," he said, pointing at a log.

They sat down. The moonlight ran like a yellow median line over the pavement-black water in front of them. He put his arm around her shoulders. "Tell me about Harry."

"Harry?" Katrine answered, taken aback. "Why?"

"Do you two love each other?"

She laughed, or coughed, she wasn't sure herself. "What on earth would make you think that?"

"I've got eyes."

"What do you mean?"

"When I saw Harry in that bar, it hit me that he's the image of Gert. Or the other way around." Arne laughed. "But don't look so alarmed, Katrine. Your secret's safe with me."

"How do you know what Gert looks like?"

"You showed me pictures. Don't you remember?"

She made no reply, just listened to the siren in the city below. It was burning somewhere, and this wasn't where she needed to be. Simple as that, but how was she to explain that to him? Could she use the cliché about it not being him but her? After all, it was true; apart from Gert she had managed to destroy everything good in her life. It was obvious that the man sitting next to her loved her, and she wished she was able to love him back. Because not only did she yearn to be loved but yearned to love someone. Just not the man now pulling her closer, the man with sad eyes who knew so much. She opened her mouth to tell him, without having decided exactly how to phrase it, just knew she had to say it. But he beat her to it.

"I'm not even sure if I want to know what it was you and Harry had. The only thing that matters to me is that you and I are together now. And that we love each other." He took her hand, brought it to his lips and kissed it. "I want you to know that I have more than enough space in my life for both you and Gert. But not for Harry Hole, I'm afraid. Is it too much to ask for you and him not to have any contact?"

She stared at him.

He was holding both her hands in his now. "What do you say, darling? Is that all right?"

Katrine nodded slowly. "Yes," she said. Arne's face lit up in a big smile and he opened the knapsack before she finished the sentence. ". . . it *is* too much to ask."

His smile faded at the edges, but he managed to retain a rictus of it in the middle.

She regretted it immediately, for now he just sat there looking like a wretched beaten dog. And she noticed that the bottle he had lifted half-way out of the knapsack was a Montrachet, the white wine he had gotten into his head was her favorite. OK, so maybe this wasn't the man for her. But he could at least be her man for one night. She could grant him that much. She could grant herself that much. One night. Then she could take stock in the morning instead.

Arne reached back down into the knapsack.

"And I brought this along as well . . ."

"Gregersen."

"Sung-min Larsen, Kripos. Sorry to call you at home on a Friday night, but I've tried all the direct lines at Krimteknisk without getting an answer."

"Yes, we've closed for the weekend. But that's OK, go ahead, Larsen."

"I was wondering about the cocaine seizure at Gardermoen, the one that landed the officers who took possession of it in trouble."

"I know the one you mean, yeah."

"Do you know who analyzed it at your end?"

"Yes, I do."

"OK."

"No one did."

"Pardon?"

"No one."

"What do you mean, Gregersen? Are you saying that batch was never analyzed?"

Prim looked at her. At the Woman, at his chosen one. Had he heard correctly? Had she said she didn't want the diamond ring?

At first, she had put her hand to her mouth, cast a quick glance at the little box he was holding up in front of her and exclaimed: "I can't accept it."

Such a spontaneous, panicky response is of course not surprising when you're taken by surprise, Prim thought. When someone holds something up in front of you, a symbol of the rest of your life, an object representing something too great to be squeezed into one sentence.

So he had allowed her to draw breath before repeating the words he had decided would accompany the presentation.

"Take this ring. Take me. Take us. I love you."

But again, she shook her head. "Thank you. But it wouldn't be right."

Wouldn't be right? What could be more right? Prim explained to her, how he had scrimped and saved and just waited for this occasion, precisely because it was *right*. More than that, *perfect*. Look, even the celestial bodies up in the velvet blackness above them were marking this as a special occasion.

"It's a perfect ring," she said. "But it's not for me."

She tilted her head and gave him this mournful look to let him know what a sorry situation this was. Or rather, how sorry she felt *for him*.

Yes, he had heard right.

Prim could hear a rushing sound. Not the swish of a gentle breeze through the treetops as he had imagined, but the sound of a TV no longer receiving any transmission, alone, without contact, without purpose and meaning. The sound continued to rise, the pressure in his head increased, though already unbearable. He needed to disappear, to be no more. But he couldn't disappear, couldn't just nullify himself. So *she* needed to disappear. She needed to be no more. Or—that was when it occurred to him—he, the other man, needed to disappear. The cause. The man who poisoned her, blinded her, confused her. The man who made it so that she was no longer able to tell the difference between his, Prim's, true love and the man's, the parasite's, manipulation. It was he, the policeman, that was her toxoplasma.

"Well, if it's not for you," Prim said, closing the box with the diamond ring, "then this is."

The eclipse had begun above them, like a ravenous cannibal the night had started to gnaw at the left edge of the moon. But there was still more than enough moonlight where the two of them sat, and he could see her pupils dilate as she stared at the knife he had produced.

"What . . ." she said. Her voice sounded dry, and she swallowed before continuing: ". . . is . . . that?"

"What do you think it is?"

He could tell by her eyes what she was thinking, saw her lips form the words, but they wouldn't come out. So he said them for her.

"It's the murder weapon."

She looked like she was going to say something but he got to his feet quickly and was behind her. Pulled her head back and pressed the knife to her throat.

"It's the murder weapon that opened the jugulars of Susanne Andersen and Helene Røed. And which will open yours. If you don't do exactly as I say."

He pulled her head so far back that he could look her in the eyes.

The way in which the two of them were viewing each other now, upside down, was probably the way they viewed each other's worlds too. Yes, so perhaps it would never have worked. Perhaps he had known that too. Perhaps that was why, despite everything, he had planned this alternative solution if she didn't accept the ring. He had expected her to look at him with disbelief. But she didn't. She looked like she believed every word he said.

Good.

"Wh-what will I do?"

"You're going to call your policeman with an invitation he can't refuse."

50

FRIDAY

Missed calls

THE HEADWAITER LIFTED THE HANDSET of the ringing telephone. "Frognerseteren Restaurant."

"This is Harry Hole. I'm trying to get hold of Inspector Katrine Bratt who's dining with you tonight."

The head waiter was taken aback. Not only because the loudspeaker on the phone was on, but because there was something familiar about the man's name. "I'm looking at the guest list now, Mr. Hole. But I can't see a reservation in her name."

"It's probably under the gentleman's name. He's called Arne, I don't know his surname."

"No Arne, but I do have several surnames here with no first names."

"OK. He's blond, might be wearing a flat cap. She's dark-haired, Bergen accent."

"Aha. Yes, they ate outside, that was my table."

"Ate?"

"Yes, they've left the restaurant."

"Mm. Did you happen to hear anything that could give you some idea where they might be going?"

The headwaiter hesitated. "I'm not sure if I—"

"This is important, it's concerning the police investigation of the murdered women."

The headwaiter realized where he had heard the name before.

"The gentleman arrived early and asked to borrow two wine glasses. He had a bottle of Remoissenet Chassagne-Montrachet and said he was going to propose to her up by Tryvann after dinner, and then I gave him the glasses. It was a 2018 vintage, you see."

"Thanks."

Harry reached out to the phone lying on Aune's duvet and ended the call.

"We need to get up to Tryvann right away. Truls, will you contact Emergency Control and get them to send a patrol car there? Blues and twos."

"I'll try," Truls said, whipping out his own phone.

"Ready, Øystein?"

"Oh, may Mercedes be with us."

"Good luck," Aune said.

The three of them were on their way out the door when Harry took out his phone, looked at the display and stopped with one foot either side of the threshold. The door swung back and knocked the phone from his hand. He bent down and picked it up from the floor.

"What's going on?" Øystein called from outside.

Harry took a deep breath. "It's a call from Katrine's number." He noticed he had automatically jumped to the possibility that it wasn't her ringing.

"Aren't you going to take it?" Aune asked from the bed.

Harry looked grimly at him. Nodded. Tapped Accept and put the phone to his ear.

"You sure?" Commander Briseid asked.

The older firefighter nodded.

Briseid sighed, glanced at the burning villa his crew were busy hosing. Looked up at the moon. It looked strange tonight, as though something wasn't right with it. He sighed again, tipped the fire helmet a little back on his head and began making his way towards the solitary patrol car. It was from the Police Traffic and Sea Division and had pulled in shortly after their own fire engines were in place. From the time the station had been alerted of the villa on fire in Gaustad at 8:50, it had taken ten minutes and thirty-five seconds until Briseid and his colleagues arrived at the scene. Not that the situation would have been critical had it taken them a few minutes longer. The house was fire-damaged from before and had been unoccupied for years, so there was little chance of lives being at risk. Nor was there any danger of the blaze spreading to the surrounding villas. Badly raised youths setting fire to houses like this wasn't that uncommon, but whether it was arson or not was something they could look at later; right now putting it out was the main concern. In that sense it could almost be deemed an exercise. The problem was the house was situated right next to Ring 3 and thick black smoke was drifting across the freeway, hence the presence of the Traffic Division. Fortunately, the usually busy traffic from out of the city on Fridays had died down, but from the hill Briseid was on he could still see the headlights of cars—those not enveloped in smoke at least—standing stock-still on the road. According to the Traffic Division there was congestion in both directions from the Smestad intersection to Ullevål. Briseid had told the female police officer that it would take time before they got the fire under control, at least until the smoke cleared, so it might be a while before people could get to where they were going. They had at any rate closed the access roads now, so no more vehicles were coming on to the freeway.

Briseid approached the police car. The female officer lowered the window.

"You should probably get some of your colleagues up here after all," he said.

"Oh?"

"See him?" Briseid pointed at the older firefighter standing over by one of the fire engines. "We call him Sniff. Because he's able to pick up that smell out of all the other smells when something's burning. Sniff is never wrong."

"That smell?"

"*That* smell."

"Which is?"

Was she slow? Briseid cleared his throat. "You have the smell of barbecue. Then you have the *smell of barbecue.*"

He could tell by her face that the penny had dropped. She reached for the police radio.

"So, what is it now?"

"What is it?" Harry's slightly bewildered voice said on the other end.

"Yes! What's up? I just turned on my phone and there's seven missed calls from you."

"Where are you and what are you doing?"

"Why do you ask? Is something wrong?"

"Just answer."

Katrine sighed. "I'm on my way to Frognerseteren station. From there I was planning to go straight home and knock back a couple of stiff drinks."

"And Arne? Is he with you?"

"No." Katrine strode downhill the same way they had come, although now at a faster pace. The moon was being slowly devoured up above, maybe that sight was what had made her decide to drop the slow torment and drive the knife right into his heart. "No, he's not with me any more."

"As in not where you are now?"

"As in both meanings."

"What happened?"

"Yeah, what happened? The short version is that Arne lives in a different, and no doubt a better, world from me. He knows everything about the elements of the universe, and yet for him the world is a rose-tinted place where you see things how you want them to be and not how they actually are. My world and yours, Harry, it's an uglier place. But it's real. In that sense we should envy all the Arnes. I thought I could put up with him tonight but I'm a bad person. I snapped and had to tell him how it was and that I couldn't stand another second."

"You . . . eh, broke up?"

"I broke up."

"Where is he now?"

"When I left, he was sitting in tears by Tryvann with a bottle of Montrachet and a pair of crystal glasses. But enough about men, why were you calling?"

"I'm calling because I think the cocaine was skimmed at Krimteknisk. And that Arne was the one who did it."

"Arne?"

"We've sent a patrol car to have him picked up."

"Have you lost it, Harry? Arne doesn't work at Forensics."

Harry was quiet for a few moments.

"Where . . ."

"Arne Sæten is a researcher and lecturer in physics and astronomy at the university."

She heard Harry whisper a quiet "shit" under his breath and shout: "Truls! Cancel that patrol car."

Then he was back on the line. "Sorry, Katrine. Seems I'm past my sell-by date."

"Oh yeah?"

"This is the third time I've gone all in and been way off the mark in this bloody case. I'm ready for the scrap heap."

She laughed. "You're just a little overworked, like the rest of us, Harry. Switch off your brain and get some rest. Weren't you going to watch the eclipse with Alexandra Sturdza and Helge Forfang? You can still make it; I see the moon is just a little more than half covered."

"Mm. OK. Bye."

Harry hung up, leaned forward in the chair and put his head in his hands. "Fuck, fuck."

"Don't be too hard on yourself, Harry," Aune said.

He made no reply.

"Harry?" Aune said cautiously.

Harry lifted his head. "I can't let it go," he said, his voice hoarse. "I know I'm right. That I'm *almost* right. The reasoning is correct, there's just one small mistake somewhere. I need to find it."

This is it, Thanh had thought as she saw his hand draw close to her face.

Exactly what "it" was, she was not entirely clear on. Just that it was something dangerous. Thrillingly dangerous. Something she should be afraid of, *had* been afraid of, but wasn't any more. Because it wasn't dangerous with a capital D, she was sure of that, everything about him told her that.

His hand had stopped. Had remained in the air, as if frozen, shaped like a gun. And then she had realized that he hadn't reached for her but was pointing. She had turned her head in the direction his forefinger was trained, had to prop herself up on her elbows to see over the ridge. Involuntarily, she had taken a deep breath. And held it.

There, bathed in moonlight in a forest clearing at the bottom of the slope in front of them she saw four, no, *five* foxes. Four cubs playing soundlessly and an adult fox looking on. One of the cubs was slightly bigger than the others and that was the one she stared at especially.

"Is that . . . ?" she whispered.

"Yeah," Jonathan whispered. "That's Nhi."

"Nhi. How did you know I called . . . ?"

"I saw you. You used the name when you played with him and fed him. You talked more to him than you did to me." In the darkness she could see he was smiling.

"But how did this . . . happen?" She nodded towards the foxes.

Jonathan sighed. "I'm the kind of idiot who takes in prohibited animals. Like that guy who had two Mount Kaputar slugs and got me to take one of them because he thought there was a better chance of at least one of them surviving if they were fed and cared for in two different locations. I should have refused. They would have closed my store down if that policeman had discovered it. And I haven't slept since I flushed it down the toilet. But at least with Nhi I had some time to think. I knew we couldn't keep Nhi hidden indefinitely, and then the environmental health authorities would put him down. So, I took him to the vet's, she pronounced him healthy, so I placed him with this pack of foxes I knew lived here. Now of course it certainly wasn't a given that they'd take Nhi in, and I know how fond you are of that cub. So I didn't want to say anything to you until after I'd made a few trips out here and was sure it was going to be all right."

"You didn't want to tell me because you were afraid I'd be upset?"

She saw Jonathan squirm slightly. "I just figured it can be painful getting your hopes up, and even more painful when things don't turn out the way you thought and dreamed they would."

Because you know quite a bit about that, Thanh thought. And that one day she would find out more about that.

But right now she didn't know if it was the darkness, the intoxicating joy and relief, the moon or just tiredness that made her want to put her arms around him.

"It's probably getting a little late for you to be still up," he said. "We can come back another day if you'd like."

"Yeah," she whispered. "I'd really like that."

On the way back, she had to hurry to keep up. Not that he appeared to be moving quickly, but he took ground-gaining strides and was clearly accustomed to being in the forest. As they were crossing the moor in the moonlight, she studied his back. His body language and bearing were also different out here compared to at the store in town. He radiated a sort of contentment and happiness, an innateness, as though this was where he felt at home. Maybe the happiness was also due to the knowledge that he had made her happy, she suspected it was. He tried to hide it of course, but now he'd been found out, and his sour face wasn't going to fool her any longer.

She increased her pace to a jog. Perhaps he thought that after just an hour in the forest she felt at home here too; he obviously didn't feel it was necessary to lead her by the hand any more at any rate.

She let out a small cry and pretended to stumble. He stopped abruptly and she was dazzled by his headlamp. "Oh, sorry. I . . . are you all right?"

"Yeah, fine," she said, and held out her hand.

He took it.

Then they walked on.

Thanh wondered if she was in love. In which case how long she had been. And—if she actually was—how difficult it was going to be to make him aware of it.

51

FRIDAY

Prim

"YOU OUGHT TO LOOK MORE relieved, Harry," Aune said. "What is it now?"

Øystein and Truls had just left room 618 ahead of him.

Harry looked down at his dying friend. "There was an old woman in Los Angeles. She got into some trouble and I've been trying to . . . well, fix things."

"Is that why you came home?"

"Yeah."

"I guessed the reason was something other than working for Markus Røed."

"Mm. I'll tell you about it next time, I'd say it'll be just a psychologist's cup of tea."

Aune chuckled and took his friend's hand. "Next time, Harry."

Harry was completely unprepared for the tears he suddenly felt welling up. He squeezed Ståle's hand. Didn't say anything because he knew his voice wouldn't hold. Buttoned his jacket and walked quickly into the corridor.

Øystein and Truls, standing in front of the elevator doors a few yards farther along the corridor, turned towards him.

Harry's phone rang. What would he say if it was the Los Angeles Police? He took out the phone and looked at it. It was Alexandra—he should of course have let her know he wouldn't make it for the eclipse. He delayed answering while he tried to decide if he could face heading up there. Right now a drink or six on his lonesome in the bar at the Thief seemed much more tempting. No, not that. A lunar eclipse from the roof of the Forensic Medical Institute. That would be nice. As he tapped to take the call, a text message appeared on the screen. It was from Sung-min Larsen.

"Hi," he said, as he began to read the text.

"Hi, Harry."

"Is that you, Alexandra?"

"Yes."

"It was just your voice," Harry said, letting his eyes wander over the text message. "You sounded so different."

The cocaine wasn't analyzed at Krimteknisk because they didn't have the capacity, so it was sent to the Forensic Medical Institute. There it was dealt with by a Helge Forfang, who has also dated and signed the analysis.

Harry felt like his heart had stopped beating. They flickered in front of his eyes, those fragmented pieces that had failed to fit with one another and which now, within a few astonishing seconds, dovetailed. Alexandra, showing him around the Forensic Medical Institute and informing him that when the Krimteknisk couldn't handle the analysis workload, they just sent it up there. Helge plainly telling Harry that the *Toxoplasma gondii* parasite was his field. Alexandra telling him she had invited Helge to the rooftop party, the sort people just crashed. The post-mortem technician could easily have placed DNA material on the corpses of Susanne and Bertine to steer suspicion towards a particular person, he could have done it in the autopsy room *after* the bodies were found. But above all: the odor of musk in the autopsy room when Helge had just been in there, and which Harry thought came from the body. The same odor as

465

when Harry leaned closer to Helge, when he had just cut open Susanne Andersen's eye and which Harry—idiot that he was—thought came from the eye.

Multiple pieces. And they all fit together to form a mosaic, a large, but clear and sharp picture. And as always when things fell into their proper place, Harry wondered how he had *not* been able to see it before now.

Alexandra's voice, so frightened that he had hardly recognized it, was there again.

"Can you come over here, Harry?"

An imploring tone. *Overly* so. Not like the Alexandra Sturdza he knew.

"Where are you?" Harry asked, playing for time to think.

"You know that. On the roof of—"

"The Forensic Medical Institute, right." Harry waved towards Øystein and Truls as he backed into 618 again. "Are you on your own?"

"Almost."

"Almost?"

"I told you that Helge and I were going to be here."

"Mm." Harry drew a deep breath and lowered his voice to almost a whisper. "Alexandra?" Harry sank into the chair next to the bed as Truls and Øystein entered the room.

"Yes, Harry?"

"Listen to me carefully now. Don't so much as bat an eyelid, and just answer yes or no. Can you get away from there without arousing suspicion, say you need to go to the bathroom or fetch something?"

No answer. Harry held the phone a little from his ear and the other three in the Aune group inclined their heads towards the Samsung.

"Alexandra?" Harry whispered.

"Yes," she said in a toneless voice.

"Helge is the killer. You need to get away. Out of the building or lock yourself inside somewhere until we arrive. OK?"

There was a crackling noise. And then another voice, a man's voice.

"No, Harry. Not OK."

The voice was familiar but unfamiliar at the same time, like another version of a person you know. Harry took a deep breath. "Helge," he said. "Helge Forfang."

"Yes," the voice confirmed. It wasn't just deeper than Harry remembered. It sounded more relaxed, confident. Like it belonged to someone who had already won. "Or actually you can call me Prim. Everyone I hated did."

"As you wish, Prim. What's going on?"

"That's exactly the right question to ask, Harry. What's going on is that I'm sitting here with a knife to Alexandra's throat wondering what the future has in store for the two of us. For the three of us, perhaps, as you're a part of this too, aren't you? I realize I've been found out, a lost position, as they say in chess. I was holding out, hoping to avoid that, but even if I'd known things would work out this way, I wouldn't have changed what I've done. I'm quite proud of what I've accomplished. I think even my uncle will be when he reads about it—*if* he reads about it. If his parasite-ridden brain manages to cling on to life."

"Prim . . ."

"No, Harry, I certainly haven't thought of avoiding punishment for what I've done. In fact, I was planning on taking my own life when all this was over, but things have happened. Things that have given me the desire to live on. That's why I'm interested in negotiating that my punishment is as lenient as possible. But in order to have a bargaining position you need to have something to bargain with, and I have a hostage that I can choose to spare or not. I'm pretty sure you understand, Harry."

"The best move you can make to get a more lenient sentence is to let Alexandra go and hand yourself over to the police right away."

"The best for you, you mean. Get me out of the way so you have a clear shot."

"A clear shot at what, Prim?"

"Don't act stupid. A clear shot at Alexandra. You've infected her, made

467

her desire you, made her believe that you have something to offer her. Like true love for example. Well, here's your chance to prove it's true. What do you say to an exchange, you swapping places with her?"

"And you'll let her go?"

"Of course. Neither of us wants Alexandra to be harmed."

"OK. Then I have a suggestion about how to go about it."

Helge's laughter was lighter than his voice. "Nice try, Harry, but I think we'll do things according to my plan."

"Mm. And that is?"

"You drive here together with one other person; you park out in front of the building so I can see the two of you—and only the two of you—get out of the car and walk towards the building. I'll open the door from here. As soon as you get out of the car, I want to see your hands being hand-cuffed behind your back. Understand?"

"Yes."

"Both of you will take the elevator up, walk to the door leading to the roof, open it a crack and let me know you're there. If you come rushing out, I'll cut Alex's throat. You understand that too, right?"

Harry swallowed. "Yeah."

"So, when I tell you, both of you will *back out* through the door and onto the roof."

"Back out?"

"That's how they do it in maximum security prisons, isn't it?"

"Yeah."

"Then you understand. You'll go first. Eight steps backwards. Then you'll stop and go down on your knees. Whoever's with you will take four steps backwards and then kneel. If that's not done exactly as—"

"I get it. Eight and four steps backwards."

"Good, you're quick. I'll put the knife to your throat while Alexandra walks to the door of the roof. Your colleague will accompany her down to the car and they will drive away."

"And then?"

"Then the negotiations can begin."

There was a pause.

"I know what you're thinking, Harry. Why swap a good hostage for a bad one? Why give up a young, innocent woman who both the police and the politicians know will stir much stronger feelings among the public than an aging, male police detective?"

"Well . . ."

"The answer is simply that I love her, Harry. And to make sure she's willing to wait for me to be a free man I must demonstrate my true love to her. I think the jury will also see it as a mitigating factor."

"I'm sure they will," Harry said. "Shall we say an hour from now?"

The high-pitched laughter came down the line once more. "Another nice try, Harry. Surely you don't think I'm planning on giving you enough time to alert the Rapid Response Unit and gather half the police force before the exchange?"

"OK, but we're some distance away. How much time do we have to get there?"

"I think you're lying, Harry. I don't think you're that far away. Can you see the moon from where you are?"

Øystein walked quickly to the window. Nodded.

"Yeah," Harry said.

"Then you can see that the eclipse is under way. When the moon is completely covered, I'll slit Alexandra's throat."

"But—"

"If the astronomers' calculations are correct, you have . . . let me see . . . twenty-two minutes. Just one more thing. I have eyes and ears in many places and if I see or hear that the police have been alerted before you arrive, Alexandra dies. OK, hurry up now."

"But—" Harry stopped and held up the phone to let the others know the connection had been broken.

He checked the time. Helge Forfang had given them just long enough; if they took Ring 3 it wouldn't take more than five or six minutes to the Forensic Medical Institute at Rikshospitalet.

"Did you all get that?" he asked.

"Part of it," Aune said.

"His name's Helge Forfang, he works at the Forensic Medical Institute and he's holding a colleague hostage on the roof. He wants to exchange her for me. We have twenty minutes. We can't contact the police, if we do there's a good chance of him discovering it. We need to go there now, but it's just me and one more."

"Then I'm coming," Truls said firmly.

"No," Aune said just as firmly.

The others looked at him.

"You heard him, Harry. He's going to kill you. That's why he wants you there. He loves her, but he hates you. He's not going to negotiate. He might have a tenuous grip on reality, but he knows as well as you or me that nobody gets a reduced sentence by bargaining over a hostage."

"Maybe," Harry said. "But even you can't be sure just how deranged he is, Ståle. He *might* believe that he can."

"That seems unlikely, and you're planning to risk your life on it?"

Harry shrugged. "The clock is ticking, gentlemen. And yes, I think an old, washed-up murder detective instead of a young medical research talent is a plus. It's simple mathematics."

"Exactly!" Aune said. "It's simple mathematics."

"Good, we agree. Truls, you ready to go?"

"We have a problem," Øystein said from the window. He was tapping on his phone. "I can see the traffic is at a complete standstill on the road down there. Unusual this late in the evening. And checking the NRK travel website here they're saying Ring 3 is closed due to smoke from a burning house. That means all the smaller roads are chock-a-block, and speaking as a taxi driver, I can guarantee we won't make it to Rikshospitalet in twenty minutes. Not thirty either."

The people in the room, Jibran included, looked at one another.

"Right," Harry said. Glanced at his watch. "Truls, would you like to abuse your non-existent authority as a policeman?"

"I'd love to," Truls said.

"Good. Then let's go down to A&E and commandeer an ambulance with lights and sirens, what do you say?"

"Sounds fun."

"Stop!" Aune shouted, slamming his fist on the bedside table, upending a plastic cup and sending water spilling onto the floor. "Aren't you listening to what I'm saying?"

52

FRIDAY

Sirens

PRIM HEARD THE SOUND OF the sirens rise and fall out in the darkening night. Soon the whole of the moon would be eaten up and the sky lit only by the yellow lights of the city below. They weren't police sirens, and neither were they the sirens of the fire engines he had heard earlier in the evening. It was an ambulance. Of course, it could be an ambulance on its way to the Rikshospital but something told him it was Harry Hole announcing his arrival. Prim had opened the bag with the police scanner and had it switched on. It was possible Harry could inform his colleagues without word of it being communicated through the ether, Prim wasn't the first criminal with access to police frequencies. But something about the peaceful and relaxed atmosphere of the radio traffic told Prim that there were at least not many police in the city who knew what was happening. The most dramatic incident of the evening appeared to be the charred human remains in a burning villa in Gaustad.

Prim had placed his chair right behind Alexandra's, so they both faced the metal door where the policeman and his companion would make their entrance. He had considered allowing only Harry to come, but he couldn't rule out needing someone else there to remove her by force if necessary. Now and again the smell of smoke was carried on a puff of wind down from Gaustad, situated only a quarter mile or so away. Prim didn't want to breathe it in. Didn't want any more of Markus Røed inside him. He was done with hate. Now love remained. All right, her first reaction had been to reject him. No wonder. The way he had blurted everything out had naturally come as a shock to her, and the automatic reaction to shock is flight. She had believed they were just friends! Maybe she had really believed that he was gay. Maybe she had mistaken it for a flirtation of sorts, an excuse for her to invite him out on the town and to parties without any ulterior motive. He had partly played along, thought maybe she needed that excuse, even admitted to having had sex with one man without mentioning his stepfather's abuse. He and Alexandra had had such a good time! The idea of him loving her needed time to mature, clearly, the business with the diamond ring had been too soon. Yes, love remained. But in order for their love to have a chance to grow, what was keeping it in the shade had to go.

Prim felt the syringe in his inside pocket. After speaking with Harry, Prim had held it up in front of Alexandra and explained. She might not have had enough insight into microbiology to be the ideal audience, but with her background in medicine she was more qualified than the average listener. Qualified enough to understand what a parasitological breakthrough it had been to create parasites that work ten times faster than the older, slower ones. But he couldn't say he had reaped the anticipated *oohs* and *aahs* when he had related how his gondii parasites had penetrated Terry Våge's brain in under an hour. No doubt she was too frightened to concentrate. She probably believed her life was in danger. And, yes, it might well have been if Harry Hole hadn't been so predictable. But Hole was going to do exactly as he, Prim, commanded, he belonged to the old school—women and children first. And he was going to get here in time. Prim was finally feeling the joy, the joy that had been so absent when he was boiling his stepfather's head. Sure, the battle was lost. Alexandra had refused the ring, and Harry Hole had found him out. But the war remained, and that he would win. The first thing to do was to eliminate his rival for good. That was how it worked in the animal kingdom, and we humans are—at the end of the day—animals. Then he would of course have to go to prison. But from there he would teach Her to love him. And she would, because with Harry defeated, she would understand that it was he and not the policeman who was her male. It was that simple. Not banal but simple. Uncomplicated. It was only a question of time.

He looked at the moon.

Only a sliver remained until it was completely covered. But the sirens were approaching, they were close now.

"Can you hear him on his way to save you?" Prim ran a finger down the back of Alexandra's jacket. "Does it make you happy? That someone loves you so much they're willing to die for you? But you must know that I love you more. I'd actually been planning to die, but I decided to *live* for your sake, and I'd say that's a greater sacrifice."

The siren stopped abruptly.

Prim stood up and took the two steps over to the edge of the roof. Yellow cones of light swept across the deserted parking lot below.

It was an ambulance.

Two people alighted from the vehicle. He recognized Hole by the black suit. The other person was wearing something light blue, resembling hospital attire. Had Hole brought along a nurse or a patient? The detective turned around so his back faced the roof, and although Prim couldn't make out the handcuffs, he saw the glint of metal from the light of the street lamps. The two people below walked slowly side by side towards the entrance, which was right below Prim.

Prim dropped Alexandra's Camel pack, watched it fall along the facade and land with a soft smack in front of the two. They gave a start but didn't look up. The man in the hospital clothes picked up the cigarette pack and opened it. Took out Prim's ID card and the note where he had written the security code, which floor they were to take the elevator to and that the door to the roof was up the stairs to the right.

Prim walked back and sat down on the chair behind Alexandra's, both of them facing the door ten yards away.

Prim pondered. Was he fearful of what was about to happen? No. He had already killed three women and three men.

But he was nervous. Because it would be his first time physically attacking someone not already reduced to a programmed, predictable robot controlled by the parasites he had infected them with. They had all been tricked into infecting themselves, so to speak. Helene Røed and Terry Våge had drunk it down with alcohol, Susanne and Bertine had snorted it at the party. And the cocaine dealer at Jernbanetorget had also snorted it from Bertine's snuff bullet. It was on the day they brought in the seizure of green cocaine that he had gotten the idea. That is to say, he had long since heard the rumors about Markus Røed's penchant for cocaine and wondered if it could provide a way to introduce the parasite into his body. But it was only when the seizure arrived, coupled with Alexandra telling him a few days previously about the roof party at Røed's, that he realized what an opportunity this was. The paradox was of course that three other people ingested the cocaine and had to pay for it with their lives before he was finally able to infect his stepfather with his *Toxoplasma gondii* variant. And then by mixing it with one of the healthiest, most natural and most life-sustaining essentials a person needs. Water. He had to smile when he thought about it. He was the one who had called Krohn to say Markus Røed needed to come to the Forensic Medical Institute to identify the body of his wife. And he had a glass of water waiting for Røed. He could even recall verbatim what he had said to get Røed to drink it before he entered the autopsy room:

"Experience suggests it can be a good idea to have fluid in the body when we're dealing with a case such as this."

The moon was almost consumed, and it had grown even darker when Prim heard slow—very slow—footsteps on the stairs.

He checked again that the syringe in his inside pocket was ready to be used.

The hinges on the metal door shrieked. It opened a crack. A hoarse voice sounded from inside.

"It's us."

Harry Hole's voice.

A strangled sob escaped Alexandra. Prim felt his anger rise and he leaned forward and whispered in her ear.

"Don't move and stay completely still, my love. I want you to live, but if you don't do as I say, you'll force me to kill you."

Prim rose from the chair. Cleared his throat. "Do you remember the instructions?" He heard with satisfaction that his own voice sounded loud and clear.

"Yeah."

"Then come out. Slowly."

The door opened.

As the figure in the suit stepped backwards over the raised threshold, Prim realized that the eclipse was total. He instinctively glanced up at the moon, vertically above the rooftop entrance. The face of the moon wasn't black but had taken on a magical red color. It looked like a pale jellyfish, desaturated, with only enough light for itself and nothing for the people down here.

The figure in the doorway took the first of the agreed eight steps backwards towards Alexandra and Prim, shuffling slowly as though wearing shackles. Like a condemned man to the scaffold, Prim thought. Trying to prolong his pitiful life by a few seconds. He could see the resignation and defeat in the now hunched form. That night Prim had spied on Harry Hole and Alexandra when they had been out and eaten dinner and had seen them walking closely together—like a couple—through the Palace Park, Hole had looked big and strong. The same as the night he had spied on them in the Jealousy Bar. But now it was as though Hole had shrunk to his actual size within his suit. He was sure Alexandra saw the same as him, that the suit tailor-made for the man she believed Harry Hole to be, no longer fit.

Four paces in front of Hole the other figure backed out with his hands folded behind his head. Did the last of the moonlight glint faintly on something? Had the man in hospital clothes a weapon in his hand? No, it was nothing, a ring on a finger, perhaps.

Hole stopped. It looked like his handcuffed hands behind his back were giving him problems getting to his knees without toppling forward. The man was already behaving like a corpse. Prim waited until the man in hospital clothes also kneeled.

Then he approached Hole and raised his right hand, holding the syringe. Aimed at the pale, almost white, sagging skin on the back of the neck above his shirt collar.

In a second it would be over.

"No!" Alexandra screamed behind him.

Prim swung his hand. Harry Hole had no time to react before the tip of the syringe hit his neck and the needle sank in. He jerked but did not turn around. Prim pressed his thumb on the plunger, knew that the job was done, that the parasites were already on their way, that he had given them the shortest route to the brain, that this could go even quicker than with Våge. He saw the other man, the one in the hospital clothes, turn in the gloom. Again, something glimmered faintly in his hand, and Prim saw it now. It wasn't a ring. It was the finger itself. It was metal.

The man had turned all the way around now. And risen to his feet. Because of the angle it had been difficult to see when they got out of the vehicle that this man was tall, taller than the man in the suit, and when they had backed onto the roof. Both of them had been walking hunched over. But Prim realized now that it was him. It was the man in the hospital clothes who was Harry Hole. And now he could see his face too, those bright eyes over a grinning mouth.

Prim reacted as quickly as he could. He had been prepared for them to try and trick him somehow or other. They had wanted to since he was a little boy. That was how it had begun, and it was how it would end. But he wanted to take something with him. Something the policeman wouldn't get. Her.

Prim had already taken the knife out as he turned to Alexandra. She had gotten to her feet. He raised the knife to strike. Tried to catch her eye. Tell her he was about to die. His rage rose. Because her gaze was directed over his shoulder, towards that fucking policeman. It was like with

477

Susanne Andersen at the rooftop party, they were always looking for someone better. Well, then Hole could watch her die, the fucking whore.

Harry's eyes fixed on Alexandra's. She could see and knew, as both of them knew, that he was too far away to be able to save her. All he had time to do was move his forefinger in a quick circle in front of his throat and hope she remembered. Saw her move her shoulder back.

There shouldn't have been enough time. *Hadn't* been enough time, he would recall afterwards. If the parasites hadn't also reduced their primary host's ability to react. Helge's body obscured his view of the blow, so Harry was unable to see if she had formed her hand into a chisel when she struck.

But she must have.

And she must have connected.

And Helge Forfang's instincts must have taken over. They didn't want her, or revenge, just air. Helge dropped the knife and the syringe and fell to his knees.

"Run!" Harry yelled. "Get away!"

Without a word Alexandra dashed past him, pulled open the metal door and was gone.

Harry walked over, stood beside the kneeling man in the suit, and looked down at Helge Forfang, who was holding both hands to his throat. He was making hissing sounds, like a punctured tire. But then he suddenly rolled over on the concrete, lay on his back staring up at Harry, once again holding the syringe with the tip pointing towards himself. He opened his mouth, plainly trying to say something but only emitted more wheezes.

Without taking his eyes from Helge, Harry placed a hand on the shoulder of the man in the suit, sitting with his head hanging down.

"How you feeling, Ståle?"

"I don't know," Aune said, in a barely audible whisper. "Is the girl all right?"

"The girl's all right."

"Then I'm good."

Harry could see it in Helge's eyes as he lay there. Recognized it. He had seen the same look in Bjørn's eyes that last night when Harry left him, when everyone had left him, and he was found the next morning in his car, where he had blown his brains out. Harry had seen it in the mirror a few too many times in the period that followed, when the thought of Rakel and of Bjørn had made him weigh up the pros and cons of such an act himself.

The syringe Helge was holding was no longer pointed at Harry but at himself. Harry watched the needle moving closer to Helge's face. Watched it cover one eye while the other stared fixedly at Harry. The outermost edge of the moon had begun to shine again, and Helge lowered the syringe just enough for Harry to see the tip of the needle press against the eyeball, the shortcut to the brain behind. He watched the eye begin to yield like a soft-boiled egg before the tip perforated the surface and the eye assumed its original form. Watched Prim guide the tip inwards. His face was expressionless. Harry didn't know how many nerves there were in the eye or behind, it probably wasn't as painful as it looked. Wasn't that difficult to do. Easy, in fact. Easy for the man who called himself Prim, easy for the victims' families, easy for Alexandra, easy for the public prosecutors and easy for the public who were always thirsty for revenge. They would all get what they wanted, and without the bad feeling even people in countries with the death penalty are left with after executions.

Yes, it would be easy.

Too easy.

Harry stepped forward swiftly as he saw Helge's thumb arch over the plunger, dropped to his knees and drove his fist into the palm of the other man's hand. Helge squeezed, but Harry's fist prevented him from sinking the plunger, his thumb hitting a rigid metal finger of gray titanium instead.

"Let me," Prim moaned.

"No," Harry said. "You're staying here with us."

"But I don't want to be here!" Prim whined.

"I know," Harry said. "That's why."

He held on tightly. Somewhere in the distance, familiar music could be heard. Police sirens.

53

FRIDAY

Fool

ALEXANDRA AND HARRY LOOKED THROUGH the window into the autopsy room where Ståle Aune was lying on a bench and Ingrid Aune was sitting on a chair next to him. The Aunes' house was only a five-minute drive away, and she had come immediately.

Helge Forfang had been driven away by the police and the Crime Scene Unit would soon arrive. Harry had called the duty desk to report a murder without telling them that the victim wasn't yet dead.

Suddenly Aune let out a coughing laugh inside and raised his voice enough for the words to be audible through the speakers. "Yes, yes, I remember it, darling. But I didn't think you'd be interested in a guy like me. Can I get it now?"

Alexandra took a step forward and switched off the sound.

They looked in at the two of them. Harry had been in the room when Ingrid arrived. Her husband had explained to her that the parasites in his system would likely take effect very quickly, and that he would prefer to

480

win the race. When Aune had said that Harry had offered to do it, Ingrid had shaken her head firmly. She had pointed at one of the bulging veins on Aune's neck and looked at Harry, who had nodded, handed her the syringe with morphine he had been given by Alexandra and left the room.

They now saw Ingrid wipe her eyes before lifting the syringe.

Harry and Alexandra walked out to the parking lot and smoked a cigarette together with Øystein.

Two hours later—after questioning and a meeting with the crisis psychologist at Police HQ—Øystein and Harry drove Alexandra home.

"Unless you're intent on bankrupting yourself at the Thief, you can stay with me for a while," she said.

"Thanks," Harry said. "I'll think about it."

It was midnight, and Harry was sitting in the hotel bar. Looking at his whiskey glass while taking stock. Because it was time for some final accounting. To tally up those he had lost and those he had let down. And the faceless people he might—but only might—have saved. But one person was still unaccounted for.

As if in response to the thought, the phone rang.

He looked at the number. It was Ben.

Harry knew with sudden certainty that now he would find out. Perhaps that's why he hesitated before tapping Accept.

"Ben?"

"Hi, Harry. She's been found."

"OK." Harry took a deep breath. Then drained the rest of his drink in one go. "Where?"

"Here."

"Here?"

"She's sitting right in front of me."

"You mean . . . at Creatures?"

"Yeah. Her and a whiskey sour. They took her phone, that's why you couldn't get her. And she came back to Laurel Canyon when she got out of Mexico. Here she is . . ."

Harry heard noise and laughter. And then Lucille's voice.

"Harry?"

"Lucille," was all he was able to say.

"Don't go soft on me, Harry. I've been thinking about what my first words to you would be. And what I came up with was this." He heard her draw breath and then, through a mixture of laughter and tears, her quivering, whiskey-sprinkled vocal cords say, "You saved my life, you fool."

54

THURSDAY

IT WAS COLD AND THE wind was blowing hard on the day Ståle Aune was buried. The hair of those in attendance was tossed this way and that, and at one point, strangely, hailstones fell from an apparently cloudless sky. Harry had shaved when he got up, and the lean face that had stared back at him from the mirror had been from a happier time. Maybe that would help. Probably not.

When he went up to the pulpit to say a few words, as Ingrid and Aurora had asked him to, he looked out over a packed church.

In the first two rows sat close family. In the row behind them, close friends, most of whom were people Harry had never met. In the row behind that again sat Mikael Bellman. Obviously Bellman was pleased that the case was solved, and the murderer Helge Forfang was behind bars, but he had kept a low profile the whole week while the newspapers had gorged on the flow of new details as the police had released them. Like Helge Forfang's account of the murder of his own stepfather. Mona Daa and *VG* had set a good example though, by not publicizing the video of a naked Markus Røed admitting the sexual abuse of his stepson, but merely referring to the content. But for those who did want to view it, the clip was of course available online.

Harry saw Katrine sitting next to Sung-min and Bodil Melling. She was still tired, there had been a lot of follow-up work to do and more remained. But naturally she was relieved that the killer had been caught and had confessed. During the interviews Helge Forfang had told them all they needed to know, most of which had matched Harry's assumptions about how the murders had occurred. The motive—to take revenge on his stepfather—was obvious.

Harry had arrived at the church in Øystein's Mercedes along with Øystein, Truls and Oleg, who had traveled all the way down from Finnmark. Truls was already back at work at Police HQ, given that he was no longer suspected of skimming and had celebrated by buying a suit for the funeral, suspiciously like Harry's. Øystein, for his part, claimed to have cut out dealing cocaine and wanted to make his living from behind the wheel of a vehicle. Said he had considered becoming an ambulance driver.

"Tell you what, hard to go back when you've switched on that siren once and seen the traffic part like the fucking Dead Sea for Moses. Or was it the Sea of Galilee? Whatever, I'll probably give it a miss though."

Truls had grunted. "Takes a lot of courses and the like before you can become an ambulance driver."

"It's not so much that," Øystein had replied. "There're loads of drugs in those vehicles, you know, and I can't be around that, I'm not like Keith. So, I said yes to the day shifts for a taxi company owner in Holmlia."

Harry's hands were shaking, causing the sheets of paper he was holding to make scratching noises. He hadn't drunk today—on the contrary, he had emptied the rest of the Jim Beam bottle into the sink at his hotel room. He was going to be sober for the rest of his life. That was the plan. That was always the plan. On Saturday he and Gert were taking the boat to Nesodden. Harry thought about that. His hands stopped shaking. He cleared his throat.

"Ståle Aune," he said, because he'd decided to begin by saying his full name. "Ståle Aune became the hero he never aspired to become. But which circumstances and his own courage gave him the opportunity to be at the end of his life. Naturally, he'd object to being called a hero if he was here. But he's not here. I don't think. And anyway his objection wouldn't meet with acceptance. When we were faced with resolving the hostage situation that all of you have read about in the papers, his was the voice that cut through the hubbub. 'Don't you all hear what I'm saying?' he shouted from his bed. 'It's simple mathematics.' Ståle Aune would claim it was pure logic, not heroism, that made him put on my clothes, take my place, take on my death sentence. The plan was for me to leave the scene with the hostage before it was discovered we'd switched places, or, if the need arose, for me to intervene should Ståle be found out. This wasn't my plan. It was his. He asked us to do him this favor, to let him exchange his last days of pain for an exit that actually had meaning. It was a good argument. But the best thing about it was that it gave us a greater likelihood of saving the hostage if Forfang concentrated on him, and I could step in if something unforeseen occurred. Ståle left behind—like most self-sacrificing heroes—people with feelings of guilt. Myself first and foremost, as leader of the group, and the intended recipient of the poisoned chalice up there on the rooftop. Yes, I'm guilty of having cut short Ståle Aune's life. Do I regret it? No. Because Ståle was right, it is actually simple mathematics. And I believe he died a happy man. Happy because Ståle belonged to that portion of humanity who find the deepest satisfaction in contributing to make this world a little more bearable for the rest of us."

After the funeral, there was a wake at Schrøder's, according to Ståle's wishes, with sandwiches and coffee also available. The place was so packed that there was only standing room when they arrived, and Harry and his companions had to hover at the far end by the door to the restrooms.

"Forfang was out for revenge and destroyed everything standing in his way," Øystein said. "But the newspapers are still writing that he was a serial killer, and he wasn't, was he? Harry?"

485

"Mm. Not in the classic sense. They're extremely rare." Harry took a sip of coffee.

"How many have you come across?" Oleg asked.

"I don't know."

"You don't know?" Truls grunted.

"After I caught my second serial killer, I began to receive anonymous letters. People challenging me, saying they had killed. Or were going to kill. And that I wouldn't be able to catch them. Most of them just got their kicks from writing the letters, I presume. But I don't know if any of them took somebody's life. Most of the deaths we discover to be murders are cleared up. But maybe they're good, maybe they make them appear to be natural deaths or accidents."

"So they might have outplayed you, is that what you're saying?"

Harry nodded. "Yep."

An elderly man, clearly a little tipsy, emerged from the bathroom. "Friends or patients?" he asked.

Harry smiled. "Both."

"Easily done," the man said, walking into the crowded premises.

"Plus he saved my life," Harry said under his breath. He raised his coffee cup. "To Ståle."

The other three raised their glasses.

"I was thinking about something," Truls said. "That saying you came out with, Harry. The one about if you save someone's life, then you're responsible for them for the rest of their life . . ."

"Yeah," Harry said.

"I checked. That's no proverb. It was just something they made up in *Kung Fu* that was supposed to sound like ancient Chinese wisdom. That TV series from the seventies, you know."

"The one with David Carradine?" Øystein asked.

"Yeah," Truls said. "Absolute shit."

"But in a cool way," Øystein said. "You should see it," he said, nudging Oleg.

"Really?"

"No," Harry said. "Not really."

"OK," Øystein said. "But if David Carradine said you have responsibility for those you've saved, then there's sure as shit *something* in it. I mean *David Carradine*, come on, people!"

Truls scratched his protruding chin. "Yeah, OK."

Katrine came over to them.

"Sorry I'm only getting here now, had to take a look at a crime scene," she said. "Seems everyone is here. Even the priest."

"The priest?" Harry said, raising an eyebrow.

"Wasn't it him?" Katrine said. "A man in a clerical collar was leaving as I arrived, in any case."

"Which crime scene?" Oleg asked.

"An apartment in Frogner. The body's chopped into pieces. The neighbors heard a motorized sound. The wallpaper in the living room looks like it was spray-painted. Listen, Harry, could I have a word in private?"

They withdrew to the table by the window, the one which had once been Harry's usual spot.

"Great to see Alexandra is already back at work," she said.

"She's a tough girl, fortunately," Harry said.

"I hear you've invited her to *Romeo and Juliet*?"

"Yeah. I got two tickets from Helene Røed. It's supposed to be good."

"Nice. Alexandra is a good woman. I asked her to check on something for me."

"OK?"

"She checked the DNA profile on the saliva we found on Susanne's breast against the database of known offenders. We didn't get any hits there, but we know it was a match for Markus Røed."

"Yeah."

"But the saliva was never checked against the database of *unknown* offenders, DNA in unsolved cases, that is. After the video where Markus Røed admitted the sexual abuse of a minor came to light, I asked her to run his DNA against that database too. And do you know what came up?"

"Mm. I can guess."

"Go ahead."

"The rape of the fourteen-year-old at Tuesdays. What did you call the case again?"

"The Butterfly case." Katrine looked almost a little peeved. "How did you . . . ?"

"Røed and Krohn claimed they were unwilling to provide a DNA sample because to do so would be to admit there were grounds for suspicion. But I suppose I guessed Røed had another reason. He knew you had DNA in the form of semen from the rape."

Katrine nodded. "You're good, Harry."

He shook his head. "If I were I would have solved this case long ago. I was wrong every step of the way."

"So you say, but I happen to know there are other people who rate you as well."

"OK."

"And it's these others I'd like to talk to you about. There's a vacancy in Crime Squad. We'd all like you to apply for it."

"We?"

"Bodil Melling and me."

"That's 'both,' you said 'all.'"

"Mikael Bellman has mentioned it might be a good idea. That we could create a special position. A freer role. You could even start with this murder in Frogner."

"Any suspects?"

"The victim had a long-standing inheritance dispute with his brother. The brother is being questioned right now, but he has an alibi apparently."

She studied Harry's face. The blue irises she had gazed into, the soft mouth she had once kissed, the sharp features, the saber-shaped scar running from the corner of his mouth up to his ear. She tried to interpret his look, the changes in his facial expression, the way he pulled his shoulders back, like a large bird before it flies away. Katrine considered herself adept at reading people, and some men—like Bjørn—she felt were like an open book. But Harry was and remained a mystery to her. And to himself, she suspected.

"Give my regards and say thanks," he said. "But no thanks."

"Why not?"

Harry gave a wry smile. "I've realized during this case that I'm only good for one thing, and that's catching serial killers. Real ones. Statistically, you'll pass a serial killer on the street just seven times in the course of a lifetime. In which case I've used up mine. There aren't going to be any more turning up."

The young clerk was wearing a tag that read "Andrew," and the way the man in front of him had just pronounced his name suggested he had spent time in the USA.

"A new chain for a chainsaw," Andrew said. "Yes, we can sort that out."

"Right away, please," the man said. "And I need two rolls of duct tape. And a few yards of strong, thin rope. And a roll of garbage bags. Would you have that for me, Andrew?"

For some reason Andrew shuddered. Perhaps it was because of the man's colorless irises. Or the soft, overly ingratiating voice with a hint of a Sørland accent. Perhaps the fact he had placed a hand on Andrew's forearm. Or simply that Andrew—in the same way some people were afraid of clowns—had always been afraid of priests.

A Note About the Author

JO NESBØ is a #1 *New York Times* best-selling author. He has won the Raymond Chandler Award for lifetime achievement as well as many others. His books have sold fifty-five million copies worldwide and have been translated into fifty languages. His Harry Hole novels include *The Redeemer, The Snowman, The Leopard, Phantom, Knife*, and most recently *Killing Moon*, and he is also the author of *The Son, Headhunters, Macbeth, The Kingdom*, and several children's books. He lives in Oslo.

A Note About the Translator

Seán Kinsella holds an MPhil in literary translation from Trinity College Dublin. His translations have been longlisted for both the Best Translated Book Award and International Dublin Literary Award. He lives in Norway.